THE ENCHANTED PILGRIM

And Other Stories

The Hyperion Library of World Literature.

CLASSICS OF RUSSIAN LITERATURE

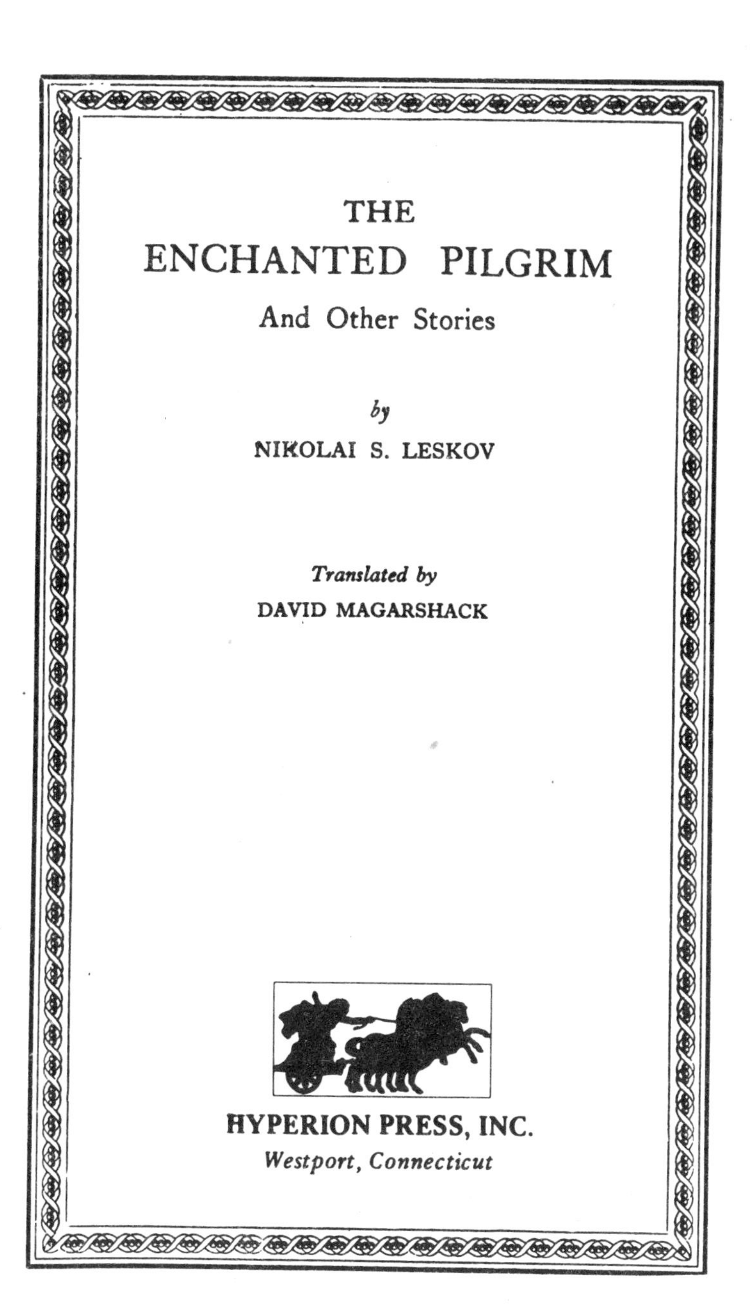

THE ENCHANTED PILGRIM

And Other Stories

by

NIKOLAI S. LESKOV

Translated by

DAVID MAGARSHACK

HYPERION PRESS, INC.
Westport, Connecticut

Published in 1946 by Hutchinson International Authors Limited
Hyperion reprint edition 1977
Library of Congress Catalog Number 76-23886
ISBN 0-88355-497-6 (cloth ed.)
ISBN 0-88355-498-4 (paper ed.)
Printed in the United States of America

Library of Congress Cataloging in Publication Data

Leskov, Nikolai Semenovich, 1931-1895.
The enchanted pilgrim, and other stories.

(Classics of Russian literature) (The Hyperion library of world literature)
Reprint of the 1946 ed. published by Hutchinson International Authors, London.
CONTENTS: The enchanted pilgrim. – Iron will. – Deathless Golovan. [etc.]
I. Title.
PZ3.L5647El12 [PG3337.L5] 891.7'3'3 76-23886
ISBN 0-88355-497-6
ISBN 0-88355-498-4 pbk.

CONTENTS

THE ENCHANTED PILGRIM

CHAPTER I

LEAVING the island of Konevetz, we sailed on lake Ladoga bound for the island of Valaam and on the way we entered the harbour of Korela, having stopped there on ship's business. Many of us were glad to go ashore and we rode on sturdy Finnish ponies to the desolate little town. On our return, our captain was ready to resume the journey and we sailed off again.

After our visit to Korela it was very natural that a discussion should have arisen about that poor, though rather ancient, Russian settlement, than which nothing drearier could be imagined. On our boat everybody was of the same opinion and one of the passengers, a man given to philosophic generalisations who fancied himself as a political wag, observed that he could not for the life of him understand why the authorities in St. Petersburg found it expedient to send undesirable characters to more or less remote places, which, of course, entailed an expense to the Exchequer on account of the cost of their transportation, when just there near the capital there was on the shores of lake Ladoga such a wonderful place as Korela where no free-thinking, nor indeed any inclination towards independence of mind, could stand up against the apathy of the population and the terrible boredom induced by surroundings so depressing and bleak.

"I'm certain," this passenger said, "it is red tape which is chiefly responsible for this state of affairs or, if not that, then perhaps lack of proper information."

Someone, evidently a man who was familiar with those parts, replied that all sorts of exiles had lived there at different times, but that, it seemed, they had not lasted long.

"One young man, a student of a religious seminary, was exiled here as a junior deacon (an exile which was to me quite inexplicable). On his arrival here the poor man did his best to keep his spirits up for a time in the hope of a turn for the better in his fortunes, but later, having sought solace in drink, he began to drink so steadily that he went off his head completely and petitioned the authorities to order him 'to be shot, or send him to the army as a private, or to condemn him to be hung for general incapacity'."

"What was the decision?"

"Well, I really don't know. You see, he didn't wait for any decision: he hanged himself of his own accord."

"He did right," said the philosopher.

"Right ?" exclaimed the man who had related the story, by the look of him a merchant who was, besides, a man of substance and religion.

"Why not ?" queried the philosopher. "At any rate, once dead there was an end to his suffering!"

"How do you mean there was an end to his suffering ? What do you suppose will happen to him in the next world ? Suicides, you know, are condemned to eternal torment. People are not even allowed to pray for them."

The philosopher smiled sardonically and said nothing, but at this point a new disputant entered the lists against him and the merchant, a man who to our surprise took the part of the unfortunate deacon who had executed his own death warrant without waiting for permission from the authorities.

This was a new passenger who had come on board at Konevetz unnoticed by any of us. He had kept silent up to now and nobody had taken any notice of him. But now we all turned to him and everyone was clearly puzzled to know how on earth we had failed to notice him before. He was a man of enormous size, swarthy and open of countenance, with thick, curly hair of the colour of lead: very striking indeed did his grizzled head appear ! He wore the short cassock of a novice of a monastery with a wide, monastic leather belt and a high, black, ecclesiastical cotton hat. Whether he was only a novice or a full-fledged monk who had taken his vows, it was difficult to say; for the monks on the Ladoga islands do not always wear skull-caps either when travelling or when going about their business on the islands, but in their rural simplicity prefer to wear tall ecclesiastical hats. Our new passenger, who later appeared to be a man of quite unusual fascination, seemed to be a man of some fifty years, but he was in every sense of the word a real giant of a man, and, moreover, a typical Russian giant, simple-minded and good-natured, who reminded you of the legendary figure of Ilya Murometz in Vereshchagin's beautiful painting or in the poem of Count Alexey K. Tolstoy. You could not help feeling that he ought not to be walking about in a cassock at all, but riding on "a dappled-grey steed" in bast shoes of enormous size, roaming through the forests and inhaling "the scents of resin and wild strawberry in the dark pine-wood."

But in spite of his undoubted good nature it did not require much observation to divine in him a man who had seen many things in his lifetime, a man who, as the saying goes, "had got about." He bore himself bravely, with self-confidence, though not with any objectionable bravado, and he spoke in a pleasant bass voice in the manner of a man who was in the habit of addressing audiences.

"All that means nothing," he began, letting fall each word lazily and softly from beneath his thick, grey moustache, which, Hussar-like, was curled upwards. "I do not agree with your views about the fate which is in store for suicides in the next world, I mean that they will apparently, according to you, never be forgiven. As for there being no one to pray for them, that, too, is nonsense, for there is a man who can improve their unhappy lot very simply and without much trouble."

Asked who the man was who had so intimate an acquaintance with the circumstances attending suicides after death and who was capable of mending them, "The man in question, gentlemen," the giant clad in the black monastic garb answered, "is a lowly village priest in the Moscow diocese, a hard drinker, who himself was very nearly unfrocked, and it is he who is exerting himself on their behalf."

"How do you happen to know about it?"

"Why, bless my soul, gentlemen, I am not the only one who knows about it: everybody in the Moscow district knows about it! For it is a matter with which no less a person than his Grace Archbishop Filaret personally concerned himself."

A short pause ensued during which someone was heard to say that the whole affair seemed rather dubious.

The black-robed novice or monk did not seem in the least put out by that remark. "To be sure," he said, "it does seem a bit dubious at first. Nor is it surprising that it should appear dubious to us when even his Grace himself would not believe it for a long time, but afterwards, having obtained all the necessary evidence, he realised that it was impossible not to believe it and he believed it."

The passengers besought the novice to tell them this amazing story. He was, indeed, very willing to do so and he began thus:

The story goes that one day an Arch-deacon wrote to his Grace the Archbishop to say, that the village priest, your Grace, is a terrible drunkard, drinks vodka day and night, and is no good in his parish. And that, his report, I mean, was in point of fact quite justified. So his Grace ordered that the humble priest should be summoned to him in Moscow. One look at the priest was quite enough to convince his Grace that he was indeed a confirmed drunkard, and the Archbishop therefore decided that the priest should be deprived of his incumbency. The poor priest was much aggrieved, so much so that he even stopped drinking. He spent all his time bewailing his unhappy lot, weeping disconsolately. "What a sorry pass have I come to," he said to himself, "and what is there left for me to do but lay violent hands upon myself? That is all that remains for me to do," he said, "for then his Grace will at any rate take pity upon my poor family and find a husband for my daughter to take my place as breadwinner and provide sustenance for my wife and children." Well, so he made up his mind without any more ado to end his wretched life and even appointed the day on which he was to do it, but, being by nature a good man, he thought to himself, "All right, suppose I do die, but what will happen to my soul then ? I am not a beast of the field, I am not without a soul, so where will my soul go to after I have done away with myself?" And thereupon he was even more cruelly distressed in his mind. Well, while he grieved and grieved, his Grace, who had decided to deprive him of his incumbency on account of his drunkenness, one day after a meal lay down on a couch with a book to rest and he fell asleep. Well, so he fell asleep or just dropped off into a doze when suddenly he saw that the door of his cell seemed to open. He naturally called out, "Who's there ?" thinking that it was probably his attendant who wanted to announce somebody's arrival, but lo! instead of his attendant who should walk in but a venerable old man, whose face bespoke infinite goodness and in whom his Grace immediately recognised one of the saints of the Church, no other than the Right Reverend Sergius himself.

So his Grace said:

"Is it thou, holy father in God Sergius ?"

And the saint replied:

"It is I, Filaret, servant of the Lord."

His Grace then asked:

"What dost thou, who art pure in heart, desire of me, thy unworthy servant ?"

And St. Sergius replied:

"I crave mercy."

"To whom dost thou want me to show mercy ?"

So the saint there and then named that same humble priest who had been deprived of his place because of his drunkenness and, after that, withdrew. But his Grace woke up and said to himself, "What can it all mean ? Was it an ordinary dream, or just an idle fancy, or a supernatural vision ?" And he began to think it over and, being a man famed throughout the world for his great intellect, he came to the conclusion that it was just an ordinary dream; for, indeed, was it possible that St. Sergius who had spent all his life in fasting and who was so strict an advocate of the good life should intercede on behalf of an ecclesiastic of a notoriously weak character who was so shockingly careless of the pitfalls with which human life is beset ? All right. So, having come to this conclusion, his Grace left the whole business to take its natural course as had been arranged from the very beginning, and he himself carried on as usual and, at the appointed hour, went to bed again. But no sooner did he fall into a slumber than again he saw a vision, and such a vision that the great spirit of his Grace was sore afflicted. Just imagine, gentlemen: a rumbling noise, such a strange noise... so strange that it is quite impossible to describe it. . . . Horses galloping . . . knights without number . . . tearing along, all accoutred in green coats of mail, breastplates and feathers, and horses like so many black lions, and in front of them their proud captain, wearing the same attire, and in whichever direction he waves his black banner, there all of them gallop, and on the banner is a dragon. . . . His Grace knew not what that procession might signify, but that proud captain roared out an order, "Tear them to pieces," he shouted, "for they have no one now to pray for them!" And after that he galloped away, and after the captain his warriors also galloped away and after them, like a flock of lean geese in springtime, there passed a whole procession of dismal spirits, and all of them nodded their heads sorrowfully to his Grace and besought him pitifully, moaning quietly through their sobs, "Let him go! He alone prays for us!" As soon as he got up, his Grace sent for the drunken little priest and began asking him what kind of prayers he was in the habit of saying and who he was praying for? The priest, weak in spirit as he was, was greatly perplexed in the presence of the Archbishop and he said, "I do everything according to the rules laid down by the Church, your Grace." It was with great difficulty that his Grace succeeded in getting him to confess. "I confess," he said, "to be guilty of one transgression. For, being weak in spirit myself and in my despair thinking that it were better to take my own life, I always during the service of the Holy Communion say a special prayer for those who die without absolution and lay violent hands upon themselves. . . ." Well, his Grace then understood what those spirits were who in his vision had sailed past him like lean geese and, not wishing to give joy to those demons who had sped before them bent on destruction, he gave his blessing to the humble priest. "Go," said his Grace, "and sin no more, and for whomsoever thou hast been praying, continue praying for them," and he sent the priest back to his parish. So he, this lowly priest, can always be useful to people who find life's struggles too great a burden to bear, for he isn't likely to prove untrue to his calling, presumptuous though it may appear, but he will go on importuning the Creator for them and He will have to forgive them.

"Why 'have to'?"

"Because 'knock, and it shall be opened unto you.' That was what He Himself commanded and that, sir, cannot be altered."

"But tell me, please: is there nobody else besides that Moscow priest who prays for suicides?"

"I really don't know what to say to that, sir. People will tell you that you shouldn't pray to God for them because they have taken the law into their own hands, but I shouldn't be surprised if there are people who, not understanding it, do pray for them. I believe that on Trinity Sunday—or is it on Whit Monday?—everybody is allowed to pray for them. They say special prayers for them on that day, wonderful prayers, so moving that I could listen to them for ever!"

"Can't you say those prayers on any other day?"

"Don't know, sir. You'd better ask those who have read a lot about such things. I expect they ought to know. You see, as I am not really interested in this matter, I haven't discussed it with anybody."

"But haven't you noticed whether those prayers are ever repeated in any church service?"

"No, I haven't, but, pray, do not take my word for it, for I don't go to church very often."

"Oh? Why not?"

"Well, you see, I'm pretty busy and I can't spare the time for it."

"Are you a monk or are you a deacon?"

"I'm neither. At present I'm just wearing a monk's habit."

"But that surely means that you're at any rate a novice, doesn't it?"

"Well . . . I suppose so. At least people regard me as one."

"They may regard you as one," the merchant remarked, "but I've known cases where men wearing cassocks have been pressed into the army."

The giant clad in the black garb of a monk was not in the least offended by that remark. He just considered it for a little while and said:

"I daresay you're right, sir. I, too, have heard of such cases, but, you see, I'm a bit too old for the army, I'm in my fifty-third year, and, besides, I'm not a stranger to army life."

"Why? Have you served in the army?"

"I have."

"As a non-commissioned officer, I presume?" the merchant asked him again.

"No, not as a non-commissioned officer."

"What were you then? A private, a quartermaster-sergeant or what? Neither fish, flesh nor fowl?"

"No, sir, you're quite wrong. I was a real army man, in fact I have been busy with regimental affairs almost since childhood."

"I see, you're the son of a regular soldier and therefore liable to military service. Is that it?" the merchant, who was beginning to lose his temper, seemed quite determined to get to the bottom of it.

"Wrong again."

"Well, blast you, who are you then?"

"I'm a connoisseur."

"A wha-a-at?"

"I am a connoisseur, sir, a connoisseur, or, to put it in plain language, I'm an expert on horses, was employed as assistant to army officers purchasing horses, acted as their adviser, I did."

"Oh, so that's it!"

"Yes, sir. I've selected and trained thousands of horses in my time. I used to break in such wild horses which, for instance, used to rear up and fall backwards with all their might and, like as not, fracture the rider's chest with the saddle bow, but no horse ever did that to me."

"But how did you tame such horses?"

"Me? Why, it's very simple really, for, you see, gentlemen, nature has endowed me with a special gift for that sort of thing. As soon as I'd jump on the back of such a wild horse, I'd give it no time to collect its wits. With my left hand I'd get hold of its ear and give it a mighty pull to one side, while at the same time I'd deal it a terrific blow with my right fist between the ears and I'd grind my teeth in a most terrifying way, so that many a poor beast would start bleeding at the nostrils and it really looked sometimes as if its brains came out with the blood. Well, of course, after that it would become as meek as a lamb."

"Well, and then?"

"Then I'd dismount, look it all over, give it a chance to have a good look at me so that it should retain a good impression of me and I'd mount it again and ride off."

"And the horse would behave itself after that?"

"Yes, it would behave itself all right, for a horse is a clever animal, it scents the kind of a man it is dealing with and it knows what he thinks about it. So far as I'm concerned, for instance, every horse formed an excellent opinion of me and, indeed, loved and regarded me. In Moscow, in a riding school, there was a horse which got completely out of hand, no rider could do anything with it, and, in addition, the savage had learnt a dastardly trick of biting through a rider's knee. The devil would seize the rider's knee with its huge teeth and bite right through the knee-cap. That horse was responsible for the deaths of many people. At that time an Englishman by the name of Raleigh was visiting Moscow, called himself the world champion tamer of wild animals, but this mean horse nearly ate him up, too, put him to shame, anyway. He only saved himself because, so I heard it said, he wore a steel knee guard, so that although it bit his leg, it couldn't bite through it and threw him instead. But for that it would have killed him. However, I put it right."

"How did you do it?"

"I did it with God's help, for, I repeat, I'm gifted that way. That Mr. Raleigh, he who called himself 'the world champion tamer of wild animals,' and the rest of them who had tried to break in that horse thought that the whole art of subduing its vicious temper consisted in the right way of manipulating the reins so that it couldn't move its head either one way or the other. But I invented quite a different method of dealing with that horse. As soon as that Englishman, Raleigh, refused to have anything to do with it, I said, 'Nonsense,' I said, 'there's nothing in it, for all that's wrong with the horse is that it is possessed with a devil. The Englishman can't grasp that, but I can and I'm quite willing to help you.' The authorities agreed. So I said, 'Take him out behind the Dragomilov toll-gate!' They took him out. All right. We led him by the halter to a gully in Fily where the gentry spend their summer holidays. I saw that the place was just what I wanted, quite big enough for my purpose, and I lost no time in getting to work. I jumped on the back of that man-eating horse, without a shirt to my back, barefooted, just in a pair of wide breeches and a cap. The only thing I wore round my naked body was a braided cotton belt dedicated to the memory of the brave and saintly Prince Vsevolod-Gabriel of Novgorod whom I had greatly admired for his valorous deeds and in whose protection I had great faith; and the belt had this inscription woven into it: '*My honour I shall yield to no one.*' In my hands I had no special implements of any kind, save, in one, a heavy Tartar riding whip with a lead head of no more than two pounds in weight, and in the other an ordinary glazed bowl with thin dough. Well, so there I was, sitting on the back of that savage horse, while four men were pulling his muzzle for all they were worth in different directions, so that he shouldn't assault any one of them with his teeth. And he, that demon of a horse, seeing that we were about to take up arms against him, started to neigh and to squeal, and he broke out into a sweat and shook all over with rage, quite intent on eating me up. I saw it plainly, so I shouted to the stablemen, 'Hurry up,' I said, 'take the bridle off the rascal!' They couldn't believe their own ears, for they never expected me to give them such an order, so they just stood there, staring at me, with their eyes popping out of their heads. I said to them, 'What are you standing about for? Come on, do what I tell you! Didn't you hear me? If I give you an order, you have to carry it out immediately!' And they replied, 'Good heavens, Ivan Severyanych, (they used to call me Ivan Severyanych in the world, Flyagin was my family name), do you really want us to take the bridle off?' I couldn't help losing my temper with them, for I could see and I could feel with my legs that the horse was getting mad with rage. So I squeezed him tightly between my knees and I bawled at them, 'Take it off!' They were going to say something, but I got so mad that I started grinding my teeth at them and they pulled off the bridle in no time and took to their heels, running off helter-skelter in all directions. Well, as soon as they had pulled off the bridle, I straightway did something that the horse did not expect: bang with the bowl on his head! The bowl broke and the dough began to run into his eyes and nostrils. The poor beast got the wind up properly, for he thought, 'What's all this?' But I took my cap off quickly with my left hand and started spreading the dough into his eyes with it, while with my right I slashed him across the side with my riding whip. . . . He just went off at a gallop, and I kept on rubbing the dough into his eyes with my cap to dim his eyesight and hitting him with the whip on the other side. . . . So I went on trouncing him mercilessly. I did not give him any time to take his breath or look round him, kept on rubbing the dough all over his face, blinding him, grinding my teeth to put the fear of God into him, frightening him, hitting him hard on both his sides with my riding whip, so that he should understand that it was no joke. . . . He did understand it all right, for he did not remain obstinately in one place, but went on galloping for all he was worth. Well, so the poor rascal kept on carrying me on his back, while I kept on thrashing him, and the quicker he ran, the more zealously did I belabour him with my whip and in the end both of us began to tire of this work: my shoulder began to ache and my arm became too limp to lift, and he, too, I could see, had stopped looking askance at me and his tongue was lolling out of his mouth. It was clear that he was on the point of capitulating, so I got off his back, wiped his eyes, took him by the forelock and said to him, 'Have you had enough, you cur, you hell-hound, you?' And I gave him such a pull that he fell down on his knees before me, and from that time he became so tractable that one couldn't ask for anything better: he would let any man mount him and any man could ride him to his heart's content, only he soon gave up the ghost."

"So he gave up the ghost after all, did he?"

"Yes, he died. You see, he was too proud a creature. Became gentle in his behaviour, but couldn't subdue his character, it seems. But Mr. Raleigh when he heard how I had tamed that horse offered me a job with him."

"Did you work for him?"

"No, sir."

"Why not?"

"Well, how am I to explain it to you? You see, in the first place, I was a connoisseur and was more used to that branch of the business. My job was to select horses and not to break them in, and he, of course, wanted me to help him with the taming of wild animals. Secondly, I didn't think his offer was quite genuine. I rather suspected him of a dark design against me."

"What kind of dark design?"

"He wanted to get my secret."

"Would you have sold it to him?"

"Oh, yes, I should have sold it to him."

"So what was the trouble?"

"I don't know. . . . I suppose he must have got frightened of me."

"Frightened of you? What kind of story is that? Tell us about it!"

"It isn't much of a story really, except that he said to me, 'Tell me your secret, my dear chap, and I'll not only give you a lot of money, but I'll also give you a job as my connoisseur.' But as I could never bring myself to cheat anyone, I said to him, 'What secret are you talking about? There's nothing in it. But he wouldn't believe me, for, being an Englishman, he naturally thought that there must be some scientific explanation to everything. 'Well,' he said, 'if you don't want to reveal your secret to me when sober,

let's have some rum first!' So after that we drank so much rum that he go
red in the face and said, not knowing any better, 'Well, now,' he said, 'ou
with it! Tell me what you did to that horse!' And I replied, 'That's what . . .
and I looked at him as fiercely as I could and ground my teeth and, no
having the bowl with the dough with me at the time, I (just for the sake o
demonstration, you understand) grabbed a glass from the table and mad
as if I was going to hit him with it, but he, of course, seeing that, just dive
under the table and then bounded for the door in double quick time and tha
was the last I saw of him. Since then he kept out of my sight and we neve
met again."

"So that's why you didn't take the job he offered you?"

"Yes, sir. For I couldn't very well take a job with him if he was afrai
to meet me, could I? Mind you, not that I didn't want the job! As
matter of fact, I wanted it badly, for I got to like him very much while w
were having that rum-drinking competition, but, it seems, no man can ru
away from his fate, and I had to follow a different calling. . . ."

"And what do you consider your calling?"

"I'm afraid, I don't quite know how to put it. . . . I wandered far an
wide, on horses and under horses, in captivity and in battle, fought agains
many people and was crippled so badly that I daresay not every man woul
have survived it."

"But when did you enter the monastery?"

"Oh, that was quite recently, only a few years after the adventurou
part of my life had come to an end."

"And, no doubt, you also felt a calling for it?"

"Well, I really don't know how to explain it to you. . . . However
I suppose I must have."

"But . . . er . . . why aren't you sure about it?"

"Because I can't be sure about it, for my past life is still a great mystery
to me."

"Why so?"

"Because much that I did, I didn't do of my own free will."

"Whose will did you obey then?"

"Well, it was all really due to a vow taken by my parents."

"And what happened to you as a result of that vow?"

"All my life I hovered on the very brink of perdition, but I did not perish
in spite of everything."

"Do you really mean it?"

"Yes, I do."

"Won't you tell us the story of your life?"

"All right, I'll do my best to tell you what I can remember, but you'll
have to listen to my story from the very beginning, for I can't tell it any
other way."

"By all means, that should be all the more interesting."

"I'm afraid I can't say whether you'll find it interesting or not, but if you're willing to listen to me, I shall be glad to tell you everything."

CHAPTER II

IVAN SEVERYANYCH FLYAGIN, ex-connoisseur, began the story of his life in these words:

I was born a serf and my parents were the personal servants of Count K., who owned estates in the province of Orel. These estates have now fallen into the hands of the young masters and have been divided up and sold, but in the lifetime of the old count they were very large indeed. The count himself lived in the village of G. in a big mansion with separate wings for guests, a theatre, a special skittle gallery, dog kennels, bear pits where bears were chained to poles, gardens; concerts were given by the count's own choir and all sorts of plays were performed by the count's own actors; the count had his own weaving sheds and other workshops, but his lordship's chief concern was his stud-farm. Each separate establishment had its own special people attached to it, but most particular attention was paid to the stables and, as in the army in the old days every regular soldier was made to send his sons into it, so at our place a coachman's son in due course became a coachman, and a groom's son became a stable-boy and was obliged to look after the horses, and a peasant whose duty it was to supply fodder for the stables had his sons assigned to the same task of bringing oats straight from the threshing floor to the stalls.

My father was the coachman Severyan and although he did not count as one of the head coachmen, for we had a great number of them, he nevertheless drove a carriage and six, and once, on the occasion of the Czar's visit, he was seventh in the rank of coachmen and was graciously presented with an ancient blue bank-note.

My mother died while I was a baby and I do not remember her, for I was her *prayed for* son, which meant that, being without children for many years, she had spent a long time praying to the Lord for a child and, when her prayer was granted, she died as soon as I was born, for I came into the world with an unusually large head, so that for that reason I was never known by my name Ivan Flyagin, but was called Golovan, being nicknamed thus from *golova*, a head.

While living with my father in the coachmen's establishment, I spent all my time in the stables and it was there that I was initiated into the mystery of understanding an animal and that, I might say, I learnt to love the horse. For even as a baby I used to crawl on all fours between the feet of horses and they did me no injury, and when I grew up I became thoroughly familiar with them.

The stud-farm on our estate was quite a separate establishment and the stables, too, were separate, and we, the stable-men, had no truck with the men of the stud-farm, but received from them the horses for training and we trained them. Every one of our coachmen and his outrider had six horses and all of them were of different breeds: there were Vyatka horses, Kazan horses, Kalmuk horses, Bityutzk horses and Don horses, and all of them had been acquired from outside, bought at different fairs. Most of our horses would naturally come from our own stud-farm, but it is hardly worth while talking about them, since stud horses are, as a rule, gentle and possess neither strength of character, nor liveliness of imagination. The others, however, the wild horses, that is, were a real terror. His lordship used to buy them wholesale, a whole drove at a time, cheap, too, about eight or ten roubles a horse, and directly we brought them home, we began to train them. We had the devil of a time of it on account of the stiff fight they would show. Half of them sometimes preferred to die rather than to submit. They would be standing in the yard unable to accustom themselves to their new surroundings and they would shy away even from the walls and all the time they would be squinting at the sky, like birds. I couldn't help being overcome by pity sometimes as I looked at one of those horses; for I could see that the poor beast would gladly have flown away, if only he had wings. . . . Such a horse would at first neither eat oats nor drink water from the trough, but would just waste away until his heart broke and he fell dead. It quite often happened that we'd lose half the horses we bought that way, particularly if they were Kirghiz horses, for they are terribly fond of their free life in the steppes. On the other hand, many of those horses which remained alive and became domesticated would be crippled in the course of their training; for there is only one way of getting the better of a horse's wildness and that is by severity. But the horses which survived all their schooling and training would turn out such capital horses that no stud horse in the world could compare with them in prowess between the shafts.

My father, Severyan Ivanych, drove six Kirghiz horses and when I grew up I was appointed outrider to his six horses. They were ferocious animals, not at all like our present cavalry horses which are ridden by officers. We used to call those officers' horses "court chamberlains" because there was no pleasure at all in riding them, since even officers could ride them; but my father's horses were just brutes: beast, serpent and basilisk all rolled into one. One look at their faces, or teeth, or legs, or manes was enough to . . . well . . . make you die of fright! They knew not what it meant to be tired: a drive of eighty, or a hundred, or a hundred and fifty *versts* from our village to Orel and back again without a stop was nothing to them. Let them get into their stride and you'd have to look out or they'd leave you miles behind!

Now at the time when I was put into the outrider's saddle I was only eleven years old, but I already had the right kind of voice for my job, a voice which according to the manners of those days was quite indispensable to an outrider of a nobleman: a most loud and piercing voice and so drawn out that I could sustain that "hi-ee-ee-o-oh!" on a high note at the top of my voice for half an hour. But I was not yet sufficiently strong in body to be able to stay in the saddle unaided on the long journeys and they used to tie me to the horse, that is to say, to the saddle and the girth; they would strap me with leather thongs to everything that would hold, and contrive it so that I could not possibly fall off. Every bone in my body would be aching horribly and quite often I'd feel so faint that I would lose consciousness for a time, but, of course, I'd go on riding in the same position and, shaken up in the saddle, I'd come round again. It was no easy job. Why, on one journey alone I'd go through those states of consciousness and unconsciousness several times, I'd faint and then I'd recover again. When I got back home, they would hoist me out of the saddle as if I were dead and they'd put me down and give me grated horseradish to smell. But I got used to it in time and took it all in my stride; and sometimes I'd even ride along and pray for a peasant to come walking on the road so that I could lay him out with a well-directed blow of my riding whip across his shoulders. That was one of the time-honoured pastimes of an outrider.

Once we were driving the count on a visit. It was a beautiful summer day and his lordship was sitting in the open carriage with his dog, my father was driving the four horses and I was streaking on ahead. We had to turn off the high-road and for about fifteen *versts* follow a lane leading to a monastery, known as the P. hermitage. This lane was made by the monks who were anxious to attract visitors by making the way to their monastery as pleasant as possible, and that was natural enough, for while the highway was covered with all kinds of filth and the willows on either side of it stuck out of the ground like so many crooked wands, the lane leading to the monks' hermitage was kept beautifully clean, swept from end to end of all dirt and dung, and shaded at the sides by large, hand-planted birch-trees, a lovely avenue of green leaves, spreading a delicious odour, and at the end of it there opened up a wide prospect of fields. . . . In a word, it looked so delightful that out of sheer gladness of heart I nearly yelled at the top of my voice, which, of course, I was strictly forbidden to do without any reason. So I kept on riding along at a gallop, but three or four *versts* before the monastery gates the road took a sudden plunge downhill and then I all of a sudden descried in front of me a black speck . . . somebody was crawling along the road just like a hedgehog. I jumped at the chance and uttered a prolonged "hi-ee-ee-o-oh!" at the top of my voice and kept it up for a whole *verst* and I got so excited that directly we began to overtake a farm-cart drawn by two horses, at which I had been yelling, I rose in the stirrups, and I saw that a man was lying on top of the hay in the cart. The man, no doubt warmed pleasantly by the sun in the gentle breeze, had fallen fast asleep, without a care in the world. He lay with his face buried in the hay and his hands were thrown far apart, and it looked as if he were embracing the cart. I could see that he would not give way, so I hugged the side of the road and, as I came up to the cart, I raised myself in the stirrups and, grinding my teeth for the first time in my life, I fetched him a terrific blow across the back with my whip. His horses just bolted with the cart down the hill and he gave a jump, such a wizened old man he was, wearing the same kind of clerical hat as myself now, and his face looked so woe-begone, like the face of an old peasant woman, frightened to death he seemed to be and tears were streaming down his cheeks, and he was writhing on the hay just like a gudgeon on a frying pan, and then, probably failing to perceive where the edge of the cart was, for he was still half-asleep, he tumbled off the cart and fell under the wheels and began to crawl in the dust . . . his feet entangled in the reins. . . . At first the way he went head over heels seemed very funny to me as well as to my father and to his lordship, but then I saw that at the bottom of the hill by the bridge a wheel caught on a projecting strip of wood and the horses stopped, but the old monk did not get up, neither did he move. . . . When we drove up, I noticed that he was all grey from the dust and that there was not even a trace of a nose left on his face, but just one big gash with blood pouring out of it. . . . His lordship ordered us to stop, alighted from his carriage, had a look at the monk and said, "Killed." He threatened to have me flogged when we came back home and ordered me to ride quickly to the monastery. From there some people were sent to the bridge and the count himself had a long talk with the abbot in the monastery and for the next few months till the autumn gifts were sent from our estate to the monastery, a whole train of farm-carts loaded with oats and flour and dried carp, and father gave me a thrashing behind a shed in the monastery with a whip across my trousers, but it wasn't a real flogging, for I had my duties to perform and get straight back into the saddle.

That was the end of the affair except that the same night the monk whom I had whipped to death appeared to me in a dream and again began crying like a silly old woman. I said to him:

"What do you want of me? Clear out!"

But he replied:

"You took my life," he said, "without giving me a chance of repentance."

"Well," I replied, "it's tough luck and I'm very sorry, but what do you expect me to do about it now? I didn't do it on purpose, did I? Besides," I said, "what have you got to grumble about? You're dead and that's that."

"Aye," he said, "that's that all right and, mind, I'm grateful to you for i but now I've come from your own mother to ask you whether you know that you're her *prayed for* son?"

"Of course I know that," I said. "My granny Fedossya has told me about it many a time."

"But do you also know," he said, "that you're a *promised* son?"

"What do you mean?"

"I mean," he said, "that you were promised to God."

"Who promised me to Him?"

"Your mother."

"Well," I said, "why doesn't she come herself and tell me that? How do I know that you've not invented it all?"

"No," said he, "I haven't invented it. You see, the trouble is your mother can't come herself."

"Why not?"

"Because," he said, "things are quite different with us here from what they are with you on earth: here not everybody speaks, nor does everybody return, for only he who has been given the gift for doing certain things, can do them. But if you want," he said, "I'll give you a sign to show you that I am speaking the truth."

"All right," I said, "but what kind of a sign is it?"

"This sign I give you," he said, "that you will encounter many hardships and adversities even to the hazarding of your own perdition, but you will not perish until the day of your real doom comes and then you'll remember your mother's promise and you'll become a monk."

"That's fine," I replied. "I consent and I shall be ready."

So he disappeared and I woke up and forgot all about it, nor did I even suspect that all those hardships and adversities were going to befall me immediately one after another.

A short time after that we went with the count and countess to Voronezh (they were taking their little daughter to the newly discovered relics of a saint to be cured of her deformed toes) and we stopped in the district of Yeletz in the village of Krutoy to bait the horses, and I fell asleep under the trough and again I saw that wizened old monk whom I had sent to his last account coming along and saying:

"Look here, Golovanka," he said, "I'm very sorry for you. Ask your master at once to let you enter a monastery and he will let you go."

I replied:

"Whatever for?"

But he said:

"I warn you, if you don't, you'll suffer many hardships."

I thought, "All right, I suppose I can hardly blame you for croaking, seeing that it was I who killed you," and with that I got up, helped my father to harness the horses and we drove off.

Now the road at that place was going downhill and the hill was exceedingly steep and on one side of it was a sheer drop into a deep ravine where hundreds of people had been killed in accidents at one time or another. His lordship said to me, "Mind, Golovan, be careful!" But I was a good hand at handling situations just like that. While it was, of course, the coachman who held the reins of the shaft-horses which had to be used in going down that precipitous hill, I knew how to be useful to my father in many ways. My father's shaft-horses were strong and very reliable when it came to getting a firm foothold on the road: they had a way of taking the carriage down by just sitting on their tails in the roadway. One of them, however, was a real villain of a horse with a predilection for astronomy: it was enough for his reins to be pulled in with some force for him to throw up his head at once, and confound his eyes if he wouldn't start scanning the skies! These astronomers are truly the worst kind of horses you could get and especially between the shafts they are a real danger! An outrider must be constantly on his guard against a horse with such a habit, for an astronomer, of course, does not look where he's putting his feet down and he usually gets himself and everybody else in a terrible mess. All this, of course, I knew about my astronomer and I'd always try to assist my father in any emergency. I would, for instance, steady my own saddle-horse and the horse next to it by grasping their reins in the crook of the elbow of my left hand and get them into such a position that they would press against the muzzles of the shaft-horses with their tails and have the shafts themselves between their cruppers, while I had my whip always poised in front of the astronomer's eyes and the moment I saw that he had begun to climb a bit too high into the sky, I'd hit him across the muzzle and he'd instantly put his head down and we would drive down the hill in fine style. So, now too, I kept my eye on the astronomer as soon as we had started taking the carriage down the hill, turning round in the saddle and steadying him with my whip. Then I became suddenly aware that the horse was no longer paying the slightest attention either to my father's reins or to my own whip. I could see that his mouth was covered with blood from the bit and his eyes were turned up, and I had hardly time to take in the situation when I suddenly heard something creak behind me and—bang!—the whole carriage lurched forward and went full tilt down the hill. . . . The brake had snapped off! . . . I bellowed to my father, "Hold on! Hold on!" and he bellowed back to me, "Hold on! Hold on!" but there was nothing to hold on to any more, for all the six horses had bolted and were tearing down the hill like mad without looking where they were going. Something flashed past my eyes and, looking up, I was just in time to see my father flung off the box: a rein had broken! And in front of us was that terrible precipice! . . . I don't know whether it was for my masters or for myself that I was sorry, but, seeing utter ruin staring me in the face, I jumped from the saddle-horse straight on to the shafts and hung on to the ends by the skin of my teeth. . . . I'm afraid I couldn't say how much I weighed at the time, but whatever my weight was I must have weighed much more in the overbalance. Anyway, I pressed the necks of the shaft-horses together with such force that their breath began to rattle in their throats and when I had summoned enough courage to look up I saw that the front horses were gone, as if somebody had cut them clean off, and that I myself was hanging over the precipice and that the carriage had stopped, having obtained a good purchase against the shaft-horses which I had almost smothered between the shafts.

It was only then that I came to my senses and I got frightened and let go my hold of the shafts and dropped into the ravine and I remembered nothing more. I don't know how long I was unconscious, but when I came to I saw that I was in a peasant's cottage, and a big peasant said to me:

"Hullo, are you really alive, sonny?"

I replied:

"I suppose I must be."

"Do you remember what happened to you?" he said.

I began to recall what had happened and I remembered how the horses had panicked and how I had jumped on to the ends of the shafts and had hung suspended over the precipice, but I couldn't remember what happened after that.

But the peasant smiled and said:

"I reckon you can hardly be expected to remember," he said, "seeing as how them horses of yours never reached the bottom of that precipice alive, got smashed up long before, they did, and you yourself was only saved by a miracle, for, you see, as you hit a lump of clay you falls down on it and slides down like as if you was on a toboggan. We thought you was as dead as mutton, but seeing you was still breathing, we reckoned you must have fainted on account of the rush of air when you was falling. And now, my lad," he said, "get up if you be feeling well enough and hurry to the saint: his lordship left money to bury you if you was to die or to send you to him to Voronezh if you recovered."

So off I went to Voronezh and I didn't speak a word, but only listened to the peasant who was driving me and who played *Mistress Mine* on his accordion all the way to the town.

When we arrived in Voronezh, his lordship summoned me to his rooms and said to her ladyship:

"Well," he said, "your ladyship, we owe our lives to this boy!"

Her ladyship just nodded her head, but his lordship said:

"Ask me anything you like, Golovan, and it shall be done."

I said:

"I don't know what to ask, sir."

And he said:

"Well, what do you want?"

So I thought and thought and then I said:

"An accordion, if you please, sir."

His lordship laughed and said:

"Well, you're a little fool, but that is neither here nor there: when the time comes, I shall keep you in mind and in the meantime," he said, "an accordion shall be bought for you immediately!"

One of the footmen was sent to a shop and he brought me the accordion in the stables.

"Here you are," he said, "now you can play it!"

I took it and tried to play, but I soon discovered that I didn't know how to, so I chucked it away at once and later it was stolen from me by some women pilgrims, who fished it out from under the shed the next day.

I should have made use of the occasion of his lordship's kindness to me and have asked him, as the monk had advised, to let me enter a monastery; but instead I had, without knowing why myself, asked for an accordion and thereby renounced my first true calling and was destined for that reason to suffer one calamity after another, undergoing greater and still greater trials, but always escaping with my life, until everything the monk had foretold in my dream had been fulfilled in my present life as a punishment for my lack of faith.

CHAPTER III

AFTER this proof of my master's singular benevolence towards me, I returned home with his lordship and his family in a carriage drawn by six horses, all of which had been newly purchased in Voronezh, and no sooner was I installed in my old quarters in the stables than I took it into my head to get myself a pair of crested doves, a cock and a hen, which I kept on a shelf. The cock had clay-coloured feathers, but the hen was a white one and with such lovely red feet, a real beauty she was! I liked them very much, especially when the cock pigeon would start cooing at night, which I found very pleasant to listen to, and in the daytime they would fly about between the horses and sit on the manger, pecking the grain and exchanging kisses with each other. . . . It is a sight that to a child is a joy to behold!

And after all that billing and cooing, they started rearing a family; they hatched out one pair and they would grow up, and then they would again start billing and cooing and hatch out some more. . . . The pigeon chicks were so tiny, and they were covered by a kind of woolly down, with no feathers at all, and so yellow, like mallow seeds you find in the grass, which children call "cheeses," but with huge beaks, not a whit worse than on the faces of Circassian princes. . . . One day I started examining those chicks and, so as not to hurt them between my fingers, I took one by his beak and could not tear my eyes away from him, such a sweet little thing he was, while the pigeon was all the time trying to get him out of my hands. So I had my fun with him, teasing him with his baby pigeon, but when I took the dear little mite back to his nest, I saw that he wasn't breathing any more. I *was* fed up with myself! I warmed him in my cupped hands for a long time, breathed on him, all the time trying to bring him back to life, but it was no use at all—he was dead and that was that! I got angry, picked him up and threw him out of the window. All right. There was another one left in the nest; the dead one a white cat, which seemed to have appeared from nowhere, picked up as she ran past the stables and carried off. I marked that cat well. I saw that she was all white except for a black spot, just like a little hat, on her forehead. Well, I thought to myself, to blazes with her, let her eat the dead chick up! But at night, as I was asleep, I suddenly heard how on the shelf above my bed the pigeon was having a ferocious fight with someone. I jumped up and looked round. It was a moonlight night and I saw the same white cat which was now carrying off my other, the live, chick.

"Well," I thought, "that is a bit too thick! Why do that?" So I threw one of my boots after the cat, but I missed her, and so she carried off my poor little pigeon and, I suppose, must have eaten him somewhere. My poor pair of doves lost their children and at first they grieved for a little while, but soon they started their billing and cooing again and once more a pair of chicks were in the nest, and that confounded cat came back again. . . . The devil alone knows how she got to know about it, must have been keeping the stables under regular observation, but, anyway, there she was dragging away another of my chicks, in broad daylight, too, and so neatly that I hadn't any time to throw anything after her. But this time I decided to teach her a lesson and I contrived such a trap on the window that as soon as she showed her face again at night, she was caught in it, and there she sat, looking very sorry for herself and miaowing. I took her out of the trap at once, thrust her face and forelegs into the top of one of my high boots, so that she shouldn't scratch me, and, taking her hindlegs and tail in my left hand, I took down a whip from the wall with my right, sat down on my bed and began to give her a good thrashing. I reckon I must have given her about a hundred and fifty strokes, with all my strength, too, until she even left off struggling. Then I took her out of my boot and I was thinking to myself, Is she alive or not? How, thought I, was I to find out whether she was dead or not? So I put her across the threshold and with my little axe I chopped off her tail. Crumpled up as she was, she gave a start and, turning over and over about ten times, ran off.

All right, I thought, now I bet you won't come stealing my pigeons again; and to frighten her off in case she did come, I went and took her tail next morning and nailed it outside my window, and I felt very pleased with myself for having done that. But an hour and certainly no more than two hours after that who did I see rushing into the stables but her ladyship's maid, who had never shown her nose in our stables before, and she was brandishing an umbrella in her hand and shouting:

"Oh, so that's who it was! So that's who it was!"

I said:

"What's the matter?"

"Was it you," she said, "who mutilated poor Zozinka? You'd better confess at once, for I can see her little tail nailed over your window!"

I said:

"Fancy making such a fuss because a cat's tail is nailed over my window!"

"How did you dare to do a thing like that?" she said.

"How did she dare to eat my pigeons?" I said.

"Who cares about your pigeons?"

"Well, if it comes to that," I said, "your cat isn't such a great lady herself!"

I was already, you understand, of an age when I was beginning to use strong language.

"Who cares," said I, "for that blasted cat of yours?"

Well, she just went at me hammer and tongs. "How dare you speak to me like that? Don't you know that it is my cat and that her ladyship herself used to stroke her?" And having said that, she slapped me across the face with her hand and I, who have since my childhood been rather quick with my hands, got hold of a dirty besom from behind the doors and, without further ado, hit her with it across the waist. . . .

Lord, what a to do there was! They took me to the manager's office to be tried, and the manager, a German, sentenced me to be soundly flogged and then to be dismissed from the stables and to be sent to the English gardens to knock stones into the paths with a mallet. . . . They gave me a terrible flogging, so that I could not even stand on my feet afterwards, and they carried me to my father on a piece of straw matting, but I didn't mind that very much; what I did mind was the last part of my sentence which condemned me to go down on my knees and knock stones into a garden path. . . . I felt so bad about it that after vainly casting about in my mind how to find a way out of my trouble I decided to do away with myself. I got myself a strong white rope, which I had obtained from one of the footmen, had a bathe in the evening and went to the aspen wood behind the threshing floor, knelt down, said a prayer for all good Christians, fastened the rope to a bough, made a noose and put my head into it. All that was left for me to do was to jump off, and that was only a matter of a second or so. . . . My character being what it is, I should have done it all, but no sooner did I take a flying leap off the tree, jump off the bough and drop than I found myself lying on the ground and in front of me stood a gypsy with a knife in his hand, laughing: I could see his snow-white teeth gleaming in the darkness of the night in that dark-skinned face of his.

"What are you up to, mate?" he said.

"Mind your own business," I said.

"Do you find life so terrible?" he kept on pestering me.

"As you see," I said, "it isn't all beer and skittles."

"Well," he said, "sooner than hang yourself by your own hand, you'd better come and live with us, perhaps you'll hang a different way then."

"And who are you and what kind of living do you make? I bet you're just thieves."

"Thieves?" he said. "Why, of course, we're thieves *and* rogues."

"I thought so," I said, "and sometimes I daresay you don't stop at cutting a man's throat, do you?"

"That, too, has happened," he said. "We don't stop at doing that, either."

Well, I thought it over in my mind and . . . what could I do? At home —to-morrow and the day after—the same old thing was in store for me: down on my knees and knock, knock, knock, all day long knocking little stones with a mallet. Already my knees were covered with callosities from that kind of work and, in addition, all I heard was how everybody was laughing at me, because a dastardly German had sentenced me to work through a whole mountain of stones and all for a cat's tail! All of them were laughing at me: "And you call yourself a life-saver," they were saying. "Saved your master's life, did you?" I just couldn't put up with that any longer and, realising that if I didn't strangle myself, I'd have to return to that kind of existence, I abandoned all hope and, after crying a little, I decided to become a highwayman.

CHAPTER IV

BUT the cunning villain of a gypsy gave me no time to collect my wits and said:

"If you want me to believe you won't go back," he said, "you must first get me a pair of horses from your master's stable and, mind, take only such horses which you know are the best so that we can ride fast and be as far away as possible from here by to-morrow morning."

This proposal made me greatly doubt whether I ought to go along with that man and to cast in my lot with him, for I hated the idea of becoming a thief. However, he needs must go that the devil drives and, knowing all the ins and outs of the stables, I experienced no difficulty at all in bringing out on the threshing floor a pair of swift horses that did not know what it meant to be tired. Meanwhile the gypsy had taken out of his pocket some wolves' teeth threaded on strings and he hung them round the necks of the horses, and we mounted and rode off. Scenting the wolves' bones on themselves, the horses carried us at such a terrific speed that at daybreak we were a hundred *versts* away on the outskirts of the town of Karachev. There we had no trouble at all in selling the horses to some house porter, and we took the money and went to a little stream to share it out. We received three hundred roubles for those horses, all of it, as was the custom in those days, in banknotes, but the gypsy gave me only one silver rouble and said:

"Here's your share."

That seemed unfair to me.

"Why," I said, "wasn't it I who stole those horses and, if caught, should I not have suffered more than you? Why, then, should my share be so small?"

"Because," he replied, "it didn't happen to grow any bigger."

"Don't," I said, "be silly. Why should you take such a lot?"

"That again," he said, "is because I'm the master and you're only my pupil."

"What are you talking about?" I said. "Pupil indeed!" And so one word followed another and we quarrelled. At length I said:

"I don't want to go along with you, because you're a rascal."

"All right," he said, "for Christ's sake don't, for you have no passport and I'll only get myself into trouble on account of you."

Thus we parted and I had half a mind to go to the justices and give myself up as a runaway serf, but first I told my story to their clerk and he said to me:

"You are just a big fool, my boy. What do you want to give yourself up for? Have you got ten roubles?"

"No," I said, "I have only got one silver rouble but I haven't got ten roubles."

"Well," he said, "haven't you got anything else on you? A silver cross round your neck, perhaps, or that thing in your ear. It's an ear-ring, isn't it?"

"Yes," said I, "it is an ear-ring."

"A silver one?"

"A silver one. And I've got a cross, too," I said. "Got it from Mitrofania. It is silver, too."

"Well, what are you waiting for?" he said. "Take them off quickly and give them to me and I'll write out a discharge for you and then you can go to Nikolayev. They want lots of people there and hundreds of our tramps have already run off there."

I gave him my silver rouble as well as my ear-ring and my cross and he wrote out a certificate for me and put the justices' seal on it and said:

"There should really be an extra charge for the seal, for everybody has to pay extra for that, but I feel very sorry for you, seeing how poor you are, and I don't want any certificate issued by me not to be in order. So off with you," he said, "and if you meet anyone who wants a certificate, don't forget to send him to me."

"All right," thought I, "what a good Samaritan you are! Takes the cross off my neck and he's sorry for me, if you please!" I didn't send anyone to him, but just trudged along, begging for alms in the name of Christ, not having a farthing to bless myself with.

I arrived in that city and went to the market-place to see if anyone would hire me. As it happened there were very few people who put themselves up for hire that day, only three men and they, too, I supposed, just half-tramps like myself. But there were hundreds of people anxious to hire us, and they just pounced on us, one man pulling one way and another another. I was pounced on by one gentleman, a big, burly man, much bigger than I. He just brushed the others unceremoniously aside and, grasping me by the hands, dragged me after him. While leading me thus, he kept on pushing the others out of the way with his fists, swearing villainously, but there were tears in his eyes. He took me to his house, built in a hurry out of some junk, and said:

"Tell me the truth: you're a runaway, aren't you?"

I said:

"Yes, sir. I'm a runaway."

"Are you," he said, "a thief, a murderer or just a tramp?"

I replied:

"What do you want to know that for?"

"Oh, just to see what kind of job you're fit for."

I told him why I had run away without concealing anything, and he suddenly embraced me and said:

"You're just the man I want, just the man I want! If," he said, "you were sorry for those pigeon chicks of yours, you'll be able to look after my child: I'm engaging you as her nurse."

I was horrified.

"How do you mean as a nurse, sir? I'm quite unequal to such a task."

"Oh, that's nothing," he said, "nothing at all. I can see that you'll make an excellent nurse. For I don't mind telling you," he said, "that I'm in an awful fix: my wife got fed up with me and ran off with a cavalry officer, an officer who buys horses for the army, and she left her baby girl with me and I can't feed her, for I have neither the time nor the food, so you'll have to nurse her and I'll give you two silver roubles a month as your wages."

"But, Lord, sir," I said, "it isn't a question of the two roubles! How shall I cope with such a job?"

"Oh, goodness gracious me," he said, "that's just nothing. You're a Russian, aren't you? Well, a Russian can cope with anything!"

"Well, sir," I said, "it is quite true that I am a Russian, but I am a man and I haven't been gifted by nature with the things that are necessary for the nursing of a baby."

"Don't you worry about that," he said. "I'm going to buy you a goat from a Jew to help you out in this matter. All you'll have to do is to milk the goat and to feed my child on her milk."

I thought it over and said:

"Of course, sir, one could nurse a child with the help of a goat, but all the same," I said, "you really ought to get a woman for such a job."

"No," he said, "don't you ever mention women to me: they're the cause of all the trouble in the world. Besides, you can't get them, anyway, and if you refuse to nurse my child, I'll go immediately and call the cossacks and I'll tell them to bind you hand and foot and to take you to the police station and from there they'll send you back to your master. Make up your mind now which you like better: to knock stones into the path of your count's garden or to bring up my child."

So I debated with myself and I decided: No, I shall certainly not go back—and I agreed to stay on as a nurse. The same day we bought from a Jew a nanny-goat with her kid. The kid I slaughtered and I made a soup with noodles with it and my new master and I ate it, and the goat I milked and I began to feed the child with her milk. The baby was very tiny and miserable and wretched: crying all the time. My master, her father, was a Pole, a civil servant, and he was never at home, the silly old bounder. He spent all his time with his cronies, playing cards, and I was left alone with my charge, the baby girl, and I was getting terribly attached to her, for time hung heavily on my hands and, having nothing else to do, I busied myself with her. I would put the baby in a wooden trough and give her a good bath, and if there should appear any rash on her skin, I would sprinkle some flour over it, or I would comb her little head, or rock her on my knees, or, if I got very tired of sitting at home, I'd put on my coat and put her inside it and go to the beach to wash her nappies, and the goat got so used to us that she, too, would go out for a walk with us. In this way I lived there until the next summer, and my baby grew up a bit and began to crawl about and even to stand on her little legs, but I noticed, as she tripped along, that she was bow-legged. I pointed it out to my master, but he didn't seem to be worried about it, merely saying:

"What can I do about it? It isn't my fault, is it? Take her to the doctor: let him have a look at her."

So I took her to the doctor, and the doctor said:

"This is the English disease, rickets. You have to cover her legs with sand."

And I did. I chose a place on the beach where there was plenty of sand, and on a fine, warm day, I'd take the goat and the little girl and would go there with them. I'd dig up the warm sand with my hands and bury the girl up to the waist in it and give her some sticks to play with and some pebbles, and our goat would walk round and round us, nibbling the grass, and I would sit and sit with my hands round my knees, until I'd fall into a doze and go to sleep.

We spent many days, the three of us, in this manner, and passing the time like that was the best remedy against low spirits that I had discovered, for, I repeat, I felt terribly dejected; and especially at that time, in the spring, when I started to bury the baby girl in the sand and to fall asleep on the beach myself, I began to be troubled by all sorts of foolish dreams. As soon as I'd fall asleep with the thunder of the waves in my ears and a warm breeze from the steppe blowing over me, something would come over with that wind, an enchantment of some kind, and I would fall under the spell of some horrible vision: I saw strange steppes and horses and all the time somebody would be calling me and luring me on and on; I could even hear him calling me by my name: "Ivan! Ivan! Come along, brother Ivan!" I'd give a start and wake up with a shudder and spit with vexation: "Blast you, can't you leave me alone? What are you calling me for?" I'd look around and see the same dreary sight before me: the goat would by then have wandered off a long way, roaming about, nibbling the grass, and the child was sitting there, buried in the sand, and that was all. . . . Ugh, how dismal! A desolate stretch of land, the sun, the estuary, and I'd fall asleep again and that strange enchantment would return with the warm breeze and again I'd hear the voice calling me, "Ivan! Let's go, Ivan! Let's go, brother Ivan!" I just couldn't help swearing, "Come on," I'd say, "show yourself for once, blast you! Who are you? What are you calling me for?" And on one occasion when I got angry like that I was sitting there half asleep and looking at the sea and I saw a small cloud rising on the horizon and coming straight for me. I said, "Whoa! You there! What are you up to? Not going to drench me by any chance, are you?" And then who did I see standing before me but that monk with the wizened face whom I had whipped to death a long time ago when I was still an outrider. I said, "Beshrew thee! Go away!" But he replied in a very kind, ringing voice, "Come along, Ivan! Come along, brother Ivan! You've got to undergo many more trials and tribulations and only then will you achieve salvation!" I cursed him in my sleep and said, "Catch me coming with you! And what kind of salvation do you want me to achieve, anyway?" But he turned into a cloud again and, through himself, showed me a most extraordinary vision, but I couldn't make head or tail of it: a steppe . . . strange, savage people . . . Saracens . . . the kind of people one finds in fairy tales about Yeruslan and Bova the Crown Prince—in huge, shaggy hats, armed with bows and arrows and mounted on wild, terrible horses. And as I beheld all that, I heard a yelling, neighing and wild laughter and suddenly . . . a sand-storm, the sand was swept up into a cloud and everything vanished, except that somewhere a bell was tolling faintly, and a big white monastery appeared on a high eminence, glowing red in the sunset, and on its walls winged angels with golden spears were walking and round about it was the sea, and every time an angel struck his shield with his spear the sea round the monastery would begin to boil and spume and from the great deep dreadful voices would set up a cry, "Holy!"

"Well," I thought to myself, "here goes that monkish business again!" And I woke up feeling greatly vexed and I was surprised to see a lady kneeling on the sand over my little girl in an attitude of great tenderness and crying as if her poor heart would break.

For a long time I gazed at that strange scene, for I naturally thought that it must still be part of my dream, but, seeing that the vision did not vanish, I rose to my feet and took a few steps towards the lady and, imagine my surprise, when I saw that she had dug the baby out of the sand and taken her in her arms and was kissing it, her face streaming with tears.

I asked her:

"What do you want?"

But she rushed towards me, holding the child tightly to her breast, and she whispered:

"This is my child, it's my daughter, my daughter!"

I said:

"Well, what about it?"

"Give her back to me," she said.

"Why do you suppose that I'd give her back to you?" I asked.

"Aren't you sorry for her?" she said, crying. "See, how she clings to me!"

"Why shouldn't she cling to you? She's just a silly child: she clings to me, too. Anyway, I can't possibly give her to you."

"Why not?"

"Because," I said, "she has been entrusted to my care. There, you see, is our goat: she always comes with us on our walks. I have to take the child back to her father."

"Very well," she said, "if you don't want to give me my child, at least be kind enough not to tell your master, my husband, that is, that you saw me and come here, to this same place, again to-morrow with my child, for," she said, "I want to hold her in my arms again."

"That," I said, "is quite a different proposition, that I promise you I'll do."

And so it was. I said not a word about it to my master, and next morning I took the goat and the baby and went with them to the beach again. The lady was already waiting for me. She was sitting in a sand pit, and as soon as she saw us, she jumped out and ran towards us, laughing and crying, thrusting toys into the baby's hands and even hanging a little bell on a red ribbon round the goat's neck, and she gave me a pipe, a pouch with tobacco and a comb.

"Smoke this pipe, please," she said, "and I'll mind the baby."

In this manner we had many meetings on the beach. The lady was always busy with the child and I was asleep most of the time, but it also happened that sometimes she would start telling me about herself, well . . . that is . . . how she had been married to my master against her will by her wicked step-mother and how she had always disliked her husband. . . . "Could never bring myself to love him," she said. But it seemed that the other one, that blessed cavalry officer of hers, she loved dearly and indeed she kept on bewailing her fate, for it appeared that she had tried hard to overcome her love for him, but couldn't. "I'm his for ever," she said, "for my husband, as you know very well yourself, lives a disreputable life, while . . ." Well, the other one, it seemed, was a paragon of virtue, but above all he had a very beautiful moustache and I don't know what else. "He's a man of very clean habits," she said, "and he cherishes me dearly, but there again," she said, "that's not enough to make me happy, for I can't live without my child. . . . Now," she said, "I've come back to this city with him and we live at the house of one of his friends, but I'm in constant dread that my husband may get to know about it. But we shall be leaving soon and, I suppose, I shall be pining away for my darling baby again ! . . ."

"Well," I said, "what's to be done about it ? If, having violated the laws of God and man, you prefer to live in sin," I said, "then you just have to suffer for it."

But she would start crying and one day her crying became more pitiful than usual and I was beginning to get fed up with her constant lamentations when, without any reason whatever, she began promising to give me a lot of money. Well, at last she came for the last time to bid us good-bye and she said:

"Look here, Ivan (she knew my name already), listen to me," she said, "listen carefully to what I'm going to tell you: to-day," she said, "*he* is coming here himself."

I asked her:

"Who's he ?"

She replied:

"Why, the cavalry officer."

I said:

"What business is it of mine whether he comes or not ?"

So she went on to tell me a whole story about how he had won a lot of money at cards the night before and how he had told her that, as he wished to please her, he had decided to give me a thousand roubles, if I, that is, gave her back her daughter.

"No, ma'am," I said, "that I shall never do."

"But why not? Why not, Ivan?" she started pestering me. "Aren't you sorry for me and for her that we should be separated?"

"Sorry or not," said I, "but I've never sold myself either for big or for little money and I never shall, so that your cavalry officer can keep his thousand roubles and I shall keep your daughter."

She started crying, but I said to her:

"You'd better stop crying, for it won't make any difference."

She said:

"You're a brute, you're made of stone."

But I replied:

"I'm not made of stone at all, I'm made of flesh and bone like the rest, only I know my duty and I shall remain true to it: I undertook to guard the child and I shall keep it under my protection."

She tried hard to persuade me to change my mind. "Can't you see that the child itself will be happier with me?" she said.

"That again," I replied, "isn't my business."

"Do you mean," she exclaimed, "do you mean that I shall have to part with my child again?"

"Well," said I, "if, having violated the laws of God and man . . ."

But I had no time to finish what I wanted to say, for at that moment I saw a sprightly Uhlan officer walking across the steppe towards us. In those days regimental officers used to walk with a swagger in a real military uniform, not at all like our present-day officers who are just indistinguishable from clerks. Well, so there that Uhlan officer was marching along, a fine figure of a man, hands pressed against his sides and greatcoat slung over his shoulders . . . not that there was any great strength in him, mind you, but plenty of dash. So I looked at that visitor of ours and I said to myself, "Why not have some fun with him? I'm bored to death and a little amusement won't do me any harm." And I made up my mind that if he said an uncivil word to me, I'd be as rude to him as possible, so that, God willing, we might have a good scrap together. That, I said joyfully to myself, would be just fine, and I didn't even listen any more to what the lady was babbling with tears in her eyes, for all I wanted then was to have some sport with that officer.

CHAPTER V

HAVING decided to provide myself with a little amusement, I began to cast about in my mind how best to provoke that officer so that he should attack me first. So I sat down, took out my comb and pretended to be combing my hair. In the meantime the officer walked up and went straight to the lady who started talking nineteen to the dozen to him: all about how I would not let her have the baby.

But he just stroked her head and said:

"Don't worry, darling, I'll find some way of persuading him. We'll show him the money and," he said, "his eyes will pop out of his head, but if that shouldn't work, we'll just take the child away from him," and with these words he walked up to me, handed me a roll of banknotes and said:

"Look here, my man," he said, "there's exactly a thousand roubles here, give us the child and you can have the money and go where you like."

But I didn't reply to him at once, for I was trying to be as rude as possible to him on purpose: I first raised myself very slowly from the ground, next I hung my comb on my belt, cleared my throat and then only did I say:

"No, sir," I said, "that won't do àt all!" And I snatched the banknotes out of his hand, spat on them and threw them on the ground, saying as if I were speaking to a dog, "Come on, Spotty, come on, sir, pick 'em up!"

He looked aggrieved, flushed a deep red and let fly at me; but, as you can judge for yourselves, gentlemen, no army officer would stand much of a chance against a man of my physique: one little push from me and he was finished—sprawling on the ground, his spurs flying skywards and his sabre wheeling sideways. I immediately stamped on that sabre of his and said:

"That's how I tread your bravery under my foot!"

But although that little cavalry officer wasn't much to look at, he had plenty of guts. Seeing that he couldn't get his sabre from me, he unbelted it and went for me with his fists. . . . Now he was asking for it and, of course, he got it good and proper. But I couldn't help admiring his spirit which betokened a brave and honourable character: I refused to take his money, but neither did he pick it up himself.

After we had had enough of fighting, I shouted to him:

"Why don't you pick up your money? It'll come in useful to pay your lordship's fares!"

Did he pick it up? No, gentlemen, he didn't: instead he ran to the child, wishing to carry her off, but, of course, as soon as he caught hold of one of her hands, I caught hold of the other.

"Come on," I said, "let's pull and see which of us gets the bigger half!"

He shouted:

"You dirty swine! You bully!" and, having said that, he spat in my face and let go of the child and was now only set on comforting the lady and persuading her to leave the beach with him, but she, in her despair, set up a most pathetic clamour and although, pulled away by force, she followed him, her eyes were beseeching me and her hands were stretched out to the child and me. And I could clearly see and, indeed, I felt it inside me that the poor lady was torn in twain, one half of her wanted to follow her lover and the other her child. . . . And at that very moment I saw my master who came running from the town. He had a pistol in his hand and he kept on firing it and shouting:

"Ivan! Ivan! Stop them!"

"Stop them?" I thought to myself. "Not likely! Not for you, I shan't! Why shouldn't they go on loving each other?" So I caught up with the lady and the Uhlan officer and I gave them the child and said:

"Take your brat, but," I said, "now you'll have to take me, too, for if you don't he'll deliver me to the officers of the law, for I have a faked passport."

He said:

"Yes, come along with us, dear Ivan. We'll go away together and you'll live with us."

So we galloped off and we took the little girl, the child left in my keeping, with us, and the goat, the money and my passport remained in the possession of my master.

All the way to Penza one thought kept on recurring to me as I sat on the box of the *tarantass* in which I was travelling with my new masters: had I done right in thrashing an army officer? After all, I said to myself, he had taken an oath of allegiance and in wartime he defended his country with his sabre and the Emperor himself quite probably addressed him as "sir," as behoved his rank, and I, fool that I was, had treated him so dishonourably! And then another thought occurred to me: what did fate have in store for me now?

There was a fair in Penza at the time and the Uhlan officer said to me:

"Look here, Ivan, I'm awfully sorry, but it seems I can't possibly let you stay with us."

I said:

"Why not?"

"Because," he said, "I am a servant of the State and you never had a passport."

"No, sir," I said, "it isn't quite correct to say that I never had a passport. I had a passport, only it was a fake."

"Well, you see, don't you?" he replied. "And now you haven't got even a faked one. Here, take two hundred roubles for your travelling expenses and good luck to you!"

Well, I don't mind confessing that I hated the very thought of leaving them, for, you see, I'd got so fond of the little girl, but I could see that there was nothing to be done about it, so I said:

"Well, good-bye, sir," I said, "and thank you very much for your kind reward, but I'm afraid there's something else that must be settled."

"What's that?" he asked.

"It's this, sir," I said. "I feel guilty before you for having had a fight with you and for having been disrespectful to you."

He laughed and said:

"Oh, that's nothing. I like you: you're a nice chap!"

"No, sir," I replied, "that has nothing to do with my being a nice chap. It can't be left like that, for it would always remain as a blot on my conscience. You're a defender of our country and I dare say the Emperor himself addresses you as 'sir.'"

"That's true enough," he said. "When we get our commission, we receive a paper on which it is written, 'Sir, we confer upon you the rank of officer and we command our people to respect and honour you.'"

"Well, you see, sir," I said, "you can hardly expect me to forgive myself for having inflicted such a dishonour on you."

"But what's to be done about it now?" he said. "That you're stronger than I can't be helped—can it?—and you can't very well take back the blows you've given me."

"That I can't take back the blows is quite true," I said, "but at least to ease my conscience, sir, I'd be obliged to you, if, whatever you yourself may feel about it, you'd hit me a few times yourself," and I blew out my cheeks and placed myself in front of him.

"But what for?" he said. "What shall I hit you for?"

"Just for no reason at all, sir," I said, "just for the sake of my conscience, so that I shouldn't have offended an officer of the Czar without proper punishment."

He laughed and I blew out my cheeks again, as much as there was breath in me, and again placed myself in front of him.

He asked me:

"What are you blowing out your cheeks for? What are you pulling faces for?"

And I replied:

"That's according to the army rules and regulations," I said. "Please, do me the favour and hit me hard on both my cheeks," and I blew out my cheeks again.

But instead of striking me, he embraced me and began kissing me.

"Drop it, Ivan, for Christ's sake, drop it," he said. "I shan't hit you for anything in the world, only go away quickly now before Mary comes back with the child, for they're sure to start crying when they see you leaving us."

"Very well, sir," I said. "That, of course, is a different matter. Why make them feel sad on my account?"

And although I did not want to go without accepting my punishment for insulting an officer's uniform, there was nothing I could do about it, so I left the house quickly without taking leave, and as I went through the gates I stopped dead in my tracks, thinking, "Where shall I go now?"

And indeed I could not help reflecting that although a long time had passed since I left my masters, I could find no place to settle down. . . . "That's the end," I thought, "I'm going to give myself up! And yet," it occurred to me, "that isn't quite right, either, for I've got money now and at the police station they're sure to take it away from me: let me at least spend some of it, let me have some tea at a tavern and some white rolls and just have a little pleasure for my money." So off I went to the fair and there I went into a tavern and asked for some tea and white rolls and I sat there drinking a long time, then, seeing that I couldn't very well sit there for ever, I went out for a walk. I walked beyond the Sura river into the steppe where the horse fair was and where the Tartars had pitched their tents. All those tents looked alike except one which was gaily coloured and round it a large number of gentlemen were occupying themselves in putting riding horses through their paces. There were gentlemen of all sorts there, civilians, army officers and landowners, who had come specially to the fair, and all were standing round, smoking pipes, and in the centre, on a beautiful rug of many colours, sat a tall, grave-looking Tartar, as thin as a reed, in a long patchwork robe and wearing a golden skull-cap. I looked round and, observing a man who had drunk tea in the same tavern with me, I asked him who that important Tartar was who was the only man to sit in that crowd of people. And the man said to me:

"Don't you know him? It is Khan Jangar."

"Who," I asked, "is Khan Jangar?"

And the man said:

"Khan Jangar," he said, "is the biggest breeder of horses in the steppe. His herds of horses are driven from the Volga to the Urals and all through the Rhyn-Sands, and he himself, this same Khan Jangar, is regarded in the steppe just like a Czar."

"Doesn't that steppe belong to us?" I asked.

"Why," he said, "of course it belongs to us, only that makes no difference because we can't do anything with it, for there's nothing there except salt marshes which stretch as far as the Caspian Sea, or else grass waving in the wind or birds flying under the heavens, and our civil servants, in particular, can't get a damn thing there and that's why," he said, "Khan Jangar lords it over everybody and, indeed, they say he has there, in the Rhyn-Sands, his own sheikhs and under-sheikhs and ulemas and imaums and hajis and mullahs, and he orders them about as he pleases, every mother's son of them, and they are glad to do as he tells them."

While listening to my new acquaintance, I noticed that a Tartar boy had driven a small white mare up to the Khan and started jabbering to him about something; the Khan got up, picked up a whip with a long handle and, placing himself right in front of the mare's head, stood still, holding the whip stretched out vertically against her forehead. How can I describe to you the way that bandit-chief was standing? Just like a beautiful statue! Aye, he was a sight to marvel at, and one look at him told you that in his leisurely way he saw right through that mare. And as I myself had since the days of my childhood been accustomed to judge the qualities of a horse at a glance, I saw that the mare herself recognised in him an expert and she stood erect before him, as if to say, "Come on, feast your eyes on me!" And it was thus that that grave-looking Tartar looked and looked at the mare, without walking round her as is the custom with our army officers who always bustle about a horse, unable to stand still for a minute; he, on the other hand, just kept on looking at her from one point and then suddenly he let fall the whip and just kissed his finger-tips without uttering a word: "A beauty!" so to speak; and he sat down again on the rug, crossing his legs, and the mare at once pricked up her ears and started to show off her high mettle.

The gentlemen who stood about now began to outbid each other: one bid one hundred roubles, another one hundred and fifty and so on, raising the bids against each other. The mare was, to be sure, a glorious animal, not too large in size, in shape somewhat like an Arab horse, but well proportioned, with a small head, a full eye, like an apple, and sharp ears; her sides were resonant, airy, her back like an arrow, and her legs light, beautifully turned, the swiftest you can imagine. I, as a lover of such beauty, could not tear my eyes away from her. Khan Jangar, seeing that everybody was bewitched by her and that the gentlemen were raising the price for her like mad, nodded to the dirty-faced Tartar boy, who leapt on to the back of the little darling and started putting her through her paces: he sat on her, you know, in his own Tartar fashion, squeezing her sides with his knees, and she just flew under him, as though she were a bird, without rolling even once, and whenever he bent over her little neck and whooped at her, she would disappear in a whirlwind of sand. "Oh, you little hussy," I thought to myself, "you little bustard of the steppe, where, oh, where could you have been born, my beautiful one?" And I felt how my soul yearned for her, for that lovely horse, with a great passion. Presently the Tartar boy brought her back and she just gave one little snort with both her nostrils, blew the breath out and shook off all weariness of body and not another breath could be heard from her, not a snort. "Oh, my darling," I thought, "Oh, my sweetheart!" Had that Tartar asked me to give up not only my soul, but my father and mother, for her, I should have gladly given them to him, but how could I hope to get such a winged courser when the gentlemen and the army buyers were just falling over each other and offering God knows what price for her! But even that was just nothing to what was to come, for before the bidding for her had come to an end and while she was still unsold, we saw a fast rider coming on a black horse from beyond the river Sura, from Selixa, and he was waving a wide-brimmed hat and, coming up like a hurricane, he jumped off his horse and made straight for the white mare and stopped dead in front of her head, just like another statue, and said:

"The mare's mine!"

But the Khan replied:

"No, sir, she's not! These gentlemen here are offering me five hundred gold coins for her."

But that rider, a huge Tartar with a big paunch, a sunburnt face, with the skin peeling off it and looking as if it had been torn off in places, and with tiny eyes, like little chinks, just shrieked:

"I'm offering a hundred coins more than anybody else!"

But the gentlemen refused to give up and began raising their bids, and that dry-as-dust Khan Jangar just sat there, pursing his lips, and from the other side of the Sura river another Tartar came riding along on a horse with a long mane, a chestnut with a whitish tail and mane, and he was a terribly lean man, yellow, all skin and bone, but he seemed to be even keener than the one who came first. He just slid off his horse and stuck like a nail in front of the white mare and said:

"Listen to me, all of you, I've made up my mind to have the mare!"

I turned to my acquaintance and asked him how he thought it would all end, and he said:

"That," he said, "depends entirely on what Khan Jangar himself decides. It isn't for the first time," he said, "that he has played such a trick on the buyers. It is his custom at every fair to dispose first of the ordinary horses he brings for sale and to keep one or two horses up his sleeve for the last day when, hey presto!—he produces them as if by magic, and the poor connoisseurs just go off their heads in their eagerness to buy them. But he, cunning Tartar that he is, has a fine time and rakes in the money, too. Knowing this habit of his everybody expects him to produce this last baby of his and so it has also come to pass now: everybody expected the Khan to leave to-day and so he will, but not before nightfall, and now he comes out with such a mare . . ."

"What a beauty of a horse!" I said.

"Yes, she's a beauty all right," he said. "He brought her to the fair in the middle of a whole herd of mares and so cunningly did he contrive it that nobody could see her for the other horses and nobody knew anything about her except the two Tartars who have just arrived and he told even them that his mare was not for sale and he sent her off to graze in a wood with a special herdsman and now he produces her just like that and offers her for sale, and you'd better watch out what wonders there will be happening on account of her and what money the cur will get for her, but if you like let's have a bet on who'll finally get her."

"How do you mean?" I asked. "How in heaven's name are we to have a bet on that?"

"Well, you see," he replied, "that's not as difficult as you think, for, mark my words, these gentlemen here are sure to back out soon and the mare will be taken by one of those Asiatics."

"Why," I said, "are they so rich?"

"Rich?" he echoed. "Why, they're rolling in money, both of them, and they're keen sportsmen, too. They bring their own herds to the fair and let them only take a liking to a horse, they'll fight tooth and nail for it. Everybody knows them: that one, the one with the big belly, the one who's face is all peeling, is called Bakshey Otuchev and the other one, the one who's all skin and bone, is Chepkun Yermucheyev, a real terror he is, but the fat one isn't a bit better. You just watch the fun that's coming. . . ."

I fell silent and saw that, indeed, the gentlemen who had been bidding for the mare had withdrawn from the sale and were just looking on, while the two Tartars kept on pushing each other out of the way and grasping Khan Jangar's hands and both of them held fast to the mare, trembling with rage and screaming at the top of their voices.

One shouted:

"I'll give you five heads (that is to say, horses) in addition to the money!"

And the other one hollered:

"The devil you will, you ugly brute! I give ten!"

Bakshey Otuchev shrieked:

"I'm giving fifteen!"

And Chepkun Yermucheyev:

"Twenty!"

Bakshey:

"Twenty-five!"

And Chepkun:

"Thirty!"

Now more than that neither of them could bid, for it seemed they had no more horses to spare. . . . Chepkun shouted: thirty, and Bakshey, too, offered thirty, and no more. Thereupon Chepkun capped his offer by the offer of a saddle and Bakshey by a saddle and a robe, Chepkun also added a robe, and once more they hesitated, trying to think how to best each other. Then Chepkun shouted, "Listen to me, Khan Jangar, directly I return home I'll fetch you one of my daughters." So Bakshey, too, promised Khan Jangar one of his daughters, and again there was a deadlock, neither of them being able to outbid the other. Here the whole Tartar mob, who had been the silent onlookers of that contest, started suddenly to shout in their own lingo, raising a hell of a din. They tried to pull the two bidders for the mare apart in order to prevent them from ruining themselves entirely, pulling them—Chepkun and Bakshey—in opposite directions, poking them in the ribs, imploring them to bethink themselves.

I asked the man standing beside me:

"Tell me, what's all the row about now?"

"Well, you see," he said, "those Tartar princes who're trying to separate Chepkun and Bakshey are sorry for them; they think that they've gone far enough, so they're trying to part them and bring them to their senses and, somehow or other, to persuade one of the two to give up the mare to the other."

"But how can you expect either of them to give up the mare, if both like her so much?" I asked. "It seems to me," I added, "that they're wasting their time."

"Not at all," he replied. "The Asiatics are a sensible people and they like to do everything without any excitement: they'll decide that it isn't fair for either of them to ruin himself and they'll give Khan Jangar as much as he asks for his mare and then put the mare up as a prize in a flogging match."

"And what," I asked, "is a flogging match?"

And the man answered:

"Don't ask so many questions! Have patience and you'll find out everything for yourself. It's something that has to be seen and it's about to start any moment now."

So I looked and I saw that both Bakshey Otuchev and Chepkun Yermucheyev were beginning to calm down a little and presently they broke loose from the Tartars who had been trying to make peace between them, ran up to each other and began shaking hands: "All right," said one, "it's a bargain!" and the other one replied in the same words, "All right, it's a bargain!"

And both of them immediately threw off their robes and their long Caucasian tunics and their morocco-leather slippers and they took off their cotton shirts and flopped down on the ground, sitting down one opposite the other like two steppe sand-pipers, and they stayed like that.

It was the first time in my life that I had happened to see such an extraordinary sight and I couldn't help wondering what was going to happen next. Well, they grasped each other by the left hand, holding on firmly, spread out their legs and put their soles and heels together, one pair against the other, and shouted:

"Come on, let's have 'em!"

I couldn't even guess what it was they were demanding to "have," but they, the Tartars, that is, shouted back to them from the crowd:

"Presently, gentlemen, presently!"

Then an old Tartar came out from that crowd, a fine, grave-looking old patriarch, and in his hands he held two mighty whips. He measured them carefully and, putting them together, showed them to the public and to Chepkun and Bakshey. "Look," he said, "they are of the same length."

"Aye," the Tartar mob shouted, "both are of equal length, we can see that, both are well made, everything's fair and above-board! Let them sit down and start!"

Bakshey and Chepkun nearly jumped out of their skins in their eagerness to get hold of those whips, but the grave old Tartar said to them, "Wait!" and then he himself handed the two whips to them: one to Chepkun and one to Bakshey and he clapped his hands softly three times: one, two, three. . . . And no sooner did he clap a third time than Bakshey struck Chepkun a mighty blow with the whip across the bare back over the shoulder and Chepkun replied in the same manner. So they went on regaling each other like that: looking straight into each other's eyes, the soles and heels of one pressed hard against the soles and heels of the other, left hands clasped firmly, and with their right hands flogging each other with leather thongs. . . . Ugh! what a lovely fight that was! One would strike a real beauty of a blow and the other would fetch an even better one. So they went on flogging each other till there was a stunned look in their eyes and their left hands went stiff, but neither the one nor the other would give in.

I asked my acquaintance:

"Do they fight one another like that just like our own gentlemen do at a duel?"

"Yes," he replied, "this is also a kind of single combat, but they don't fight to save their honour, but to save their money."

"Can they go on flogging one another like that a long time?" I asked.

"Just as long as they please," he said, "and as long as their strength holds out."

Meanwhile those two went on flogging each other and the people began to argue among themselves, some saying, "Chepkun will outflog Bakshey," and others saying, "Bakshey will outflog Chepkun," and those who were of the sporting fraternity laid bets against each other, either for Chepkun or Bakshey, all depending on whom they pinned their hopes as the winner. They'd look into their eyes and examine their teeth with an expert air and they'd also glance at their backs and they seemed to be able to judge by certain signs who was the more likely winner and that one they would back. The man with whom I had been talking was also one of these experts and, at first, he was all for Bakshey, but later he changed his mind and said:

"Ah, well, I've lost my twenty copecks! Chepkun's sure to beat Bakshey!"

But I said:

"How do you know that? It's quite impossible to tell yet: both are sitting tight!"

But he answered:

"It's true," he said, "that both are sitting firmly, but their methods are different."

"If it comes to that," I said, "Bakshey's strokes are much more vicious."

"That's the trouble," he said. "Yes, sir, my twenty copecks are as good as lost. Chepkun will flog him to a standstill."

"That's a strange business," I thought. "My acquaintance seems to be all wrong and yet," I said to myself, "he must be an old hand at that kind of fight or he wouldn't bet."

So my curiosity was rather roused, you know, and I kept on worrying my friend:

"Please be so good as to explain to me," I said, "why you're so apprehensive about Bakshey ?"

And he said:

"What a country simpleton you are! Just have a look at Bakshey's back!"

I looked and there seemed nothing wrong with his back: it was a lovely back, a strong back, big and plump as a cushion.

"But can't you see how he's hitting ?" he said.

I looked again and I could see that he was hitting out viciously, so that his eyes were popping out, and every time he hit his opponent, he'd draw blood.

"Now just try to think what's happening inside him."

"How do you mean, inside him ? All I can see is that he's sitting up straight and that his mouth is wide open and that he's taking in the air in quick gasps."

My acquaintance then said:

"Well, that's the trouble, you see. He has a large back and every blow across it goes home, he hits fast and he's therefore getting winded, he's breathing through an open mouth and that means that he'll burn up all his inside with the air."

"So you think that Chepkun is more likely to win ?" I asked.

"Of course he's more likely to win," he replied. "Have a good look at him: there's not a drop of sweat on him and his bones have no fat on 'em, just skin and that's all, and that back of his is just like a scooped-out wooden spade, no blow can possibly fall on it fully, but it will strike him only in places, while he, you see, is hitting Bakshey steadily, not too fast, but with a pause between each blow, so that the whip doesn't descend with a crash, but just strongly enough to raise a weal on the skin. That's why that one's back, Bakshey's, I mean, is all swollen and is as black as a kettle and there's not a drop of blood on it, which means that all the pain remains inside his body; but the skin on Chepkun's back is cracked like the skin of a roasted sucking pig, and it breaks, so that all the pain will go out with his blood and he's bound to give Bakshey the beating of his life. Do you see it now ?"

"Yes," I said, "I see it now," and, indeed, now I grasped the whole secret of that Tartar sport and began to be greatly interested in it and, particularly, in the question what was the best thing to do in such a contingency.

"And, mind, the most important thing," my acquaintance told me further, "is that that damned Chepkun keeps good time with that ugly face of his. Look! Do you see? He strikes, then he takes his punishment in his turn and each time he shuts or opens his eyes as the case may be. That's much easier than having your eyes popping out of your head all the time. Chepkun has clenched his teeth and bit his lips and that, too, makes it easier for him, for by holding his mouth shut he prevents any unnecessary burning inside him."

I made a mental note of all those interesting points and, as I looked more and more closely at Chepkun and Bakshey, I began to see for myself that Bakshey was bound to collapse, for his eyes had already glazed over and his lips had distended into a thin line, baring all his teeth. . . . And so it was: Bakshey struck Chepkun about twenty more times and every time the force of his blow got weaker and weaker, then—wallop!—he suddenly swayed backwards, let go of Chepkun's left hand, while still moving his right one up and down as if he were continuing to deal blows with it, but he was already unconscious and in another moment he passed right out. Well, my acquaintance then said, "It's all over! Good-bye to my twenty copecks!" Here all the Tartars started talking at once, congratulating Chepkun and shouting:

"A clever chap, Chepkun Yermucheyev! Oh, what a brainy fellow! Knocked Bakshey right out! Now the mare's yours. Come on, get on her back!"

And Khan Jangar himself also got up from his rug, sucked his lips and said:

"It's yours, it's yours, Chepkun. The mare's yours. Mount her and have a ride on her, you can have a rest on her back."

Well, so Chepkun got up. The blood was streaming down his back, but he showed no sign of feeling any pain. He put his robe and tunic over the mare's back and jumped on her, lying flat on his belly, and rode off like that, and I was beginning to feel depressed once more.

"Well," I thought, "now that's finished I'll start worrying about my position again," and I just hated to think about it.

But, luckily, that acquaintance of mine said to me:

"Wait, don't go. Something more's sure to happen."

I said:

"What's going to happen now? It's all over."

"No," said he, "it isn't over. Look," he said, "do you notice the way Khan Jangar is smoking his pipe? He keeps on puffing away at it, that's a sure sign that he's contemplating some other Asiatic trick!"

So I thought to myself, "If only something of the kind were to happen again and somebody were to back me by a promise to pay for the horse, I'd never let him down!"

CHAPTER VI

AND would you believe it? Everything came to pass exactly as I wished. Khan Jangar was blazing away at his pipe and from a near-by wood another Tartar boy came galloping towards him, but this time not on a mare like the one Chepkun had won from Bakshey in a public contest, but on a bay colt which defied all description. Have you ever watched a corncrake flying over the boundary between two fields? If you have, you must have noticed how he spreads out his wings while his tail—unlike other birds—is not spread out in the air at all, but hangs down, and his legs, too, he lets droop, as though he had no use for them, and you get the impression that he is riding on air. So did that new horse, like that bird, seem to tear along driven by some power not his own.

It is the honest truth I'm telling you when I say that the colt didn't even fly, but that it looked as if the earth was gaining on him. Never in my life had I seen such lightness, and I did not even know what price to set on such a horse, what treasure to give for him and who was the man worthy to own him, what Crown Prince he should belong to, and least of all did I dream that I might myself become its owner.

"Did you become its owner?" the surprised passengers interrupted the novice.

"Yes, he became mine, mine according to all the rules, but for one minute only, and how it all happened, gentlemen, you will hear, if you will be kind enough to give me your attention."

As was to be expected, the gentlemen began to haggle over the horse, and my cavalry officer, to whom I had given the child, also joined in the bidding; but against them all, as though he were their equal, a Tartar started bidding for the horse, a Tartar by the name of Savakirey, a stocky sort of chap, a little man, but of strong build, with a devil of a temper, his head shaven, as if turned on a lathe, and round like a firm cabbage fresh from the field, and a face like a red carrot, and altogether he looked like a fine, fresh vegetable. "Why waste money for nothing?" he hollered. "Let anybody who likes put down as much money as the Khan asks and let him have a flogging match with me and the winner takes the horse!"

Well, the gentlemen naturally would not accept such a challenge and they at once withdrew, for how, indeed, could they even think of entering a flogging contest against that damned Tartar who was quite certain to og the whole lot of them to death? And my cavalry officer was not xactly rolling in money at the time, for he had again lost a lot of money t cards in Penza, and I could see that he wanted that horse badly. So pulled him by the sleeve from behind and said to him, Don't offer any ore money for the horse, but just give as much as the Khan asks and t me have a go at Savakirey at that flogging match of theirs. He would ot hear of it at first, but I persuaded him to let me have a try, saying:

"Do me a favour, sir, I'd like to very much."

And so he did.

"And you and that Tartar . . . Did you really flog each other?"

"Yes, we did flog each other according to their custom, in public, and got the horse."

"Then you won?"

"Yes, I won. Mind you, it was no easy victory, but I did get the better f him in the end."

"But the pain must have been terrible."

"Well . . . how shall I put it? . . . At the beginning, yes, the ain was rather bad, especially as I wasn't used to it and, besides, he, that Savakirey chap, also knew all about hitting your back so that it swelled p, but did not bleed. However, I used a trick of my own against his lever art: every time he had a crack at me I'd pull up the skin on my back nder the whip and I got so clever at it that I'd tear the skin and in that way I escaped the danger of a swollen back and I myself flogged that Savakirey to death."

"How do you mean? Actually to death?"

"That's right. You see, through his own pig-headedness and through what he thought was clever policy on his part he brought things to such a pass that he departed this world for good and all," the novice replied quite good-humouredly and rather casually, but seeing that the passengers looked at him, if not in terror, then in mute bewilderment, he seemed to feel the need of adding a gloss to his story.

"You see," he said, "that was his look out, not mine, because he was famed far and wide throughout the Rhyn-Sands as one of their strongest men and, being naturally ambitious of his title, he would not give in to me for all the world. He wanted to bear his punishment honourably, so as not to be the means of discrediting the whole Asiatic nation, but, poor chap, he just couldn't bear it, I suppose, couldn't stand up against me and I suspect, gentlemen, that was chiefly because I had a farthing in my mouth. You can't imagine what a great help that is! I kept on biting on it so as not to feel the pain and to distract my thoughts I counted the blows in my head so that I didn't mind it very much."

"And how many blows did you count?" one of the passengers interrupted him.

"That I couldn't tell you for certain, sir. All I remember is that I counted up to two hundred and eighty and then I seemed to have had a kind of fainting fit and I got confused in my head for a moment and lost count of the blows and didn't bother to count any more and, anyway, soon after that Savakirey aimed his last blow at me, but had not the strength to hit me and fell forward like a doll on top of me. They looked him over, but he was dead. . . . Oh, what a fool I was! To think what it was I had stuck it out for! I nearly landed in jail on account of him. The Tartars, mind you, didn't care a bit: if you've killed him, you've killed him, for according to the rules he could have flogged me to death, too. But our Russians were quite hopeless. Really, I was terribly disappointed in them: they didn't seem to grasp the situation at all! Made such a fuss! I said:

"What do you want? What are you getting so worked up about?"

"What do you mean?" they said. "You killed an Asiatic, didn't you?"

"So what if I did kill him? Wasn't it done according to the rules? Would it have been better if he had killed me?"

"He could have killed you," they said, "and gone scot-free, because he isn't a Christian, but you," they said, "are a Christian and you'll therefore have to be put on trial according to the Christian laws. Come on," they said, "to the police station with you!"

But I said to myself, "Oh, no, my dear friends, you're as likely to put the wind on trial as me," and as in my opinion there can't be anything less wholesome than the police, I just dodged behind one Tartar and then behind another and I whispered to them:

"Save me, princes! You saw yourselves how it all happened. It was a fair fight. . . ."

Well, they just closed up their ranks and pushed me from one to the other and so they concealed me.

"Forgive me, but how do you mean they *concealed* you?"

"I ran away with them to their steppe for good."

"To their steppe?"

"Yes, sir. As far as the Rhyn-Sands."

"And did you stay there long?"

"For ten whole years: I was twenty-three when I reached the Rhyn-Sands and I ran away from them in my thirty-third year."

"Did you like life in the steppe or didn't you?"

"No, I didn't. What is there to like about it? I was terribly homesick all the time I was there, but I couldn't get away earlier."

"Why not? Did the Tartars keep you at the bottom of a well or did they mount guard over you?"

"Oh, no, nothing of the sort. They're kindly folk and wouldn't permit anyone to treat me so dishonourably as to throw me into a well or put me into stocks, but they just said to me, We want you to be our friend, Ivan. We love you dearly, they said, and we want you to live with us in the steppe and be a useful man, cure our horses and help the women."

"And did you cure their horses?"

"Yes, I did. As a matter of fact, I was their only doctor and I took care of their health as well as of the health of their cattle, their horses and their sheep, but most of all I would give treatment to their wives, the Tartar ladies."

"And did you cure their illnesses?"

"Well, I don't rightly know what to say. . . . You see, there isn't much in it when you come to think of it, is there? If any of them got ill, I'd give them some aloes or the root of galanga and it would pass off. Luckily, they had plenty of aloes: a Tartar found a whole sackful of them in Saratov and he had brought it home with him, but before I came to live with them, they didn't know what to do with it."

"So you settled down among them?"

"No, I didn't. I was always trying to get back."

"And did you really find it so hard to get away from them?"

"No, I shouldn't have found it so hard if my feet were in good shape. I should have gone back to my country long before."

"What was the matter with your feet?"

"I was bristled up after my first attempt."

"What's that? Pardon us, but we don't quite understand what you mean by saying you were *bristled up!*"

"Oh, that's one of their usual tricks: if they take a liking to a person and want to keep him and if that person is feeling down in the mouth and tries to escape, they do something to him to prevent him from running away. The same thing happened to me after I had tried to run away and lost my way in the steppe. They caught me and said, Look here, Ivan, they said, we want you to be our friend and to make sure that you won't run away again we're going to take the skin off your heels and shove some bristles in and then sew it up again. Well, in this way they crippled my feet and I had to crawl on all fours all the time."

"How do they perform this terrible operation?"

"Quite simply. About ten of them threw me to the ground and told me, Shout, Ivan, shout as loud as you can when we start cutting your flesh: you'll feel much better then! And they sat on top of me and one of them, a past-master in this art, cut away the skin of my heels in less than no time and put in some hair from a horse's mane, which had been cut up very fine, and, putting back the skin on top of the bits of hair, he sewed it up with some gut. After that, I admit, they did keep me bound hand and foot for a few days,

for they were afraid that I might interfere with my wounds and get rid o
the bristle by making them matter. But as soon as the skin healed up
they let me go, saying, Welcome to our tents, Ivan, for now you're ou
friend for better or for worse and you will never leave us again! I trie
to get up, but as soon as I stood on my feet, down I went again, for th
cut-up hair under the skin of my heels hurt terribly because it pierced int
the living flesh and I couldn't take a single step. However hard I tried
I couldn't think of a way of standing on my feet. I had never cried in m
life before, but just then I couldn't help bawling at the top of my voic
and I said to them, What have you done to me, you damned Asiatics
I'd rather you'd killed me outright than crippled me for the rest of my day
and made it impossible for me to stand on my feet! But they said to me
Don't cry, Ivan, there's nothing to worry about. Why are you kickin
up such a row over nothing at all ? But I said, What are you talking about
Do you call crippling a man nothing and do you really expect me not t
kick up a row about it ? And they said, Get used to it, don't step on you
heels, but walk about in a bandy-legged fashion by stepping on your ankl
bones ! Oh, you rascals, I thought to myself, and I turned away from
them and spoke no more, but I made up my mind that I'd rather be dead
than follow their advice and walk on my ankle bones in a bandy-legged
way. However, after lying about for some time I felt as melancholy as
a cat and I started getting used to walking about in a bandy-legged way
and by and by I was hobbling about on my ankles. They laughed at me
a lot on account of that and they even had the effrontery to tell me, That's
very nice, Ivan, you can walk beautifully now!"

"What an awful thing to happen to you! Did you try to run away a
second time and did they catch you again ?"

"No, I didn't do anything of the kind. You see, it was quite impossible.
The steppe is flat, there are no roads and one has to eat. . . . The first time
I had walked for three days and I had grown so weak that I could hardly drag
my feet. I caught some bird with my hands and I ate her raw and then again
hunger and thirst. . . . How was I to go on ? . . . In the end I collapsed
and they found me, brought me back and bristled me."

One of the passengers remarked in regard to that "bristling" that it
must have been very awkward walking on one's ankles.

"At first it is rather a bit of a nuisance," Ivan Severyanych replied,
"and even later on when I got the knack of it, I found it quite impossible
to walk very far. But to give them their due, those Tartars after that
appreciated the awkwardness of my situation and they did their best to
make life tolerable for me. They said to me, You can hardly manage for
yourself now, Ivan: you can't fetch any water for yourself, nor can you
cook yourself any food, so why don't you take a Natashka to help you ?
Choose any Natashka you like and we'll be glad to give her to you. But

I said to them, Why waste my time choosing, if there's only one thing they're good for, anyway? Let's have any one you like. So without any more ado they married me."

"What? Do you mean they married you to a Tartar woman?"

"Well, of course they married me to a Tartar woman. First to one, the wife of Savakirey whom I had flogged to death, but she, this Tartar woman, was not to my taste at all: a queer one she was, and she seemed to be scared of me and was no fun at all. I don't know whether it was that she was longing for her husband or whether it was something else that made her so broken-hearted, but directly the Tartars saw that she was more of a burden than a delight to me, they brought me another one, a little girl she was, no more than thirteen years old. They said to me, Take this Natashka for your second wife: she'll be more fun for you. So I took her."

"And was she more fun?" the passengers asked Ivan Severyanych.

"Yes," he replied, "she was more fun, she'd amuse me a lot sometimes, but at other times she'd just get my goat by her naughty ways."

"What kind of naughty ways?"

"Well, all sorts. . . . Just as her fancy took her: she'd jump on my knees, for instance, or when I'd be asleep she'd scoop up my skull-cap with her feet and send it flying all over the tent, laughing her head off. I'd start scolding her, but she'd go on laughing and running about like a blessed pixie and, crawling on all fours, I couldn't catch her and I'd slip and start laughing myself."

"And did you shave your head and wear a skull-cap there in the steppe?"

"Yes, I shaved my head."

"But why did you do that? Did you want to please your wives?"

"I hardly think so, more for the sake of cleanliness, for, you see, they have no baths there."

"So that you had two wives at the same time?"

"Yes, two in one steppe, but afterwards when I lived with another Tartar chief, Khan Agashimola, who had carried me off from Yermucheyev, they gave me two more."

"But," one of the passengers could not help interjecting, "how did they manage to carry you off?"

"By a stratagem. From Penza I had run away with the Tartars of Chepkun Yermucheyev and for five years I lived with the Yermucheyev crowd and it was there that all the Tartar princes and ulemas and sheikhs and under-sheikhs used to forgather in celebration of some feast, including even Khan Jangar and Bakshey Otuchev."

"Is that the one Chepkun had flogged?"

"Yes, the same."

"But how's that? Didn't Bakshey bear a grudge against Chepkun?"

"Why should he? They never bear a grudge against each other for such a thing: the winner in a flogging match gets the prize and that's all there is to it. Khan Jangar, though, did say to me once, Oh, Ivan, Ivan, what a stupid idiot you are, Ivan, to have sat down to that flogging match with Savakirey when I was just going to enjoy a good laugh at your prince, watching his highness himself take off his shirt. But I told him, You'd never have lived to see that. So he asked me, Why not? And I replied, Because our princes are faint-hearts and have no pluck at all and their strength isn't anything to boast about, either. He understood and he said to me, I could see that there were no real sportsmen among them and that if they wanted a thing, they expected to get it for money. And I said, That's true enough: they can't do anything without money. Anyway, that Khan Agashimola belonged to a distant Tartar tribe and his herds of horses grazed somewhere near the Caspian Sea. He liked to doctor himself, it was quite a hobby with him, and he asked me to come and see if I could cure his wife and promised many heads of cattle to Yermucheyev if he let me go. So Yermucheyev let me go with him. I took with me my aloes and the galanga root and went off with him. But once he got me, Khan Agashimola moved off with all his tribe to some other grazing grounds, for eight days we galloped before we came to them."

"Did you go on horseback?"

"Why, yes."

"And what about your feet?"

"What about them?"

"But didn't that chopped-up hair in your feet trouble you at all?"

"Not in the least. You see, they had thought it out very cleverly. They put the bristle under a man's heels so that he can't walk, but such a bristled man can ride a horse better than ever before, because he has got used to walking in a bandy-legged way and he holds his legs always in a crooked position. He therefore finds it an easy matter to get a firm grip on the horse's sides as with a hoop and no horse can throw him."

"Well, and what adventures did you have while living with Khan Agashimola?"

"I suffered worse and worse trials and tribulations."

"But you didn't perish."

"No, I did not perish."

"Won't you tell us what further trials you had to undergo with Khan Agashimola?"

"Gladly, gentlemen."

CHAPTER VII

"As soon as Agashimola's Tartars brought me to their tents, they broke camp and away they went to look for new pastures and they would not let me go back. They said to me, Why do you want to go back to Yermucheyev, Ivan? Yermucheyev is a thief. You'd better stay with us, we'll take you hunting with us and we'll give you lovely Natashas. You had only two Natashas there, but we'll give you more. But I refused, saying, I don't want any more of them, what shall I do with more of them? But they said, You don't understand, Ivan: the more Natashas you have, the better it is for you, for they'll bear you more Kolkas who'll all be calling you daddy. But I didn't consider the prospect of bringing up lots of Tartar children particularly inviting and I told them so. I said, If I could have baptised them and made sure that they received the Holy Communion, it would be a different matter, but in my present circumstances however great a number of children I had they would still be yours and they would not be Orthodox Christians and—who knows?—they might even grow up to cheat Russian peasants! So I only took two more wives and no more, for if there are too many women about, they start quarrelling among themselves, Tartar women though they be, and I'd have had my work cut out keeping them in order."

"Well, and did you love those new wives of yours?"

"How do you mean?"

"Did you love your new wives?"

"Love them? Oh, I see, you mean *that?* Well, there was one I got from Agashimola and she always tried to please me and . . . well . . . I did take pity on her."

"And that girl, the young one who had been your wife before, didn't you like her even more?"

"Yes, I reckon I took pity on her, too."

"Didn't you miss her when they abducted you from one tribe to another?"

"No, I don't think I missed her particularly."

"But didn't you have any children by those first wives of yours?"

"Why, of course, I had. Savakirey's wife bore me two Kolkas and one Natashka and the other one, the little one, bore me six in five years, for she brought me two Kolkas at the same time."

"Why, pray, do you always call them 'Kolkas' and 'Natashkas'?"

"That's a Tartar custom. They have only one name for Russians: a man they call *Ivan* and a woman *Natasha* and boys *Kolkas*, so my wives, although they were Tartar women, were considered to be Russians by them because I was a Russian and they called them Natashkas, and my boys they called Kolkas. I am, mind you, talking of them as my children only in a manner of speaking, for as they had never received any sacraments of the Church, I, for one, never considered them as my children."

"Why didn't you consider them as your children? Whose children were they then?"

"I couldn't very well consider them as my own, if they had not been baptised and anointed with myrrh."

"But what about your parental feelings?"

"What would that be?"

"Didn't you love those children of yours? Didn't you ever fondle them?"

"How should I have fondled them? Sometimes when I was sitting alone and one would run up to me, I . . . well . . . I'd stroke his head or say to him, 'Go to your mother!' But that didn't happen very often, for I couldn't be bothered with them."

"But why not? Were you so very busy?"

"No, I wasn't busy, but I was always brooding, wanted to go home to Russia very badly."

"So even in ten years you couldn't get used to the steppes?"

"No, I couldn't. I wanted to go home. . . . I'd be overcome by melancholy thoughts, especially in the evenings, and sometimes even in the daytime when it happened to be a very fine day, very hot, and everything in the camp was quiet, for on a hot day the Tartars keep to their tents, going to sleep, but I would raise the flap of my tent and look out on to the steppe . . . one way and another . . . it was all the same. . . . A fiery furnace, pitiless. . . . For miles and miles the horizon stretched without a break; grass—everywhere, feather-grass, white and tufted, waving like a silver sea and scenting the air with the breeze; there was a smell of sheep, and the sun would be blazing from a clear sky, burning, and wherever I looked there was no end to the steppe as there's no end to life's sorrows, and as there was no bottom to my heartache. . . . I looked without knowing myself where I was looking and suddenly I would behold a monastery or a church and I would remember my own Christian land and I would start shedding tears. . . ."

Ivan Severyanych stopped and, overcome by his memories, heaved a deep sigh, then he went on:

"It was much worse among the salt marshes close to the Caspian Sea: the sun glared, baked, and the salt marsh sparkled and the sea sparkled. . . . You'd get dizzier from that sparkling than from the feather-grass and then you wouldn't know where, in what part of the world, I mean, you were, whether you were numbered among the living or you were among the dead and were being tormented in hell without hope of redemption. In the steppe, which is covered thickly with feather-grass, it is, at any rate, more agreeable; occasionally in some ravine there you can at least catch a glimpse of the bluish mist of blossoming sage or else, now and then, small bushes of wormwood and savory dazzle the eye with a splash of whiteness! But here there is nothing but that sparkling. . . . There, the grass would sometimes be set ablaze and a trail of fire would pass across the steppe—a general hubbub would arise: great bustards would rise in the air, little bustards and steppe snipe, and we'd have some sport. The great bustards we'd overtake on our horses and start killing them with long whips; and, as likely as not, we'd have in the end to take to our heels ourselves, fleeing on our horses from the flames. . . . All that would, to a certain extent, break the monotony of our existence. And then wild strawberry would again begin to flower on the burnt-out patches of steppe; all kinds of birds would come flying there, mostly small birds, and there'd be a constant chirping in the air. . . . And then again, here and there, you'd come across some shrubs: queen-of-the-meadows, wild peach, field southernwood! . . . And when at the rising of the sun the mist descended and covered the grass with dew, there'd be a pleasant coolness in the air which would be full of the fragrance of plants. . . . No doubt even then one felt sick at heart, but all that would make life at least bearable, but God preserve any man from spending a long time among those salt marshes! The horse finds life quite pleasant there for a time: he licks the salt and that makes him drink a lot and get fat, but no man can live there for long without perishing. There's no wild life of any kind there, except, funnily enough, one little bird, a redpoll, like our swallow, a most ordinary bird except for that red streak round its beak. Why she should go to the shores of that sea I don't know, but as there's nothing there on which she can alight, she just drops on the salt marsh and sits there on her rump and, lo! up she rises again and off she flies. But you can't even do that, for you have no wings, and you stay there and there's neither life, nor death, nor repentance for you, and if you die, they'll put you, like mutton, in salt and you'll lie there till the end of the world like a piece of salted meat. But, if anything, it is even worse to spend a winter on those dismal grazing grounds. There isn't much snow about, just enough to cover the grass and then it hardens. The Tartars spend all their time in their tents over a fire, smoking, and out of sheer boredom they often flog each other. If you leave your tent there is nothing to look at: the horses walk about with their heads hanging down, shrivelled up and their ribs showing, their tails and manes alone streaming in the wind. They can hardly drag their feet, they rake up the frozen snow with their hooves and swallow the frozen grass, which is the only fodder they get. It's enough to drive you crazy. . . . The only distraction you get is when a horse is seen to be getting too weak to rake up the snow with his hooves and nibble the frozen grass, for then they stick a knife into his throat, take off his hide and eat his flesh. It's rotten meat, though: sweet, just like a cow's udder, except that it is tough. You eat it, of course, but that's only because you have to, for it just turns your stomach. One of my wives, fortunately, knew how to smoke a horse's ribs: she'd take a rib just as it was, with the meat clinging to the bone on both sides, put it inside a large gut and smoke it over the hearth. That wasn't so bad, you could eat it with some relish, for the smell at least reminded you of smoked ham, but it turned your stomach all the same. Well, I'd be chewing that bit of carrion and, suddenly, the thought would cross my mind: Oh, to be at home now in my village! Christmas would be coming soon and everybody would be plucking ducks and geese, slaughtering pigs, cooking cabbage soup with stuffed birds' necks, as fat as anything! And father Ilya, our priest, such a dear old soul, would soon be leading a procession to glorify Christ the Lord and with him in that procession would be his deacons, the priests' ladies and the deacons' ladies, walking side by side with the seminary students, and all of them a bit tipsy. . . . Father Ilya himself can't hold much drink: at the hall the butler would offer him a glass of vodka on a tray and at the office the manager would send out the old nurse with another, so father Ilya would get a bit fuddled and he'd totter along to the servants' quarters, hardly able to drag his feet, drunk as a lord, poor soul! In the first cottage, at the edge of the yard, he'd somehow manage to sip another glass, but that would be his last, and every other glass offered to him he would be emptying into a bottle which he carried under his chasuble. Being a most devoted family man even where food was concerned, father Ilya, if he should happen to see a tasty morsel lying about, would never miss the chance of begging for it. Wrap it up in a newspaper, he'd say, and I'll take it home with me! Generally, such a request would bring forth the reply, We have no newspaper, father! But he wouldn't get angry and would take it as it was, without bothering to wrap it up, but handing it to his wife just as it was, and he would continue on his way, as serenely as ever. . . . Oh, gentlemen, when all those happy memories of my childhood would come crowding into my head and oppress my soul and weigh heavily upon my liver, I'd say to myself, What a dog's life you're leading now, far away from all that happiness, bereft of spiritual consolation for so many years, you live unwedded and you'll die unmourned! . . . And I'd be overcome by such melancholy that, as soon as night came, I'd steal quietly out of the camp, away from the sight of my wives and children and all the other heathens, and I'd start to pray . . . and I'd pray and pray and I wouldn't even notice that the snow under my knees had melted and where my tears had dropped I could see the grass next morning. . . ."

The novice fell silent and sank his head. No one disturbed him, for all felt deeply moved by the sacred sorrow of his last memories; but after a short time Ivan Severyanych heaved a sigh, with which he seemed to dismiss the whole thing, took off his monastic hat and, crossing himself, said:

"Well, everything passed off all right, the Lord be praised!"

We gave him time to rest a little and then ventured to ask more questions about how he, our enchanted hero, managed to get rid of the bristles in his crippled heels and how he succeeded in fleeing from the Tartar steppe, from his Natashkas and Kolkas, and entering a monastery.

Ivan Severyanych satisfied our curiosity with great frankness, from which, indeed, he was quite incapable of departing.

CHAPTER VIII

As we set great store on consecutive order in the development of the story of Ivan Severyanych, which we had found so fascinating, we asked him to tell us first of all by what unusual means he had rid himself of the bristles and how he had managed to flee from his captivity. He gave us the following account of his adventures:—

I completely despaired of ever returning home and seeing my native land again. The very thought of it seemed a waste of time to me and my homesickness began gradually to die down. I went on living like some lifeless statue and that was all. But sometimes the thought would occur to me that at home in our church the same father Ilya who used to ask for newspaper to wrap up some delicacy with, would pray during the divine service for "all that travel by land, or by water, and all sick persons and *captives*," and that I, hearing that prayer, would always wonder: "Why? Are we at war now that he should be praying for captives?" Now I understood why those prayers were said in church, but what I could not understand was why those prayers were not of the slightest use to me and, to tell the truth, although I am not an unbeliever, I am sometimes perplexed, and so I stopped saying any prayers.

"What's the use of praying," I said to myself, "when nothing comes of it anyway?"

In the meantime I suddenly noticed one day that the Tartars were in a state of great excitement.

I said:

"What's the matter?"

"Oh, nothing much," they said, "except that two mullahs have arrived from your country with a safe conduct from the White Czar and they're going on a long journey to spread their gospel."

I just gasped and I said:

"Where are they?"

They pointed out a tent to me and I went where they had shown me. When I entered the tent I saw that a large number of sheikhs and under-sheikhs had gathered there as well as imaums and dervishes and all of them were sitting cross-legged on rugs and among them were two strangers, who though dressed in travelling clothes were obviously men of the cloth. Both of them were standing in the midst of that mob and were preaching the gospel to the Tartars.

As I beheld them, I greatly rejoiced to see two of my fellow-countrymen and my heart leapt within me and I fell down at their feet and wept. They, too, rejoiced to see me prostrate myself before them and both exclaimed:

"Well, brethren, do you see how wonderfully the grace of God works? Behold, one of your own kith and kin has already become converted and renounced Mahomet!"

But the Tartars replied that it did not seem to have worked at all, for that man, they said, was just one of your own Ivans who lived as a captive among us.

The missionaries were greatly displeased with that. They would not believe that I was a Russian, so I roused myself and said:

"Yes," I said, "I am truly a Russian! Fathers," I said, "servants of the Church, have mercy upon me, save me, help me to escape from here! I've been held captive here for over ten years and you can see for yourselves that I've been crippled and cannot walk on my feet."

But they paid little heed to my words and turned away and carried on with their business: they went on preaching!

So I thought to myself, "I have no right to murmur against them, for they are on an official mission and, perhaps, they find it a bit awkward to treat me otherwise in the presence of the Tartars." I therefore left the tent and chose a more auspicious time when they were alone in a tent and I went to them and told them frankly all about myself, what a cruel fate had befallen me, and I besought them:

"Dear fathers," I said, "put the fear of our great White Czar into them, tell them that he has forbidden the Asiatics to keep one of his own subjects in captivity, or, what would be more to the point, offer them a ransom for me, and I will follow you and become your servant. Living among them," I said, "I have learnt to speak their language like a native and I could be very useful to you."

But they replied:

"We are very sorry for you, my son, but we have no ransom to offer and," they said, "we are strictly forbidden to threaten the infidels, for they are, as it is, a cunning and treacherous people, and as for our being civil to them, it is just politics."

"Do you mean," I said, "that I have to perish utterly here by remaining with them all my life because of those politics of yours?"

"Well, my son," they said, "it matters little where a man perishes. What we'd advise you to do is to pray: our Lord is a Lord of mercy. He will, perhaps, devise some way of delivering you."

"I have prayed," I said, "but my strength is at an end and I've given up all hope."

"You must not despair," they said, "for that is a grievous sin."

"I do not despair," I said, "but . . . how can you treat me like this? . . . I'm deeply grieved that you, Russians and fellow-countrymen of mine, should refuse to stretch out a helping hand to me."

"No, my son," they said, "do not try to involve us in this business. We are one body in Christ, and in Christ there are neither Jews nor Gentiles: our fellow-countrymen all obey the law of Christ. To us all are alike, all are equal."

"All?" I said.

"Yes," they replied, "all. That is the teaching we have received from St. Paul the Apostle. Wherever we go, we avoid trouble . . . it doesn't become us to be mixed up in any trouble. You are a servant of the Most High and you just have to suffer, for," they said, "according to St. Paul the Apostle, servants must be obedient. You have to remember that you are a Christian and that, therefore, we have no further business with you, for the pearly gates are even without our help open to admit your soul, but these people here will abide in darkness if we do not convert them, so it is with them that our business lieth."

And they showed me a book.

"Do you see how many people are put down in this register?" they said. "All of them have been converted to the true faith by us."

I did not waste any more words on them, nor did I see them again, except one of them and that, too, by mere accident. One day one of my sons came running from somewhere and said to me:

"There's a man lying by our lake, daddy!"

I went to have a look. I saw that the socks were torn off from his knees downwards and the gloves taken off from his hands and arms up to the elbows: the Tartars are past-masters at that sort of thing—they make a cut round the arm or leg and tear the skin off. The head of the man was lying a few paces away and on his forehead a cross was cut.

"Oh," thought I, "you refused to do anything for me, fellow-countryman of mine, and I blamed you for it, but now you have been thought worthy of a martyr's crown and you have sealed the testimony of your faith with your blood. Forgive me, I pray, for Christ's sake!"

And I made the sign of the cross over his body, put his poor head near his trunk and, making a low obeisance, I buried him and said the Lord's prayer over his grave; but what had happened to his companion I never could find out. I reckon he, too, must have ended up by winning a martyr's crown; for afterwards the Tartar women in our camp had a large number of holy icons to amuse themselves with, the same icons which those two missionaries had brought with them.

"But do missionaries usually go as far as the Rhyn-Sands ?"

"Of course they do, but it doesn't make much difference."

"Why not ?"

"They don't know how to deal with them. An Asiatic can be converted to the faith by fear, he must be made to tremble with fear, and those missionaries are preaching to them about a God of love. That spoils everything from the start, for an Asiatic will never respect a meek God who doesn't threaten and they will kill those who preach His gospel."

"What a band of cut-throats!"

"Yes, sir. The same thing happened to a Jew while I was still living with them. One day a Jew appeared heaven knows from where and he, too, started preaching his faith. He was a good man and, evidently, a great believer in his religion, and he was dressed in such rags that you could see his naked flesh through them. He began preaching his faith with such fervour that I could have listened to him for ever. At first I tried to argue with him. I said to him, What kind of religion is yours if you have no saints? But he said, We do have saints, and he began to read from the Talmud all about the kind of saints they had, very interesting it was, and the Talmud, he said, was written by Rabbi Joash ben Levi who was such a learned man that sinful men could not look at him, for one look at him and they would fall dead and that was why God called him before Himself and said, Listen to me, O, Joash ben Levi, it is a good thing to be as learned as you are, but it is neither good nor proper that all my Jews should die because of you, for it wasn't for that that I led them through the desert with Moses and helped them to cross the sea: you must therefore leave your native country and live in a place where no man can see you! So Rabbi ben Levi went and wandered about till he came to the very place where Paradise had been and there he buried himself up to his neck in sand and spent thirteen years in the sand, but every Saturday he would prepare a lamb for himself which was roasted by a fire that descended from heaven. And if a gnat or a fly would alight on his nose to feed on his blood, it was also instantly devoured by a fire from heaven. . . . The Asiatics liked the story about the learned Rabbi very much and they listened a long time to the Jewish preacher, but afterwards they set about finding out where he had buried his money. The Jew called heaven and earth to witness that he had no money, and he asserted that God had sent him to them with his wisdom only, but they did not believe him and, raking out the coals, they put a horse's hide on the burning embers and began to toss him about on it. Again and again they demanded that he should tell them where he had hidden his money and when they saw that he had gone black all over and had stopped screaming, they said, Stop, let's bury him up to the neck in sand, perhaps that will make him change his mind. And so they buried him, but the poor Jew died, buried like that, and for a long time his blackened head remained sticking out of the ground; as the children, however, were rather frightened of it, they cut it off and threw it into an empty well.

"So that's what comes of preaching to them!"

"Yes, it is a very difficult job, but the Jew, you know, did have money after all."

"Did he?"

"Yes. You see, after a time the wolves and jackals began to pull him about and they dragged him out of the sand bit by bit until at last they came to his boots. When they started pulling those to bits, seven silver coins fell out of the soles. They were picked up later."

"Well, and how did you escape from them?"

"I was saved by a miracle."

"Who performed this miracle for you?"

"Talafa."

"And who's Talafa? Is he also a Tartar?"

"No, he belongs to quite a different race, an Indian, and he isn't just any Indian, either, but one of their gods, who descended to earth."

In compliance with the entreaties of the passengers, Ivan Severyanych Flyagin told the following story about this new act in the tragi-comedy of his life.

CHAPTER IX

ABOUT a year had passed since the Tartars had got rid of the missionaries and it was winter again and we drove our horses to new grazing grounds, in a southerly direction, nearer to the Caspian Sea. It was there that one day towards evening two men—if indeed one could call them men—suddenly appeared in our camp. Nobody knew what kind of men they were, or whence they came, or to what tribe they belonged, or what their calling was. They couldn't even make themselves understood properly either in Russian or in Tartar, but spoke one word in our own tongue and another in the Tartar tongue, and to each other they spoke in a lingo of their own which neither the Tartars nor I could understand. Neither of them was old. One of them had black hair and he had a big beard and he wore a long robe, rather like a Tartar, except that his robe was not of many colours, but all red, and on his head he wore a pointed Persian hat; the other one was red-haired and he also wore a long robe, but he seemed to be a tricky customer; he had all sorts of boxes with him, and whenever he found himself alone and nobody looking, he would immediately take off his robe and remain in a short coat and trousers of a cut worn by the Germans employed in the factories in Russia. He would keep on sorting and turning over the articles in his boxes, but what those articles were the devil and himself only knew. It was rumoured that they had come from Khiva to buy horses and that they were contemplating going to war against somebody or other in their own country, but who they wanted to go to war against they did not say, and all the time they were inciting the Tartars against the Russians. The red-haired one—so I was told—didn't say much (he wasn't much of a linguist), but every time he pronounced the Russian word for governor, he'd spit: but they brought no money with them, for, being Asiatics themselves, they knew perfectly well that anyone who came to the steppe with money took his life into his hands and that it was a hundred to one that he would not come out of it alive; they were trying to persuade the Tartars to drive their herds of horses to the river Darya and they promised to settle their accounts there. The Tartars were in two minds about it, not knowing whether to accept their offer or not. They thought and they thought, taking their time like people searching for gold in the sand, but it was clear that they were afraid of something.

At first those two tried to persuade the Tartars by saying that, being men of honour, they'd never let them down, but later they changed their tune and began to put the wind up them.

"You'd better get a move on," they said, "or something terrible will happen to you: for our god Talafa has sent his fire with us and heaven forbid that he should get angry."

The Tartars had never heard of that god and they were in doubt whether he could do anything to them in the steppe in winter, but the man with the black beard who had come from Khiva in a red robe said, "If you're still in doubt, then Talafa will reveal to you the glory of his power even to-night, but I warn you," he said, "don't run out of your tents whatever you may see or hear, or he'll burn you to ashes." Now all that sounded very exciting to us, for we were badly in need of some distraction from the monotony of our life in the steppe in winter, and while we were also a little afraid of the terrible things that might happen, we were no less glad of the opportunity of finding out what that Indian god could really do: how and by what kind of a miracle he would reveal himself.

We went to our tents with our wives and children early and waited. . . . Everything was quiet and dark as on any other night, but no sooner had I fallen asleep than I suddenly heard a high wind rising with a hiss in the steppe and then something exploding with a bang and through my sleep it seemed to me as if sparks were falling from the skies.

I bestirred myself and I saw that my wives were all in a flutter and the children began to howl.

I said:

"Hush! Shut up, the lot of you! Suckle them and don't let me hear a sound from them!"

So the little ones sucked away and everything became quiet again, but presently a ball of fire went up with a hiss in the dark steppe . . . and again there was a bang. . . .

"Well," thought I, "it seems Talafa means business!"

A little later he began to hiss again, though in a different manner, and he flew upwards like a fiery bird with a tail, which was also fiery, and the fire was such an unusual one, red as blood, and when it burst everything turned yellow and then blue.

Everything in the camp, I noticed, had grown as still as the grave. For anybody not to have heard that racket was, of course, impossible, but all of them, I could only suppose, must have been terrified and they were lying huddled up under their sheepskins. All one could hear now was how the ground would suddenly tremble and shake and then everything would be quiet again. That, I surmised, must have been the horses shying and crowding together in a panic. Then I heard those Khiva men or Indians rush somewhere and again a fire swept over the steppe like a dragon. . . . The horses just gave one terrified neigh and bolted, whereupon the Tartars forgot their terror, scampered out of their tents, jerking their heads about and bellowing, "Allah! Allah!" and away they went in pursuit of the horses. As for the men of Khiva, they just disappeared, vanished without a trace, leaving one of their boxes behind as a memento. . . . So, as all our able-bodied men had gone after the herd and left only the women and old men in the camp, I went to have a look at the box: what, I wondered, had they got in it? I began to investigate and I found that it contained different kinds of earths and medicines and paper tubes. I was examining one of those tubes at the camp fire and, as I brought it a little too close to the fire, it suddenly exploded, nearly burning my eyes, and up it went into the sky and there—bang!—burst into a shower of stars. . . . "Oho," I thought to myself, "so it isn't a god after all, but only common or garden fireworks which we used to let off in our public park!" So I let off another and, lo and behold, the Tartars, the old men who had stayed behind, all fell down on their faces and lay flat on the ground, every man where he fell, wriggling like eels. . . . At first I almost got the wind up myself, but when I saw them writhing on the ground I felt quite differently inclined and, for the first time since my captivity, I ground my teeth and began roaring a string of meaningless words at them:

"Parlez-bien-comme-ça-chirez-mir-verfluchtur-min-adieu-m'sieu!"

And I let off another firework, a Catherine wheel this time. . . . Now when they saw the Catherine wheel scouring along and leaving a fiery trail behind, they all seemed to give up the ghost. . . . The fire went out, but they continued to lie on the ground, and then one of them raised his head a little, but immediately bobbed down again, and kept on beckoning to me with a finger, indicating that he wished to talk to me. I went up to him and said:

"You damned scoundrel, which do you prefer—life or death ?" for I saw that they were mortally afraid of me.

"Have mercy on me, Ivan," he said, "don't kill me! Please, let me live!"

And from all over the place they started beckoning to me in the same way and all implored me to forgive them and spare their lives.

I could see that my affairs had taken a favourable turn at last: I must have atoned for all my sins by my sufferings, so I prayed:

"Holy Mother of God and you, St. Nicholas, take pity on me, oh, my adored ones, stretch out a helping hand to me, oh, my benefactors!"

And, turning to the Tartars, I asked them in a stern voice:

"What do you want me to forgive you for and why do you ask me to spare your lives ?"

"We want you to forgive us," they said, "for not believing in your God."

"Aha," thought I, "so that's how scared you are of me now!" and I said, "Oh, no, my dear people, this time you won't get off so easily: I shall never forgive you for your hostility to the true faith!" and I ground my teeth again and let off another firework.

This time it was a rocket: there was a terrific explosion and a huge flame.

Then I yelled at the Tartars:

"I give you one more minute to make up your minds: if you still refuse to believe in my God, I shall destroy the whole lot of you!"

"Don't destroy us, please," they replied. "We all agree to submit ourselves to your God."

So I stopped letting off more fireworks and baptised them in a near-by brook.

"Do you mean you baptised them there and then ?"

"Yes, sir, on the spot! You see, I didn't want to waste much time, for I was afraid they might change their minds. I sprinkled their heads with water over a hole in the ice, said, In the name of the Father and the Son, put round their necks the crosses left by the missionaries, told them to honour the murdered missionary as a martyr and pray for him, and I showed them his grave."

"And did they pray ?"

"They did."

"But they did not know any Christian prayers, did they ? Did you teach them some ?"

"No, I had no time to teach them any prayers, for I saw that now was my chance to escape. All I did was to tell them: Carry on as before, say your old prayers, but don't you dare to call upon Allah in future, but address yourselves only to Jesus Christ! And it was this profession of faith that they accepted."

"But how did you afterwards manage to run away from those newly converted Christians in spite of your crippled feet and how did you cure yourself?"

"Afterwards I found in that box with the fireworks a kind of corrosive earth: as soon as you applied it to your body, it would begin to burn you terribly. I applied it to my heels and pretended to be ill, and while lying under the rug, I kept on applying it to my heels and during the next two weeks I had applied it with such good effect that the flesh on my feet was covered with festering sores and the bristles which the Tartars had put there ten years ago were carried away with the pus. I got well as speedily as I possibly could, but I didn't tell anybody about it, but pretended to be feeling worse and I told the women and the old men to pray as hard as they could for me, for, said I, I am dying. In addition, I imposed a fast upon them as a kind of penance and ordered them not to leave their tents for three days and, to make doubly sure, I let off one of the biggest fireworks in the box and went away. . . ."

"And they didn't catch you?"

"No, they couldn't very well catch me, for I had so scared them and so weakened them by the fast that I expect they were too glad not to put their noses out of their tents for three days and when they did go out afterwards I was gone too far for them to overtake me. My feet, after I had got rid of the bristles, healed up completely and they were so light that, having started to run, I ran and ran till I had run from one end of the steppe to the other."

"And all on foot?"

"Naturally! How else? There are no roads there and you don't meet anyone on the way and if you do happen to meet someone, you aren't always pleased in the companion you have acquired. On the fourth day of my journey I came across a Chuvash tribesman who was driving five horses. He said to me, Get on one of my horses! But I thought it over carefully in my mind and decided that it would be much safer not to."

"What were you afraid of?"

"I wasn't afraid of anything in particular. . . . He just didn't look trustworthy to me and, besides, I couldn't find out to what religion he belonged and, unless you know that, it isn't safe in the steppe. He kept on shouting like a fool:

"Get on," he shouted, "it'll be merrier to ride along together!"

But I said:

"Who are you? Have you a god or not?"

"Of course I have," he said. "The Tartar has no god, he eats horse-flesh, but I have a god."

"Who's your god?" I asked.

"Why," he replied, "everything is a god to me. The sun's my god and the moon's my god and the stars are my god . . . everything's my god. What do you mean: have I got a god?"

"Everything? Hmm. . . . Everything, you say? And what about Jesus Christ," I said, "isn't He your god?"

"Why, yes," he said. "He, too, is my god and the Holy Virgin is my god and Nicholas is my god. . . ."

"Which Nicholas?" I asked him.

"Why," he said, "the one who lives in summer and the one who lives in winter!"

I could not help congratulating him upon his respect for the Russian saint, Nicholas the Miracle-Worker.

"Honour him always," I said, "because he is a Russian," and I was about to declare myself completely satisfied with his religion and to accept his invitation to go along with him, but, luckily, he went on talking and revealed himself in his true colours.

"Indeed," he said, "I honour Nicholas. I may not kneel to him in summer, but in winter I always give him a twenty-copeck piece to keep an eye on my cows. Not that I put my entire trust in him alone! No, sir! I also offer up a bullock to Keremetee."

I just couldn't help getting angry at that.

"How dare you not to put your trust in St. Nicholas the Miracle-Worker and give him, a Russian, a twenty-copeck piece only, while you give a whole bullock to that heathen goddess of yours, the thrice-accursed Keremetee! Away with you," I said, "I shan't go with a man who shows so little respect for St. Nicholas the Miracle-Worker!"

And I didn't go with him; I took to my heels and, before I knew, towards the evening of the third day after my meeting with the Chuvash, I saw water in the distance and some people. I hid myself in the long grass as a precaution and looked out to see what kind of people they were, for I was afraid to fall into worse captivity, but I saw that they were cooking a meal: they must be Christians, I thought to myself, and I crawled a little nearer and then I saw that they were crossing themselves and drinking vodka, and that settled it: they were Russians all right! So I jumped out of the grass and I revealed myself. I discovered that they were fishermen: they were casting nets into the river. They gave me a great welcome as behoved fellow-countrymen of mine and said:

"Have a drink of vodka!"

I replied:

"Thank you, dear friends, but I've spent many years with the Tartars and I've quite lost my taste for it!"

"No matter," they replied, "you're among your own folk now, your own nation, and you'll soon get used to it again. Come on, have a drink!"

I poured myself out a glass, thinking, "Now then, praise the Lord for your safe return!" and drank it, but the fishermen—what splendid fellows they were!—insisted on my having another glass.

"Have another drink," they said; "see how weak you've grown without it."

I permitted myself another glass and I became very talkative and I told them everything. I went on talking to them throughout the night, sitting at the camp fire, drinking vodka and feeling so happy because I was in Holy Russia again, but towards morning when the camp fire began to go out and almost all who had been listening to me were asleep, one of them, a member of the team of fishermen, said to me:

"But have you got a passport?"

I said:

"No, I haven't."

"If," he said, "a passport you can't show, it's to jail you're sure to go."

"If that's so," I said, "I shan't leave you. I dare say one can live with you without a passport, can't one?"

And he replied:

"To be sure, you can live with us without a passport, but you can't die without one."

I said:

"Why's that?"

"That," he said, "is very simple, for how can you expect the priest to register your death if you have no passport."

"What's going to happen to me in that case?" I asked.

"Oh," he said, "we shall throw you into the river to feed the fish."

"Without a priest?"

"Without a priest."

Being a little tipsy, I got terribly frightened of that and I began to weep and bewail my fate, but the fisherman laughed:

"I was only pulling your leg," he said. "Don't be afraid to die: we shall bury you in good old mother earth."

But I was very cross with him and I said:

"What a joke! If you go on cracking any more jokes like that I shan't live to see another spring!"

No sooner had the last fisherman fallen asleep than I got up quickly and made off and I came to Astrakhan, where I earned a rouble as a day labourer and immediately took to drink and drank so heartily that I couldn't remember how I got to another town, where I found myself in jail and from there they sent me under police guard to my own part of the country. They brought me to our town, gave me a good flogging at the police station and sent me to our estate. Her ladyship the countess who had ordered me to be flogged for the cat's tail had died, and the count alone remained, but he had grown very old and had become a devout churchman and given up hunting altogether.

When my arrival was announced to him, his lordship remembered me and he ordered that I should be flogged again at home and that I should then go to father Ilya for confession. Well, they gave me a good, old-fashioned sort of flogging at the records hut and I went to father Ilya and he started to hear my confession and, having heard it, refused to grant me absolution for the next three years. . . .

I said to him:

"Oh, dear," I said, "what am I to do now, father? I haven't partaken of the sacrament for so many years and . . . I had thought that . . . having waited so long . . ."

"That you've waited so long," he said, "is neither here nor there. You'd better tell me," he said, "why you've kept so many Tartar women as wives? You must understand," he said, "that I'm really doing you a great favour in refusing you the sacrament, for if you were to be dealt with properly according to the rules laid down by the Holy Fathers of the Church, you should have been set on fire alive and your clothes burnt off you, but," he said, "you needn't be afraid of that because that is no longer permitted by our penal code."

"Well," I said to myself, "as I can't do anything about it, I'll have to do without the sacrament, stay at home a little and have a rest after my captivity," but his lordship wouldn't allow that. His lordship was so good as to say:

"I cannot allow a man who has been refused absolution by the Church to live near me."

So he ordered the manager to give me another thrashing, this time in public as an example to the world at large, and then let me go a free man provided I paid a certain sum each year as a tax. And so it was done: they administered another flogging to me, but in quite a new way, on the top of the steps in front of the office and in the presence of all his lordship's servants, and they gave me a passport. I felt very happy to be a free man at last after so many years and to be in possession of a legal paper, and so I went away. I had no definite plans for my future, but the Lord soon provided me with a job.

"What sort of job?"

"In my old line again: horses. I started from the bottom, without a penny, but very soon I obtained a very good situation and I could have done still better for myself, were it not for one thing."

"And may we ask what that thing was?"

"I became greatly possessed with evil spirits and evil passions and with one more unseemly thing."

"What was that?"

"Magnetism, gentlemen."

"Wha-at? Magnetism?"

"Yes, gentlemen. The magnetic influence of one person."

"How did that influence manifest itself over you ?"

"A stranger's will had the whip-hand over me and I was made the stalking horse of another man's destiny."

"So it was there that your *own* doom overtook you after which you realised that you had to fulfil your mother's promise and you entered a monastery ?"

"Oh, no, all that came later. Until then many other adventures befell me, before, that is, I was granted perfect understanding."

"You wouldn't mind telling us your adventures, would you ?"

"Why, not at all, gentlemen! With great pleasure!"

"Please, do."

CHAPTER X

TAKING my passport, I went off without any definite plans about my future, and I came to a fair and there I saw a gypsy exchanging a horse with a Russian peasant and deceiving him disgracefully. He began to show off his horse's strength and he harnessed it to a cart loaded with oats, while the peasant's horse he harnessed to an apple cart. There was, of course, the same draught in both the carts, but the peasant's horse was sweating because it was overcome by the smell of the apples, for there is nothing more disagreeable to a horse than that smell; besides, I also saw that the gypsy's horse was subject to fits, for it had a certain mark on its forehead, showing that it had been branded with fire, but the gypsy said, It is a mole. Well, I was of course sorry for the peasant because he would not be able to do his farm work with a horse suffering from fainting fits, for it might collapse and that would be the end of it, and, besides, I conceived a great hatred of gypsies at that time, seeing that it was a gypsy who was the first to give me a taste for the life of a tramp and I must, I suppose, have also had a premonition of something else which indeed came to pass. So I revealed to the peasant the fraud about that horse, and when the gypsy started arguing with me, insisting that the mark on the horse's head was not due to branding, but was a mole, I, to prove my point, prodded the horse with an awl in the kidney and it immediately fell to the ground in one of its convulsive fits. So I went and chose a good horse for the peasants, in accordance with the knowledge of such things that I had acquired, and they treated me to vodka and to a fine spread and they also gave me money, twenty copecks in silver coins, and we all had a good time. That, gentlemen, was the beginning of it: my capital began to grow and so did my addiction to drink, and barely a month had passed when I saw that I was making good; I hung all sorts of metal plates over myself and the various appurtenances of a horse-doctor and went tramping from one horse fair to another, and everywhere I tipped the wink to poor and ignorant people and I was gathering up a competence for myself and was only too glad to allow my clients to stand me drinks, as is the custom at horse fairs; in the meantime I became to all the gypsies who were eager to defraud, beguile and overreach the people in buying horses, a veritable wrath of God and I had been tipped off that they were plotting to give me a beating. I began to shun them, for I was one and they were many, and they could never light on me alone and give me a sound drubbing, which they durst not do in the presence of the peasants, who always stood up for me, being highly appreciative of my virtues. Instead, the gypsies spread an evil rumour abroad to the effect that I was a sorcerer and was such a good judge of horses only because I was assisted by the devil; but, of course, all that did not matter in the least since, as I have already told you, gentlemen, I have a way with a horse, having been gifted by nature in that respect, and I was always ready to share my secret with any man, except that it would not have been of any use to him whatsoever.

"Why wouldn't it have been of any use?"

"Because nobody could grasp it, since for that sort of thing one must be gifted by nature, and there were many cases where I revealed my secret and all in vain, but with your permission, gentlemen, I shall tell you about it later."

Well (the novice went on), when my fame had spread far and wide across all the fairs of the land and I had become known as a man who could see through a horse, one purchaser of horses for the army, a prince, came and offered me a hundred roubles.

"Tell me your secret, my dear fellow," he said, "your secret about understanding the way of a horse, for such a secret is worth a lot of money to me."

And I replied:

"I have no secret, my lord," I said. "It is just a natural gift."

But he wouldn't leave me alone.

"Tell me," he said, "how you go about it, and that you should not think that I want to get your knowledge from you for nothing, here's a hundred roubles for you."

What was I to do? I shrugged my shoulders, tied the money up in a rag and said:

"I'll tell you all I know with pleasure, but you, sir, would do well to give me all your attention and apply your mind to what I'm going to tell you, for I must warn you that if, having learnt all I can teach you, you still derive no profit whatever from it, I, for one, shall not hold myself responsible for it."

However, he was satisfied with that, saying:

"It isn't your fault if I'm slow to learn. All I want is for you to tell me all you know."

"The very first thing," I said, "a man must bear in mind if he really wants to know what sort of a horse he's buying is what is the best way of examining a horse and, above all, he must never shirk such an examination. The first thing to do is to look at its head and that not anyhow, but with understanding; the next thing is to cast a quick glance all over the horse, from head to tail, and one must never paw the horse about as army officers usually do. An army officer, as a rule, begins his examination of a horse by touching its crest, its forelock, its muzzle, its windpipe, its chest and, indeed, anything else, but all to no purpose. That's why a horse-dealer is so fond of cavalry officers: it is their habit of running their fingers all over the horse that pleases him. Directly a horse-dealer notices this kind of pawing by military men, he starts to turn the horse round, keeping it constantly on the move, but you can be sure that if there's any blemish he doesn't want to show, he won't show it for anything in the world, and it is in the part he conceals that the fraud lies, and there is no end to such frauds: say, if a horse is lop-eared, they'll cut an inch of hide out of its neck, pull it together, sew it up and smear it over, and that's why the horse keeps its ears straight, but not for long, for the skin will soon stretch and its ears will hang down again. Or, if a horse's ears are too long, they'll cut them and to make them, stand upright they'll insert bits of horn into them. Should a man be anxious to purchase a well-matched pair of horses and supposing only one of the horses has a star on its forehead, the dealers will do their best to provide the other one with a similar star: they'll rub the hair with pumice stone, or apply where necessary a hot, baked turnip, to make white hair grow, and it does grow, but anybody who takes the pains to examine such hair closely will find that it is always longer than the natural hair and that it curls like a beard. The dealers deceive the public even more shamefully about a horse's eyes: one horse may have little cavities above its eyes which spoil its looks, but the dealer will prick the skin with a pin, apply his lips to the place and blow for all he's worth and to such good effect that the skin will lift up and the eye will immediately look fresh and beautiful. This can be done easily, for a horse enjoys the sensation of warmth such breathing gives it and it will stand stock-still, but the air is bound to escape sooner or later and the horse will again have cavities over its eyes. There's only one way of detecting such a fraud: feel near the bone to see whether there's any air under the skin! But even funnier is the way horse-dealers sell blind horses: it's a real treat, that is. The cavalry officer waves a straw in front of the horse's eyes to find out if the horse can see it, but what he himself doesn't see is that when the horse might be expected to shake its head, the dealer gives it a prod with his fist under the belly or in its side; and even if he strokes it gently, he has a nail hidden in his glove and only pretends to stroke it, but in reality pricks it."

I told the prince ten times as much as I have told you here, but for all the good it did him I might as well not have said a word. Next day when I saw him again he had bought such horses as I should have been ashamed to be seen with: one jade worse than the other, and he actually called me to come and admire them, saying:

"Well, my dear fellow, aren't I clever to have learnt to know a good horse so quickly!"

I just glanced at them and laughed and replied that there was nothing, so to speak, to look at.

"That one's shoulders," I said, "are too meaty, she'll be constantly tripping over, and that one is too low in girth—touches her belly with her hoof and within a year, if not sooner, she's sure to get a rupture, and that one stamps her foreleg when eating her oats and knocks her knee against the stall," and in this way I found fault with his entire purchase and I was right about everything and it turned out exactly as I said it would.

So next day the prince said to me:

"No, Ivan, I can see that I shall never be able to acquire your gift. What about taking a job with me as my connoisseur and choosing the horses yourself and I'll pay you for it?"

I agreed and for the next three years I lived in peace and contentment, not as a servant or as a hired labourer, but rather as a friend and assistant, and but for my drinking bouts during my days off, I could have saved up a tidy bit, for it is the custom among the army horse-buyers that every time a horse-breeder arrives on a business visit, he himself goes to spend his time with the army buyer, while sending a trustworthy man to the connoisseur to get the connoisseur on his side by hook or by crook, for the horse-breeders know very well that everything depends not on the horse-buyer, but on the connoisseur, if, that is, the horse-buyer employs the right man for that job. And being, as I told you, a born connoisseur, I performed my duties in the most exemplary way, being deeply conscious of the debt I owed to nature in this respect: I was incapable of deceiving the man I served and the prince knew that I wouldn't deceive him for anything in the world and he respected me highly, and indeed we treated each other with the utmost frankness. Sometimes, if he happened to have lost a lot of money at cards the night before, he would come to see me in the stables directly he got up in the morning, in his short Oriental coat which he wore instead of a dressing-gown, and he'd say:

"Well, my demi-semi-honourable Ivan Severyanych, how are you this morning? Are your affairs prospering?"

He used always to joke like that, calling me his *demi-semi-honourable*, but he respected me highly, as you will see.

I knew very well what it meant if he addressed me in that jocular vein and I'd answer:

"I'm very well, thank you, sir. My affairs, too, thank God, are in excellent order. How are your lordship's affairs ?"

"My affairs," he'd reply, "are so bad that I don't think they could be worse."

"Why, what's the matter, sir ? Did you lose a fortune last night as usual ?"

"You've hit the nail on the head, my demi-semi-honourable sir. I've lost a fortune all right."

"And how much money has your lordship been relieved of ?" I'd ask.

He would tell me at once how many thousands he had lost and I'd shake my head and say:

"All you want now, my lord, is a good hiding. What a pity there isn't anyone to give it to you!"

He'd laugh and say:

"That's the trouble, my dear sir. I wish there was!"

"Well," I'd say, "that can be easily remedied, my lord. Just lie down on my bed and I'll put a clean, rolled-up straw-mat under your lordship's head and give you a good beating."

Well, so he'd naturally try to make up to me, doing his best to persuade me to lend him some money to try his luck again.

"No, sir," he'd say, "don't flog me, but let me have a little of what's left over from your expenses: my luck's sure to change to-night and I'll clean out the whole lot!"

"No, thank you, my lord," I'd say. "Try your luck by all means, but don't expect it to change."

"What are you thanking me for ?" he'd begin with a laugh and end up by getting really angry. "Don't forget yourself, please," he'd say. "Stop pretending to be my guardian and give me the money!"

We asked Ivan Severyanych if he had ever given any money to his prince to try his luck at cards again.

"Never," he replied. "I'd either tell him a lie, say that I had spent all the money on oats, or just run away from the house."

"But wasn't he angry with you for letting him down ?"

"Yes, he was angry all right. He'd say to me without any further beating about the bush: 'You're fired! You're no longer in my employment, my demi-semi-honourable one!' "

I'd reply:

"Very well, my lord. May I have my passport ?"

"All right," he'd say. "Collect your things, will you ? I'll give you your passport to-morrow."

But to-morrow he'd forget all about it and we'd never mention the subject again; for barely an hour later he'd come to me in quite a different frame of mind and say:

"Thank you, my overmuch-little-significant sir, for having been so firm with me and for having refused to give me any money to try my luck at cards again."

And so well disposed was he to me afterwards that if anything happened to me on my days off he, too, would treat me like a brother.

"And what happened to you?"

"Well, I told you that I used to take days off."

"And what do you mean by *days off?*"

"I used to go out to have a good time. Having got a taste for vodka, I didn't drink it every day, nor did I ever drink it in moderation, but if something happened to distress me, I'd get a terrible desire for drink and I'd immediately take a few days off and disappear. And such moods came upon me without any reason at all; for instance, when we used to send away our horses—and they were not exactly my own flesh and blood, were they? —I'd start drinking, especially if I'd part from a horse that was very beautiful, for I just couldn't get him out of my head and he'd always be there before my eyes, so much so that I'd try to escape from him as from some ghostly apparition, and I'd take some days off."

"You mean you'd get drunk?"

"Yes, I'd leave the house and start drinking."

"For how long?"

"Well, that depended on the kind of day off it was: sometimes I'd go on drinking till I had spent all the money I had on me and either someone would knock me about or I'd beat someone up myself; another time it wouldn't last so long—I'd spend a night at a police station or have a good sleep in a ditch and everything would be all right again and it would pass off. In such cases I'd stick to a certain rule and whenever I got restless and felt that I had to take a day off, I'd come to the prince and say, I'm feeling restless, sir, please take care of my money and I'll make myself scarce. He wouldn't even try to dissuade me, but just took the money or asked me, Does your honour expect to be away long? And I'd go and he would be left to look after things at home and he would wait patiently for me until my *day off* came to an end, and everything would go off well; but I was beginning to feel terribly fed up with that weakness of mine and I made up my mind to get rid of it; it was then that I took such a last day off that the memory of it makes my hair stand on end even now."

CHAPTER XI

NEEDLESS to say, we did our best to persuade Ivan Severyanych to put the finishing touch to his kindness by giving us a full account of this new unhappy episode of his life and he, out of the goodness of his heart, did not in any way refuse our request, and he told us the following story about his last *day off*:

We had a mare by the name of Dido which we had bought from a stud-farm, a young, golden bay mare, destined for an officer's saddle. She was a dream of a horse: a lovely head, comely eyes, subtile and wide-open nostrils, breathing without any effort, a light mane, the chest between the shoulders sitting easy, like a sailing ship, and her back was slender, her pasterns white and her feet so light that when she began to fling them about it looked as if she were playing with them. In a word, no lover of a horse who had been endowed with an eye for beauty could take his eyes off such an animal and would certainly not easily forget it. I conceived so great a liking for her that I wouldn't even leave the stables while she was there and I went on caressing her out of the sheer joy of it. Sometimes I'd groom her myself and rub her all down with a white cloth so that there wasn't a speck of dust left on her coat, and I'd even kiss her on the forehead, on that sweet little curl of hers, where her golden coat parted. At that time there were two fairs on at one and the same time: one at L. and the other at K., and the prince and I had parted company—I going to one fair, while he was doing business at the other. Suddenly I received a letter from him in which he wrote to say, Send me such and such horses, including Dido. I did not know what he wanted my beauty for, the lovely mare to which I had taken such a fancy. But I naturally surmised that he must have exchanged my favourite for another horse, or sold her, or more likely lost her at a game of cards. . . . So I let Dido go with some stablemen and, being consumed with a terrible longing for her, a great desire came upon me to take a day off. But my position at the time was rather a peculiar one: as I told you, I had made it a rule that whenever I became obsessed with a desire to take a day off I'd go to the prince, hand him all the money of which I always had a large amount on me and say, I'm going to disappear for so-and-so many days. But how was I to arrange things now that the prince was away? So I said to myself, No, sir, this time you're jolly well going to abstain from drink because your prince is away and you can't possibly have your day off as you used to, for you have no one to leave the money with, and you have a considerable sum of money on you, over five thousand. Well, having made up my mind that it just couldn't be done, I stuck to my guns and did not give in to my craving to go on a spree and kick over the traces. But all the same I could feel no weakening of my desire, which, on the contrary, seemed to grow more and more powerful. At last I could think of nothing else but how to arrange things in such a way that I could both satisfy my passion for a drink and assure the safety of the prince's money. With that aim in view I began to hide the money and I hid it in the most unlikely places where no man would ever have dreamt of putting any money. . . . I thought to myself, What can I do? It is pretty clear that I shan't be able to master my desire, so I must at least—so I thought—put the money away in a safe place where nothing could happen to it, and then I'll give in to my craving and take a day off. But I was greatly perplexed: where could I hide the confounded money? For wherever I put it, the thought would occur to me before I had gone a few steps from the place of hiding that someone was sure to pinch it. I'd go back, take it out quickly and again hide it somewhere else. . . . I got sick and tired of hiding it in the haylofts, in the cellars, under the eaves and in every imaginable unlikely hiding-place, for as soon as I'd go away, I'd fancy that someone had seen me hiding it and I'd go back again and once more I'd get it out and carry it about on my person, thinking to myself, No, it just can't be done, it isn't my fate to satisfy my desire this time. Then suddenly a divinely inspired idea occurred to me: why, I said to myself, who else but the Devil would be tormenting me by such desires and, if so, why not get rid of the scoundrel by throwing myself upon the mercy of the Lord? So I went to early mass, said my prayers, made sure of my deliverance and, as I was going out of the church, I saw on the wall a painting of the Last Judgment and on it angels were chastising the Devil in hell with chains. I stopped to have a good look at it, prayed even more fervently to the Holy Angels and, as for the Devil, I just spat at him and, thrusting my fist under his snout, said, Here's a fig for you, take it and buy yourself anything you like with it! After that I was no longer troubled and, having seen to everything at home, went to a tavern and ordered tea. . . .

In the tavern I noticed standing among the company a sort of tramp, an absolutely contemptible specimen of a man. I had seen him before and I looked on him just as a charlatan or clown, for you could always see him knocking about at fairs where he annoyed the gentlemen by asking them for help in French. He seemed to belong to the gentry himself and was said to have served as an officer in the army, but to have squandered all his money at cards, and he now lived by begging. . . . Here, in the tavern where I had come to have my tea, the waiters were trying to chuck him out, but he refused to go, and just stood there and said:

"Don't you know who I am? I am not a nobody like you! I used to own serfs myself and I used to flog chaps like you in the stables just for my amusement. It is true I lost my fortune, but it was God's will that I should and I still bear a special mark of His wrath and that's why nobody dares to touch me."

The waiters did not believe him and they laughed at him, but he went on to tell them of the fine style in which he used to live, the fine carriages he used to drive about in and the way he used to throw the civilian gentlemen out of the public park and how he had once stripped and paid a visit stark naked to the governor's wife, "and now," he said, "I've been cursed for my presumption and my entire nature has been turned into stone and I have to keep on softening it with drink, so, come on, give me some vodka! I can't pay for it because I have no money, but I'm quite willing to eat the glass after I've drunk it."

So one of the gentlemen ordered a glass of vodka to be given to him, for he wanted to see how he would eat the glass. He at once emptied the glass in one gulp and did as he promised and began to crunch the glass with his teeth—fair and square—and ate it in front of everybody, and all the people were amazed at it and burst out laughing. But I was sorry for him, for I thought: here was a well-born man and yet so addicted was he to drink that he didn't mind sacrificing his bowels for a glass of vodka. So I made up my mind at least to let him wash down the broken glass by another drink and I ordered a second glass to be given to him at my expense, but I did not insist on his eating the glass. I said, Don't! Don't eat it! He was deeply touched by that and gave me his hand.

"I suppose," he said, "you originally belonged to a gentleman's servants."

"I did," I said.

"I could see at once," he said, "that you were not one of those swine. *Grand merci*," he said, "for that."

I said:

"Don't mention it, go in peace!"

"No," said he. "I'm very happy to have a chat with you. Move up a little and I'll sit down beside you."

"All right," I said, "sit down beside me by all means."

So he sat down beside me and began to tell me what a noble family he had sprung from and what a fine education he had had and again he said:

"What are you drinking? Tea?"

"Yes," I said, "tea. Won't you have some with me?"

"Thank you," he said, "but I'm afraid I can't drink any tea."

"Why not?"

"Because," he said, "my head isn't made for tea, my head's made for desperate things. I'd rather you told them to give me another glass of vodka!"

And in this way he made me treat him to one, then two and three glasses of vodka and I was beginning to get fed up with standing him drinks. But what I disliked most about him was that he told so many lies, showing off all the time and boasting about what an important person he was, and suddenly abasing himself and crying, and all for nothing.

"Do you realise," he said, "what kind of a man I am? Why," said he, "I was created by God in the same year as the emperor and I'm of the same age as he."

"So what about it?" I asked.

"What about it? Do you think it's fair that I should have come down in the world as I did in spite of that? Yes, sir, in spite of all that," he said, "I am a man of no consequence and I've turned out to be a nonentity and, as you saw just now, am despised by everybody." And, having said that, he called for more vodka, but this time he asked for a whole decanter of it, and himself went on to tell me a long story of how the merchants made fun of him in the taverns and, finally, he said:

"They're an uneducated lot," he said. "They think it's an easy job to go on drinking and eating the glass as a kind of *hors d'œuvre*. But it's a very hard profession, my dear fellow, and I'm quite sure many people wouldn't be able to carry on with it at all. But I've trained myself for it because I realise that a man has to go through everything, and I'm carrying on."

"But why," I argued, "are you so devoted to this habit of yours? Why not give it up?"

"Give it up?" he exclaimed. "Oh, no, my dear fellow, I just can't give it up!"

"Why not?" I said.

"I can't give it up for two reasons," he replied. "In the first place because without drinking I should never go to bed, but would go on wandering about the streets, and secondly and principally because my Christian sentiments do not permit me to do it."

"What are you talking about?" I said. "I can well believe that you wouldn't go to bed, for you'd be roaming about the town in search of drink, but that your Christian sentiments won't allow you to drop such wickedness, that I cannot possibly believe."

"I see," he replied; "so you can't believe it, can you? Well, everybody else says the same thing. . . . But have you ever thought what would happen if I ever dropped that drinking habit of mine? Why, somebody else would be sure to pick it up! Now tell me honestly, do you think he'd thank me for it or not?"

"God forbid!" I said. "I certainly don't think so."

"Well, then," he said, "so you see how it is, don't you? And since it's necessary that I should suffer, then you ought to honour me for that at any rate and tell them to bring me another decanter of vodka!"

I banged the table for another decanter and I sat and listened to him, for to tell the truth I found his talk very entertaining, and he went on:

"It is right that I should endure this cross and that it shouldn't fall upon anyone else's shoulders, for I," said he, "am a man of good family and I have received an excellent education, so that I could say my prayers in French when I was a little boy, but I was very unkind and I inflicted all sorts of tortures on people, lost my serfs at cards, separated mothers from their children, married a rich woman and made life so unbearable to her that she soon died and, finally, being myself the cause of all my troubles, I even murmured against God for having given me such a nature. And that's why he has punished me and given me a different nature, so that I haven't got a vestige of pride left in me: spit in my eyes or slap my face and I don't mind so long as I can get drunk and forget all about myself."

"And now," I said, "don't you ever murmur against Him for giving you such a character?"

"I do not," he replied, "for although it is worse, yet it is better."

"What do you mean?" I asked. "I don't know what you're talking about: it's worse, yet it's better!"

"That's quite simple," he replied. "For, you see, now I only know one thing and that is that I'm destroying myself, but at least I can no longer destroy others, for everybody turns away from me. I," said he, "am now like unto Job smitten with sore boils and therein," he said, "lies my happiness and my salvation," and with these words he drank up the last glass of vodka and asked for another decanter, saying:

"And you, my dear friend, remember: never scorn any man, for nobody can tell the reason why a man is tormented by any desire, nor why he suffers. We, the possessed, suffer these things so that it shall be easier for the rest. And if you yourself be afflicted by some desire, do not wilfully abandon it lest another man pick it up and be tormented, but rather look for a man who would be willing to take upon himself this wickedness of yours."

"But where can I find such a man?" I asked. "No man will ever agree to do such a thing."

"Do you really think so?" he replied. "Why, you haven't even to go far to find such a man, for such a man is now before you. I am that man!"

I said:

"Are you joking?"

But he suddenly jumped to his feet and said:

"No, I am not joking, but if you don't believe me, you can test me!"

"But how am I to test you?" I asked.

"That's easy," he said. "Do you want to know what kind of gift I possess? For, my dear fellow, I possess a great gift. As you see, I am drunk now. . . . Am I or am I not drunk?"

I looked at him and I could see that his face was purple and that he was quite fuddled and that he was swaying on his legs, and I said:

"Yes, of course you're drunk."

But he replied:

"Now turn away for a minute to that icon and say the Lord's prayer to yourself."

I turned away for a minute towards the icon and had just time to say the Lord's prayer to myself when that down-at-heel gentleman again commanded me:

"Well, have a good look at me now: am I drunk or not?"

I turned round and, indeed, he looked as sober as a judge and there he stood, smiling.

I said:

"What does it mean? What kind of magic is that?"

And he replied:

"That," he said, "is no magic, but it's called magnetism."

"What's that?" I asked.

"It is such a will which is given to a man," he said, "and it can be neither lost by drinking, nor in sleep, for it is a gift. I have demonstrated it to you," he said, "so that you should understand that if I wanted to I could stop drinking straight away and never taste another drop of liquor in my life, but I don't want any man to start drinking instead of me while I, having mended my ways, should again forget God. But I'm ready and willing to release any man from his desire for drink in one minute."

"Do me a favour," I said, "and do this for me!"

"But do you drink?" he asked.

"I do indeed," I said, "and there are times when I drink like a fish."

"Well," said he, "do not be downhearted. It is in my power to do it and I shall do it gladly, for I want to repay you for treating me to-night. Yes, I shall release you from your addiction to drink, my dear fellow, and I shall take it upon myself."

"Do me the favour, sir. Please, I pray you, set me free!"

"With pleasure, my dear fellow," he said, "with pleasure," and having said that, he shouted for more vodka and for two glasses.

I said:

"What do you want two glasses for?"

"One," he said, "is for me and the other—for you."

"But I'm not going to drink," I said.

"Whisht! Silence! Not a word! Who are you, tell me? A patient?"

"All right," I said, "have it your own way. I am a patient."

"And I," said he, "am a doctor and you have to carry out my orders and take your medicine," and with that he poured me out a glass and himself a glass and started to wave his hands over my glass like some precentor.

He waved and waved and then ordered:

"Drink!"

I had my misgivings at first, but, to be quite frank, I badly wanted a drink of vodka myself and, as he had ordered me to drink, I said to myself, Let's drink it just to see what happens, and I drank.

"Well," said he, "did you like it? Did it taste good or was it bitter?"

"I'm hanged if I know," I said.

"That," he said, "means that you haven't had enough," and he poured me out another glass and started again waving his hands about. He waved and he waved and then, with a final shake, he again made me drink this, the second, glass, and again he questioned me: "How was that?"

I pulled his leg. I said:

"This one seemed a bit heavy."

He nodded and at once started waving over the third glass and again commanded, "Drink!" So I drank and said:

"This one was lighter," and thereupon I myself got hold of the decanter and began treating him and pouring one out for myself, and so we went on drinking. He did not try to stop me, except that he wouldn't permit me to have a single glass before he'd waved over it, and as soon as I'd get hold of it he'd take it out of my hand and say:

"Whisht! Silence. . . . *Attendez!*" and he would first wave his hand over it and then say, "Now it's ready and *thou canst receive it as it is written.*"

And thus I underwent my cure with the down-at-heel gentleman at that inn till the evening, and I didn't have any qualms of conscience about it, for I knew that I was drinking not for the sake of indulging myself, but for the sake of denying myself. I'd put my hand inside my coat to make sure that the money was still there and, having made sure that everything was in order, I'd go on drinking.

The gentleman who was drinking with me went on telling me all about how he had led a life of sin and debauchery and he spoke particularly about love and he ended up by trying to pick a quarrel with me on the score that I knew nothing about love.

I said:

"It isn't my fault that I don't know anything about all that nonsense, is it? You should be glad that you do know all about it and that that's why you've turned out such a fine specimen!"

But he said:

"Whisht! Silence! Love is a sacred thing!"

"Rubbish," I said.

"You're a yokel," he said, "and a rascal, too, if you dare laugh at one of the most sacred feelings of the human heart and speak of it as rubbish."

"What else is it," said I, "but rubbish?"

"But don't you understand the meaning of 'beauty, nature's perfection' at all?" he said.

"Yes," said I, "I can understand the beauty of a horse."

Whereupon he jumped to his feet and wanted to box my ears.

"Is a horse," he said, "beauty, nature's perfection?"

But as it was getting rather late by that time, he had no time to prove his point to me, for the barman, seeing that both of us were the worse for drink, winked at the chuckers-out and they, six hefty men of them, rushed up to us and said, "It's time for you to go, gentlemen," and they took us under the arms and put us out into the street, slamming the doors behind us and locking them for the night.

And then it was that I suffered such bedevilment that although a great many years have passed since that amazing chapter of accidents, I cannot to this day render a clear account to myself of what really took place and by what force it worked upon me, but such temptations and adventures which I underwent that night, I am sure, no saint or martyr ever underwent, not, at any rate, one whose life is described in the Book of Saints.

CHAPTER XII

THE first thing I did after I had been thrown out of the inn was to feel inside my coat to see if my wallet was still there. Well, it seemed that it was. "Now," thought I, "I must be careful to bring it home."

The night was very dark, as dark as can be. In summer we get such nights near Kursk, you know, pitch dark, but very warm and tranquil: in the sky the stars are hung like so many icon lamps and down below the darkness is so dense that you get the impression as if someone were feeling you all over, touching you. . . . And during a fair hundreds of wicked people of every description roam about the streets and there had been many cases of robbery and murder. In spite of the fact that I knew myself to be a man who was a match for anybody in physical strength, I could not help thinking that, in the first place, I was drunk and, secondly, if ten or more men were to attack me, even my powerful physique would not avail me against being robbed and, furthermore, brave as I was and ready to take on anybody, I couldn't help recalling that every time I got up and sat down to pay for the drinks, my companion, that beggarly gentleman, could see that I had a flush of money on me. And that was why, you know, it suddenly occurred to me: was he perhaps contemplating some treachery against me to my utter undoing? Where was he, anyway? We had been thrown out of the inn together, hadn't we? So where, in heaven's name, did he disappear to so quickly?

I was standing there and, peering quietly round me, I called to him softly, not knowing his name, thus:

"Eh, you," I said, "you magnetiser, where are you?"

And he suddenly burst upon my sight like some hobgoblin and said:

"Here I am!"

I couldn't recognise his voice and in the pitch darkness even his face did not seem his own.

"Come nearer," I said, and, as he did so, I took hold of his shoulders and began peering down at him, but I couldn't for the life of me make out whether it was he or not: for directly I touched him I lost my memory, just suddenly like that, for no reason at all. All I could hear was that he was mumbling something in French: "Dee-ka-tee-lee-ka-tee-pé," and I could not understand a word of it.

"What are you mumbling about?" I said.

But he said again in French:

"Dee-ka-tee-lee-ka-tee-pé."

"Stop it, you silly fool," I said. "Answer me in Russian who you are, for I've forgotten all about you."

He replied:

"Dee-ka-tee-lee-ka-tee-pé: I'm the magnetiser."

"Oh, to hell with you, you rogue," I said, and for a fleeting moment I seemed to remember who he was, but as soon as I'd begin to look closely at him, I'd see that he had two noses! . . . Yes, two noses! And no sooner had I begun to think about it than I'd forget again who he was. . . .

"Oh, confound you!" thought I. "Where could I have picked up a rascal like you?" And once more I asked him, "Who are you?"

He said again:

"The magnetiser."

"Get away from me," I said. "How do I know you're not the devil?"

"Not exactly," he said, "but not far off, either."

I punched him on the nose and he got cross and said:

"What are you hitting me for? I'm doing you a great favour, curing you of your drinking habits, and you can do nothing better than hit me."

But however hard I tried, I just could not remember him, and I said:

"But who the devil are you?"

He said:

"I'm your faithful friend."

"All right," I said, "supposing you are my friend, would this prevent you from doing me harm?"

"No," he said, "but I'm going to show you such a *petit-comme-peu* that you'll feel quite a different man."

"Stop telling fibs," I said.

"Truly," he said, "truly, such a *petit-comme-peu*. . . ."

"What the devil are you talking French to me for?" I said. "I don't know what your *petit-comme-peu* is!"

"I'll give life a new meaning for you," he said.

"All right," I said, "that's different. But what kind of new meaning can you give me?"

"Such a one," he said, "that you'll comprehend beauty, nature's perfection."

"But how am I to comprehend it so suddenly?"

"Come along with me," he said, "and you'll see."

"All right," I said, "let's go!"

So off we went. We walked along, the two of us, unsteadily, it is true, but walk along we did, but where we were going to I did not know, and then I'd suddenly remember that I did not know who my companion was and I'd say again:

"Stop! Tell me who you are, or I shan't go another step!"

He would tell me and I'd seem to remember it for a little while and I'd ask:

"Why do I keep on forgetting who you are?"

And he would reply:

"That," he said, "is due to the action of my magnetism, but don't be afraid of it, it'll soon pass off, only let me give you another dose of magnetism, a bigger dose this time."

And he suddenly turned me with my back to him and started fumbling about with his fingers in the hair on my neck. . . . Uncanny, that's what it felt like: he seemed to rummage about there as if he wanted to crawl into my head.

I said:

"Look here, whoever you are, what are you burrowing there for?"

"Wait a minute," he said, "and stand still, will you? I'm introducing into you the whole force of my magnetism."

"That's right," I said, "let's have the whole of it by all means, but are you sure that you don't want to pinch my money?"

He denied it.

"All right," I said, "wait till I find out."

I put my hand inside my coat: the money was safe.

"Now I can see that you are not a thief," I said, but I had again forgotten who he was and I could not even remember how to ask him about it, for I was wholly preoccupied with the curious sensation I had that he had crawled through the back of my neck right inside me and was looking at the world through my eyes and that my eyes were just like windows to him.

"Good heavens," I thought, "what a dirty trick to play on me!" and I asked:

"What's happened to my eyesight?"

"You haven't any left now," he said.

"What are you talking about?" I said. "How do you mean I haven't any?"

"What I mean," said he, "is that all you'll see with your eyes now is what isn't there."

"What kind of wonder is that?" I said. "Very well, let's try!"

So I opened my eyes wide and peered for all I was worth and I seemed to see all sorts of horrible faces on little legs staring at me from behind dark corners, darting across my path and standing on the cross-roads, waiting and saying, "Let's kill him and take away his treasure!" And my little gentleman was there again before me, his hair bristling and his face lit up by some inner light, and behind me I heard an awful din and uproar, voices and twangling instruments and wild shouts and screams and merry laughter. I looked round and I realised that I was standing with my back against some house with open windows and everything bright inside and that it was from there that all that noise came and the voices and the melancholy strain of a guitar, and in front of me I again saw the gentleman in the tattered clothes and he was waving his hands in front of my face and making passes over my chest, stopping at the heart and pressing against it, and seizing my fingers and giving them a slight shake, and again waving and working away with his hands with such zeal and abandon that I could see that he was all covered with sweat.

But as the light began to shine forth from those windows and I felt that I was regaining consciousness, I stopped being afraid and said:

"Listen to me, whoever you are, devil or Satan himself or just a hobgoblin out of hell, do me a favour and either wake me or vanish out of sight!"

And he said in reply to that:

"Wait," he said, "the time hasn't come yet: there's still the danger that you won't be able to stand it."

I said:

"What is it that I won't be able to stand?"

"That," he said, "which is now happening in the heavenly spheres."

"What is happening there?" I asked. "I can't hear anything in particular."

But he insisted that I wasn't listening properly and he spoke to me in the language of Holy Writ.

"To hear it," he said, "thou must imitate the one who playeth the harp, him who inclineth his head towards the earth and straineth his ear to the singing and striketh the strings with his hand."

"Well," I thought, "what's all this about? That isn't at all like the speech of a drunken man, the way he talks now!"

And he went on looking at me and waving his hands over me quietly, while himself continuing to exhort me to do as he wished.

"Hearken unto the strings," he said, "and see how cunningly they are struck one after the other and, as they are struck, the harp bursteth forth into song and the harp player rejoiceth in the honeyed sweetness of its sounds."

I tell you, gentlemen, it was as if I heard no words at all, but as if the waters of a living stream came rippling by my ear and I said to myself, "Is this a drunkard? See how well he can talk in the tongues of angels!"

In the meantime my gentleman stopped fidgeting about and spoke as follows:

"That'll do for you. Now awaken," he said, "and fortify yourself!"

And with these words he bent down and for a long time he tried to get hold of something in the pocket of his torn trousers and at last he got it out. I looked and saw that it was a little lump of sugar, all covered with dirt from lying so long in his pocket apparently. He removed the dirt with his nails, blew on it and said:

"Open your mouth!"

I said, "What for?" and just opened my mouth wide. He pushed the lump of sugar into it and said:

"Suck," he said, "suck and fear not: this is a magnetic sugar-mentor and it will fortify you."

I realised, of course, that if he used French words, it was all about magnetism, so I didn't ask him any more questions, but was entirely preoccupied with sucking the lump of sugar and, anyway, I could no longer see the man who had given it to me. Whether he went away somewhere and vanished in the dark or whether he just sank through the ground, the devil alone knew: all I knew was that there I was quite alone and that I was completely restored to my senses. Well, I thought, "What's the use of waiting for him here? I must go home now." But the trouble was that I didn't know in what street I was and what kind of house it was beside which I was standing. So I said to myself, "Is this a house at all? Maybe I'm just seeing things, maybe it's nothing but a piece of witchcraft. . . . It is night, everybody's asleep, so why's there a light here? But why not try? . . . Let's go in, have a look what's happening there: if there are people in this house, real people, I'll ask them the way to my home and if it is only a delusion and a dream and not living people at all, then what's there to be scared of? All I have to do is just to say, 'This ground is holy: get thee behind me, Satan!' and everything will vanish. . . ."

CHAPTER XIII

THUS fortified in spirit, I walked up the front steps, crossed myself, uttered a short prayer and—nothing happened! The house remained standing, it didn't even sway and I saw that the doors were open and that at the end of a very long passage a lantern with a lighted candle hung on a nail in the wall. I looked more closely and I noticed that to the left there were two more doors, both covered with matting, and above them were strange kinds of candlesticks with mirrors in the shape of stars under them. "Well," I thought, "what sort of a house could this be? It doesn't look like an inn, and yet one can see that it is a house of entertainment," but what kind of entertainment I couldn't make out. But as I listened, I heard the strains of a song coming from behind one of the doors covered with matting . . . such a sweet song, too, a song that made your heart stand still, and the voice that sang it was as clear as a bell, a voice that just took your breath away, that bewitched your soul. So I listened and I didn't move from my place, and at that moment a door opened somewhere at the end of the long passage and I saw a tall gypsy coming out in wide silken breeches and a velvet cossack coat and showing somebody out of the house through a special door under that distant lantern, a door I hadn't even noticed at first. Although, to be quite frank, I wasn't able to make out who was the man he had shown out of the house, I did get the idea that it was none other than my magnetiser and I heard the gypsy saying to the man:

"All right, all right, don't be so angry about the fifty copecks, but call in again to-morrow and if we get some profit out of *him*, we'll give you more for bringing him to us."

And with those words he bolted the door and rushed towards me, pretending to have only just noticed me, and, opening the door under one of those curiously wrought mirrors, said:

"Welcome to our house, sir! Come and hear our songs! We have beautiful singers."

And without giving me time to reply, he quietly flung the door wide open in front of me. . . . I don't know what happened to me at that moment, gentlemen, but everything seemed so familiar to me that I suddenly felt quite at home there. The room was very big, but rather low and the ceiling seemed to give in the middle, as though thrusting downwards with its belly, and the walls looked so dark, as if covered with soot, and the tobacco smoke was so thick that the large chandelier under the ceiling did not shed any light and but for the fact that it was alight, one would not notice that it was there at all. And below in that dense smoke a crowd of people . . . hundreds and hundreds of them, and in front of them a young gypsy girl was singing in that beautiful voice which I had already heard. As I entered, she was just finishing her song and her voice died down on a last note of great tenderness and fell silent. . . . And as that sweet voice of hers fell silent, everything in the room seemed to fall silent, too, as if the people there were dead. . . . But in another moment everybody jumped up like mad and began to clap and to shout. But as I looked in sheer bewilderment at those crowds of people I wondered where they had all come from; for as I stood there, more and more faces were constantly appearing through the smoke. "Heavens above," thought I, "are they really human beings or demons in human shape?" But presently I began to recognise among that vast crowd many horse-breeders and horse-buyers, known to me personally, and other well-to-do merchants and landowners whom I knew to be keen horsemen, and among them all a gypsy girl was moving about, such a . . . but it is quite impossible to describe her, she didn't seem to be a woman even, but like some gaily-coloured serpent she seemed to be moving about on her tail, her whole slender body bending lithely and a fire blazing in her black eyes. A fascinating figure! She carried a large tray with glasses of champagne round the edge and in the middle a great pile of money. There was no silver in that pile: only gold and banknotes—blue tits and grey ducks and red heath-cocks, everything except white swans. Every time she offered a glass to a man, he'd drink the wine and throw some money on the tray, each man indulging his own fancy in this matter and parting either with a gold piece or with a banknote, and then she'd kiss him on the lips and curtsy to him. Well, so she walked round the first row and the second—the people sat in a kind of semi-circle—and then she walked round the last row, behind which I stood, and, having walked round it, she was about to turn back, not wishing to offer me any drink, but an old gypsy who walked behind her, suddenly shouted at her, "Grushka!" and he motioned her with his eyes in my direction. She just lifted her eyelashes at him. . . . Lord, what lovely eyelashes they were! Long and black, and they seemed to be alive and move by themselves like birds. . . . And I saw that, as the old man shouted his order to her, her eyes blazed out as if her whole being reared up in anger! She got angry, you see, because she had been ordered to offer me a drink. However, she did as she was told. She went up to me behind the last row, bowed and said:

"Won't you drink my health, sir?"

And I couldn't even reply to her: so instantly did she bewitch me! Immediately, that is, as she bowed before me over the tray and I saw how the parting on her head ran between her black hair like a thread of silver and disappeared at the back, I seemed to go stark, raving mad and to lose my reason entirely. I drank the wine she had offered me, while looking at her over the rim of the glass and I couldn't tell whether her skin was dark or fair, but I could see distinctly how underneath her thin skin the colour glowed, as in a cherry in sunlight, and how on her lovely temple a vein was beating. . . . "So that's what real beauty is," thought I, "which is called nature's perfection! The magnetiser spoke the truth: it isn't at all like the beauty of a horse, an animal that is bought and sold."

And so I drained the glass and set it down with a crash on the tray, and she stood waiting to see how much I esteemed her kiss to be worth.

I put my hand quickly into my pocket to get some money to put down on the tray, but all I could find there was a few silver coins and other small change. "It isn't enough," I thought. "It won't do to give so paltry a present to so alluring a snake and, besides, I shall lower myself in the estimation of all the people here!"

In the meantime I could hear the gentlemen saying to the old gypsy, without even pretending to lower their voices:

"Really, Vassily Ivanov, why do you order Grusha to treat that lout? We can't help resenting it!"

And he replied:

"We make no distinction between one guest and another, gentlemen. Everybody is welcome and everybody is treated honourably in this house. I'm sorry you should feel resentful, but that's, I suppose, because you fail to realise that even a plain man knows how to value beauty and talent. I've seen many examples of that, gentlemen."

And I, hearing that, thought:

"Oh, to hell with you! Do you think that because you're richer you have more refined feelings than I? No! What will be, will be. I'll pay the prince back later, but now I shall neither disgrace myself, nor cheapen that paragon of beauty by my stinginess."

No sooner said than done: I put my hand at once inside my coat, took out a hundred-rouble swan from my roll of banknotes and flipped it down on the tray. The gypsy girl immediately took the tray in one hand and with the other wiped my lips with a white handkerchief, and she didn't even kiss me, but just seemed to touch my lips with hers lightly, and as she did so, she seemed to smear them with a kind of poison, and then she went away.

She went away and I would have remained standing where I was had not the old gypsy, Grusha's father, and another gypsy taken me under the arms and dragged me forward and made me sit down in the first row next to the captain of police and other gentlemen.

To tell the truth, I did not particularly relish it and I didn't want to stay, but wanted to leave, but they would not let me, entreating me and calling on Grusha:

"Grusha, darling, don't let our dear guest depart!"

And she came forward and . . . the devil alone, I suppose, could tell what power there resided in those eyes of hers: one glance and she seemed to have injected some paralysing venom into my eyes, and she said:

"Do not offend us, sir! Please, stay a little longer at our house!"

"Well," I said, "who would dream of offending you?" and I sat down.

And she kissed me again, and again I had that curious sensation as if she touched my lips with a poisoned brush and sent a hot stream of blood racing to my heart so that it seemed to be set on fire and contract with pain.

After that the singing and the dancing began again and, once more, a gypsy girl went round with the champagne, but this time it was a different girl. She, too, was beautiful, but not a patch on Grusha! She wasn't half as lovely, and to show how little I thought of her as compared with the other, I just grabbed a handful of silver coins from my pocket and sent them rolling on the tray. . . . The gentlemen thought it a great joke and laughed heartily, but I didn't care, for all I cared for was to keep my eyes on her, on Grusha, waiting for her to sing alone without the choir, but she did not sing. She was sitting among the other gypsies, joining in the refrain of their song, but she would not sing a solo, and I couldn't hear her voice and only saw her sweet little mouth with the white teeth. . . . "Oh," thought I, "miserable wretch that I am! I came in just for a minute and lost a hundred roubles and now I won't even hear her sing again!" But, as good luck would have it, I was not the only one among that large company who wanted to hear her sing: the others, too, all the important gentlemen in the room, after an interval joined in a universal shout:

"Grusha! Grusha! 'The Skiff!' Grusha! 'The Skiff!' "

Well, the gypsies cleared their throats, and her young brother touched the guitar and she began to sing. You know . . . their singing is usually very sensitive and it goes to your heart and when I heard her voice, which had sounded so alluring to me even behind the door, I could not help feeling deeply moved. It was lovely! She began, perhaps, a little harshly, a little too boldly, something like this: "The sea's ro-o-o-oaring, the sea's mo-o-o-oaning. . . ." And you really felt how the sea was moaning and how it dashed the little skiff, which was caught up in it, now one way and now another. But when she appealed to the star, there was a sudden change in her voice: "Sweetest, dearest star of morning, twinkling up so high, human sorrow cannot touch me while thou sailest up the sky!" And then a new surprising change, something you didn't expect. All their songs are full of those appeals: now they weep, sunk into the deepest melancholy, throwing you into such a black dejection of spirits as if your soul is about to part from your body, and then, suddenly, they burst out in quite a different key and your heart feels merry again. . . . So also in that song she began by dashing the skiff against the raging waves, and the others suddenly burst out on a high note all together:

Ja-la-la, ja-la-la,
Ja-la-la, pringala!
Ja-la-la pringa-la!
Hey da chepuringala!
Hey hop-hi, ta hara!
Hey hop-hi-ta hara!

After the song Grusha went round with the tray again, offering wine and kisses, and I gave her another swan from the inside pocket of my coat. . . . People began looking askance at me, for I was lowering their prestige by my munificence, and they felt ashamed to give anything after me; but I didn't care a fig for my money any more, for I wanted to show what I felt in my heart, I wanted to fling my soul wide open and I did fling it open. Every time Grusha sang a song, I'd give her a swan for it, and I had even stopped counting how many I had given away, but handed them out without a thought and that was why when anybody else asked her for a song she would excuse herself, saying that she was feeling "tired," but I had only to wink at the old gypsy, "Can't you make her sing?"—so to speak, and he would look at her with such eyes that sing she would. She sang many songs that night, one song more entrancing than the other, and I had thrown to her without counting I don't know how many swans, until at last—I couldn't tell what hour it was, but the day was beginning to break by then—she was really and truly tired and, looking very wan, she threw a meaning glance at me and began to sing, "Go away, look no more, vanish out of my sight." With those words she seemed to entreat me to go, but with the other words she seemed to search my mind: "Dost thou want with my brave heart to play, till with my beauty's splendour I thee slay?" And so I thrust another swan upon her! She kissed me again, unwillingly, and I felt as though she had stung me, and her eyes blazed angrily, and the other gypsies, in that evil hour, burst out in a farewell refrain:

Darling, don't you feel at all,
How much, sweet, I'm in your thrall!—

and all joined in that chorus and looked at Grusha, and I, too, looked at her, humming, "Don't you feel at all?" Then the gypsies burst forth, "Go away, cottage, go away, stove, pity the master, who can't move," and all suddenly began to dance. . . . The gypsies danced and the gypsy girls danced and the gentlemen danced: they were all caught up in one dance and indeed it did look as if the whole cottage had started to move. The gypsy girls went skipping in front of the gentlemen, who tried to catch up with them and raced after them, the young ones with a wild shout and the older ones with a suppressed groan. . . . I looked round at the seats: there was not a man left there. . . . Even those among the men who had reached the age of discretion and whom I hardly expected to see indulging in such high jinks, even those had all risen from their seats. One of the more solid citizens would remain in his seat for a little while, at first clearly rather ashamed to join in the riot and either looking on or just pulling at his moustache, but presently one devil would start jerking his shoulder and another pull at his leg and, lo, he'd suddenly jump to his feet and start throwing his legs about in a way that was hardly becoming to his station in life. The police captain, a man of immense girth with two of his daughters married, joined the throng of revellers with his two sons-in-law and went round the room gasping for breath, like a sheat-fish, and lifting his feet heavily, as though he were pulling them out of a bog; and a hussar officer, a rich captain who was a horse-buyer for the army, a dashing dancer and a fine, upstanding young fellow, put everybody else in the room to shame: arms akimbo, he sent his heels flying and crashing on the floor—just showing off, and every time he got near to the gypsy girls he'd spread out his arms as if about to enfold them, and every time he got near enough to Grusha, he'd toss his mop of hair, throw his cap at her feet and shout, "Step on it, crush it, oh, sweetheart mine!" and she . . . Oh, what a lovely dancer she was! I remember seeing actresses dancing on the stage, but, goodness me, compared with her it was just like some army officer's horse without a scrap of imagination cavorting on the parade ground and prancing through the regulation steps just for the sake of show, without a spark of life! But that beauty—no sooner had she joined in the dance, than she went sailing like a swan and she moved with such magnificent ease, her body swaying neither to the right nor the left, that one could almost hear how inside her—inside that serpent—the little bones moved and how the marrow passed from one bone to the other, and when she stopped dead, she would arch her back, move a shoulder and her eyebrow would be in line with the toe of her foot. . . . A picture! Just to see her dance was enough to turn the head of every man in the room: they were all drawn irresistibly towards her, in a headlong rush: some had tears in their eyes, others bared their teeth, and all shouted in one voice, "Take all we have: only dance!"—and they just threw their money at her feet, some gold pieces, others banknotes. The dance went on, and the crowd of dancers grew more and more dense, only I alone was still sitting down, but even I did not know how long I'd be able to hold out, for I could not bear to see how again and again she would step on the cap of that hussar officer. . . . Every time she stepped on it the devil would tear at my heart; she'd step again, and again he would grip my heart, and at last I said to myself, "Why go on tormenting yourself for nothing? Why shouldn't your soul rejoice as much as it wishes?" So up I jumped, brushed the hussar out of my way and away I went kicking up my heels in front of Grusha. . . . And to make quite sure that she, Grusha, would not step on the hussar's cap again, I resorted to a stratagem: "All of you," I said to myself, "go on yelling that you don't mind giving away all you have, but I am not deceived by that cry of yours, for I shall presently prove to all of you by deeds and not by words that I, for one, don't mind giving everything away!" So I bounded in front of her and, taking a swan out of the inside pocket of my coat, I flung it under her feet, shouting, "Crush it! Step on it!" At first she wouldn't . . . notwithstanding that my swan was a damn sight more valuable than the hussar's cap, she wouldn't even look at it and was all for following the hussar, but the old gypsy—good man!—saw it in time and he just stamped his foot at her. . . . So she took the hint and followed me. . . . She was sailing after me, her eyes cast on the ground, blazing with anger and almost setting the ground afire like the dragon in the fable, and I was leaping like a hobgoblin in front of her and every time I leapt, I flung a swan under her feet. . . . While I held her in such reverence that I kept on saying to myself, "Hast thou not, accursed one, created heaven and earth?"—I did not hesitate to shout brazenly at her, "Come on, faster, faster!" and all the while I was flinging swans under her feet and, then, I put my hand inside my coat to get another one and I found that there were only about ten of them left. . . . "Well," thought I, "the devil take you, the lot of you!" and I crumpled them all in my hand and just flung them in one heap under her feet and, having done that, I snatched up a bottle of champagne from the table, knocked its neck off and roared, "Make way, my soul, or I'll drown you!" and I drank it all in one gulp to her health, for after the dance I felt a terrible thirst upon me.

CHAPTER XIV

"Well, and what happened after that?" we asked Ivan Severyanych with bated breath.

"After that everything really did happen as *he* had foretold."

"Who had foretold?"

"Why, the magnetiser, of course, who had cast that spell on me: as he had promised to release me from the power of the devil of drink, so he did get rid of him for me and I have not tasted another glass since. He did it remarkably well."

"Well, ye-e-es. . . . But how did you settle with your prince for the swans you had set free?"

"That, gentlemen, was settled so simply that I can hardly believe it myself even to this day. How I got back home from those gypsies I couldn't say myself, nor how I went to bed. The first thing I knew was that the prince was knocking at my door and calling to me. I wanted to get up from the wooden chest on which I slept, but, try as I might, I couldn't find the edge, so I naturally couldn't get off it. I would crawl to one side of it, then turn to the other, but I just could not find the edge. . . . I seemed to have lost my way on that chest and I could do nothing about it. The prince would shout, Ivan Severyanych! and I would reply, One moment, sir! and just kept on crawling about without being able to find the edge of my bed and at last I said to myself, Well, if I can't get off it, I'd better jump off it!—but as I took a flying leap, intending to jump as far as possible, something hit me in the face and everything round me began to ring and crash to the ground and behind me, too, everything rang and crashed to the ground, and I heard the prince's voice saying to his orderly, Get a light, quick! I stood still, not wishing to move, for I didn't know whether all that was really happening or whether I was seeing it in a dream, for I believed myself still lying on the wooden chest, having been unable to reach the edge, but instead, when the orderly had brought in a lighted candle, I saw that I was standing on the floor and that I had crashed through the glass door of a cupboard and had broken all the china in it. . . ."

"How did you manage to lose your bearings like that?"

"Quite simply: I thought that I was as usual sleeping on the wooden chest, but on returning home from the gypsies I must have fallen asleep on the floor and I kept on crawling about looking for the edge of the chest and then I took that flying leap and . . . crashed through the china cabinet. I was wandering about all over the room because he, the magnetiser, that is, had removed the devil of drink from me, but had left the roaming devil with me. . . . I at once remembered the words he had said to me, Mind, you may find things much worse, if you leave off drink!—and I went in search of him, for I wanted to ask him to demagnetise me to my old state, but I couldn't find him. It seemed he had taken too much upon himself and he couldn't stand it, poor man, drank so much at the pub opposite the gypsies' house that he died."

"So you remained magnetised like that?"

"Yes, so I remained."

"But did that magnetism work a long time on you?"

"Why only a long time? It's probably still working to-day."

"But how did you settle with the prince? Didn't you have to give him some explanation about those swans?"

"Why, of course I had to give him an account of what I did with them, only it didn't matter one way or the other. You see, the prince himself came back without a penny, having lost his shirt at cards. He began asking me for some money to try his luck again, but I said:

"You're wasting your time, sir, I have no money."

He thought that I was joking, but I said:

"No, sir, it's the truth I'm telling you. While you were away I had rather an expensive day off."

He asked:

"How could you possibly have spent five thousand in one day off?"

I said:

"I gave them all to a gypsy girl. . . ."

He didn't believe me.

I said:

"All right, don't believe me, but I'm telling you the truth."

He lost his temper and said:

"Shut the door and I'll show you how to waste Government money," but then he suddenly changed his mind and said, "Never mind, I'm as big a wastrel as you."

So he lay down in the room to finish his night's sleep and I, too, went to sleep in the hayloft. When I came to, I found that I was in a hospital and I was told that I had had an attack of delirium tremens and had tried to hang myself, but, thank God, they put me into a strait-jacket. Later when I got better, I went to see the prince in his village, for he had resigned from the army in the meantime, and I said:

"I want to work for you, sir, until I've paid you the money I owe you."

But he said:

"Go to hell."

Well, I could see that he was very cross with me, so I went up to him and bowed my head before him.

"What are you up to now?" he asked.

"Give me a good beating, at any rate, sir," I said.

But he said:

"Why do you assume that I'm angry with you? Perhaps I don't even consider you to have been at fault."

"Goodness gracious, sir," I said, "how am I not at fault if I have wasted such a vast amount of money? I know very well, sir, that hanging is too good for a villain like me!"

He, however, replied:

"But, my dear fellow, what could you do about it if you are an artist?"

"How do you mean, sir?" I said.

"I mean what I say," he replied, "my dear Ivan Severyanych, my semi-honourable one—an artist."

"I'm afraid, sir," I said, "I don't understand."

"Don't think it is anything bad," he said, "for I, too, am an artist."

"Well," I thought to myself, "I can see that all right: it isn't only I who drank myself into delirium tremens!"

But he got up, knocked out his pipe and said:

"I don't wonder that you should have flung all the money you had on you before her, when I, my dear fellow, gave for her more than I have and more than I have ever had."

I just glared at him.

"For pity's sake, sir," I said, "what are you saying? Just to hear you talk like that, sir, frightens me!"

"There's no need to be frightened," he said, "for the Lord is merciful and I may be able to extricate myself somehow or other, but the fact is that I've paid fifty thousand to the gypsy camp for that Grusha."

I just gasped.

"Do you really mean it, sir ?" I said. "Fifty thousand for a gypsy girl! But the trollop isn't worth it, sir!"

"Now," he replied, "my semi-honourable friend, you're talking like a fool and not at all like an artist. Not worth it ? Why, a woman is worth everything one has in the world, for she puts such a curse on you that you can't get rid of it for a whole kingdom, but she can rid you of it in a second."

Well, I couldn't help thinking that that was true enough, but all the same I went on shaking my head and said:

"What a lot of money! Fifty thousand!"

"Yes, sir," he said, "and, please, don't rub it in, for I was jolly glad they had accepted that much for her, or I should have had to give them more . . . I'd have given them everything in the world for her!"

"You should have just spat and that's all, sir."

"I couldn't do that, my dear fellow," he said. "I couldn't just spit."

"Why not ?"

"Because she had stung me by her beauty and her talent and I had to get cured or I'd have gone mad. But, tell me the truth, she is beautiful, isn't she ? Eh ? It's true, isn't it ? She has something to drive a man mad, hasn't she ?"

I just bit my lips and nodded silently: "It's true, all right," was what I implied.

"You know," the prince said, "I shouldn't hesitate for a minute to die for a woman. Can you understand that ? Can you understand that one wouldn't mind dying for a woman ?"

"Well," I said, "there's nothing incomprehensible about it: beauty's nature's perfection."

"What do you mean by that ?"

"I mean," I said, "that beauty is nature's perfection and to a man who falls under its spell death itself may be . . . happiness!"

"You're a fine fellow, my demi-semi-honourable and all-too-much-little-significant Ivan Severyanych!" my prince exclaimed. "Yes, yes, one may be even happy to die and that's why I'm so glad to have turned my life upside-down for her: I've resigned from the army and mortgaged my estate and I shall be living here from now on and see no one, but just keep on looking at her!"

Here I lowered my voice even more and said in a whisper:

"What do you mean by . . . looking at her, sir ? Is she here ?"

And he replied:

"What else do you think ? Of course, she's here."

"Is it," said I, "possible ?"

"You wait here," he said, "and I'll bring her at once. You are an artist and I shouldn't dream of hiding her from you."

And with these words he left me and went out. I stood there waiting and thinking to myself:

"That's bad! To say that you don't want to look at any face but hers is a bad sign: it means that you'll soon get tired of her!" But I didn't enter into all the implications of the prince's words, for as soon as I'd remember that she was there, I'd feel hot all over and my head would begin to swim, for I couldn't help thinking, "Shall I really see her now?" And then both of them suddenly came in, the prince walking ahead of her, carrying in one hand a guitar with a wide, scarlet ribbon and dragging poor Grusha with the other, clasping both her hands in his, and she was walking with her head downcast, resisting him and without looking and only those long, black eyelashes of hers fluttered like the wings of a bird.

The prince brought her into the room, picked her up in his arms and set her down like a child on a wide, soft divan with her feet towards a corner, put one velvet cushion under her back and another under her right arm; then he put the ribbon of the guitar across her shoulder and placed her fingers on the strings and, sitting down himself on the floor beside the divan, he leant his head against her scarlet, morocco-leather shoe and nodded to me: "Sit down, too," so to speak.

So I, too, crossed my legs and let myself down quietly on the floor by the door and there I remained sitting, looking at her. There was an uncanny stillness in the room. I sat there for a long time, till my knees began to ache, but every time I looked up at her she was sitting in the same position and when I happened to look up at the prince I saw that he had almost gnawed through his moustache from sheer agony of soul, but he spoke no word to her.

So I nodded to him: "Ask her to sing!" so to speak. And he, too, gave me to understand in pantomime that, so to speak, she wouldn't listen to him.

So the two of us went on sitting on the floor and waiting, and then suddenly she started to sigh and to sob, but she seemed to be doing it in a kind of a delirium, and a tear rolled down her cheek and her fingers began to move over the strings of the guitar like wasps and to hum. . . . And all at once she began to sing in a very soft voice and it sounded as if she were crying, "Good people, hear my sorrow and my heartache. . . ."

The prince whispered to me, "Well?"

And I replied to him in French, also in a whisper:

"*Petit comme peu,*" I said, and I could say no more, for at that moment she suddenly cried out, "But for my beauty they'll sell me, they'll sell me . . ." and she hurled the guitar from her lap, far into the room and tore her kerchief from her head and, throwing herself down on the divan, she buried her face in her hands and began to sob, and I, looking at her, began to cry, too, and the prince . . . he, too, began to cry and, picking up the guitar, he did not seem to sing so much as to chant, as though intoning a verse at divine service, and to moan, "If only thou'dst see my heart on fire, my soul consumed with longing for thee . . ." and the rest was drowned in his tears. So he went on singing and crying, "Comfort me, the comfortless one, bestow the happiness of thy love upon me, the unhappy one. . . ." So great was the wretchedness of his spirit that she, I saw, was beginning to take heed of his tears and his mournful singing and was growing more composed and resigned, and, then, suddenly, she withdrew her hand from her face and put her arm round his head with great tenderness, like a mother. . . .

Well, of course, I realised that she must be very sorry for him at that moment and that she would comfort him and gladden his soul consumed with longing. So I got up and left the room unobserved.

"Was it then that you entered the monastery?" one of the passengers asked.

"No, sir, not then, but much later," Ivan Severyanych replied, adding that first of all he was destined, while still in the world of men, to see a great deal of that woman and to be with her until everything fate held in store for her came to pass and his own destiny, too, was fulfilled.

The passengers very naturally besought him to tell them the story of Grusha, even if only in bare outline, and Ivan Severyanych did as they asked him.

CHAPTER XV

YOU see, gentlemen (Ivan Severyanych began), my prince was a good man, but his character was very unstable. If he wanted a thing, he had to have it at any price, you just had to give it to him or he'd go off his head, and in those years he would not hesitate to give anything in the world so long as he got it, but when he got it, he did not appreciate his good fortune. That was exactly what happened between him and the gypsy girl, and her father (Grusha's father, that is) and the rest of the gypsies belonging to his camp had a pretty shrewd idea about the prince's character and that was why they had asked such a terrific price for her, more than his property warranted, for although his estate was quite big, it was burdened with debts. Such a sum as the gypsy camp had asked for Grusha was more than the prince had in cash at the time and he had to raise it as a loan and to resign from the army.

Knowing all his weaknesses, I did not expect much good from him for

Grusha and my expectations were fully justified. For a time he waited on her hand and foot and would not let her out of his sight, unable, it seemed, to draw his breath without her, but suddenly he fell to yawning in her presence and he began asking me to share their company.

"Sit down," he used to say, "and listen."

I would take a chair, sit down somewhere near the door, and listen. But it also frequently happened that when he asked her to sing, she would say:

"Who shall I sing to? You," she would say, "have grown cold and I must have someone whose soul will be set ablaze and be tormented by my song."

So the prince would at once send for me, and he and I would listen to her together; and after a time Grusha herself began to remind him to send for me, and she grew to be very friendly with me and after her singing I would quite frequently have tea in her apartments with the prince, but, of course, either at a separate table or somewhere by the window, except when she was alone, in which case she would always insist that I should sit beside her without any ceremony. Many days passed like that and the prince was getting more and more worried and one day he said to me:

"Do you know, Ivan Severyanych, things are not going well with me, my business is very bad."

I said:

"It couldn't be as bad as all that, sir. Thank God, sir, you live as a gentleman of your position should and you have everything you want."

Well, he just got angry with me.

"What a blithering idiot you are, my semi-honourable one," he said. "I have everything forsooth! What is it that I *have?*"

"Everything you want," I said.

"It isn't true," he said. "I've grown as poor as a church mouse. Why, I have to think twice before I can treat myself to a bottle of wine for dinner. Is that life? Is that life, I ask you?"

"Goodness gracious," I said to myself, "so that's what is worrying you, is it?" and I said aloud, "Well, sir," I said, "even if you can't afford a bottle of wine occasionally, it's nothing to make a fuss about, for after all, sir, you've something that's sweeter than wine or honey."

He understood that I was referring to Grusha and he seemed to be a little ashamed before me and he began to pace the room and wave his hands about, saying:

"Of course . . . of course . . . naturally . . . but only . . . You see, I've spent the last six months here and I haven't seen a living soul. . . ."

"But what do you want to see people for, sir, if you've got someone you desire more than anyone in the world?"

The prince reddened.

"You don't understand anything, my dear fellow," he said. "One thing's good only if one has the other."

"Aha," I thought, "so you've changed your tune, have you?" and I said, "What do you intend to do now, sir?"

"Let's start dealing in horses," he said. "I'd like to see horse-breeders and army buyers in my house again."

Horse-dealing is an unprofitable business at the best of times and it is certainly not a fit occupation for a gentleman, but I thought, "Humour the child—no matter what it does, so long as it doesn't cry," and I said, "By all means, sir, let's."

So we opened up stables and began to keep all sorts of horses which we were supposed to get in good shape for the fairs. But no sooner had we started than the prince got completely carried away by that new passion of his: he would raise some money and immediately spend it all on the purchase of horses, buying any horse that caught his fancy without listening to my advice. So we bought a whole multitude of horses, but when it came to selling them we just couldn't find any purchasers. . . . The prince soon got tired of it, anyway, and dropped his horses and began to do anything that came into his head: one day he'd get all excited about some new and wonderful flour mill which he would start building immediately, next day he'd open a saddler's shop, and the outcome of all his activities would be more losses and greater debts and, what was more serious, there was a change for the worse in his character. He never stayed at home for any length of time now, but kept rushing off to one place or another, always on the look out for something, while Grusha was left alone and in such a condition, too, for the poor girl was with child. Time would hang heavily on her hands. "I don't see much of him now," she used to say, but she went on showing a bold front to the world and in her relations with the prince, in particular, she'd try to be as little exacting in her demands as possible: as soon as she noticed that he was beginning to get tired of staying at home after a day or two, she'd immediately say:

"Why don't you go somewhere, my precious jewel? Go out and enjoy yourself. Don't sit about with me: I'm such an ordinary woman, without any proper education."

The prince would be full of contrition at those words of hers, and he'd kiss her hands and hold out for another two or three days, but when he kicked over the traces after that, there'd be no holding him, but her he'd leave under my personal supervision.

"Take good care of her, my semi-honourable Ivan Severyanych," he'd say. "You're an artist, you're not a good-for-nothing wastrel like me, an artist of the first water, and that's why it seems you know how to talk to her and you find each other such congenial company. As for me, I'm getting sick and tired of her 'precious jewels'."

I said:

"Why should you, sir? It's just a word of endearment."

"It may be a word of endearment," he said, "but it's stupid and tiresome all the same."

I said nothing, but after that I went to see her as a matter of course: whenever the prince was away I'd visit her twice a day in her apartments, just for a cup of tea, and I'd try to cheer her up as much as possible. And I felt she needed cheering up, for every time she started talking to me, she'd begin to complain bitterly.

"My dearest friend, Ivan Severyanych," she would say, "the green monster, jealousy, is eating me up."

I, of course, did my best to comfort her.

"Why be eaten up by jealousy so much," I'd say, "if wherever he goes he always comes back to you?"

But she'd start crying and she'd smite her breast and say:

"Please, tell me the truth, my dear friend, don't hide it from me: where does he spend all his time?"

"Why," I'd say, "with his friends in the country and in town."

"But are you sure," she'd say, "that he hasn't got anyone, some woman who keeps him away from me? Tell me, wasn't he in love with some woman before he met me and has he now gone back to her, or does he intend to marry her perhaps, the wretch?" And her eyes, as she would say that, would blaze with such hatred that I felt frightened of what might happen if her suspicions were justified.

I comforted her as best I could, but I could not help thinking, "Who can tell what his lordship may not be up to?" For it was very rarely that we saw him at all at that time.

Well, when the thought that the prince might be contemplating marriage occurred to her, she began plaguing me to find out what he was doing in town.

"Please," she said, "my dear, dear friend, Ivan Severyanych, go down to town and find out everything for certain and come back and tell me about it without concealing anything from me."

She kept on plaguing me more and more persistently and in the end made me feel so sorry for her that I thought, "Come what may, I'll go and find out, although if I do discover that the prince is unfaithful to her, I shan't tell her everything, but, at least, I'll have a look and clear the matter up one way or the other."

I thought of a good excuse for going to town: I said that I had personally to buy all sorts of medicaments for the horses from herbalists. So early one morning I set off, but I didn't set off just anyhow—oh, no!—I devised a cunning plan of my own.

Grusha did not know, and the servants had been strictly forbidden to tell her, that before he met her the prince had had another mistress in town, a woman of good family, Yevgenia Semyonovna, the daughter of a secretary in some government department. She was well known throughout the town as a fine pianist and she was altogether a very kind-hearted lady, good-looking, too, and she had had a daughter by the prince, but she grew rather fat and it was said that the prince had left her because of that. However, being still very rich at the time, he had bought a house for the lady and her daughter and they lived on the income that house brought in. After rewarding her in that way, the prince never visited Yevgenia Semyonovna again, but our servants, for old times' sake, remembered her for her kindness and every time they chanced to go to town, they'd stop at her place, both because they loved her and she was very nice to them and because she loved to find out about our prince from them.

So on my arrival in town I went straight to her, to this kind-hearted lady, and I said:

"I'd like to stay at your house, if I may, madam."

She replied:

"Yes, of course, but why don't you stop at the prince's flat ?"

"Has he a flat in town ?" I asked.

"Yes," she replied. "He's been staying there for more than a week. He's starting some new business, I believe."

"What kind of business ?" I asked.

"A cotton mill," she said. "I understand he's taking it on a lease."

"Goodness me, madam," I exclaimed, "what has he thought up now ?"

"Why ?" she said. "Is there anything wrong ?"

"Not that I know of," I said, "except that I'm rather surprised at him doing that."

She smiled.

"That's nothing," she said. "There's something you really ought to be surprised at: I've received a letter from the prince in which he writes to say that he intends to pay me a call to-day. It seems he's longing to see my daughter."

"And did you give him your permission, ma'am ?" I asked.

She shrugged her shoulders and said:

"Why shouldn't I ? Let him come and have a look at his daughter," and, having said that, the poor lady sighed and fell into thought and so she sat with head bowed, still so young and fair and robust-looking and, besides, her manners were so different from Grusha's. . . . Grusha knew nothing better than her "precious jewel," but this one, this one was quite different. . . . So I grew quite jealous of her on Grusha's account.

"Oh," thought I to myself, "I only hope that when he looks at that child of his, he won't cast a look at you, too, with that insatiable heart of his, for if he does, nothing good would come of it to my dear Grusha."

Revolving these thoughts in my mind, I was sitting in the nursery where Yevgenia Semyonovna had asked the old nurse, Tatyana Yakovlevna, a very talkative old lady, a native of Moscow, to treat me to a cup of tea, when suddenly I heard a ring at the front door and presently the parlour-maid rushed in and said to nurse:

"The prince has just arrived!"

I was about to get up to go to the kitchen, but Tatyana Yakovlevna who had a real passion for gossiping and hated to be deprived of a listener, said to me:

"Don't go, Ivan Golovanych, we can both retire to the dressing room and sit down behind the wardrobe. She'd never bring him in there and we shall be able to have a cosy little chat together."

I gladly agreed to her suggestion, for I hoped to learn something useful for Grusha from Tatyana Yakovlevna who, once she started talking, would never stop; and as Yevgenia Semyonovna had sent me a little eau-de-Cologne bottle with rum for my tea, I decided, being myself already a strict teetotaler at the time, to pour it into nurse's tea; for I was anxious to do everything possible to encourage her natural talkativeness in the hope that the dear old lady—bless her heart!—would tell me something which she would not otherwise have told me.

We left the nursery and esconced ourselves behind the cupboards in the dressing room, which was very narrow, more like a passage than a room, with a door at one end and, as luck would have it, that door led straight into the room where Yevgenia Semyonovna had received the prince, and the couch on which they had sat down was standing against that door. In a word, only that door, hung with a curtain on the other side, separated me from them, but it was really as if I were in the same room with them, for I could hear every word they said.

As soon as he entered the room, the prince said:

"How do you do, my dear and trusted friend?"

And she replied:

"How d'you do, prince? To what do I owe the pleasure of your visit?"

And he said:

"We shall talk about it later," he said. "Let me have a look at you first, let me kiss your head, my dear," and I could hear how he gave her a smacking kiss on the head and then asked about his daughter.

Yevgenia Semyonovna replied that she was at home.

"How is she?"

"She's quite all right, thank you," she said.

"She must have grown up, eh?"

Yevgenia Semyonovna laughed and said:

"Of course," she said, "she's grown up."

The prince said:

"You don't mind my seeing her, do you?"

"Of course not," she said, "I'd be delighted!" and she got up, went into the nursery and called the nurse, Tatyana Yakovlevna, who was having such a grand old time with me.

"Please, nurse," she said, "bring darling little Lyuda to the prince."

Tatyana Yakovlevna was terribly fed up. She put down her saucer of tea on the table and said:

"What a nuisance they are, to be sure! A body can't sit down to have a nice talk to a man but they start shouting for her and spoil all her pleasure!" She then covered me up quickly with her mistress's skirts which hung on the wall and said, "Wait for me here," and went to fetch the little girl.

I stayed behind the cupboards and I could hear how the prince kissed the child twice and dandled her on his knees and said:

"Would you like, *mon enfant*, to go for a ride in my carriage?"

The little girl said nothing, whereupon the prince said to Yevgenia Semyonovna:

"*Je vous prie*," he said, "please, let her have a ride in my carriage with nurse. I'm sure she'll like it."

Yevgenia Semyonovna started objecting in French, why and *pourquois*, and so on, but, he too, said something in French, something to the effect that it was "absolutely necessary," and having exchanged a few words in this way, she at last very reluctantly agreed to fall in with his suggestion and said to nurse:

"Dress her and go for a ride with her."

So for a ride they went and those two remained together and I was eavesdropping on them, for I could not possibly leave my hiding place behind the cupboards and, besides, I said to myself, "Now is my chance to find out the truth and know for certain whether either of them has in mind any harm to Grusha."

CHAPTER XVI

HAVING made up my mind to eavesdrop, I did not content myself with that, but I also wanted to see what I could with my own eyes and I contrived it so that my wish was fulfilled to my entire satisfaction: I climbed very quietly on a stool and I soon discovered a chink in a groove above the door and pressed my eye eagerly to it. I saw that the prince was sitting on the divan and that Yevgenia Semyonovna was standing by the window and . . . yes . . . watching her little darling being put into the carriage.

After the carriage had driven off, she turned to the prince and said:

"Well, prince, I did all you wanted me to do : tell me now what business brought you here."

And he answered:

"Damn the business! . . . There's plenty of time to discuss my business: it isn't a bear, it won't run away into the wood. First of all, come here, darling, sit down beside me and let's have a good talk, as we used to do, you and I, in the old days."

Yevgenia Semyonovna, however, did not budge from her place by the window, leaning against it with her hands behind her back. She was silent, knitting her brows. The prince implored her:

"What's the matter, darling ? Won't you sit down beside me ? I want to talk to you!"

She obeyed him and came up; seeing that, his lordship at once said again jokingly:

"That's right," he said, "let's sit down as we used to, darling," and he wanted to embrace her, but she pushed him away and said:

"Tell me your business, prince! What is your business ? What can I do for you ?"

"Goodness gracious me," said the prince, "do you want me to put all my cards on the table without any preliminaries ?"

"Of course," she said, "tell me straight what you want. We're old friends, aren't we ? So why stand on ceremony ?"

"I want money," said the prince.

Yevgenia Semyonovna just looked at him and said nothing.

"A lot of money," said the prince.

"How much ?"

"At the moment only twenty thousand."

Yevgenia Semyonovna again said nothing and the prince went on to describe in very eloquent language how he was buying a cotton mill and how he hadn't a penny to bless himself with, "but," said he, "if I succeed in buying it, I shall be a millionaire, for," he said, "I intend to modernise the whole works, get rid of the old machinery and everything and I'll start manufacturing beautifully coloured cloths and sell them to the Asiatics in Nizhny. I'll manufacture it all out of rubbish and dye it in bright colours and it'll sell like hot cakes and I'll make a lot of money, but now I only want twenty thousand which I have to pay as a deposit for the factory."

Yevgenia Semyonovna said:

"But where can you get all that money ?"

And the prince replied:

"I'm damned if I know, but I must get it, for I've thought everything out most beautifully. You see, I have a man, Ivan Golovan, an army connoisseur, not very bright, but a fine fellow, as honest as they make them and very dependable, and he was for many years a prisoner among the

Asiatics and he knows all their tastes well. There's a fair in Nizhny now, so I'll send down Golovan there to get me contracts and take samples of the sort of stuff they want and I'm quite sure there'll be plenty of orders. . . . Well, then . . . first of all I'll immediately repay those twenty thousand . . ."

Here he stopped and Yevgenia Semyonovna, too, was silent for a moment, then she just sighed and said:

"Your plan, prince," she said, "is excellent."

"Yes, isn't it?"

"It certainly is excellent," she said. "You *will* do that. You'll pay the deposit for the factory, then everybody will look on you as a manufacturer, they'll start saying in society that your affairs have improved . . ."

"Yes, you've got it, darling!"

"Thank you, but I haven't finished yet. Then . . ."

". . . Golovan will get hundreds of orders and deposits in Nizhny and I'll repay my debt and be a rich man!"

"No, please, don't interrupt me: you'll first of all throw dust in the eyes of the President of the Noblemen's Chamber and while he regards you as a rich man, you'll marry his daughter and, then, having made sure of her dowry, you will indeed be a rich man!"

"So that's what you think, darling?" said the prince.

And Yevgenia Semyonovna replied:

"Why? Don't you think so, too?"

"Well," said he, "if you can see through it all, then may the Lord hearken unto your words and bring us joy everlasting."

"*Us?*"

"Of course," his lordship said, "for then we shall all be in clover: you'll mortgage your house for me and I'll pay your daughter ten thousand interest for the twenty thousand!"

Yevgenia Semyonovna said in reply:

"The house is yours. You gave it to her and you can take it back, if you want to."

He began to object. "No, no," he exclaimed, "the house isn't mine, but as you are her mother I ask you . . . I mean, of course, if you trust me. . . ."

But she said:

"Really, prince," she said, "is that all I have trusted you with? Haven't I trusted you with my honour and my life?"

"Oh, I see," he said, "you mean . . . Well, thank you, thank you . . . You're such a darling. . . . So I may send the mortgage to you for your signature to-morrow, mayn't I?"

"Yes," she said, "send it and I'll sign."

"But aren't you afraid?"

"No," she said, "after what I've lost already, I've nothing to be afraid of any more."

"But aren't you sorry? Tell me, aren't you sorry? I presume you still love me a little, don't you? Or do you just pity me? Eh?"

But she merely laughed at his words and said:

"Stop talking nonsense, prince! Won't you have some stewed cloudberries with sugar? They're delicious just now!"

Well, the prince seemed to have been hurt by that offer of hers, doubtlessly expecting something quite different, so he got up and smiled.

"No, thank you, my dear," he said, "you can eat your cloudberries yourself: I don't feel like indulging in a sweet just now. Good-bye, darling, and thank you," and he began kissing her hand and in the meantime the carriage returned.

Yevgenia Semyonovna got up and gave him her hand as a farewell gesture and said:

"But what are you going to do with that black-eyed gypsy girl of yours?"

Well, the prince just struck his forehead and said:

"Good heavens, I'd forgotten all about her! What a clever woman you are, darling! Believe it or not, but I cannot ever forget how clever you are and thank you for having reminded me of that precious jewel of mine!"

"Had you really forgotten all about her?" she said.

"On my word of honour, I had," he said. "It just slipped my mind, but, of course, I shall have to do something for that silly fool."

"Do something by all means," said Yevgenia Semyonovna, "only let it be something good: remember, she isn't a Russian girl: a mixture of tepid blood and new milk. She won't take things lying down, she'll never forgive you for old times' sake."

"Don't you worry," he said, "she will."

"Is she in love with you, prince? I'm told she's terribly in love with you."

"Oh, I'm sick and tired of her, darling, but, thank God, she seems to be very fond of Golovan."

"How will that help you?" Yevgenia Semyonovna asked.

"Well, I'll buy them a house, register Ivan as a merchant and they'll get married and live happily ever after."

But Yevgenia Semyonovna shook her head and said, smiling:

"Oh, my poor prince, what a silly man you are! Where's your conscience?"

And the prince said:

"Leave my conscience alone, please. I've no time for it just now: I have to send for Golovan to come to town to-day, if possible."

So, of course, Yevgenia Semyonovna told him that I was in town already and, she said, "he's staying at my house." The prince was very glad to hear that and he asked her to send me to him as soon as possible, and he himself left immediately.

After that things began to move fast, just as in a fairy tale. The prince loaded me with all the necessary legal documents to show that I had complete powers to act for him and that he was the owner of a cotton mill and he taught me to say what kind of cloths his factory was manufacturing and he sent me straight from town to the Nizhny fair, so that I had no time even to see Grusha, but all the time I was very cross with the prince, for how could he have said that she would be my wife? At the Nizhny fair I struck lucky. I got hundreds of orders and samples and money from the Asiatics and the money I sent to the prince and I myself went back to the estate and I just couldn't recognise it. . . . Everything seemed to have changed as if by magic: everything had been redecorated like a peasant's cottage for the high holidays and of the wing where Grusha had had her apartments not a trace could be seen: it had been levelled to the ground and where it stood a new building had been erected. I just gasped with astonishment and rushed to see where Grusha was, but not a soul could tell me anything about her; the servants were all new, all of them had been hired and were not the prince's own, and all of them gave themselves such airs and they wouldn't even let me get near the prince. Before the prince and I were just pals, like two army men, but now everything was in a grand style and if there was anything I wanted to tell to the prince I had to do it through his valet.

I never could put up with that sort of thing and I shouldn't have stayed another minute there if I hadn't felt so sorry for Grusha. But, try as I might, I couldn't find out what had happened to her. If I tried to question some of the old servants, they would shut up and I could see that they had received strict orders not to tell me anything. It was with the greatest difficulty that I at last succeeded in persuading an old maidservant to tell me that Grusha had only left a short while ago, "it's only a matter of some ten days," she told me, "that she left in a carriage with the prince and did not come back." So I went straight to the coachmen and tried to find out from them where the prince had taken her to, but they wouldn't tell me anything. All they would say was that the prince had changed his horses at the first stage of the journey and had sent them back, leaving with Grusha for some place they knew not on hired horses. Wherever I went, I could pick up no trace of the poor gypsy girl and that was all: whether the villain had stuck a knife into her or shot her with a pistol and had thrown her body into a ditch somewhere in a wood and covered it up with dry leaves or whether he drowned her in a pond or a river, it was impossible to say, but all that might have easily have happened, seeing what a slave he was to his passions; for she certainly stood in the way of his marriage, as Yevgenia Semyonovna quite rightly warned him, because Grusha loved him, villain that he was, with all the passion of her unrestrained gypsy heart and it was not like her to put up with his foul treachery and meekly to bear her burden, like Yevgenia Semyonovna, who was indeed a true Christian lady, sacrificing her life for him as she did, just letting it burn out like a lamp before an icon. I fancied that when the prince told Grusha about his intended marriage, the gypsy blood in her must have blazed up like a flame through the smoke of a camp fire and she must have uttered God knows what threats and so he had murdered her.

So the more I considered it, the more convinced did I become that that was what had actually happened and I just could not bring myself to watch all the preparations for the prince's forthcoming marriage to the daughter of the President of the Noblemen's Chamber. And when the day of the marriage came and the maidservants were given brightly coloured kerchiefs to wear and the menservants were all dressed up in new liveries, each according to his duties, I refused to put on my new suit of clothes, but took everything to my little store-room in the stables and left it there and from early morning betook myself to the woods where I wandered about, without knowing myself to what purpose, till the evening, hoping against hope to stumble against her dead body. When evening came I left the woods and sat down on the steep bank of the little river, and beyond the river I could see the prince's mansion glittering with lights and I could hear the noise of merriment coming from there. The guests were enjoying themselves and the band was playing and the music and the sounds of revelry could be heard a long way away. I sat there, no longer even looking at the mansion, but my eyes fixed on the water where the lights were reflected in the rippling waves and the columns of the house were swaying to and fro, like the columns of some watery palace. And I felt so miserable, so sick at heart that I did what I had never done before, not even in the days of my captivity: I began to talk to the unseen powers and, as in the fairy tale of Sister Alyonushka, whom her brother went on calling, I called to my poor Grusha, the dear sister of mine, in a grief-stricken voice:

"Oh, my dear sister," I said, "my poor little Grusha, answer me, speak to me, say just one word to me, appear to me just for a minute!"

And imagine my surprise, gentlemen, when after calling her three times like that in a mournful voice, it seemed to me that someone was running towards me and I felt terrified, for I could hear clearly how somebody had run past me once, then begun to circle round me, whisper in my ears, peer into my face over my shoulder and, all at once, rushed at me out of the darkness of the night! . . . and hung round my neck, shaking convulsively. . . .

CHAPTER XVII

I WAS frightened out of my wits and nearly collapsed on the ground, but I did not lose consciousness, and I felt that somebody—alive and light—was fluttering on the ground like a wounded crane, sighing, but uttering no word.

I said a silent prayer and looked up: and there before me was poor Grusha's face!

"My dear," I said, "my poor, poor darling! Are you alive or have you come to me from the next world? Don't be afraid to tell me the truth," I said, "for I shan't be afraid of you, my poor little thing, even if you are dead!"

And she heaved a deep sigh—it seemed to come out of her very heart—and said:

"I am alive."

"Well," said I, "thank God for that."

"But," said she, "I have come here to die."

"Good heavens, my dear Grusha," I said, "what are you saying? Why should you die? Let us live together happily: I shall work for you, I shall build a little house just for you, my poor little one, and you'll live with me in place of my own dear sister."

But she answered:

"No, Ivan Severyanych, no, my dear one, my dearest friend, thank you very much for your great kindness to me, a poor, unhappy creature, but I, miserable gypsy girl that I am, cannot go on living, for if I do I might bring death and ruin to an innocent soul."

I questioned her:

"Who are you talking about? Whose soul are you so sorry for?"

And she answered:

"I'm sorry for her, the young wife of my seducer, for she is so young and innocent, poor dear, and my jealous heart will never reconcile itself to her happiness and I shall kill both her and myself."

"You mustn't talk like that," I said. "Cross yourself, do! You were baptised, weren't you? Think what will happen to your soul!"

"No," she said, "I shan't even be sorry for my own soul: let it go to hell, for here it is worse than hell!"

I could see that the poor girl was beside herself and that she did not know what she was saying, so I took her by the hands and held them closely and looked at her. I was amazed to see how terribly changed she was and I could not help wondering where her beauty had gone to. Even her body seemed to have shrunk to a shadow and only her eyes were blazing in her dark face, like the eyes of a wolf at night, and they seemed to me to be twice as large as before, and her belly bulged terribly, for her pregnancy was drawing to an end, and her poor little face was no bigger than a fist and her black locks fell over her cheeks. I looked at the dress she was wearing and I saw that it was a cheap cotton one, of a dark colour and all in holes, and her shoes she wore on bare feet.

"Tell me," I said, "where have you come from? Where have you been and why have you lost all your looks?"

She smiled suddenly and said:

"Why? Am I not beautiful? Beautiful! This is what my sweetheart has done to me for the great love I bore him, for giving up my lover for him, for giving myself entirely to him, body and soul! He locked me up in a safe place and he set guards on me and he commanded them to keep a good watch over my beauty. . . ." And then she burst out laughing suddenly and said wrathfully:

"Oh, you stupid fool of a prince! Is a gypsy girl one of your young ladies that she can be kept under lock and key? Why, if I were so minded I'd go straight to your young wife and bite her throat out!"

I saw that she was all convulsed by her jealous fit and I thought, "Let me try to distract her thoughts not by the fear of hell, but by sweet memories," and I said:

"But think how dearly he loved you, Grusha, how he loved you! How he used to kiss your feet. . . . Do you remember how he used to kneel in front of the couch while you were singing and kiss your scarlet slipper all over, top and bottom? . . ."

She began to take notice of my words and her long black eyelashes fluttered over her dry cheeks and, looking down at the water, she said in a hollow voice:

"Yes," she said, "he loved me, the villain, he loved me, he didn't begrudge me anything while I didn't care for his love, but as soon as I fell in love with him, he jilted me. And who did he leave me for? Is she, my rival, better than I, or will she love him more than I? . . . Oh, he is so foolish, so foolish! The sun in winter doesn't warm as much as the summer sun, nor will he ever again taste love such as mine. You'd better tell him that, tell him: before her death Grusha prophesied that about you and said that that would be your destiny!"

I was glad that at last she had become so talkative and I started questioning her and said:

"What did happen between you and the prince and why did it all happen?"

She threw up her hands and said:

"Oh, it didn't happen for any reason at all, except because of his treachery. . . . He got tired of me, that is the only reason," and while saying this, she began crying bitter tears. "He bought me dresses according to his taste," she said, "dresses which were no good to a pregnant woman, dresses with narrow waists. I would put them on to please him, but he'd get angry and say, 'Take it off: it doesn't suit you!' But if I didn't put them on and came out to him in a loose dress, he'd get even angrier . . . he'd say, 'What an awful sight you are!' It was then that I understood that I had lost him for good, that I had become odious to him. . . ."

She began to sob now and she looked straight ahead and whispered:

"I have felt it coming a long time," she said, "I knew that he wasn't fond of me any more, but I wanted to see what kind of conscience he had. I thought: I mustn't plague him, I must make him pity me, but he had no pity for me. . . ."

Then she told me such a strange, silly story about her last parting from the prince that I couldn't understand and I cannot still understand how a little thing like that could make even a wicked man betray and ruin a woman for ever.

CHAPTER XVIII

GRUSHA told me everything, how "after you," she said, "had gone away and disappeared"—that was when I had gone off to the Nizhny fair—"the prince did not return home for a long time and I heard rumours that he was going to be married. . . . I cried a lot because of that and lost my good looks. . . . My heart ached and I felt how my child pressed against it. . . . I thought: it will die in my womb. Then, suddenly, I heard them say, 'He's coming!' I trembled all over and I rushed to my rooms to get myself up as nicely as possible for him. I put on my emerald ear-rings and I took down from the wall, from behind a sheet, a dress trimmed with lace and with a low bodice, which he liked better than any of my other dresses. . . . I was in such a hurry to put it on that I couldn't get the back fastened, so I left it unfastened and just threw a red scarf over it, so that he shouldn't notice that it wasn't fastened, and I rushed out to meet him on the steps. . . . I was all of a tremble and before I knew what I was doing I had exclaimed, 'Oh, my darling, oh, my sweet, my fair, my precious jewel!' and I threw my arms round his neck and fainted. . . ."

The poor thing nearly fainted again as she told me of it.

"When I came to," she went on, "I was in my room . . . lying on a divan and trying to remember whether I had really embraced him or whether I had only dreamt about it. . . . I felt awfully weak," she said, "and did not see him for a long time . . . I kept on sending for him, but he wouldn't come. . . ."

At last he did put in an appearance and she said to him:

"Have you thrown me over altogether? Have you forgotten me?"

And he said:

"I am very busy."

She said:

"What are you so busy about now, why weren't you so busy before, my precious jewel?"

And she stretched out her arms again to embrace him, but he made a wry face and pulled with all his might at the silken ribbon round her neck.

"Luckily," she said to me, "that silk ribbon round my neck wasn't very strong, it had become frayed and it broke, for I had been wearing an amulet on it for many years, or he would have strangled me, and I expect that was what he had intended to do, for he got quite white in the face and he hissed out at me:

" 'Why are you wearing such a dirty ribbon?'

"I said, 'Why are you so concerned about my ribbon? It was clean, it has got dirty now because I worry such a lot, it has got dirty from the heavy sweat on my body.'

"But he just spat and went out and late in the afternoon he came back, looking angry, and said:

" 'Let's go for a ride in my carriage!' and he pretended to be nice to me and he kissed me on the head and I, suspecting nothing, sat down in the carriage with him and we drove away. We drove a long time, changing horses twice. He would not tell me where we were going, but I saw that we got to some woods, it was a marshy, wild and dreadful place. And in that forest we soon came to some beehives and behind those beehives was a cottage and there three strong, young girls in madder red dresses met us and they addressed me as 'madam.' As soon as I got out of the carriage, they took me under the arms and dragged me into a room which was all ready for me.

"All that troubled me greatly and my heart contracted with pain, but I was particularly frightened of those young girls.

" 'What kind of an inn is this?' I asked the prince.

"But he replied:

" 'It isn't an inn. This is where you are going to live from now on.'

"I began to cry and to kiss his hands, imploring him not to leave me there, but he showed no pity: he pushed me away from him and went away. . . ."

Here poor Grusha fell silent and bowed her head, then she sighed and said:

"I wanted to run away, I tried a hundred times to escape, but I couldn't, for those girls kept watch over me and didn't let me out of their sight. . . . I felt so wretched there and in the end I made up my mind to deceive them and I pretended to be carefree and happy and told them that I wanted to go for a walk in the woods. They took me for a walk, but they wouldn't take their eyes off me. I kept on looking at the trees, at the top branches and the bark, to find out which way the sun was shining at noon, and all the time I was trying to think of a way of giving those girls the slip, and yesterday I carried it out. After dinner I went out with them to a clearing in the wood and I said:

" 'Come on, sweethearts, let's play blindman's buff in this clearing!'

"They agreed.

" 'But instead of binding our eyes,' I said, 'let's tie our hands and catch each other with our behinds.'

"They did not object to that, either.

"So we did. I tied the hands of one of them very tightly behind her back and rushed off with another behind a bush and tied her up there and the third I just overcame by main force in the sight of the other two; they screamed for help, but I ran away swifter than a racehorse, pregnant though I am, keeping to the woods all the time and so I ran for a whole night and in the morning I collapsed by some old beehives in a thick part of the wood. Here an old man approached me and started talking to me, but I could hardly make out what he was saying with those toothless gums of his. He seemed all covered with bees-wax and he smelt of honey and in his yellow eyebrows bees were swarming. I told him that I wanted to see you, Ivan Severyanych, and he said to me:

" 'Call him, my pretty maid, once with the wind and once against the wind, and then he'll feel a longing for you and he'll start looking for you and you'll meet.'

"He gave me some water to drink and some honey and cucumber to strengthen myself with. I drank the water and ate the cucumber with the honey and went on my way again, calling you all the time, once with the wind and once against the wind, and so we met. Thank you," she said, and she embraced me and kissed me and said, "You're like a dear brother to me!"

I said:

"And you're like a dear sister to me," and, overcome by my feelings, I began to shed tears.

And she, too, wept and said:

"I know, Ivan Severyanych, I know everything and I realise that you alone really loved me, my dear, dear friend. Prove to me that you still love me and do what I shall ask you in this fateful hour."

"Tell me what you want me to do," I said.

"No," said she, "you must first swear to me by all that you hold sacred in the world that you will do what I ask of you."

So I swore to her by the salvation of my soul, but she said:

"That's not enough: for my sake you might even break that oath. No," she said, "swear to me by something which is even more sacred."

"But," I said, "I can't think of any more terrible oath than that."

"Well," she said, "I thought of something for you and you say it quickly after me and don't try to think about it at all."

I promised her that, fool that I was, and she said:

"Damn my own soul as you have damned yours if you will not do as I tell you."

"All right," I said, and straightway I damned her soul.

"Well, listen to me now," she said, "for now you can become the real saviour of my soul. I have no more strength," she said, "to go on living and tormenting myself, seeing how shamelessly he has treated me and how he has heaped dishonour upon me. If I live for one more day, I shall surely kill *him* and *her* and if I take pity on them, I shall kill myself and damn my soul for evermore. . . . So do you take pity upon me, my dear, dear brother: thrust a knife into my heart!"

I started back from her and began making the sign of the cross over her, trying to get as far away from her as possible, but she threw her arms round my knees, and she wept and prostrated herself before me, saying:

"You," she said, "will live and obtain forgiveness from God for my own soul and for yours, but if you force me to lay hands on myself, you'll condemn me to eternal damnation. Won't you do it? . . ."

Ivan Severyanych knit his brows in his great distress at the recollection of that scene and, biting his moustache, he seemed to bring the words out from the bottom of his tortured heart, and he sighed rather than spoke:

"She took my knife out of my pocket . . . opened it . . . straightened the blade . . . and put it into my hands . . . and she carried on in a way that I could not bear to see."

"If you don't kill me," she said, "I shall repay you all by becoming a harlot!"

I trembled all over at those words of hers and told her to say her prayers, but I did not stab her: I just threw her over the steep bank into the river. . . ."

Hearing this last confession of Ivan Severyanych, all of us for the first time began to doubt the veracity of his story and there was a great silence for a time, but at last somebody cleared his throat and said:

"Did she drown?"

"The water swallowed her up," replied Ivan Severyanych.

"And what did you do after that?"

"How do you mean, sir?"

"I suppose you must have suffered a lot."

"Of course I did."

CHAPTER XIX

I RAN from that place without thinking and without giving myself an account of what I was doing or whither I was going and all I remember is that someone seemed to be running after me, someone who was terribly tall and big and shameless and naked and his whole body was black and his head was small as an onion and he was all covered with hair, and I reckoned that if it was not Cain, it was Satan himself, the foul fiend of hell, and I kept on running away from him and called upon my guardian angel for succour. I came to myself when I was already on the highway, sitting under a willow tree. It was an autumn day, dry, the sun shone, but it was cold and the wind raised clouds of dust and yellow leaves were tossed about in it. I did not know what hour of the day it was or what place it was or where the road led to, and there was a horrid emptiness in my soul: not an inkling of an idea what I had to do. All I was thinking about was that poor Grusha's soul was doomed now and that it was my duty to suffer for her and to save her from everlasting hell. But how I was to do it, I didn't know and that filled my mind with distress and anguish, but, suddenly, something touched me on the shoulder: I looked up and I saw that it was a dead twig that had fallen from the willow tree and was being carried far away by the wind, and I followed it with my eyes and then suddenly I saw Grusha walking, only she was very small and looked no more than six or seven years old, and behind her shoulders there sprouted little wings. As soon as I saw her, she flew away from me like a bullet and there was only a swirl of dust and dry leaf left behind her.

I thought: that must certainly be her soul following after me and she has gone ahead to show me the way. So I went. I walked for a whole day without knowing myself whither I was going, and I was dead tired, and then some people overtook me, an old man and an old woman travelling in a cart together, and they said:

"Sit down in our cart, stranger, and we'll take you on your way."

I sat down in the cart and they went on and I could see that they were greatly distressed.

"We are in great trouble," they said. "Our only son is being taken away into the army and we have no money and cannot hire another man in his place."

I was very sorry for the old couple and I said:

"I'd gladly oblige you and go instead of your son, but I have no papers."

But they said:

"That's nothing: leave that to us. All we want you to do is to take our son's name and to call yourself Peter Serdyukov."

"All right," I said, "that suits me. I shall continue to pray to my own saint, St. John, and I don't mind what I call myself."

So we agreed on that and they took me to another town and enlisted me there in the army in place of their son and gave me on the way twenty-five roubles in silver and promised to help me while they lived. I gave away the money they had given me, the twenty-five roubles, to a poor monastery to offer prayers for Grusha's soul and myself petitioned the army authorities to send me to the Caucasus where I could die for my faith as soon as possible. So it was done, and I spent more than fifteen years in the Caucasus and revealed my real name and occupation to no one and was known as Peter Serdyukov and only on St. John's day did I pray for myself to God through the intermediary of the saint, the blessed Evangelist. And I had almost forgotten my past life and occupation and was serving in this manner my last year in the army when, as it came to pass, on that very day, St. John's day, we were in pursuit of the Tartars, who had given us a lot of trouble and had gone beyond the river Koys. There are several rivers of that name in those parts: one of them flows along the Andian valley and is known as the Andian Koys, and a second along the Avarian valley and is known as the Avarian Koys, and a third and a fourth are known as the Korikumuyskaya and Kuzikumuyskaya, and all of them meet and where they meet the river Sulak begins. But all four of them are very rapid and cold, and especially the Andian one, behind which the Tartars had fled. We had killed a great number of those Tartars there, so many that we couldn't even count them, but some of them succeeded in crossing the Koys river and they hid themselves on the other side behind boulders and as soon as we exposed ourselves they started firing at us. But there was great cunning in the way they fired, for they did not waste a single shot, but kept back their fire until they were certain that each bullet would find its mark, for they knew that we had a lot more ammunition than they and so keen were they on inflicting certain harm on us that although we were all in full view of them, those devils would not fire in our direction even once. Our colonel was a man of great courage and he liked to fancy himself another Suvorov and he always said "Bless my soul," and taught us to be brave by his own example. So he just sat down on the bank, bared his legs and put them into the ice-cold water up to the knees and began praising it up to the skies.

"Bless my soul," he said, "how warm this water is! Just like new milk in a pail under the cow! Will any of you, my friends, volunteer to swim to the other side with a rope so that we can put a bridge across?"

While our colonel sat there chatting like that to us, the Tartars put out the barrels of two rifles through a slit between two boulders, but did not shoot. As soon as two soldiers had volunteered and began to swim across, however, they began firing at them and those poor devils just disappeared under the waves. We pulled out the rope and another pair took to the water, while we opened a murderous fire upon those boulders behind which the Tartars were hiding, but we couldn't do them any harm, for our bullets hit the stones and those confounded demons just let go at the swimmers and the water became red with blood and the soldiers again disappeared. A third pair followed, but neither did they reach the middle of the Koys, the Tartars sending them to the bottom of the river. Well, after the third pair there were no more volunteers, for everybody could see that that was no longer war, but just plain murder. But as the murderers had to be punished, the colonel said:

"Listen to me, dear friends, isn't there one among you who has committed a mortal sin and who would like to expiate his crime for his soul's sake? Bless my soul, what a splendid chance he has now of washing away his offence by his blood!"

Well, I thought to myself, "What better chance can I have for ending my life?" and I stepped forward and took off my clothes. I said the Lord's Prayer, prostrated myself on every side before my comrades and my superiors, said to myself, "Well, Grusha, dear sister of my heart, may my blood expiate your sin," and then took the string, which was tied to the rope by one end, into my mouth and, taking a flying run from the bank, plunged into the river.

The water was terribly cold: I had shooting pains under my armpits and my chest contracted painfully and I got a cramp in my legs, but I carried on. . . . Above me our bullets were whizzing past and round me Tartar bullets went on plopping into the water, but they did not hit me. I did not know, however, whether I was wounded or not, but I did reach the other bank. . . . There the Tartars could no longer fire at me, for I was separated from them by one side of a ravine and to shoot at me they would have had to show themselves under the hail of bullets which our soldiers kept up from the other bank. So there I was standing under the rocks and pulling away at the rope. I pulled it across and then we threw a bridge over the river and our men were quickly across, but I was still standing there, hardly realising what was happening under my very eyes, for I was thinking all the time: did anybody see what I saw? For, as I swam, I saw Grusha flying above me and she was now a girl in her teens, just about sixteen, I should say, and she had large wings already, bright wings, spanning the whole river, and she protected me with them. . . . However, as nobody said a word about it to me, I said to myself, "It seems I shall have to tell about it myself." So when the colonel started embracing me, kissing me and extolling me to the skies, saying:

"Bless my soul, what a gallant fellow you are, Peter Serdyukov!" I replied:

"I am not a gallant fellow, sir, but a great sinner and neither earth nor water wants to receive me!"

He began to question me:

"What sin did you commit?"

And I replied:

"I have sent to their doom many innocent souls in my time," and that very night in his tent I told him what I have just told you, gentlemen.

He listened to me very attentively, then he fell into thought and, finally, he said:

"Bless my soul, the things you have gone through! But all the same, my dear fellow, whatever you may say, I am going to recommend you for a commission. I shall send in my report about it right away."

I said:

"Just as you please, sir, but won't you send also an inquiry to that town I told you of to find out whether or not it is true that I killed a gypsy girl?"

"All right," he said, "I shall make that inquiry."

And so he did, but the inquiry the colonel sent went from one town to another and came back with an answer that my whole story was a lie. The police authorities where the prince's estate was situated declared that "we know nothing about any gypsy girl" and that Ivan Severyanych "of whom we do know that he was employed by the prince, a long time ago obtained his freedom as a serf and later died at the house of the State-owned peasants Serdyukovs."

Well, what more could I do to prove my guilt?

The colonel said to me:

"Don't you dare to tell any more lies about yourself, my dear fellow. You must have got a bit befuddled in your head as you swam across the river. You are suffering from the after effects of the cold water and fright. For my part," he said, "I'm glad that what you've told me is just a pack of lies. Now there's nothing to prevent you from becoming an officer. Bless my soul, that's capital!"

Well, I don't mind confessing that I myself got a bit muddled up there. Did I really push Grusha into the water or had I imagined it all that night, overcome as I was by so strong a longing to see her?

So they made me an officer for my bravery, but as I insisted on telling all and sundry the whole truth about myself, they discharged me from the army with a Georgyev Cross, so that I should no longer worry myself over the whole business.

"Accept our congratulations," the colonel said, "you are now a member of the nobility and you can get a job in the Civil Service. Bless my soul, what a glorious life you're going to have," and he gave me a letter to an important man in St. Petersburg. "Go and see him," he said, "he'll help you with your career and see you're all right."

So I eventually got to St. Petersburg with this letter, but I had no luck with my career.

"Why not ?"

"You see, I couldn't get a job for a long time and then I got mixed up with Theta and that brought me more troubles."

"What do you mean by getting mixed up with Theta ? What is theta, anyway ?"

"The man to whom I was sent about my career got me a job at the Noblemen's Registration Office as an information clerk, and at that office each clerk is given his own letter and all persons whose name begins with that letter have to go for information to him. Now, some letters are very good letters, for instance, the letter B or P or K, for a great many family names begin with those letters and the clerk derives a good income, for the inquirers are naturally anxious to reward him for his zeal on their behalf. But I was given the last and the most insignificant letter of the Russian alphabet, the letter Theta, which is pronounced the same as the letter F, and there are very few people whose names begin with it and even those whose names should rightly begin with it, try their best to wriggle out of it and to disown it and any one of them wishing to take out a registration of nobility pretends that his name really begins with an F. While you're wasting your time looking for his name under theta, the rogue goes and registers himself under F. So, naturally, there's very little profit in such work, while, of course, it means that you have to be at the office all the time. Well, I saw that things couldn't be much worse and I tried to get another job and what better job could I wish for than that of a coachman ? But nobody would employ me. "You're an officer," they said to me, "and you have a military order and we can't very well swear at you or knock you about!" I was in such a terrible fix that I almost thought of hanging myself, but, thank God, I always stopped short of committing such a folly, desperate though I was. But to save myself from death or starvation, I took on a job as an artist."

"What kind of an artist were you ?"

"I acted parts."

"Oh ? At what theatre ?"

"At a side-show on Admiralty Square. There they did not scorn the nobility and accepted everybody: there were army officers there and heads of civil service departments and students, but especially former officials of the High Court of Justice."

"And did you like that life ?"

"No, not very much."

"Why not ?"

"Well, in the first place, you see, we had to rehearse and learn our parts during the Holy Week or during Shrove-tide when they sing in the churches: 'Open, ye gates of repentance,' and, secondly, my part was a very difficult one."

"Oh?"

"Yes. I had to play Satan."

"Why was it so difficult?"

"Well, just imagine, gentlemen, I had to dance during two intervals and turn somersaults, and the turning of somersaults was a particularly tricky business, for I was covered from top to toe in the shaggy coat of a grey goat and I had a long tail on a wire, which would always get between my legs, and the horns on my head would get mixed up with every blessed bit of property on the stage, and, besides, I was getting on in years, I was no longer young and I had lost my youthful lightness, and, to make things worse, I had, according to the book, to be beaten all through the play. Well, all that is awfully tiresome, gentlemen. I admit, the sticks they beat me with weren't real sticks, but were made out of canvas and were hollow inside with some cotton wool in the middle, but, all the same, I got tired of being constantly knocked about and some whose business it was to beat me, whether because of the cold or just for fun, got very clever at beating me quite hard. They were mostly ex-high-court officials who seemed to have developed quite a knack at delivering a succession of heavy blows. You see, they were a terribly clannish lot and when they got a chance of playing tricks on an army man they would let themselves go and be an awful nuisance, for they had to start beating me in front of the public from noon, as soon as the police flag was hoisted, to midnight, and all the time the man whose turn it was to beat me rained as hard blows as possible on me to amuse the public. There was not much fun for me there. And on top of it all a rather unpleasant incident occurred after which I was forced to give up my part."

"What happened?"

"I had boxed a prince's ears."

"Which prince?"

"I don't mean a real prince, of course, but a theatrical one. He was one of those ex-high-court officials, but he played the part of the prince at our theatre."

"What did you box his ears for?"

"Because he deserved it. He was an incorrigible buffoon, always up to all sorts of silly tricks, liked to play practical jokes on everyone."

"On you as well?"

"Yes, on me, too. He was an awful nuisance, played the deuce with my costume, in the warming-up room where we used to sit over a coal fire and drink tea he'd steal behind me and fasten my tail to my horns or do something else to raise a laugh and I wouldn't discover it till I had run out in front of the public, and our manager would be cross with me. However, I let him off so long as it was only me that he annoyed, but he soon began to molest one of our fairies. She was such a young girl, belonged to an impoverished nobleman's family, and she played the goddess Fortune who had to save the prince from my hands. She had a part in which she had to appear in a dress of glittering tulle material with wings and we had very hard frosts at the time and her hands, poor thing, used to get quite blue, pinched, and he would keep on worrying her, thrusting his attentions on her, and once at the climax of our show, after the three of us had fallen through a trap-door into a cellar, he began to pinch her. Well, I naturally felt very sorry for the poor little thing and I gave him a thrashing."

"And how did it all end ?"

"Oh, the whole thing blew over. You see, there were no witnesses in the cellar except the little fairy, so he couldn't very well bring an action against me, but our high-court mob went on strike and demanded that I should be dismissed and as they were the chief actors there, the manager, to please them, gave me the sack."

"And where did you go after that ?"

"Well, for a time I had nothing to eat and no roof over my head, but that little fairy was so grateful to me that she used to give me food, but of course my conscience wouldn't let me be fed by a poor girl who had hardly enough to eat herself, so I kept on racking my brains how to get out of such as situation. I did not want to go back to that Theta business and, besides, the poor thing had already to provide for another man who was also down on his luck, so I decided to enter a monastery."

"Was there nothing else you could do ?"

"What could I have done ? I had nowhere to go to and life in a monastery appealed to me."

"So you got to like life in a monastery ?"

"Yes, very much. Everything was quiet there, just like in my old regiment. You'd be surprised how much life in a monastery resembles life in the army. Everything's provided, clothes, footwear, food, and the authorities look after you and demand strict obedience."

"But don't you find this obedience a bit irksome ?"

"Not at all. Why should I ? The more obedient a man is, the easier everything in life is for him. No, I have nothing to find fault with in my present position as novice at a monastery: I am not forced to attend the divine service unless I want to and I perform my duties as in the old times. If they tell me, 'Harness the horses, Father Ishmael' (they call me Ishmael now), I harness the horses, and if they tell me, 'Unharness the horses, Father Ishmael,' I unharness them."

"So (said we) it seems that in the monastery you got your old job back?"

"Yes, I was given the job of coachman from the start. You see, in the monastery they don't mind my officer's rank, for although I'm not a full-fledged monk yet, not having taken my monastic vows, I am treated as if I were a real monk."

"And when do you intend to take your monastic vows?"

"I shan't take them at all."

"Oh? Why not?"

"So . . . I don't consider myself worthy."

"Because of your old sins and transgressions, you mean?"

"Yes, I suppose so. But why should I, in any case? I feel very happy in my present position and I live in peace."

"But have you ever told the whole story of your life as you've told it to us to anybody else?"

"Why, yes. I've told it to many people, but what's the use if I have no documents to prove it? They just don't believe me, and so, it seems, I've brought with me the worldly lies into the monastery where, incidentally, they are convinced that I must be of noble birth. It doesn't make much difference, one way or another, for I am getting old and it's only a question now how much longer I shall live."

The story of the enchanted pilgrim was evidently drawing to a close now. All that was left for us to find out was how he had fared at the monastery.

CHAPTER XX

As our pilgrim had reached his journey's end, namely, the monastery, to which he seemed to have been destined from birth, being of so sincere and religious a cast of mind, and as everything seemed to go so swimmingly with him there, we were at first inclined to think that Ivan Severyanych had not stumbled against any more misfortunes; but in that we were deceived. One of our passengers remembered that, according to legends, novices were in constant trouble because of the unending machinations of the devil and he asked:

"Didn't the devil try to tempt you in the monastery? I'm told that he is very fond of tempting monks!"

Ivan Severyanych looked calmly from under his eyebrows at the questioner and replied:

"Tempt me? Of course he did. Why, if St. Paul the Apostle himself could not escape from him, for doesn't he write in his epistle to the Romans that 'there was given me a thorn in the flesh, the messenger of Satan to buffet me,' then how could I, poor and miserable sinner that I am, hope not to be tormented by him ?"

"What particular torments did he inflict on you ?"

"Oh, all sorts."

"But what ?"

"Various abominations and at first, before, that is, I got the better of him, he even tried to lead me into temptation."

"But you did get the better of *him*, the devil himself ?"

"Of course, what else did you expect ? It is our special calling in a monastery to frustrate the devil and his works, but, to be quite frank with you, gentlemen, I don't think I should have been able to do it unaided, without the help, that is, of an old hermit who had had great experience in that kind of work and who knew a remedy for every temptation under the sun. As soon as I told him that Grusha appeared to me so vividly all the time that the air round me seemed to be full of her, he at once thought it over and said to me, James the Apostle saith, 'Resist the devil and he will flee from you,' so all you have to do, he said, is to resist! And he also told me how to do it, saying, As soon as you feel that your heart begins to burn within you and you remember her, you must understand that it is Satan who is drawing nigh unto you and you must immediately gird up your loins and be ready to battle against him: first of all fall down on your knees, for, he said, a man's knees are the first instruments against the devil, since as you kneel your soul immediately flies upwards and, being thus exalted in spirit, you keep on prostrating yourself as much as there is strength in your body and indeed carry on with it until you are worn out, and furthermore, he said, wear yourself out with fasting even unto starvation, for the devil, when he sees that you are ready to win a martyr's crown to defeat his knavish tricks will never let you go as far as that, but will run off at once because what he fears most is to bring a man by his machinations to the bosom of Christ sooner than necessary and he usually says to himself, 'I'd better leave him alone and tempt him no more, for he will be more likely to stumble that way.' And I did as he told me and so indeed it came to pass."

"Did you have to torment yourself like that long before the devil finally left you alone ?"

"Yes, a very long time, and it was by starvation alone that I conquered the fiend, for, it seems, he fears nothing else: I used to prostrate myself about a thousand times and would entirely abstain from food and drink for four days on end, it was then only that *he* realised that I was a match for him and he lost heart and weakened. As soon as he saw me throwing out my little bowl with food through the window and taking up my beads to count the number of genuflexions, he'd understand that I was in dead earnest and ready to win a martyr's crown, if need be, and he'd run away, for he is terribly afraid of bringing a man to the point where he begins to partake of the consolations of joy everlasting."

"Well, yes . . . er . . . *he* would hardly . . . But even if you did conquer him, you had to suffer a great deal at his hands, didn't you ?"

"Yes, but after all it was I who was oppressing the oppressor and I did it without suffering any particular inconvenience."

"And have you got rid of him completely now ?"

"Yes, completely."

"And he no longer appears to you at all ?"

"No, he never appears to me any more in the seductive shape of a female and if he does now occasionally appear somewhere in a corner of my cell, he looks a pitiful sight: squeaking just like a little pig who is being slaughtered. I have even stopped tormenting the rascal. I just cross myself and prostrate myself once and he stops squealing."

"Well, thank God, you managed it so well."

"Yes, indeed. Still, while it is true that I've conquered the temptations of the big devil, I must confess to you, gentlemen, although it is strictly against the rules, that I'm getting sick of the silly tricks the little devils are playing upon me."

"Oh ? Have the little devils also been annoying you ?"

"Of course. . . . I admit that according to their rank they're rather an insignificant lot, but they don't give me any rest all the same. . . ."

"What exactly do they do to you ?"

"Well, they're only children, of course, and, besides, there are so many of them in hell and, not having to worry about board and lodging, they've nothing much to do, so they're constantly asking for permission to go down to visit the earth and create confusion and, having obtained that permission, they just enjoy themselves: the more important the position of a man, the more they annoy him."

"But what, for instance . . . How do they annoy people ?"

"Well, they shove something in your hand or put something in your way and you knock it down and break it and thereby annoy or anger someone: that they consider a great lark and it makes them very happy and, indeed, so pleased are they that they start clapping their hands and rush off to their superior, 'Look,' they say, 'we have made a Christian lose his temper, give us a penny for it!' That's really all they're after. . . . Just a lot of kids. . . ."

"But what, for instance, did they do to you to annoy you ?"

"Well, there was one instance when a Jew hanged himself in a wood near our monastery and all our monks began to say that it was really Judas Iscariot and that he walked about our monastery at night and groaned, and there were many who had seen him with their own eyes. I didn't care a brass button about him, for I said to myself, 'Haven't we enough Jews left?' But one night as I was asleep in the stables, I suddenly heard someone come walking past and put his head through the door over the crossbeam and start to groan. I immediately said a prayer, but he remained standing there. So I made the sign of the cross, but still he stood there groaning. 'Well,' I said to myself, 'what can I do for you? I can't possibly pray for you, for you are a Jew, and, besides, I have no special dispensation to say prayers for suicides. Get out of here,' I said, 'back to your forest or the desert!' And I put such a curse on him that he trotted off and I fell asleep again, but next night the rascal was there again and again he started groaning. . . . Wouldn't let me go to sleep, confound him! I did my best to take no notice, but I couldn't! 'How do you like the nuisance,' I said to myself, 'isn't there enough room for him in the wood or on the steps of the church that he must come crashing into my stables? Well, it seems it can't be helped, I shall have to devise some effective means of getting rid of you!' So next morning I drew a large cross on the doors with a clean piece of charcoal and at night I lay me down to sleep calmly, trusting that he wouldn't come again now, but no sooner had I fallen asleep than there he was again: standing by the doors, if you please, *and* groaning! 'Hang thee for a jailbird,' I said to myself, 'will nothing avail thee?' So he kept me in a sweat all through the night and in the morning as soon as the bell began to toll for morning mass, I jumped up and rushed off to lodge a complaint with the abbot, but on the way I met our bellringer, brother Diomedes, and he said to me:

"What do you look so scared for?"

So I told him all about it. "That's what I had to put up with last night," I said, "and I'm going to the abbot to complain about it."

But brother Diomedes said:

"Don't waste your time going to the abbot," he said. "for he has been putting leeches to his nose all night and is now in *a very bad temper* and will do nothing for you in this matter, but, if you want me to, I shall be able to be of greater help to you than he."

"It makes no difference to me," I said. "I'll be very glad indeed if you can help me and I'll give you my old warm mittens for that: you'll find them a great comfort when you have to ring your bells in winter."

"All right," he said.

So I gave him my mittens and he brought me from the belfry a door from an old church on which was painted the Apostle Peter with the keys from the heavenly gates in his hands.

"That," brother Diomedes said, "is the most important part of it, the *keys*, I mean. All you have to do is to put this door against the door of the stables, for nobody can pass through that."

I was so overjoyed that I nearly fell at his feet and I thought, "Why put this door in front of the stable doors and then have to remove it again when I can fasten it there so that it can always serve me as a barrier ?" And so I did and I hung this door on strong hinges and to make doubly sure I attached a heavy block to it with a big stone on a rope. All this I contrived very quietly during the day and by the evening it was all ready and when night came I lay down to sleep. Well, what do you think happened ? That night I woke up again and blessed if somebody wasn't breathing there! I couldn't believe my own ears, but, no, I wasn't imagining it: there it stood and breathed! And that wasn't all, gentlemen, not by a long chalk! For not only did it breathe, but it was also trying to burst the door open! My old door had a lock on the inside, but that one I didn't provide with a lock, for I depended entirely on its sacred nature to keep the fiend out, and, anyway, I had hardly had time for it. So he went on pushing it more and more till I could distinctly see his snout coming through it, but the door, being wide open now, suddenly slammed to on account of the block. . . . He jumped back and I thought I could hear him scratching himself, but after a little time he began pushing the door open again, more vigorously this time, and again I just caught a glimpse of his snout before the block once more slammed the door to with a bigger bang than ever. I suppose he must have got a proper bang on the head that time, for he quietened down and stopped pushing the door open and I fell asleep again, but after a little time I woke up and I saw that he had resumed his work, the rascal, and with greater vigour than ever. This time he didn't just butt the door with his horns to try to push it open, but he went about his task with great deliberation, pushing the door slowly with his horns. . . . So I covered my head with my sheepskin, for I was properly scared by that time, but he just tore the coat off me and licked me on the ear. . . . Well, I couldn't put up with such impudence any longer, so I put my hand down under my bed, got hold of an axe and—smack!—I just heard him utter one bellow and then collapse on the floor. 'Serve you right!' I thought. But imagine my surprise, gentlemen, when next morning instead of the Jew I beheld our monastery cow, which those little devils had put there in his place, the confounded imps!"

"Did you hurt it ?"

"Hurt it ? I killed it with my axe. There was a terrible to-do in our monastery about it, I can tell you!"

"You must have had a lot of unpleasantness because of it!"

"I should think so. The abbot said that I had just imagined it all and he thought it was because I didn't go to church frequently enough, so he gave me his blessing and told me to stand by the screen where the candles are lit every evening after I had finished with the horses, but they, those mischievous little devils, did something to me which brought utter disgrace upon me. On the night of Shrove Tuesday during the Holy Communion service when the father abbot and the dean of the church stood, as behoved their respective ranks, in the centre of the church, an old lady of the congregation gave me a candle and said to me, 'Put it up for me, father, and may the Lord bless you!' I went up to the lectern where the icon Saviour of the Waters was hanging and began to fix the candle, but I brushed against another and it dropped to the floor. I bent down to pick it up and was about to fix it when I brushed against two more and they straightway dropped to the ground. I started fixing them and, lo! four fell down! I just shook my head at that, thinking, 'Well, that's those little urchins again playing their pranks on me and tearing the candles out of my hands! . . .' I bent down again to pick them up, but as I raised myself quickly with the fallen candles I hit the back of my head a terrible blow against the candlestick and . . . the candles just showered down on the floor! Well, then I got mad and knocked the remaining candles off myself with my hand. 'If they are *that* impudent,' I thought, 'then I'd better knock them all down myself as quickly as possible' !"

"And what happened to you then ?"

"They wanted to put me on trial for that, but our hermit, the blind old monk, Syssoy, who lives in our monastery in strict seclusion from the rest of the monks, interceded for me. 'Why are you going to put *him* on trial,' he said, 'when it is Satan and his attendants who brought about his downfall ?' The abbot listened to him and he gave me his blessing and ordered that I should be lowered into a pit and that I should stay there, and this he did without any trial."

"Did they keep you long in that pit ?"

"When he had blessed me the abbot did not say how long I was to remain there. All he said was, 'Let him be put there,' so I was kept there the whole summer until the first sharp frosts set in."

"Didn't you find it even drearier and more heartbreaking in that pit than in the steppe ?"

"No, I shouldn't say that, you can't even compare the two. Here I could hear the church bells and some of my friends among the monks would come to see me. They would come and stand over the pit and we would talk to each other, and the father treasurer ordered a hand-mill to be lowered to me on a rope to grind salt for the kitchen. How can you compare it with the steppe or indeed any other place ?"

"But why did they take you out ? Was it because the frosts came and it got too cold ?"

"No, not for that reason at all, but for quite a different reason, for, you see, I began to prophesy . . ."

"Prophesy ?"

"Yes. While I sat in that pit I fell into thought and I kept on thinking what a paltry spirit I had and how much I had had to suffer on account of it and how I seemed incapable of improving myself, and I sent one of our novices to that old man, the hermit, to ask him to pray to God to grant me a more accommodating spirit. And the hermit sent me back an answer, saying, 'Let him pray well and then wait for what he has no right to expect'. So I did as I was bid: three nights I knelt in my pit on those excellent instruments of penitence, my knees, and I prayed most fervently and I began to await a sign of grace which should work a miraculous change in my soul. And we had another novice by the name of Gerontius, a man who had read a prodigious number of books and subscribed to newspapers and once he gave me to read the life of the Very Reverend Tikhon Zadonsky and whenever he happened to pass my pit he would always take a newspaper from under his cassock and throw it down to me. 'Read it,' he used to say, 'and perhaps you may find something in it that may be of use to you and, anyway, it will help to while away your time in the pit.' So while waiting for the unlikely realisation of my prayer, I began in the meantime to occupy myself with reading: as soon as I had finished grinding the salt which had been given to me for my day's task, I would begin to read, and I usually began with the life of the Very Reverend Tikhon and there I read how the Holy Mother of God, accompanied by St. Peter and St. Paul, had visited him in his cell one day. It is written that the saint asked the Holy Virgin to prolong peace on earth, but St. Paul said to him in a loud voice, 'This sign I give thee when peace shall come to an end: when,' said he, 'everybody will be saying, It is peace, and confirm it, then suddenly dire ruin will befall them.' And I began to reflect on those apostolic words and at first I couldn't understand the meaning of the revelation the apostle had given to the saint. But then I read in the papers that both in our own country and in foreign parts people kept on saying that an era of eternal peace was being established throughout the world, whereupon my prayer was granted to me and I suddenly obtained understanding that what was said was about to be fulfilled, namely, 'When everybody will be saying, It is peace, then sudden ruin will befall them,' and I was filled with fear and trembling for my Russian nation and I began to pray and whoever came to visit me I implored with tears in my eyes, saying, 'Pray that under the rule of our Czar every enemy and evil-doer may be vanquished, for the day of dire ruin is nigh!" And it was granted to me that the tears I shed were wonderfully prolific . . . for it was for my country that I wept. So they went and told the abbot, saying, 'Our Ishmael is shedding many tears in his pit and he is prophesying war.' The abbot then gave me his blessing and ordered that I should be transferred to the empty hut behind the kitchen gardens and to put therein the icon Sacred Silence on which the Saviour is presented in the shape of an angel with gently folded wings, not with his crown of thorns, but as the Lord of Hosts, with His hands crossed serenely over His breast. And I was bidden to prostrate myself daily before that icon until I lost my spirit of prophecy. So they shut me up in that hut and I remained locked up there until spring, praying all the time to Sacred Silence, but directly I beheld a man the spirit of prophecy would again descend upon me and I would start prophesying again. It was at that time that the abbot sent a doctor to have a look at me to see whether I was quite right in my head. The doctor spent a long time with me in my hut and, having listened to my story just as you are doing now, gentlemen, he just spat and said, 'What a drum you are, my dear fellow: they beat you and beat you and they can't finish you off!' So I said, 'What can I do about it? I suppose it has been ordained that way.' But the doctor, having heard all I had to tell him, said to the abbot, 'I can't make out what's the matter with him,' he said. 'Is he just a harmless, good-natured soul, or is he a lunatic, or, maybe, really a prophet? That, however,' he said, 'is for you to say, for I know nothing about prophecies, but my advice to you is to send him away: let him go and visit remote places, perhaps he's been too long in one place.' So they let me go and now I am on my way to the Solovsky monastery to pray at the tombs of St. Zossima and St. Sabbatai, for which I have obtained the blessing of the abbot, for I want to kneel to them before I die."

"But why before you die? Are you ill?"

"No, I am not ill, but just in case it may be necessary to fight again."

"Are you again talking about war?"

"Yes, I am."

"So Sacred Silence didn't do much good?"

"I can't say: I am doing all I can to keep silence, but the spirit overcomes me."

"What exactly does he tell you?"

"He's always saying to me, 'Take up arms'!"

"But why? You aren't going to fight, too, are you?"

"Of course I am! What else would you have me do? I want to die for my people."

"But not in your cowl and cassock?"

"Why, no. I shall take off my cowl and cassock and put on my old uniform again."

Having said that, the enchanted pilgrim seemed again to feel the spirit of prophecy coming upon him and he fell into a quiet meditation which none of his fellow passengers dared to interrupt by any more questions. And, indeed, what more could we have asked him? He had told us the adventures of his past life with all the frankness of his simple soul, and his prophecies remain for the time being in the hands of Him Who hides the future from both the wise and the foolish and reveals it only now and then unto babes.

IRON WILL

CHAPTER I

WE had been having a violent discussion during which the point of view was put forward with some persistence that the Germans possess an iron will and we do not. It was further maintained that for that reason we, being men of infirm purpose, should think twice before engaging in an argument with Germans, for we should be certain to get the worst of it. In short, the subject of our debate was hardly original and, to be quite frank, somewhat boring, but it was one that could not be dismissed off-hand.

Of our whole company only one elderly man, Fyodor Afanassyevich Vochnev, took no part in the discussion. He went on quietly pouring out the tea, but when all our glasses had been filled and we had helped ourselves to them, Vochnev said:

"I have listened very carefully to what you have been saying, gentlemen, and in my opinion you were just engaging in an empty war of words. Supposing the Germans do possess a firm will of their own and that we are rather lackadaisical in that respect, there's absolutely no reason in the world why we should be so upset about it, none in the world. I'm neither extolling nor decrying my own fellow-countrymen, I'm merely saying that they are quite capable of standing up for themselves and, whether wise or foolish, can take care of themselves. If you find it difficult to agree with me, gentlemen, but if the subject nevertheless interests you, that is to say, if you'd like to know how such differences of national character are adjusted in life, I'd be glad to tell you a story about a man, a German, who had an iron will."

"But mind it isn't too long, Fyodor Afanassyevich!"

"Dear me, no. As a matter of fact, it is a very short story which can easily be told over a cup of tea."

"Well, of course, if it is a short story, then carry on by all means. We don't mind listening to a short story even about a German."

"Very well, then, gentlemen. Quiet, please, for the story is about to begin."

CHAPTER II

SOON after the Crimean war (it isn't my fault, gentlemen, if all our stories nowadays invariably start with that) I succumbed to one of our modern crazes for which I've had many opportunities of being sorry afterwards: I mean I gave up my job in the Civil Service, although I had made quite a good start in it, and I accepted a post with a private firm which was at the time newly established. The firm went broke long ago, and, I might add, sank into oblivion without raising a ripple of scandal. By working for a private company, I had hoped to earn an honest living without being subject to the unaccountable whims of my superiors in the Civil Service, and those unpleasant surprises which lie in wait for every civil servant in our country as a consequence of the well-known rule, according to which he can be given the sack without any explanation. In a word, gentlemen, I thought that I had achieved freedom, as if freedom can be had for the asking outside the gates of every Government building—but that is another story.

The owners of the firm where I had obtained a job were Englishmen: there were two of them, both married and each with a large family; one of them played the flute and the other the 'cello and they were first-rate fellows, both of them, and quite practical, too, which I conclude from the fact that, having utterly failed in their first enterprise, they realised that Russia possessed certain peculiarities of her own which could be overlooked only at one's peril: so they started from scratch again, but this time they conducted their business in the simple Russian fashion and they got rich again in the purely English fashion. However, when my story begins they were still inexperienced, or, as we say, "raw," and they went on spending the capital they had brought with them with the most injudicious self-confidence.

Our business operations were large and extremely complicated: we ploughed the ground and sowed sugar beet and we intended to run a sugar factory, a distillery, a saw mill, carpenter's shops for the manufacture of barrels and parquet flooring, a saltpetre factory, in a word, our intention was to exploit every industrial possibility that our district offered. We started on all those various enterprises at the same time and soon work on all of them was in full swing: we ploughed and dug, put up brick walls, erected monumental chimneys and employed every kind of worker under the sun, mostly foreigners, though. Of the Russian employees, my job carried the biggest salary, chiefly because part of my duties consisted in travelling all over the country on business, which I, of course, could do much better than any foreigner. On the other hand, the foreigners employed by our firm were so numerous that they formed a colony of their own. Our employers built a number of rather uniform, but quite beautiful and comfortable cottages for us round the huge old country mansion: which was occupied by the two principals of our firm and their families. The mansion, built according to the freakish whim of a rich Russian landowner, was so huge and spacious that even two large English families could be easily accommodated in it and enjoy all the amenities to which they were accustomed. Over the house towered a semi-circular cupola, surmounted by an Aeolian harp which had long ago lost all its strings, and below the cupola was a big concert hall where in former days serfs, since sold one by one as the rumours about their forthcoming emancipation looked like being realised, used to show off their prowess as musicians and singers.

My employers used to give concerts of Haydn quartets in that hall at which all their employees, including the various managers, clerks and book-keepers, were expected to turn up and form the audience. All that was done with the laudable intention of "improving public taste," but that excellent object was never achieved, because Haydn's classical quartets were caviare to the general and even bored them to tears. They openly complained to me that they were "fed up with having to listen to that rubbish," but listen to "the rubbish" they had to nevertheless, until fate provided us with another entertainment, a much more enjoyable one, which happened with the arrival from Germany of a new "colonist," the engineer Hugo Karlovich Pectoralis, who came to us from the little German town of Doberan, situated by the lake of Plau in Mecklenburg-Schwerin, and his very arrival aroused great interest among us all.

As Hugo Pectoralis is the hero of my story, I'd better tell you about him at greater length.

CHAPTER III

PECTORALIS was part of a consignment of machines ordered from Germany. He was supposed to bring those machines, start them going and look after them. Why the Englishmen should have employed a German and not one of their own people or, indeed, why they should have ordered those machines in the little German town of Doberan, I don't really know, but I believe it all happened because one of the Englishmen had seen the machines made by that particular firm somewhere and, taking a fancy to them, had most regrettably failed to take into account certain considerations of a purely patriotic character. After all, business is business, and even patriotic Englishmen have to act accordingly. However, do stop me if I seem to digress too much.

The machines were to be used for our steam flour-mill and saw-mill and, as the two buildings had already been put up, we were very anxious to get them as well as the engineer. The German firm had let us know that the machines had already been dispatched by sea via St. Petersburg; as for the engineer for whose arrival before the machines we had particularly asked, for he had to make the necessary adjustments in the buildings which were to house them, we were informed by the Doberan people that they were sending one of their own men whose name was Hugo Pectoralis and who was particularly fitted for the job, since he possessed an iron will which made him carry out everything he set his mind on.

I was at the time away on the firm's business in St. Petersburg and it fell to me to get the machines through the customs and send them off to our remote rural parts. I was further instructed to take charge of Hugo Pectoralis and bring him back with me. Hugo Pectoralis was supposed to be arriving shortly and, on his arrival in St. Petersburg, he had to call on the firm of Asmus Simonsen & Co., which acted as the agent for the ancient German settlement on the Volga founded in the eighteenth century with the blessing of the Empress Catherine II, and the chief centre of which was the town of Sarepta. The firm of Asmus Simonsen & Co. was therefore known as Sarepta House, and since the main business of the Volga "Moravian brothers" was the sale of the produce of their two large mustard factories, their mustard being famous throughout Russia, Sarepta House was popularly known as the Mustard House. But there occurred some kind of *quid pro quo* in the dispatch of the machinery and the engineer: the machines came late and the engineer, contrary to our expectations, arrived in St. Petersburg before his appointed time. In fact, when I arrived at Mustard House to leave my address for Pectoralis, I was told that he had already left St. Petersburg a week before.

This event, which was rather an unpleasant shock to me and which was fraught with all sorts of dangers for Pectoralis, occurred towards the end of September, which in that year happened to be, as though on purpose, particularly inclement and harsh. There was no snow or frost as yet, but it rained cats and dogs and the rains alternated with piercingly cold fogs; the northerly winds blew with such force that they chilled you to the marrow and the streets were covered knee-deep in mire and it didn't take much imagination to guess in what a state the muddy country roads were at the time. The position of an imprudent (so it seemed to me) foreigner who at such a season ventured alone on a long journey without a knowledge of either our roads or our customs, was, I thought, perilous to a degree, and I was not far wrong in my supposition. Indeed, what happened actually far exceeded my worst fears.

I inquired at the Mustard House whether Pectoralis knew any Russian and was told he didn't. Not only did Pectoralis not speak Russian, he didn't know a single word of Russian. When I asked if at least he had enough money on him, I was told that he had been given "on behalf of the company" his travelling expenses and, in addition, his daily expenses for ten days and that he hadn't asked for more.

The affair was getting more and more complicated. Taking into consideration the way people used to travel in those days of stage coaches, the constant changing of horses usually involving endless delays, Pectoralis could easily have got stranded somewhere and might even be forced to resort to begging.

"Why didn't you stop him? Why didn't you persuade him to wait for the man who was to accompany him on his journey ?" I kept on expostulating with the people at the Mustard House.

But they replied that they did their best to persuade him to wait and explained to him the difficulties of such a journey for a foreigner, but that he insisted that, having given his word to travel without stopping on the way, he would carry out his promise, and he added that he was not afraid of any difficulties because he had an iron will.

Greatly worried, I wrote to the principals of my firm a detailed account of what had happened and I asked them to do everything they possibly could to avert any misfortune that might befall the unfortunate traveller; but, to be quite frank, while writing that letter I hardly knew myself what could be done to intercept Pectoralis on the way and bring him to his destination under the protection of a reliable guide. I myself could not possibly leave St. Petersburg at the time, being detained there by very important business which required my personal attention and, besides, he had left such a long time ago that I could hardly hope to catch up with him. If, however, anybody else was sent to meet the man with the iron will, how was one to ensure that the messenger would meet Pectoralis *and* recognise him ?

At that time, of course, I did not know that anybody meeting Pectoralis would be sure to recognise him. That misconception arose in my mind because the Germans at the Mustard House I had asked for information about him, could not give me any distinguishing marks by which he could be recognised. Conscientious as they were in supplying me with the necessary data, they lacked imagination and they gave me only a general description of his features, a sort of description one usually finds in a passport and which could apply to any man. According to them, Pectoralis was a young man of twenty-eight or thirty, slightly over medium size, with black hair, grey eyes and a cheerful, very firm expression. I'm afraid there's nothing in such a description to recognise a man by if one meets him for the first time. The only thing in the description which stuck in my mind was the "cheerful and very firm expression," but, after all, what average man is such an expert in facial expressions that he could immediately recognise a man by such a description and say, "Pardon me, sir, aren't you Mr. Pectoralis ?" Moreover, couldn't even such an expression change, couldn't it droop and sag in the Russian autumnal damp and cold ?

It therefore appeared to me that except for writing a voluminous letter about that eccentric individual, I couldn't do anything more for him that would be of the slightest use to him and, willy-nilly, I had to rest satisfied with that and, besides, just at the time I had received an unexpected call to go south immediately to visit different towns, and I had no time even to think of Pectoralis. In the meantime October and half of November had gone: I received no news of Pectoralis during my constant peregrinations and it was almost the end of November when I was on my way home, having visited a large number of towns in between.

The weather had undergone a great change for the worse during that time: the rains had come to an end, it was bitterly cold, dry and frosty, and every day there was a fall of hard, fine snow.

In Vladimir I recovered my *tarantass* which could still be used on the roads, for it was more comfortable to travel in a carriage than in a sledge, and I started on my journey home. I had to cover a distance of about a thousand *versts* and I hoped to do it in six days, but the constant jolting shook me up so badly that I permitted myself frequent intervals for rest and I travelled much more slowly than I had intended. On the fifth day I just managed to get as far as Vassilyov Maydan and it was there that I had quite an unexpected and quite an incredible meeting.

I don't know what Vassilyov Maydan is like now, but in those days it was a cold, bleak station, standing by itself far from any human habitation. It was a hideous-looking place with a deal roof and sides and two "official" columns at the entrance and it gave one a most unpleasant feeling of discomfort and, indeed, from what I had been told, the station enjoyed the uneviable reputation of being one of the coldest in Russia; but I was so tired that I nevertheless decided to spend the night there.

Although the light which twinkled dimly in the windows of the passengers' waiting-room told me that there were travellers inside who had probably already packed up for the night, nothing could shake my resolution to get some rest and I was amply rewarded for it by a most pleasant surprise.

"Did you meet Pectoralis there?" somebody interrupted the narrator eagerly.

"Whoever it was I met there," Vochnev replied, "I must ask you, gentlemen, to wait patiently until you have heard the whole story from me and to listen without interruption."

"But, good lord, man, you can't expect us not to interrupt you if your story is interesting, can you?"

"That's all the more reason why you shouldn't interrupt me. Instead you'd better write it down and send it to one of our more popular newspapers. The question of German will power and our lack of it is one of the most debated topics throughout Russia to-day and we might be able to supply the public with some not entirely uninteresting reading matter."

CHAPTER IV

HAVING asked my servant to take my felt rug, my fur coat and whatever else was necessary into the station, I told the coachman to leave the *tarantass* in the yard and myself groped my way through the large, dark entrance hall of the station and tried to open the door of the passengers' waiting-room. I found it with great difficulty and began to pull at it, but it had so much expanded with the damp that it would not open. However much I pulled away at it, I should hardly have been able to open it by my own efforts, had not someone else's welcome hand or rather foot come to my aid; for the door was opened for me from the inside by somebody who had applied his foot to it with such vigour that I had barely time to jump back. I saw in the doorway a man wearing a city silk hat, a very wide oilskin cloak and an umbrella which was suspended from a button of his cloak, at the collar. I couldn't very well make out the face of the stranger at first, and, I confess, I nearly swore at him for almost knocking me down with the door. But what surprised me most about him and made me pay particular attention to him was that he did not walk out of the door, as I might have expected, but, on the contrary, went back into the room and began calmly to perambulate up and down, from one corner to another of that dismally empty room which was only lit by a guttered candle.

I asked him if he knew where I could find the station-master or any other living human being.

"*Ich verstehe gar kein russisch,*" the stranger replied.

I began to speak to him in German.

He seemed to be overjoyed to hear the sounds of his native tongue and he told me that the station-master was not on the premises, having gone off somewhere some time ago.

"I expect you're waiting for your horses here ?"

"Oh, yes, yes, certainly. I'm waiting for my horses."

"But aren't there any horses ?"

"I don't know. I just can't get them."

"Have you asked for them ?"

"No. You see, I can't speak any Russian."

"Dear me," I said, "not a word ?"

"Well, yes, I can say—'can,' 'cannot,' 'carriage' and 'customs . . .' " he murmured, having evidently exhausted the entire vocabulary of the Russian words he knew. "When they say 'can,' I carry on with my journey, when they say 'cannot,' I stay where I am, and when they say 'carriage,' I pay what is required of me, and that's all. . . ."

"Merciful heavens," I thought, "what an extraordinary individual!" And I started looking him over. What strange clothes he wore! His high boots were quite ordinary, but out of their tops there protruded the longest imaginable, coarse woollen stockings which covered his legs above his knees and which were held up half-way up his thighs by blue garters; from under his waistcoat a knitted red sweater fell over his stomach and over his waistcoat could be seen a grey coat of thick woollen cloth, usually used for dressing-gowns, with a green braid binding, and on top of all that he wore an oilskin cloak, which was hardly the kind of garment to wear at that time of the year, and the umbrella, which hung from a button at the neck.

The entire luggage of the traveller consisted of a little cylindrical parcel in an oilskin cover and, on top of it, an ordinary note-book—and that was all!

"That's wonderful!" I exclaimed and I nearly asked him, "Are you really travelling like that?" but I immediately suppressed my curiosity, not wishing to appear uncivil, and, turning to the station-master who had just entered, I asked him to put the *samovar* on the table and light a fire in the fireplace.

The foreigner went on pacing the room, but as soon as he saw that they had brought in some logs and were lighting a fire, he said, looking very pleased:

"Oh, I see, so they 'can' and I've been here for three days and every day I pointed to the fireplace, but they always said 'cannot'."

"You don't really mean to say you've been here for three days?"

"Oh, yes, sir, for three days," he replied calmly. "Why? What's the matter?"

"But why should you have stayed here for three days?"

"I don't know. I've always to wait like that."

"How do you mean 'always'? At every station?"

"Why, yes, sir. At every station. Since I left Moscow, I've had to wait like that at every station and then I'd carry on with my journey again."

"And at every station you had to wait three days?"

"Yes, sir, three days. . . . But no, that's not quite true. At one station I had only to wait two days—it's all written down in my journal—and at another station I had to wait four days: I've written that down, too."

"And what do you do at the stations?"

"Nothing."

"Excuse me, sir," I said, "but are you making a study of our customs and is that why you put everything down in your diary?"

That was the fashion in those days.

"Yes," he replied. "I just make a note of everything they do to me."

"But why do you let them do this to you?"

"Well, sir, I can't help it, can I? You see, I can't speak any Russian and I just have to do what they tell me, but afterwards . . ."

"What will you do afterwards?"

"Afterwards they'll have to do what I tell them!"

"Oh?"

"Yes, sir, most decidedly so!"

"But why did you start on such a journey without any knowledge of the language?"

"That was absolutely necessary, sir. I have undertaken to travel without stopping and I do travel without stopping. I always carry out what I promise," the stranger said and, as he said it, his face, which until then did not strike me as in any way unusual, assumed "a cheerful and very firm expression."

"Dear me, what a strange fellow," I thought and I said, "Excuse me, sir, but do you really regard the way you are travelling as 'travelling without stopping' ?"

"Of course I do. I keep on travelling, I'm always on my way. Directly they say 'can' I start on my journey and, as you see, to be always ready to start at any moment I never even take off my clothes. Oh, I haven't taken off my clothes for days and days!"

"Well," I said to myself, "I can imagine how clean you must be!" and I said aloud:

"I hope you don't mind my saying so, sir, but I can't help feeling that you do things in rather an extraordinary way."

"Why ?"

"You should have looked for some Russian in Moscow who was travelling the same way as you and then you would have travelled much faster and much more comfortably."

"That may be so," he replied, "but I'd have had to stop there for some time to find such a companion for my journey."

"But you'd have quickly made up for the lost time, wouldn't you ?"

"Having given my word, I resolved not to stop."

"Still according to your own account you are stopping at every station, aren't you ?"

"Yes, sir, that is so, but I can't help that."

"Agreed, but why do it ? And, anyway, how can you stand it ?"

"Oh, I can stand anything, for, you see, sir, I have an iron will!"

"Dear me," I exclaimed, "you have an iron will ?"

"Yes, sir, I have an iron will and my father also had an iron will and so had my grandfather, and so I, too, have an iron will."

"An iron will! You are not by any chance a native of Doberan in Mecklenburg ?"

"Yes, sir, I am a native of Doberan."

"And you are on your way to R. to take charge of some factories there, aren't you ?"

"Yes, I am on my way there."

"And your name is Hugo Pectoralis, isn't it ?"

"Yes, yes, I am engineer Hugo Pectoralis! But how do you know that, sir ?"

I just could not contain myself any longer, so I jumped up from my seat, embraced Pectoralis as if he were an old friend of mine, dragged him to the *samovar*, warmed him up with some hot punch and told him that I recognised him because of his iron will.

"Oh, so that's how you recognised me!" he exclaimed, looking as pleased as Punch and, raising his hands aloft, he said, "Oh, my father, oh, my *grossvater*, did you hear that and are you satisfied with your Hugo now?"

"I'm quite sure they're satisfied with you," I said. "But do sit down at the table and warm yourself with a cup of tea. I expect you must be frozen to the marrow."

"Yes, sir," he said, "I am feeling rather chilly. It's cold here, devilishly cold! I've got it all down in my diary."

"Even your clothes aren't the kind you should have had: they can't possibly keep you warm."

"That's quite true, sir," he said, "my clothes don't warm me at all. The only things that keep me warm are my socks, but I have an iron will and you can see for yourself, sir, what an advantage it is to have an iron will."

"I'm afraid," I said, "I can't see it."

"What do you mean you can't see, sir? I'm known before I arrive, I keep my word and I'm still alive and I can die without losing my self-respect, without any sign of weakness."

"But if you don't mind my asking, to whom did you give the word which you say you have kept?"

He stretched out his hand and, pointing a finger slowly at his breast, replied:

"To myself."

"To yourself? But, my dear sir, that's sheer obstinacy!"

"Not at all, sir, it is not obstinacy."

"Promises are made in accordance with certain considerations and they are carried out according to circumstances."

The German looked at me with the utmost disdain and said that he did not recognise such a rule: that whatever he promised, he carried out and that it was only thus that one acquired an iron will.

"Learn to be your own master first and then you'll become a master over others, that's what should be done and that's what I intend to do and what I shall always endeavour to do!"

"Well, my dear fellow," I thought, "I can see that you've come here to surprise us all, but take care you're not surprised by us yourself!"

CHAPTER V

I SPENT the night with Pectoralis and hardly slept a wink. The shivering German occupied the armchair in front of the fireplace and, as he wouldn't budge from his chair for anything in the world and kept on scratching himself like a flea-infested poodle, his chair kept up an uninterrupted squeaking throughout the whole of the night and I was constantly wakened by that noise. I did my best to persuade him to lie down on the couch, but he would not hear of it. We got up early next morning, had tea and drove away. In the first town we came to I sent my servant with him to the public baths with the order to see that he had a good wash and that he put on clean linen and after that we continued on our journey without a break and he no longer scratched himself. I also got Pectoralis out of his oilskin cloak, wrapped him in my servant's spare sheepskin and he got thoroughly warm and became extremely lively and talkative. During his slow journey across Russia, the German had not only got frozen, but also hungry, for he had spent all his travelling money (he had sent part of it home to Doberan immediately he had received it) and for the rest of the journey he seemed to have lived almost entirely on his iron will alone. But to offset those bodily discomforts, he had made a great many observations which he had put down in his note-book, and they were not entirely lacking in originality. What struck him most during his journey across Russia was what nobody else had noticed before, namely, what amazing things could be performed in our country by skill, pertinacity and, above all, iron will.

I enjoyed his company very much, and I was particularly pleased when I thought of all the other members of our colony whom I hoped to present with an object of considerable amusement in the person of this queer individual, who was already hoping to make a big fortune for himself in Russia, mainly with the help of his iron will.

What sort of fortune he actually did make you will see from my story, but now I'd better carry on with it just as it happened.

Well, in the first place, this Pectoralis proved himself to be a good and, if not an original, then at any rate an experienced, knowledgeable and skilful engineer. Thanks to his pertinacity and firmness, the business which he had come to do throve beyond all expectations and in spite of many unexpected snags. The machines, which he had arrived to install, turned out to be defective in many of their parts and of inferior material to boot. We had no time to write to Germany about it, or to demand new parts to replace the faulty ones, for our flour mill had to start grinding the corn, and so Pectoralis had to do many things himself. The faulty parts were somehow or other recast at the small and far from perfect foundry in our town, owned by an artizan of the name of Safronov, a well-known loafer and ne'er-do-well, and Pectoralis himself put the finishing touches to them at a home-made lathe. To accomplish all that successfully one had to have an iron will. Proper notice was duly taken of Pectoralis's services which were rewarded by a rise in salary, amounting now to one thousand five hundred a year.

When I told him of his rise, he thanked me in a highly dignified manner and immediately sat down at the table and began adding something up, then he fixed his gaze on the ceiling and said:

"This means that without having to alter my decision, the time is reduced exactly by one year and eleven months."

"What were you adding up?" I asked.

"Oh," he said, "I'm just calculating something. . . ."

"I'm sorry, old chap," I said. "I shouldn't be so inquisitive."

"Oh, don't apologise," he said. "It's just that I have certain expectations which depend on my being able to raise a certain sum of money."

"And this rise which I was glad to be able to tell you about will, I suppose, shorten the time of waiting?"

"Yes, you've got it, old man," he said. "It shortens it by exactly one year and eleven months. I must write to Germany about it immediately. When do they take the post to town?"

"To-day."

"To-day? What a pity! I shan't have time to describe everything as I ought to."

"My goodness, what nonsense!" I said. "Surely it wouldn't take you such a long time to write a business letter to your partner or your firm?"

"My firm?" he echoed me and, smiling, added, "Oh, if you only knew what kind of a firm it is!"

"Oh? Is the head of your firm such an awful stickler for dry formality?"

"Why, it isn't the head of my firm at all: it is a young and beautiful girl!"

"A girl? You miserable old sinner! So that's the kind of peccadillo you keep up your sleeve?"

"Peccadillo?" he repeated, looking puzzled, then he added, shaking his head, "I was never guilty of any peccadilloes, I assure you. I couldn't possibly have ever been guilty of any, either. That's a very important highly reliable and absolutely unimpeachable affair which depends entirely on my getting three thousand *thalers*. Then you'll see me . . ."

". . . on the top of the world?"

"Oh, dear, no! Not quite on top, but near enough. I shall be on top of the world only when I have ten thousand *thalers*."

"Doesn't it mean in plain language, my dear chap, that you're making arrangements for your marriage and that in Doberan or somewhere not very far from it there's a lovely young maiden who possesses part of your iron will?"

"Quite, quite. . . . You're absolutely right."

"And being both of you people of firm will you promised each other to postpone your wedding day until you got your three thousand *thalers*. Isn't that so?"

"Quite, quite. . . . You're a marvellous guesser, old man."

"Well," I said, "it isn't so difficult to guess, is it?"

"But," said he, "do you think such a thing would be possible in Russia, taking into consideration the Russian character, I mean?"

"Good heavens," I said, "how can we with that Russian character of ours even hope to emulate such wonderful constancy? Why, we're not worthy of sitting at the same table as you considering that we can't even pull as long a face as you!"

"But that's not all, old man," he said. "I mean you haven't guessed everything."

"Oh?" said I. "What else is there to guess?"

"Oh," he said, "that's something important, highly important, something for which, you see, I keep myself under such strict discipline."

"Keep yourself," I thought to myself, "keep yourself by all means, my dear chap!" and I went away, leaving him to write his letter to his far-away fiancée.

In about an hour he appeared in my room with his letter which he asked me to send off and, staying for a cup of tea, he talked nineteen to the dozen, but from time to time he'd fall silent, carried away by his dreams into a world of his own and, as he day-dreamed, he would smile to himself as though he saw a million beckoning to him from behind a rose-coloured cloud. The blighter was so happy that it was positively indecent and I couldn't help wanting to say something that would make him squirm. Frankly, I could not resist the temptation to bring him down to earth with a bump, so when Hugo, without rhyme or reason, put his arm round my shoulders and asked me whether I could imagine what would be the outcome of the union of a man and a woman who both possessed such firm characters, I replied:

"I can."

"Well, what do you think?"

"I think that maybe nothing will come of it."

Pectoralis looked at me with astonishment and asked:

"Why do you think so?"

I felt sorry for him and I said that I was just joking.

"Oh, you were joking," he said, "but that's no joking matter, it really could happen! Still I admit that it is a very, very important matter for which a man needs all the iron will he's got."

"To blazes with you," thought I, "I'm not even interested in unravelling your mystery," but I should never have guessed it, anyway!

CHAPTER VI

MEANWHILE Pectoralis's iron will, which was of such great benefit to our firm wherever pertinacity was demanded of him and which promised to play such an important part in his own life, caused among us, in our Russian simplicity, much amusement and innocent merriment, being regarded, I'm afraid, rather as a big joke. And what was even more remarkable, we had to admit that it couldn't be otherwise: for things inevitably worked out that way.

Infinitely stubborn and pertinacious, Pectoralis was stubborn about everything and pertinacious both in big and little things. He was preoccupied with his iron will as some people are preoccupied with their physical fitness, and he trained himself in it systematically and persistently, as though it were his only worth while calling in life. His considerable victories over himself made him unreasonably self-reliant and sometimes put him either in rather melancholy or highly comic situations. Thus, for instance, he taught himself Russian, supported solely in that herculean task by his iron will, and he learnt it very quickly and according to the best rules of grammar; but before he had mastered it completely, he went through all sorts of unnecessary sufferings because of that iron will of his, and his sufferings were so real and tangible that they left their mark on his health with rather serious consequences later.

Pectoralis had vowed to learn Russian in six months and to learn it correctly and grammatically, and on the appointed day he suddenly and to everybody's surprise began to talk Russian. He knew that Germans spoke Russian in a very funny way and he did not want to be funny. He learnt Russian by himself, without any teacher, and he did it, moreover, in dead secret so that none of us even suspected it. Until the appointed day Pectoralis did not speak a word of Russian. He seemed even to have forgotten the four words he knew, namely, "can," "cannot," "carriage" and "customs." But one fine morning he suddenly entered my room and said, not without a certain effort, it is true, nor absolutely correctly, but quite easily and enunciating every word clearly:

"Good morning, how are you getting on?"

"Good boy, Hugo Karlovich!" I exclaimed. "Fancy playing such a trick on us!"

"Playing a trick?" he repeated reflectively and, I'll say that for him, he got it immediately. "Oh, yes, yes . . . that's it! You were surprised, weren't you?"

"Of course, I was surprised," I said. "Fancy you talking Russian like that!"

"Oh, but it had to be like that."

"Why 'had to,' old chap? Has the gift of tongues suddenly descended upon you?"

He thought it over, then he murmured to himself, "The gift of tongs?" and fell into thought again.

"The gift of tongues!" I repeated.

Pectoralis understood immediately and answered in excellent Russian:

"Oh, no, not at all, not a gift, but . . ."

". . . your iron will!"

Pectoralis pointed with dignity at his chest and said:

"Yes, sir. That's what it is."

And he went on to tell me, as one friend to another, that he had always intended to learn Russian, for although he had noticed that certain of his fellow-countrymen domiciled in Russia carried on excellently without any knowledge of the language, he had come to the conclusion that, being civil servants, they could do without it, but that he, being in private employment, had to behave differently.

"It is impossible to get on without it," he went on it, "for without it you can't possibly make sure that your business will prosper and, besides, I don't intend to be deceived by anybody."

I was simply dying to tell him that "the time will come, old chap, when they'll deceive you even with a knowledge of Russian," but I didn't want to distress him: why shouldn't he go on feeling happy?

Since that day Pectoralis always insisted on speaking Russian with Russians and if he made mistakes, his mistakes were of an unconscious kind. Thus, for instance, he would say something which he didn't really want to say, but he stuck to his guns for all that and whatever unpleasantness his error might involve him in, he put up with it without a murmur, thanks to that iron will of his, and never went back on a single word spoken by him. It was there that the real punishment for his perverse obstinacy began. Like any other man who insists on acting according to his own sweet will, Pectoralis never noticed when he became the slave of somebody else's opinions. Afraid of making a fool of himself over some trifle, he forced himself to do what he never intended to do and could not possibly have wished to do, but *that* he would not admit for anything in the world.

Soon, however, people got wind of that peculiarity of his and poor Pectoralis became the butt of the most cruel practical jokes. His verbal slips usually occurred when he had to reply quickly to some question without having time to grasp the full meaning of it. It was then that he often said something which was quite contrary to what he really wanted to say. He would be asked, for instance:

"Do you like strong or weak tea, Hugo Karlovich?"

On the spur of the moment he didn't get the meaning of "strong" and "weak" in such a connection.

"Strong," he'd reply. "Oh, yes, very strong!"

"Very strong?"

"Yes, very strong."

"You mean *very* strong, don't you?"

"Oh, yes, I mean very strong!"

So he was poured out a cup of tea which was as black as ink and he would be asked again:

"Are you quite sure it isn't a little too strong for you?"

Now, of course, Hugo could see quite plainly that the tea was very strong, that, in fact, it wasn't at all what he wanted, but that iron will of his would not let him admit that he had made a mistake.

"Oh, not at all," he would reply, and drink his frightful tea; and when surprise was expressed that he, a German, could drink such strong tea, he had the pluck to reply that he simply loved it.

"Do you really like it?" he was asked.

"Oh, yes, I like it frightfully," Hugo replied.

"But it can't do you any good, you know."

"Oh, not at all! It'll do me all the good in the world."

"But, really, haven't you made . . . er . . . made a . . . ?"

"Haven't I made what?"

"Are you sure you haven't made a mistake?"

"Oh, dear, no!"

So while being simply unable to stand strong tea, he went on assuring everybody that he liked it "frightfully" and he was taken at his word, the whole company at the tea-table falling over each other to treat him to a cup of tea. In that way he was forced to imbibe innumerable cups of strong tea and that popular Russian beverage became a veritable nightmare to poor Hugo. But he continued making a martyr of himself and went on drinking tannin instead of tea, until one day he suffered a nervous breakdown.

The poor German spent a whole week in bed, unable to move or talk, but on getting back the gift of speech the first thing he murmured was something about his iron will.

When he recovered, he said to me:

"I'm very pleased with myself," and he pressed my hand with his weak hand.

"What are you so pleased about?"

"I was true to myself," he said, but he did not explain what there was so remarkable about his perseverance.

But his illness, at any rate, brought his tea torture to an end, for he was forbidden to touch tea altogether and all he had to do to save his face now was to pretend to be sorry to have to do without tea. To compensate him for that loss, however, the same thing repeated itself in connection with the French mustard "Diafan." I can't remember how it all began, but I suppose it must have happened in the same way as with the tea. Anyway, Hugo soon became known as a great admirer of the excellencies of the French mustard "Diafan," which was pressed upon him with every dish and the poor man consumed tons of it, smearing it even on his bread instead of butter and praising it up to the skies, declaring that it was simply delicious and that he liked it "frightfully."

The experiment with the mustard ended in the same way as the earlier experiment with the tea: Pectoralis nearly died of acute gastric catarrh and although he got over it, it left its trace throughout the life of the poor stoic and even played its part in his tragi-comic death.

There are many other instances of a similar funny and lamentable character. I can't possibly remember them all, nor would it be worth while recounting them in detail, but I can still recall three instances where Hugo, a martyr to his iron will, could not possibly pretend that he was doing what he really wanted to do.

That, I suppose, was a phase in his life which he had to go through until it reached its climax and, then, little by little it passed on inexorably to its anti-climax.

CHAPTER VII

THE new phase began during the first summer Pectoralis spent with us and it started with an invention by Hugo of a new type of carriage. I should perhaps have told you before that it was about forty *versts* from our colony to the nearest town. There was a short-cut through the woods, however, a path rather than a road, which cut the distance almost by half. But, unfortunately, the path was too narrow for an ordinary four-wheeled carriage, and even in their two-wheeled carts our peasants had the greatest difficulty in using it. Hugo wanted to use that short-cut through the woods and he refused to be jolted in a peasant's cart, so he set his mind to work and designed an extraordinary chariot of his own: it was a common or garden arm-chair with a spring cushion placed on a frame which was attached to the fore-part of an old four-wheeler. The resulting carriage was a very ingenious contraption, indeed, and it had such a curious appearance that the peasants nick-named Pectoralis who drove it a "Mordvin idol"; but what was much worse was that the arm-chair, deprived of its firm resting place on the floor of a room, steadfastly refused to travel and, unable to stand the constant jolting, it would very often fly off the frame with the result that Pectoralis's horse used to arrive home without him and poor Hugo followed it in about an hour or even two, limping and carrying his arm-chair on his back. And sometimes even worse accidents would happen: once he was flung into a swamp with his arm-chair and he had to wait until his rescuers arrived and dragged him out, bringing him home in a most wretched condition.

Hugo could not very well say that he had intended such an accident to happen to him, but he continued to use his contraption, unwilling to admit himself beaten, and he did it with a pertinacity that was simply amazing.

Then there was the incident with the wasps. One day Hugo, drenched to the skin after a shooting expedition, was dragged by one of the principals of our firm straight to a tea-party. It was a very agreeable party and we were all enjoying ourselves, chatting round the tea-table. Hugo was given a hot drink of wine and water and the assembled company began to ply him with questions about the success of his shoot. Hugo was a keen sportsman and he did not tell too many lies, but as even in sport his iron will played an important part, his story, for all its innocence, did not lack an amusing side. We listened to him, laughing up our sleeves, but to our great chagrin the fun of our conversation was spoilt by hundreds of wasps which seemed to appear out of nowhere. It was quite an extraordinary business, and we just couldn't understand where those wasps came from. Although the windows of the room we were sitting in were wide open, the wasps did not come from the garden, for it was raining outside, a pleasant summer shower it was, and those vicious insects do not as a rule fly in swarms in a rain. Where on earth could they be coming from? And they went on buzzing about, appearing like rabbits out of a conjurer's hat: they crawled up the legs of the table, went for a walk on the tablecloth, explored our plates, swarmed all over Hugo's back and, finally, very provokingly, stung our young hostess on the head.

Our delightful party came to a sudden end, for any further conversation now became impossible: there was a terrible to-do and the resulting commotion was made a hundred times worse by feminine nervousness and masculine eagerness to protect the fair sex. The most drastic measures were immediately taken: everybody began to dash about all over the room, one trying to swat a wasp with his handerkerchief, another chasing them with a napkin and the rest defending themselves as best they could against the concerted assaults of the insects. Hugo alone did not take part in all that rushing about and general excitement—and he alone knew the reason. He stood motionless at the chair on which he had until then been sitting and he looked a terrible sight: his face was covered by a deathly pallor, his lips trembled, his hands twitched spasmodically and his whole coat and, especially, his back was alive with wasps.

"Merciful heavens," we exclaimed, surrounding him from all sides, "why, Hugo Karlovich, you're a veritable wasps' nest."

"Oh, no," he said, hardly able to bring the words out of his mouth, "I am not a wasps' nest, but I am carrying a wasps' nest!"

"A wasps' nest?"

"Yes. You see, I found it, but it was very wet and, as I wanted to examine it, I took it with me."

"But where have you got it?"

"It's in my back pocket."

"So that's what it is!"

We pulled off his coat (the ladies had left the fiendishly uncomfortable room long ago) and we saw that the entire back of Hugo's waistcoat was thickly covered with wasps which were crawling upon it, and, having got warmed up, were taking wing, while out of his pocket there came an endless procession of more and more wasps.

The first thing we did was to throw Hugo's luckless coat on the floor and destroy the wasps' nest, which was the cause of all that commotion, by trampling upon it; then we turned our attention to poor Hugo himself who had been stung all over so badly that he could hardly move, but he stood there uncomplainingly without uttering a sound. We got rid of the wasps for him (the insects had even crawled under his shirt), smothered him in butter like a sausage and, laying him on a divan, covered him up with a sheet. He began to swell in less than no time and he quite obviously suffered terribly, but when one of the Englishmen, out of compassion for him, said that the man really possessed an iron will, Hugo smiled and, turning to us, said:

"I'm very glad that you no longer have any doubts about it."

He was left by himself to admire his iron will and nobody spoke another word to him. Poor man, he never suspected how much we laughed at him; but a new adventure was in store for him, an adventure in which his iron will scored another great victory, though hardly to his benefit.

CHAPTER VIII

HERE I should like to mention that if Hugo was not exactly a miser he was very careful and thrifty and as his thrift was merely a means to an end, the end being the saving up of three thousand *thalers*, and as in pursuit of that end he had mobilised all the formidable forces that were at the disposal of his iron will, his thriftiness was quite indistinguishable from the most insane miserliness. He absolutely begrudged himself everything that he could possibly do without: he did not spend anything on new clothes for himself and he did not employ a valet, preferring to clean his boots himself. But there was one thing on which he had to spend money, the expense being necessary for the sake of still greater economy. Hugo, in short, decided not to go on spending any more money on the hire of a horse, but to acquire a horse of his own. Having made up his mind to buy a horse, he did not, however, proceed to do it in an ordinary way. We had hundreds of stud farms in our district, both large and small, but among the horse breeders there was one by the name of Dmitry Yerofeyich, a middling sort of landowner, who was well known as a man who cheated for the sheer joy of cheating. Nobody in the world could play such tricks with a horse as

Dmitry Yerofeyich who, when he cheated a man, did it not as any common or garden horse dealer would do it, but like a real artist who took a great pride in his art and was anxious to show the whole world what a clever fellow he was. The more a purchaser laboured under the delusion that he was an expert where horses were concerned, the more brazenly did Dmitry Yerofeyich cheat him. He used to jump out of his skin for joy whenever he happened to light upon such an expert and he would shower all sorts of compliments on him, assuring him again and again that there could be nothing more pleasant than to do business with a man who understood everything about horses. And on such an occasion Dmitry Yerofeyich was usually very reserved about the horse he intended to palm off on the expert. He would never praise it. On the contrary, he used to remark rather disdainfully:

"Oh, it's not such a bad horse, you know. It's true there's nothing special about him, and I, for one, would never dream of sending him to a horseshow, but won't you have a good look at him yourself? After all, I don't want to sell you a pig in a poke!"

And while the expert looked, Dmitry Yerofeyich would shout to his groom:

"Stop spinning that horse round! What are you spinning round and round with him for like the devil before early mass? We're not gypsies, are we? Stand still and let the gentleman examine the horse properly! I'm afraid he hurt a leg rather badly the other day, sir. I wonder if it's better now."

"Where did he hurt it?" the purchaser would ask.

"Oh, on the pastern, I believe."

"It wasn't this horse, sir," the groom would remark.

"Not this horse? Well, bless my soul, I really can't remember now which horse it was. Take a good look at him, sir, anyway. I don't want you to make a mistake. It's true you're getting a bargain, but you wouldn't like to waste your money on something you don't want, would you? Money's very scarce nowadays, sir. Oh, well, I'm afraid you'll have to excuse me. I must be going back now, I'm dead tired."

And he would go away and, after he had gone, the purchaser would very carefully examine the horse's pastern which, of course, had never had anything wrong with it and he'd fail to notice the horse's real shortcomings.

The man would be cheated and Dmitry Yerofeyich would calmly say:

"Ah, well, business is business, sir, and besides, you should not have boasted that you were an expert on horses. Let this be a lesson to you for bragging about things you don't know anything about."

But Dmitry Yerofeyich also had his weak point, his Achilles' heel, where he was very vulnerable. As every human being longs for something he hasn't got, so Dmitry Yerofeyich liked people to trust him. He had got a taste for that sort of thing a long time ago and he had even invented a kind of jingle for a rule which he would enunciate on every possible occasion:

"Don't look, don't gaze, don't be too clever, but remember ever on me to rely, then everything'll be hunky-dory and I'll give you a horse worth five hundred for a hundred."

And so it actually happened. For Dmitry Yerofeyich this was a *point d'honneur*, an iron will of a kind. But as his secret soon became public property and many horse buyers exploited this weakness of his rather shamelessly, Dmitry Yerofeyich began to lose heavily because of that *point d'honneur* of his and he had been intending a long time to give up that vexatious habit of his, but couldn't quite pluck up enough courage to do it. But when the Lord sent him Pectoralis, Dmitry Yerofeyich plucked up courage. As soon as Hugo approached him about his intention of becoming the owner of a horse and appealed to the horse-breeder's conscience to give him a good one, Dmitry Yerofeyich said:

"My dear chap, don't talk to me of conscience, for it's a commodity that doesn't exist to-day. I've hundreds of horses, choose whichever you like, but don't appeal to my conscience."

"Oh, that's quite all right, Dmitry Yerofeyich, I rely on you absolutely and I'm quite ready to trust you."

"Take my advice, my dear chap, and don't trust anyone or rely on anyone. Why should you rely on somebody else? Are you a fool or what?"

"Well, just as you like, sir. I've made up my mind and here's one hundred roubles and let me have a horse for them. You can't possibly refuse me that, can you?"

"Why should I refuse? A hundred roubles is good money, of course, so why shouldn't I take it? But I can't help feeling, my dear chap, that you'll be sorry and I'm rather worried about it, you know."

"I shan't be sorry."

"What do you mean you won't be sorry? You're not exactly rolling in money, are you? It's hard-earned money, isn't it? And if I give you a rotten horse, you'll be sorry all right and I daresay you'll even start abusing me into the bargain, won't you?"

"I shan't abuse you, sir. I promise you that."

"I know, my dear chap, you just say that now, but when it comes to the point you'll be calling me all sorts of names. When you start thinking how I have cheated you, you'll be abusing me right and left."

"I give you my word of honour that I shall never say a bad word about you to anybody."

"Will you take your oath on it?"

"I'm afraid we don't take an oath on such things in my country, Dmitry Yerofeyich."

"Well, you see—don't you?—you don't even take an oath! How am I to believe you?"

"You can trust my iron will, sir."

"All right, have it your own way," Dmitry Yerofeyich gave in at last and, while entertaining Pectoralis to supper, he called for his groom and said:

"Harness Okryssa to Hugo Karlovich's sledge, please."

"Okryssa, sir?" the groom said in surprise.

"Yes, Okryssa."

"You mean, sir, that I should harness her to the sledge?"

"Good God, man, what do you keep asking me for? Are you deaf? I told you to harness her, so go and do it!" And turning away with a smile from the groom, he remarked to Pectoralis, "I'm giving you a fine mare, my dear chap, young and big and of an excellent breed and a golden coat. A lovely coat, my dear chap, a beauty. I'm sure you'll be grateful to me all your life."

"Thank you, thank you, sir," said Pectoralis.

"You'd better keep your thanks till after you've driven about for a bit, but if there's anything about her that you don't fancy, remember our agreement: don't swear at me, don't abuse me, for, my dear chap, you can't possibly expect me to know your own particular taste in horses."

"I shall never say a cross word about you to any living man, sir. I promise you that and you can absolutely depend on my iron will."

"Well, in that case, I must say you're a fine fellow! Alas, my dear chap, I have no will at all. Made up my mind again and again to deal fairly with people, but I just can't do it. What would you advise me to do about it? It is true, I usually tell everything to the priest at confession, but unfortunately the harm's been done already. But you Lutherans don't confess your sins, do you?"

"We confess our sins to God, sir."

"Well, well, what a strong will you must have, to be sure. You don't take an oath and you don't go to confession, but, of course, you don't have any priests, either, do you? And, I suppose, no saints, for all the saints are Russian, anyway, aren't they? Well, farewell, my dear chap, go and take your seat in your sledge and drive to your heart's content. As for me, I'll go and say my prayers and then to bed."

And so they took leave of each other.

Pectoralis knew that Dmitry Yerofeyich liked to play jokes on people and he was quite convinced that the horse-dealer was just joking; he put on his hat and overcoat, went out, sat down in his sledge, but no sooner had he taken up the reins than the horse rushed forward precipitously and knocked her forehead against a wall. He pulled her to the other side of the yard, but she rushed forward again and once more knocked her forehead against a wall, this time of a locked-up shed, and she gave herself such a terrific bang that she began to jerk her head about.

For a long time the German couldn't understand what was the matter with the mare, nor would he have been able to get anyone to explain it to him, for while his horse was rushing headlong all over the yard, every sign of life in the house had disappeared, all the lights were extinguished and every living soul seemed to have hidden itself away. Everything indeed was dead as in an enchanted castle, only the moon shone from a clear, pale sky, shedding its ghostly light over the fields which could be seen beyond the gates, closed for the night, and an icicle would suddenly fall with a sharp snap from some roof or a twig would crack in the frost.

Hugo looked one way, then another, and he realised that things could not possibly be worse, so he turned the mare's head towards the moon and a cold shiver ran down his spine: the huge, white, sightless eyes of poor Okryssa stared at the moon, dull and dead, like two opaque mirrors, and the light of the moon was reflected in them as in metal.

"The horse is blind," Hugo at last divined the truth and once more he looked round the yard.

In one of the windows he thought he could see the long figure of Dmitry Yerofeyich, who most probably had not gone to bed yet and was standing there admiring the moon or, perhaps, getting ready to say his prayers. Hugo sighed, took the horse by the bridle and led her out of the yard. . . .

As soon as the gates closed behind Pectoralis, a gentle light appeared in the window of Dmitry Yerofeyich's room: the old man must have lit the lamp before the icon and knelt down to say his prayers.

CHAPTER IX

POOR Hugo had been cruelly and shamelessly deceived, the injury done to him rankled in his mind, the loss he had suffered and the unbearable sense of disappointment weighed upon his heart and, moreover, his present plight in the open country-side was desperate in the extreme, but he put up with it all, put up with it patiently and uncomplainingly and trudged along in the snow for forty *versts*, leading the blind horse, behind which his sledge dragged along empty. And how did he propose to give vent to his feelings and what did he intend to do with the horse? The horse vanished and he told no one what he had done with it (he must have sold it to the Tartars in Ishima). He continued to pay his usual visits to Dmitry Yerofeyich, on whom all of us used to call, without showing the slightest change in his attitude to the man who had cheated him. Dmitry Yerofeyich would not for a long time receive him, but at last they did meet and Pectoralis never mentioned the horse.

In the end Dmitry Yerofeyich could hold out no longer and he broached the subject himself.

"I say, my dear chap, I always forget to ask you how that horse of yours is getting on."

"Thank you," Pectoralis said, "she's getting on very nicely."

"Well, of course, I expected as much, for she's a splendid animal, but I'm rather curious to know how she behaves between shafts."

"She behaves beautifully, thank you."

"Ah, that's fine! You know, I knew she'd make an excellent horse between shafts. But you don't seem to have been driving her to-day, have you?"

"No, sir. You see, I'm taking very good care of her."

"That's right, my dear chap, take good care of her, she deserves to be taken good care of. A wonderful mare! It would be a mortal sin not to take good care of her."

And he would tell his servants that Hugo Karlovich was very satisfied with "our" Okryssa, while himself, however, he could not help thinking, "What's the matter with that German? Good Lord, such a thing has never happened to me before: I cheated the man shamelessly and he doesn't even call me names or complain to people about me!"

This unnatural behaviour of Pectoralis began to prey on Dmitry Yerofeyich's mind. He tried to figure out what it could mean, but he just couldn't find any explanation for it. He himself began to tell everybody how he had cheated the German and he would complain bitterly, explaining how deeply hurt he was that Pectoralis did not abuse him. But Hugo was game to the last and, learning what Dmitry Yerofeyich was saying about him, merely shrugged his shoulders and muttered:

"The man has no guts."

Now Dmitry Yerofeyich was undoubtedly a rogue, but he was also a coward at heart as well as superstitious and pious; it therefore occurred to him that Pectoralis was hatching some deep plot against him and, to put an end to all his worries, he one day sent the German a wonderful horse worth about three hundred roubles and asked Pectoralis to accept it with his compliments and to forgive him. Pectoralis reddened, but absolutely refused to accept the horse. He ordered it to be taken back and, by way of an answer, wrote:

"I am ashamed of you. You don't seem to have any will at all."

And presently this man who had performed so many amazing experiments with his iron will, suddenly came very near to the realisation of his long-cherished dream: the new year brought him another rise in salary which, together with his savings, put him in possession of a sum which even exceeded his wished-for three thousand *thalers*.

Pectoralis thanked his employers and immediately set about making all the necessary preparations for a trip to Germany whence he promised to return in about a month's time with his bride.

His preparations didn't take long, and off he went, leaving us in suspense until he returned with his wife who, according to our anticipations, should be something quite extraordinary.

But in what way extraordinary?

"She'll be an awful sell, gentlemen," Dmitry Yerofeyich affirmed stolidly.

CHAPTER X

We were not left long without news from Pectoralis: about a month after his departure he wrote to tell me that he had been joined in holy matrimony with Klara Pavlovna (he referred to his wife in the Russian fashion), and after another month he got back home to us with his wife whom we, to be quite frank about it, were expecting rather impatiently. We were all dying to see her and for that reason we studied all her good and bad points with rather immodest curiosity.

In our colony where everybody was well acquainted with the prodigious and not so prodigious feats performed by Pectoralis, the opinion generally prevailed that his marriage ought also to turn out to be a kind of nine days' wonder.

It actually turned out to be one, as we shall see later, but at first we didn't know what to make of it.

Klara Pavlovna was a typical German woman, large and to all appearances healthy, though her face was rather unnaturally red, and she possessed one remarkable feature: the whole of the left side of her body was much more massively built than the right side. It was particularly noticeable about her somewhat swollen left cheek, which seemed to be affected by some chronic gumboil, and about her extremities. Both her left hand and her left foot were considerably larger than the right ones.

Hugo himself drew our attention to that extraordinary phenomenon and was apparently very pleased about it.

"Look," he said, "this hand is the larger and that one the smaller. That doesn't often happen, does it?"

When I beheld this strange freak of nature for the first time, I was rather sorry for poor Hugo, thinking that instead of having to buy one pair of shoes and gloves for his wife, he would have to buy two pairs; but it seemed I pitied him a little too soon, for *Madame* Pectoralis managed the whole business differently. She bought both her shoes and gloves of the larger size and consequently one of her shoes fitted her perfectly, while the other always fell off her foot, and the same thing applied to her gloves.

None of us took to the lady who, to tell the truth, hardly deserved to be called a lady, for she was exceedingly coarse and common, and many of us could not help wondering what exactly Pectoralis could have seen in that vulgar German woman and whether it had been really worth while carrying out all those vows he had made to lead her to the altar. And to think that he had had to go on such a long journey to Germany to fetch her! We felt like singing to him a couplet from the well-known song:

Where the devil didst thou roam?
We'd have married thee at home.

Klara's virtues, it was only to be supposed, were well hidden from the eye of a stranger and might very well have lain in her remarkable will. We, naturally, asked Hugo about it.

"Has Klara Pavlovna a firm will?"

"Oh," he replied without a moment's hesitation, "a devilishly firm one!"

Klara Pavlovna did not at all fit into the society of our English ladies, some of whom were very clever and highly educated females. She herself as well as her husband were quite aware of it, but Pectoralis in particular was not at all upset about it and, generally, did not care a fig what impression his wife made on us. Like a real German, he considered that his wife was entirely his own affair and as it was he who had to keep her, his employers had to put up with her, so that the discordant note she introduced in her environment did not worry him in the least. She had that which he wanted most: an iron will which, combined with his own iron will, was certain to produce some miracle in his offspring—and that was quite enough for him!

But what did surprise us a little was that so far none of us observed any manifestation of those combined wills. Klara Pavlovna lived just like any other German woman: she cooked soup for her husband, fried him *klops*, knitted and darned his socks and in her husband's absence (Pectoralis had at the time to be away on business for long periods) she spent all her time with the German mechanic Offenberg, a stupid, wooden-faced German from Sarepta.

There isn't much I need tell you about Offenberg: he was the type of youth whom, I think, all actors who play the part of the workman seduced by his mistress in the play "The Miller's Wife of Marly" might do well to copy. We all regarded him rather as a fool, although he did seem to possess a certain streak in his character, something calculating and rather villainous, which is typical of all those apparent simpletons one meets in the Jesuit houses in the *Rűe de Serves* and similar places.

Offenberg was taken on as Pectoralis's assistant not so much as a mechanic as an interpreter whose duty it was to convey Hugo's orders to the workmen, but even in that capacity he wasn't altogether satisfactory and was very often the cause of a lot of quite unnecessary confusion. Pectoralis, however, put up with him and found him even useful after he had learnt to speak Russian himself. More than that: for some reason Hugo got very attached to the fool of a mechanic and spent all his leisure time with Offenberg, shared the same quarters with him and slept in the same room with him until the arrival of his wife, played chess with him, went out shooting with him and kept a fatherly eye on his morals, claiming that the lad's morals had been specially entrusted to his care by Offenberg's parents and by the heads of the Sarepta Moravian brothers. Altogether Pectoralis and Offenberg seemed to be great pals and it was not very often that one found them out of each other's company. Now of course all that had changed, for Pectoralis had to be frequently away on business, but that did not in the least imperil Offenberg's morals, over which Klara Pavlovna in the absence of her husband kept constant watch. Thus both of them proved very useful to each other, for Offenberg kept Klara amused, while she shielded him from all the temptations and pitfalls to which youth is exposed. And one must admit that Pectoralis had managed it all very cleverly, but the devil must have got very envious of this state of affairs and he made Offenberg commit a piece of folly which, thanks to the frankness and originality of our wonderful Hugo, got rather unnecessary publicity and turned the whole place upside down.

According to our ladies, Hugo alone was to blame for the episode which I am about to relate to you; but have you ever heard of any lady blaming anybody else but the husband for any discord that arises in a family? Now you'd better listen carefully and judge for yourselves without being in any way biased by the ladies.

CHAPTER XI

A YEAR had passed since Pectoralis's marriage, then another and, finally, a third. A sixth year might have passed without any particular change, and an eighth and even a tenth, if that third year had not turned out to be exceedingly profitable to Pectoralis from the financial point of view. It was just that piece of great good fortune that was responsible for the great misfortune about which you are going to hear now.

I believe I have told you already that Pectoralis was a real expert at his job and, being extremely efficient and pertinacious by nature, as a result, no doubt, of his iron will, he performed all he undertook with the utmost expedition and reliability and, one need hardly say, very conscientiously. That gave him such an excellent reputation in our district that he was soon besieged with requests to put one machine right here, to set up another there and to repair a third somewhere else. The principals of our firm did not object to his taking on all those various outside jobs and he was always successful in whatever he undertook to do and his earnings were quite considerable. In fact, his capital had grown so greatly that he was beginning to wonder whether it wouldn't pay him to hand in his resignation to his Doberan employers and to start his own machine-shop in the centre of our industrial district in the town of R. It was an ambition that was obvious and natural to any man, for who does not want to give up his position as mere employee of a firm and become the independent owner of a business of his own? But it seemed that Hugo Karlovich had his own strong reasons for a step of that kind, for to him a business of his own was inextricably bound up with an enlargement of his personal rights. I'm afraid you may not quite understand what I mean by that, but I hope you won't mind if I keep the explanation of it a secret for a little while.

I can't remember now how much money Pectoralis thought would be sufficient to enable him to start his machine-shop, but I believe it was somewhere between fifteen and twenty thousand, and as soon as he got the last penny of the required sum he put a full stop to one period of his life and announced the beginning of another.

This new period of his life came into being in three different stages, the first of which began with his announcement that he was about to resign from his present job and open up a factory of his own in town. The second began with the opening of his factory, for which he had first, however, to find a proper site, which, needless to say, had to be both cheap and suitable for his purpose. There weren't many such sites to be had in a small town and of those which were available only one fully corresponded to Pectoralis's demands: he therefore made up his mind to acquire that site by hook or by crook.

It was, as a matter of fact, a splendid site of the right depth, one side of which converged on the market-place and the other on the river. There were furthermore large stone buildings erected on it which could at a small cost be converted into workshops. Unfortunately, half of the site had been many years ago taken on a very long lease by a certain small manufacturer by the name of Safronov, who actually owned a little foundry of his own. Pectoralis knew about that foundry and he had also made the personal acquaintance of Safronov whom he had great hopes of inducing to sell out his business. Now it was true that Safronov himself did not encourage any such hopes and was even heard to declare most definitely that he would never give up his place; but Pectoralis had devised a scheme against which, he was sure, Safronov could not possibly do anything. And so, relying on that scheme of his, he bought the freehold of the site and one fine day he returned to us, to his old home that is, with the deed of purchase and in a most happy frame of mind. Indeed, so happy was he that he permitted himself to depart from his usually reserved mode of behaviour and he embraced his dear wife in the presence of us all, kissed the principals of our firm, took hold of Offenberg's ear and gave it a mighty tweak and then announced that he had got his new establishment in the town, that he was deeply grateful to us for the hospitality we had offered him for so many years and that he would soon depart for good to R. to start his business.

It seemed to me that Klara Pavlovna went rather white in the face at that announcement and that Offenberg, too, was a bit upset by it, and indeed Hugo himself did not fail to notice it and, laughing heartily, said:

"Aha, you didn't expect it, my poor chap, did you ?"

And with those words he pulled the wooden-faced Moravian brother towards him, patted him on the shoulder and said:

"Never mind, Offenberg, my dear boy, don't look so upset about it, for I have thought of you, too! I shan't leave you, never you fear. I'll find you a job at my factory, but now off to town with you, my lad. Bring the Champagne and everything else I bought there, and here's the list of my purchases."

The list contained every possible delicacy that Pectoralis had bought and left in town, including, wines, all sorts of refreshments, etc.

Pectoralis evidently wanted to throw a party in our honour and, to be sure, next day when all the groceries had safely arrived from town, he went round inviting one and all to his place in the evening for a great spread on the occasion of his marriage.

At first I thought that I must have misheard him, so I said to him:

"You are giving the party on the occasion of your departure and in celebration of your new start in life as an independent industrialist, aren't you ?"

"Oh, no," he said, "I intend to give another party in town to celebrate that once my new business begins to thrive, but now I'm giving a party in honour of my marriage to-day."

"You're going to get married to-day ?"

"Yes, yes, yes! . . . To-day Klara Pavlovna and myself . . . are going to get married."

"What are you talking about, old man ?"

"I know what I am talking about. I'm telling you I'm going to get married."

"Get married ? But you've been married these three years already, haven't you ?"

"Yes, yes, of course, but you don't expect me to go on as I did during the last three years do you ? I admit it could have gone on for another thirty years if I had not got the money to launch out on my own but now . . . no, sir! Klara Pavlovna, you can be quite sure, will become my wife to-night. Don't you understand what I'm talking about?"

"I'm afraid, old man, I . . . I don't."

"Well, it's really quite simple. You see, I had to agree with dear Klara that when I got my three thousand *thalers*, we should have our wedding, just a wedding, you understand, and nothing else, but when I became my own boss, we'd really get married. Do you follow me now?"

"Dear me," said I, "I'm really beginning to be afraid for you now that I realise that for the past three years you . . . you haven't been married!"

"Of course I haven't been married! Didn't I just tell you that if I had not got a business of my own I shouldn't have been married for another thirty years?"

"You are a remarkable man!"

"Yes, aren't I? Of course I realise that I'm a remarkable man! You see, I have an iron will! Didn't you understand what I meant when I told you a long time ago that when I got my three thousand *thalers* I shouldn't be on the top of the world, but very near it?"

"No," I said, "I certainly didn't understand what you meant then."

"But now you understand, don't you?"

"Yes, I understand now."

"Oh, I knew you weren't a fool old man. And what do you really think of me now? I'm my own boss and I can afford a family of my own and I certainly am determined to have all I want."

"Bravo," I said, "you're a fine fellow and no mistake. A fine fellow, damn you!"

And during the whole day until the evening I just couldn't help feeling excited by the amazing piece of information imparted to me by Pectoralis. "Confound him," I thought, "what a blasted German, eh? Why, he puts our own Chichikov to shame!"

And as Heine seemed to have been obsessed by his dream of the Prussian eagle grasping the whole of Germany in its claws, so I simply could not get out of my mind the German who was to become the husband of his wife after three years of married life. And indeed what hardships couldn't such a man be expected to undergo and what couldn't he achieve after that?

This question kept on recurring to me all during the feast which went on for a very long time and was worthy of the King of Prussia himself. Both the Russians and the Englishmen and the Germans got dead drunk and kept on embracing and kissing each other and everybody was throwing out broad hints to Pectoralis to the effect that the prolongation of the party was robbing him of his long-wished-for moments of bliss, but Hugo remained adamant: he, too, was as drunk as a lord, but he kept on saying:

"I'm not in a hurry, I'm never in a hurry and I always get there in time.

So please, please keep your places and help yourselves to more drinks, for, remember, I have an iron will."

Poor chap, in those moments he didn't even suspect how much he'd need that iron will of his and what awful trials were in store for him.

CHAPTER XII

NEXT day I overslept a good half hour thanks to the carousal of the night before and even when I woke I found it hard to get up in spite of the annoying insistence of my servant who had wakened me. It was only the importance of the business he had told me about and which I couldn't at first grasp that forced me to make the necessary exertion and get out of bed.

"What is it all about ?" I kept on asking, sitting up in bed and trying hard to keep my eyes open.

It was all about Hugo Karlovich, as though the rowdy party given by him had not been enough. It seemed that about an hour after the departure of his last guest, at the break of the greyish day, Pectoralis had appeared on the front steps of his cottage, let out a long-drawn whistle and said:

"That's the limit!"

After a few minutes he repeated his oracular saying in a louder voice and then again a few times more, every time in a louder and still louder voice:

"That's the limit! That's the limit!"

One of the night-watchmen came up to him and said:

"What's the matter, sir ?"

"Send me that limit!" said Hugo rather enigmatically.

The night-watchman looked at the German and said:

"You'd better go back to bed, sir." And then, as Hugo repeated his request, he added, "Is anything wrong, sir ?"

"You're a blasted fool," replied Hugo. "Fetch me the limit at once! Go to that cottage, there . . . where the locksmiths live, wake him and tell him to come here immediately!"

"Drat those drunken infidels!" thought the night-watchman and went to wake up Offenberg. "He's a German," he said to himself, "and he ought to be able to find out what that other German wants."

Offenberg had also taken a drop too much at the party and it was with a great effort that he roused himself, but he got up, dressed himself and went to see what Pectoralis wanted. Hugo had been standing on the steps all that time, and, on seeing Offenberg, he gave a violent start and again shouted:

"That's the limit!"

"What do you want ?" asked Offenberg.

"It's the bally limit," said Pectoralis, "for what I want I can't have and that's the limit!" And changing his tone, he said sharply, "Follow me!"

He then shut himself up with Offenberg in his office and since then they had been fighting with each other.

I was just too dumbfounded for words, but my valet insisted that he was telling me the truth and he added that Pectoralis and Offenberg were fighting in good earnest. They had locked themselves in so that it was impossible to find out what was actually happening, but there could be no doubt from the noise they were making that a battle royal was taking place in that office and above the noise of battle one could hear that Mrs. Pectoralis was sobbing bitterly.

"You ought to go there at once, sir," my servant said, "for all the gentlemen have been there for some time already. They are afraid a murder might be committed, but they can't do anything about it, for they can't get into the room."

I at once rushed to Pectoralis's cottage and I found that indeed all our company was gathered there, crowded round the front door, which, as I said, was locked on the inside. Something unusual was certainly taking place behind that door: there was a terrific row going on in there and we could hear how one of the combatants was administering heavy blows to the other and then dragging his body about on the floor. He'd hit out a few times, then begin dragging the body, then fling it to the floor, then start punching it again, then there would be an interval of dead silence during which we could hear the suppressed crying of a woman, and, finally, it would start all over again.

"I say," I shouted, "haven't you had enough of it, gentlemen? Open the door!"

"Don't answer!" Pectoralis's voice was heard, followed by a resumption of the fighting.

"Stop it, stop it, Hugo Karlovich!" we all shouted in chorus. "Stop it or we'll break the door in!"

Our threat apparently worked: the fighting went on for another minute and then suddenly stopped and immediately the door was unlocked and out rushed Offenberg, quite obviously aided in his precipitous flight by some extraneous force.

"What's the matter, Offenberg?" we all shouted in one voice, rushing up to him, but he didn't say a word, but ran off as fast as his legs would carry him.

"My dear Hugo Karlovich," I said, "what did you beat him black and blue for?"

"He knows," replied Pectoralis, who bore as many scars of the battle as Offenberg.

"Whatever he did to you, I don't think you ought to . . . you ought to have done that."

"Why shouldn't I?"

"But why beat up a man so mercilessly?"

"Why not? He beat me up, too. We conducted a Russian war on equal terms."

"So you call it a Russian war, do you?"

"Yes, of course. That was the condition I made: fight a Russian war and don't shout."

"Dear me," I said, "whoever heard of a Russian war without shouting? I'm afraid, old man, this is all your own invention and has nothing to do with anything Russian."

"Bash his face in!"

"Well, what about bashing his face in? It isn't only Russians who fight that way, is it? And furthermore what did you want to fall foul of each other like that for?"

"What for? He knows that," replied Pectoralis, and with these enigmatic words he summed up the whole tragic essence of his situation which, apparently, had been rather an unpleasant shock to the poor fellow.

Soon after that Russian war between two Germans, Pectoralis left for his new place in the town and, taking leave of me, he said:

"Do you know, old man, I've been cruelly deceived."

I was silent, for I guessed of course what he was referring to, but Pectoralis bent over to my ear and whispered:

"I'm afraid dear Klara hasn't got the iron will I had expected of her and she didn't look after Offenberg at all as she ought to have done."

When he left, he took his wife with him of course, but he did not take Offenberg. The poor lad stayed with us until he had recovered from the injuries he had received during the Russian war, but he uttered not a word of complaint against Pectoralis, merely remarking that he couldn't for the life of him understand what that war was all about.

"He called to me," he said, "and shouted, 'That's the limit!' and then, 'Come on,' he said, 'let's fight a Russian war and if you won't hit me, I'll hit you all the same.' Well, I put up with his blows for some time and then I started hitting back."

"But what did he mean by 'that's the limit'?"

"I don't know, sir. That's all he would say and I'm afraid I don't know anything about it."

"But that *is* rather the limit, don't you think?"

"I daresay it is the limit, sir, and it was rather painful, too."

"But are you quite sure you haven't been making up to Mrs. Pectoralis?"

"No, sir. I certainly haven't been making up to her."

"And you're as innocent as a babe?"

"I am, sir."

So there the matter rested and it was a bit doubtful to what extent this Joseph could be considered the guilty party, but there could be no doubt whatever that Pectoralis had received a very cruel blow and that his iron will was somewhat shaken; and although it hardly becomes one to rejoice at the misfortunes of others and indeed it is a sin to do so, I must nevertheless confess quite frankly to you that I could not help—shall I say ?—deriving a certain satisfaction from the fact that my conceited German friend had suffered such a shocking blow to his high opinion of himself by the discovery that his Klara's will was so disappointingly weak.

This disappointment may have dented his iron will a little, but it did not shatter it and when the time came for it to be shivered, it happened in a most tragi-comic way and as a result of quite different circumstances after Pectoralis had found himself involved in another Russian war, but this time with a Russian.

CHAPTER XIII

PECTORALIS had enough will power to recover from the shock he had suffered from the discovery of insufficient will power in his better half. Naturally it was not so easy for him to swallow his pride, if only for the reason that he had now to give up one of his most cherished dreams to see the fruit of the union of two people distinguished by their iron will; but, being a man of great strength of mind, he suppressed his pain and threw himself wholly into his business.

He was making arrangements for starting his machine-shop and he did his best not to injure his reputation as a man who was not the slave of circumstance and who always achieved what he set out to do.

I have already told you that Pectoralis had acquired the freehold of a site the rear part of which was occupied by the foundryman Safronov, who had a long lease on his premises and steadfastly refused to sell out his business and vacate his house.

Thriftless, lazy and slow-witted, Safronov never budged from the position he had taken up and vowed that he would not give up his lease until the day when he was bound to surrender it and the courts, recognising that he had a legal right to do as he pleased, could do nothing about it.

But with his wretched workmen and no less wretched business he interfered and could not help interfering with Pectoralis's orderly and well-conducted business, for, among other things, he had to use the German's front yard as a way of communication with the outside world. And that was not by any means all. There was something even more intolerable in that situation: for Safronov, feeling himself in the right, began to talk big and show off and say to everybody he met:

"I don't give a damn for that blasted German. I love my country, I am a patriot and I shan't budge. If he wants to take an action against me in the courts, I have a friend, a former clerk at a court, Zheega his name is, and he'll knock him into a cocked hat."

That, of course, Pectoralis could not put up with, for his vanity was badly hurt by such talk and he decided to get rid of Safronov in his own way, in a way that was a hundred per cent certain of coming off—and to achieve his purpose he spread out his nets so cleverly that there could be little doubt that the Russian numskull would get himself inextricably entangled in them.

Indeed, Pectoralis acted in this matter with such great foresight that, in spite of his undoubted legal rights, Safronov was entirely at his mercy and he only realised that when the whole thing had been brought to a successful conclusion, or at least so it seemed.

This is how he brought it about.

Pectoralis worked by the sweat of his brow and grew richer and richer, while Safronov was lazy, drank and was bringing inevitable ruin upon himself. With such a competitor on his doorstep, Safronov could not help blundering hopelessly and facing a prospect of utter penury, but he clung obstinately to his back premises and refused to move.

I well remember that poor, timid soul with his typically Russian trait of bearing no malice, of being over-confident and careless.

"What is going to happen to you, Safronov?" people would ask him, pointing out to him that his business was continually shrinking and had indeed been reduced almost to nothing as a result of the inroads made into it by Pectoralis. "Look what your carelessness has done for you! Your competitor is taking all your customers away from you right under your nose."

"What are you so concerned about, gentlemen?" the thriftless Safronov would reply. "What are you trying to frighten me with that German for? I assure you, I have nothing to fear, and, besides, a German isn't a dog, is he? A German, too, has to eat. As for me, gentlemen, I shall manage somehow!"

"But he's taking all your work away from you!"

"Well, what can I do about it? Maybe it's right that he should be working for me, but I shan't give up my home! No, sir, I shan't give up my home!"

"But why shouldn't you give it up? He'll pay you a good premium for your premises."

"No, sir. I shan't go. And anyway where could I go even if I wanted to? Everything I have in the world is there and, besides, there are the women and all sorts of odds and ends, pots and pans, tubs and vats, cupboards and shelves, not to mention crockery—how do you expect me to move all that ?"

"Don't talk so daft, Safronov! You know perfectly well that it wouldn't take you long to move all that."

"I don't know anything of the sort. It may not take so long to move it all, but you have to consider, gentlemen, that all our things are so old and fragile: they're all right so long as you don't touch them, but try to move them and the whole lot will fall to pieces."

"Why not buy new things then ?"

"New things ? But why should I buy new ones, if the old ones can still be used ? Just waste money ? Besides, one has to take care of one's old things, for he who takes care of his things is taken care of by the Lord. Anyway, my friend Zheega, the old lawyer's clerk, you know, has told me quite definitely not to move. 'Don't move,' he said to me. 'I'm giving you this advice after careful consideration. We shall get the better of that German,' said he, 'by just sitting tight and refusing to budge.' "

"Well," he would be warned, "you'd better look out, Safronov! That Zheega of yours is probably leading you up the garden path."

"Goodness gracious, why should he want to lead me up the garden path ? If he'd said it to me when he was sober, he might, in his weakness, have told me a lie, but I'm telling you he was drunk when he gave me his advice: 'Give praise to the Lord,' he said, 'and shout Hosanna in the Highest, for these things are not done unto thee for thy undoing, but for thy greater glory and well-being!' "

These boastful speeches of Safronov naturally came to the ears of Pectoralis and vexed him exceedingly until, at long last, his patience gave out completely and made him take rather drastic action.

"Very well," Pectoralis said, "if he wants to set his will against mine, then it's high time I showed him that he can't get the better of me by just sitting tight. I've had enough of it," Hugo Karlovich exclaimed, "watch me finish him off, gentlemen!"

"He's going to finish you off," Safronov was duly informed.

"Is he really ? Well, God's in His heaven and all's right with the world. Zheega told me, 'Wait, he'll find you a hard nut to crack!' "

"Will he, though ?"

"Why, no doubt about it, gentlemen, he certainly will. Zheega said quite rightly, 'We are Russians,' he said, 'our heads are bony, though our rumps may be fleshy: we're not like a German sausage which can be eaten all of a piece—something is sure to be left over from us.' "

This opinion met with general applause.

But the very next day after this conversation Mrs. Safronova woke up her husband and said:

"Get up quickly, you good for nothing loafer, and see what that German has done to us!"

"Don't nag, woman," Mr. Safronov replied. "I told you I'm much too bony for any pig to eat me all up."

"Well, you'd better go and have a look for yourself: he's blocked up our gates and our wicket-gate. I got up to fetch some water from the river for the *samovar*, but the gates are nailed up and we can't leave our house at all now, for they refuse to open them. They told me Hugo Karlovich had ordered them not to—he has nailed them up for good!"

"Well," said Mr. Safronov, "I wonder what he will be thinking of next," and he went outside to examine the fence. He tried to open the wicket-gate and the big gates and, sure enough, they would not open. He started knocking, but there was no reply. The man of flesh and bone, it seems, had been locked up in his own backyard as in a box. So Vassily Safronov climbed on the top of the shed, looked over the fence and saw that both the wicket-gate and the big gates had been nailed up by planks from the other side, from the side of Hugo Karlovich's backyard, that is. Mr. Safronov immediately raised the alarm, called for anybody he could think of in Pectoralis's house, but got no reply at all. Not a man came to his rescue, but after a time Hugo Karlovich himself appeared in the yard with his vile German cigar and he said:

"Well, sir, what are you going to do now?"

Mr. Safronov then got the wind up properly.

"Dear Mr. Pectoralis," he said to Hugo Karlovich from the roof of the shed, "do you realise what you're doing? You can't do such a thing to me. I have a lease," he said, "and what you've done is against the law."

"Well, well," said Pectoralis, "and I, you know, am thinking of putting up another fence to give you even greater legal protection."

So they were standing there, one on the roof and the other in the yard, arguing with one another.

"But," said Mr. Safronov, "how do you expect me to go on living like that? Don't you realise that I can't leave my house now?"

"Of course I realise that, my dear man: that's exactly why I did it. I want to prevent you from leaving your own house."

"But what am I to do? Why, even a cricket must have his chink and how am I to manage without one?"

"Well, think it over and discuss it with that lawyer friend of yours. But I must warn you: I have a right to stop up all your holes, for your lease contains no clause against that."

"Oh dear," exclaimed Mr. Safronov, "are you sure?"

"Positive! So there you are, my dear sir, that's the position!"

"But," objected Mr. Safronov, "that's impossible!"

"Don't argue, my dear man. Get off your roof and have a look at the lease yourself."

"All right," said poor Mr. Safronov and got off the roof.

He went back to his house, took out the lease he had got from the former owner of the property, put on his glasses and began to read it. Well, he read it through from beginning to end and, lo and behold, Pectoralis was quite right, his position was a parlous one and no mistake; for the lease said nothing about such a situation where, if the freehold of the site had been sold to another person, that person had no right to block up all the entrances and exits of the leaseholder of the back property and thus deprive him of all egress therefrom. But who but a German would ever have thought of it?

"Oh, may the Lord destroy thee as thou hast destroyed me," said Mr. Safronov and went out and started knocking at the fence, calling upon his other next door neighbour.

"Dear Mrs. N.," he said to her, "would you mind very much if I put up a ladder against your fence so that I can walk through your yard into the street?" And he told her what had happened. "That's what that cold-hearted German has done to me," he said. "He has locked me up in my house, caught my legs in a deadly noose so that I can't even run for advice to my lawyer. Until the courts decide whether he has a right to do this to me or not, let me use your yard and save me and my little ones from death, for otherwise we shall all surely perish of hunger and thirst. Give me permission to climb over the fence until I get the law on that bandit."

The neighbour, a small shopkeeper, took pity on him and gladly permitted him to use her yard as an exit to the world outside.

"Why," she said, "dear Mr. Safronov, of course I shan't keep you off my yard. You're a good man, you are, so put up your ladder on your side of the fence by all means, for it won't cost me anything, will it? And I'll tell you what I'll do to help you: I shall put up a ladder on my side of the fence and then you'll be able to go on climbing over my fence as much as you like and use my yard as if it was the street itself until you get the law to decide between you and that wicked German. Mark my words, the law won't let him carry on like that, German though he is."

"It won't, my dear Mrs. N., I'm sure it won't."

"But in the meantime, dear Mr. Safronov, go and see Zheega immediately! He's sure to put everything right."

"So he will. I'll go to him at once."

"Hurry, dear Mr. Safronov, there's not a minute to lose. He's a cunning devil, Zheega is, up to all sorts of tricks and he's sure to help you, if not with one thing, then with another, or again with something else. In the meantime I'll let you use my fence and give you a chance, poor dear, to do your best."

Safronov felt much better: a chink was opened up for him!

So they put up one ladder on one side of the fence and another ladder on the other and the Safronovs obtained a laborious, but at least some sort of way of communicating with the outside world. Mrs. Safronov went to fetch a pail of water from the river and Mr. Safronov scurried off to the former clerk of the court, Zheega, who had many years ago drawn up the lease for him and, crying bitterly, told the old lawyer about the grievous injury Pectoralis had done to him.

"You told me I should get the best of it in my feud with the German and that's what he does to me now and it's all your fault and because of your rotten advice my wife and my little ones," said he, "will perish of hunger. That's the kind of glory and well-being you've brought upon me."

But the former clerk of the court just smiled.

"What a fool you are, Vassily Safronov, my dear chap, and what a coward! An unexpected piece of good fortune comes your way and you get in a dither because of it."

"Oh dear, oh dear," said Safronov, "what kind of good fortune is it when my family and I have now to climb over somebody's else fence? I have never asked for that kind of good fortune! And, moreover," he said, "my children are still very small and, God forbid, if I should send one of them on an errand he may get a splinter in his belly or fall off and break a leg and sometimes my wife, according to the law of wedlock, gets big-bellied and I couldn't very well expect her to go on jumping over the fence then, could I? How can we go on living, besieged as we are? Not to mention my work, for now I shan't be able to get any, for I shan't be able to get anything out of my foundry now, not even a harrow, let alone a steam boiler."

But Zheega went on repeating:

"Oh, what a fool you are, Vassily Safronov, what a fool you are!"

"What's the use of calling me a fool? Stop calling me names for a moment, and say something to comfort me for a change."

"What kind of comfort do you want if the Lord has already rewarded you more than your deserts?"

"I don't know what you're talking about," said poor Mr. Safronov.

"That's what I've been saying. You don't know what I'm talking about because you're a fool and such a fool, too, that I'm ashamed to waste my wisdom on such folly by talking to you. But I do reply to your foolish chatter because the good fortune that hath befallen you is so great that my heart rejoiceth at the thought of what a glorious life you'll be living from now onwards. Don't you forget me now, don't get too big for your shoes, don't get too stingy to stand me a drink."

"Are you pulling my leg?"

"Have you lost your wits completely that you don't understand plain language any more? What kind of a leg-pull is that? I'm talking business to you. Why, you're the luckiest man in the world now, if you don't drink yourself to death."

Poor Vassily Safronov couldn't understand a word his lawyer had been telling him, but Zheega did nothing to enlighten him.

"Go home now," he said, "and take the long way over the fence and remember one thing: don't ask the German for any favour and don't make peace with him and the Lord forbid that your neighbour should withdraw her permission for you to climb over her fence and you just carry on as you do now, climbing over the fence, as agreed between you and your neighbour, for there can be no luckier way for you than that."

"Oh dear, oh dear, so I shall have to go on climbing over the fence, shall I?"

"Why, what's wrong with that? Yes, by all means go on climbing and see that you don't do anything to improve your present situation, for one ought not to tamper with such a blessing from heaven. And now go home, dear friend, and send out for a pint of vodka and a little bottle of Kizlyara liqueur for this evening, for I, too, am going to climb over that fence of yours to pay a call on you, and to celebrate your good fortune we shall drink to the health of the German."

"I don't mind your coming to have a drink with me," said Mr. Safronov, "but don't expect me to drink that man's health. I'd rather he came to my funeral dinner and choked himself with a pancake."

And the merry lawyer comforted him and said:

"That, too, may come to pass, my dear chap, indeed everything, everything may happen now! But let us drink to the health of the German just the same, seeing the kind of jolly business he has started, and it may very well be that he will come to your funeral repast and that a pancake will stick in his throat. For as you know the Scriptures say, 'He made a pit and digged it, and is fallen into the ditch which he made.' Or do you think he won't fall into it?"

"Fall into it? What a hope! He's getting mighty strong now."

"'Let not the strong ones rejoice in their strength!' Where was that said? Oh, you men of little faith, how can I live with you and put up with your folly? Take a lesson from me, see how I put my trust in the Lord! Why, I was thrown out of the Civil Service fourteen years ago, but I just go on drinking vodka. At times, it is true, I do weaken and am about to murmur against Him, but something always turns up and I start drinking again and praising Him. Everything in life, my dear friend, hath its ebb and flow, it is you alone who have now been vouchsafed happiness everlasting, yea, even unto the grave, so go now and wait for me and don't forget to gape as wide as you possibly can at the wonderful things we shall now do to that German. One thing, though, you'd better pray for. . . ."

"What's that?"

"That he should outlive you."

But instead of a reply, Mr. Safronov just spat out of sheer vexation of spirit.

"Don't spit," said Zheega, "but do as I tell you: pray! Because it is faith that you want now more than anything else, for the German, poor chap, is in for a lot of trouble!"

CHAPTER XIV

It was in such perplexing riddles that Zheega spoke.

Mr. Safronov walked off to his locked-up home, going the long way and climbing over the fence, and he sent off one of his children the same way to fetch some sustenance for his lawyer, and he waited for him in great distress of mind which he could do nothing to overcome in spite of his lawyer's boastful utterances.

Zheega, for his part, did not let the grass grow under his feet. He rigged himself out in his old russetty civil service uniform, put a cloak over it, covered his bald head with a hat of the same colour as the uniform and went straight to Hugo Karlovich's house where he asked for an interview with the German. Pectoralis had just had his dinner and was picking his teeth with a feather toothpick which he kept in a little bead-work case which he had received as a present from Klara Pavlovna in those far off blissful days when happy Hugo was not yet afraid of her presents and when he still firmly believed in her iron will.

Hearing about the lawyer's visit, Hugo Karlovich who was already beginning to play the big man in his own home would not receive him for a long time, but when the ex-court official sent in a message to say that he had come on important business, he said:

"Show him in."

Zheega entered and began to bow very low to Pectoralis who liked it so much that he said:

"Sit down, my dear sir, take a seat, *bitte*."

But the old lawyer replied:

"God forbid, Hugo Karlovich," he said, "that I should sit down in your presence. I've got a pair of Russian legs, sir, legs of oak, and I don't mind standing before an honourable man like you."

"Aha," thought Pectoralis, "that old lawyer realises all right the kind of important man I am and he knows his place, too," and he said again to Zheega, "No, no, my dear sir, I must insist that you take a seat."

"Really, Hugo Karlovich, I'd rather remain standing before you. We are taught to stand up straight from our childhood and to foreigners in particular we must always be civil."

"Oh, what a funny fellow you are," Pectoralis said jokingly, and he laughed happily and himself got up and forced his visitor to sit down.

All Zheega could do to show his respect was to wriggle forward in the arm-chair and to sit on the very edge of it.

"Now tell me what you want," Pectoralis said. "But if you've come here to ask me to help you because you're poor, then I must warn you that I don't hold with helping the poor, for the poor have only themselves to blame."

The old lawyer covered his mouth with his hand and, looking up in all humility at Pectoralis, replied:

"You're quite right, sir. The poor have only themselves to blame. There are of course some people to whom God Himself does not grant any sustenance, but they, too, have only themselves to blame."

"But why so, my dear sir? Why should such unfortunate ones blame themselves?"

"Because they don't know what they ought to do. We had such a case in our town: a regiment was quartered here, or whatever they call it . . . on horses, you know."

"Cavalry."

"That's it, sir, cavalry. . . . Well, a captain of that regiment one day taught me the whole philosophy of life."

"A captain of cavalry never teaches philosophy."

"That one did, sir. You see, sir, it so happened that he was able to teach me."

"Well, in an exceptional case, of course."

"Yes, it was an exceptional case, sir. You see, they were all drawn up on parade, waiting for their commanding officer. So there they were, sitting on their horses and smoking cigarettes when a poor German went up to them and said, '*Seien Sie so gut*,' and so on, telling them a long story about how poor and destitute he was. The captain said, 'Are you a German?' and he replied, 'Yes, I am a German.' So the captain said, 'There's no need for you to go begging, just join our regiment and you'll be a general in no time, like the general we're expecting,' and he refused to give him anything."

"So he gave him nothing, eh?"

"Not a thing, sir, and that poor German, sir, really joined the regiment and I'm told on good authority, sir, that he became a general and cashiered that captain from the army."

"A fine fellow!"

"That's right, sir. He was a fine fellow, I quite agree, and that's why I'm always very respectful when I'm talking to a German, for one never knows what he mightn't become."

"What a nice fellow," Pectoralis thought, "what an exceptionally nice fellow this lawyer is!" And aloud he said:

"Your story is a very excellent story, but what is the business you want to see me about?"

"It's about your business, sir."

"My business?"

"Yes, sir."

"But I don't think I have any action pending in the courts."

"You will have, sir."

"Not with Safronov by any chance?"

"Yes, sir, with Safronov."

"But he hasn't a leg to stand on. All his lease says is that there should be a fence between his property and mine and there is a fence between them."

"Yes, sir, there certainly is a fence between them."

"His lease says nothing about the gates."

"No, sir. Not a word about the gates, but there's going to be an action in the courts all the same, sir. He came to me and said: 'I'm going to take legal action.' "

"Let him."

"That's exactly what I said to him, sir. 'Take legal action,' I said, 'but remember your lease says nothing about the gates.'"

"Quite right, too."

"Yes, sir, but he said . . . You'll forgive me, sir, if I tell you what he said, won't you?"

"Why, of course, I'll forgive you."

"He said, 'Even if I lose all I now possess. . . .' "

"But he has lost it already, his work isn't of any use and his boilers whistle."

"Yes, sir, they whistle all right."

"He's finished now, his job's gone."

"Yes, sir, he's finished all right and his job's gone, too. Well, so I said to him, 'Your business has gone bust,' I said, 'nobody can do anything for you any more, you can't take anything through or carry anything out of your gates.' But he said, 'I'd rather be dead than give in an inch to that *verfluchter* German.'"

Pectoralis wrinkled his forehead and got very red in the face.

"Did he say that?"

"Would I tell you a lie, sir? That's what he said, *verfluchter* . . . you're a *verfluchter* so and so and he said it in the presence of many witnesses, in fact, almost in front of all the merchants of our town, for our talk took place at an inn, in the part reserved for the exclusive use of gentlemen, and they were all having tea at the time."

"What a scoundrel!"

"Yes, sir, he's a scoundrel all right. Mind you, sir, I wanted to stop him. 'Vassily Safronov, my dear chap,' I said, 'you must not speak so disrespectfully of the German nation,' I said, 'for many of them occupy important positions in our country.' But he then lost his temper completely, sir, and carried on in such a disgraceful way that the gentlemen forgot all about their tea and just listened to him and, I'm afraid, sir, not without approval!"

"But what exactly did he say?"

" 'Oh, that,' he said, 'is quite new. I,' he said, 'am an upholder of our old ways and in the olden times,' said he, 'for so it is written in the books of Czar Alexey Mikhailovich, when Germans came to live in Moscow, they were told to live in a special quarter and not all over the place and to register themselves in a special merchants' and tradesmen's guild, known as the Black Hundred.' "

"Hm. . . . Was there such a law?"

"According to some books, sir, there was."

"It wasn't a very good law, was it?"

"That's what I said, sir. That was a rotten law, I said, and, besides, why talk of what happened so many years ago and in the presence of so many people and in a public place, like a saloon for gentlemen in an inn, where people talk of all sorts of things and where they are particularly fond of talking politics?"

"The rascal!"

"Well, of course, sir, you could hardly call him an honest man, that's what I told him."

"You told him that?"

"Yes, sir, I did tell him that, but, I'm afraid, it all ended up in a frightful row. We started abusing each other and . . . well . . . it went even further. . . ."

"You mean you fought a Russian war?"

"Yes, sir. I'm afraid it all ended up in a Russian war."

"And did you give him a good thrashing?"

"Oh, yes, sir. I gave him a thrashing and he gave me a thrashing, too, just according to all the rules of Russian warfare. But, of course, he was greatly handicapped in trying to get the better of me, for as you see, sir, I've lost most of my hair from too much study and the few hairs you can still see on my crown I really get from my loans department, I mean, I comb it up from my reserves at the back of my head, while he's a shaggy brute, has a beautiful head of hair on him. . . ."

"Yes, a shaggy devil."

"Yes, sir. So, of course, sir, as soon as I saw that peace was about to be broken and war about to be declared, I returned my hair to the loans department and just grabbed him by his mop of hair."

"And did it work?"

"Well, yes, sir. It worked all right, only I'm afraid he gave me a beating, too."

"Oh well, that's all in the game, I suppose."

"It may be, sir, but it hurt all the same."

"Don't worry, my dear fellow, I'll pay you for any medical treatment you may need and here's a rouble, to begin with."

"Thank you, sir. I counted on your kindness, sir, only I'm afraid I did a very silly thing."

"Oh?"

"Yes, sir. You see, after our first encounter, we concluded a short truce, for we were, of course, separated and an argument started between us. I really don't know how I could have been so mad, but I just couldn't help taking your part, sir, and I said all sorts of things about you."

"About me?"

"Yes, sir. I took on a wager about you. Start your action, I said, but you won't change Hugo Karlovich's mind, for he has an iron will, and you won't make him unlock your gates."

"Does he think he'll make me, the donkey?"

"Oh, he's quite convinced of it and, mind you, sir, the others, too, were quite sure of it."

"The others, too?"

"Yes, sir. All of them, absolutely unanimous."

"Oh, well. We shall see, we shall see. . . ."

"How they'll hug themselves if you do give in, sir."

"I give in?"

"Yes, sir."

"But didn't you say yourself that I had an iron will?"

"Why, yes, I did say that, sir, and it was in that belief that I took such a frightful risk. You see, sir, I took on a wager that you would never open those gates and I got so excited that I wagered a hundred roubles. I promised to deposit my bet as soon as possible."

"Well, deposit it, my dear sir, you'll get back two hundred."

"You see, sir, I told them all at the inn that I was going home for the money, but instead I came straight to you, for to tell you the truth, sir, all the money I've got at home is about two roubles and fifty copecks, not a copeck more."

"Hm . . . That's bad. Why haven't you got any money?"

"I'm a hopeless fool, sir, that's why I haven't got any money. What can you expect of a country such as ours, sir, a country where you can't live honestly?"

"Yes, I suppose that's true enough."

"Of course, it's true, sir. So being a man of sterling honesty, I have to eke out a miserable existence."

"Don't let that bother you, my dear sir. I'll give you the hundred roubles."

"Oh, thank you, sir, thank you. That's very handsome of you, sir, and, besides, the money will be safe, for it all depends on you whether I get the money back or not."

"You'll get it back all right. Yes, sir, take my word for it. So when you get the two hundred roubles, you take one hundred for yourself and pay me back the other hundred."

"Why, of course, I shall pay you back, sir."

Pectoralis gave a hundred rouble note to Zheega who, as soon as the front door was shut behind him, laughed so much that it was with great difficulty that he found his way in the darkness to the yard next door and he climbed over the fence to Safronov to enjoy his well-earned drink.

"Rejoice," he said, "you Russian simpleton! I've tied that German up in such a knot that Satan will sooner break his chains than he'll untie it."

"Stop talking in riddles," Safronov besought him.

"I shan't say another word about how we've caught him except that he's been caught in the noose of his pride and that's the most fatal noose there is."

"Not he!"

"Silence, you man of little faith, silence! Don't you know that an angel once went riding on that horse and that he was cast into utter darkness, so how could that German even hope to escape ruin ?"

So they drained their cups and sat down to draw up their plaint, and Safronov himself took it to the court next morning, going the long way over the fence, and although he both believed and disbelieved the old lawyer that "this action will bring you undreamt of felicity," he felt, at any rate, much easier in his mind.

Safronov let the furnace go out, returned all his orders, dismissed all his workmen and waited to see what the issue of his action would be. Zheega alone did not seem to worry at all about the action and he spent all his time in pubs, making merry on the hundred roubles he had obtained by fraud from Pectoralis and boasting in his cups—to the greater joy and temptation of all who heard him and to Hugo Karlovich's still greater injury—how cruelly he had cheated the German.

All this, of course, created such excitement in our town that there was not a man in it who did not wait with bated breath for the hearing of the action brought by Safronov against Pectoralis. And as time passed, Pectoralis went on blowing himself up like the frog who tried to emulate the bull, and Safronov wore all his clothes to a thread in climbing over the fence and, in the end, losing courage, he kept on sending his wife and children to Pectoralis, without telling Zheega about it, imploring him to change his mind about the gates and come to some kind of understanding.

But Hugo was inflexible.

"No," said he, "I shall do no parleying with him. I shall only accept one invitation from him—to eat pancakes at his funeral dinner and, till then, let the whole world know what an iron will means."

CHAPTER XV

AND so in due course Safronov and Pectoralis received their official notices and on the day appointed for the hearing of their action both of them appeared in court.

The court-room was, needless to say, packed, for, as I told you, that ridiculous affair had become known all over the town. There was not a soul who did not know all the particulars about it, not excluding the incident between Safronov's lawyer and Pectoralis, for Zheega himself told everybody with the utmost frankness the whole story of the dishonest trick he had played on the German. And we, Hugo's old comrades-in-arms, and the two principals of our firm also turned up in court to see how Pectoralis would fare and how it would all end.

Pectoralis and Safronov arrived without any barristers to plead their cause. Pectoralis was evidently absolutely certain of the justice of his case and was furthermore convinced that no man could plead his cause better than himself; as for Safronov, he was just unlucky, for his old lawyer who had faithfully promised to appear for him in court, had made such thorough preparations for seeing him through that, on the night before the action was to come up for decision, he fell off the bridge into a ditch, being in a state of blind intoxication at the time, and nearly died the death of "the king of the poets." As a result of that mishap Safronov lost heart completely and sat in court with his head bowed, while Pectoralis held his up high and drew great comfort from his enemy's moral collapse. He was clad from top to toe in the shining armour of his iron will, which was now to be displayed not only before some private individual or, at most, a small family circle, but before the citizens of an entire town. One look at Pectoralis was enough to convince anybody that he, at least, was fully aware of the tremendous importance of that solemn hour, and there could therefore be no doubt at all that he would make full use of it, that he would show himself, present himself to his fellow-citizens as a man of steadfast purpose, a man worthy of general respect and admiration and, as it were, cast his countenance in bronze for the acclamation of future generations. In short, it was, to use a favourite expression of Russian army officers, a "moment" upon which everything depended.

Pectoralis knew that the strange double event of his wedding and marriage had given rise to a multitude of funny stories about him in which his iron will had become the common talk of the populace. All sorts of apocryphal additions were tacked on to the true events of his life, beginning with his two months' journey in winter in an oil-skin cloak and ending with his Russian war with Offenberg and the thoughtless way in which he had fallen a victim to the fraudulent trick of a disreputable lawyer, and those additions were usually embellished by hundreds of the most fantastic details. And, truly, Pectoralis was himself beginning to suspect that fate was playing all sorts of cruel jokes on him and (as it invariably happens with people who have a run of bad luck) he even accused it of depriving him of those qualities which formed the sheet anchor of his character, namely, his business flair, his knowledge and his common sense. Only a short time ago he had been doing up his town residence and he wanted to surprise everybody by the modern comforts of his new home by the installation of a central-heating system with warm air; he must have made some bad miscalculation, however, for while the boiler in his cellar got red hot and was in danger of falling to pieces, the rest of the house was freezing cold. Pectoralis froze himself and he froze his wife, but to conceal from the whole world the true state of affairs he wouldn't admit anybody to his house and at the same time went about boasting how wonderfully warm and snug his house was. But in our town rumours were rife that he had gone mad and was heating his house with wind, and those who were telling the story thought themselves very clever. It was also said that the chariot in which Pectoralis continued to drive about the country-side like "a Mordvin idol," had played a dirty trick on him and fallen to pieces just as he was fording a stream. The armchair—the story went—fell off and his horse bolted home with the two wheels, leaving him stranded in the chair in midstream. He remained sitting there until a police captain happened to drive by and, seeing him, shouted:

"Who's the fool who puts an arm-chair where it doesn't belong?"

The fool, it appeared, was Pectoralis.

The police captain took Pectoralis off the arm-chair and brought him to dry himself in his cold house; the chair was seen later apparently by many people in the stream and the country people, it was said, now referred to that place as "the German's ford." How much truth there was in that story and how much of it was fiction and which was which, it was difficult to say. But there could be no doubt that Pectoralis did have an accident with his chariot, was stranded in the stream and rescued by the police captain who himself told the story. Anyway, the chariot of the "Mordvin idol" had never been seen since.

As misfortunes never come singly, but always in crowds, all that, as I said, just descended in a cloudburst over poor Pectoralis and also simultaneously surrounded him with a kind of aura of a buffoon. That did a lot of harm to his reputation as an enterprising and reliable business man, a reputation which seemed to have gone almost as soon as it had come.

Dear old Russia where great reputations are so easily achieved and even more easily lost was beginning to leave her mark on Pectoralis. Only a short time ago his word in his particular line of business was regarded as law by everybody, but now, after Zheega had cheated him so shamelessly, people had lost confidence even in that. The captain of the rural constabulary who had rescued him from his chariot in the stream, asked him to advise him about a house he was planning to build for himself in the country.

"I'd be glad, my dear fellow," he said to Pectoralis, "if you'd draw up a plan for me according to which the house would have a frontage of sixty-three feet—I'm afraid that's all the site will allow—with six windows and a door in the middle of the balcony."

"You can't have so many windows," said Pectoralis.

"Why can't I?"

"Because the scale won't allow it."

"I'm afraid you must have misunderstood me, old man," the police captain said. "It's a country house I'm talking about."

"Makes no difference," Pectoralis replied, "whether in the country or in town. You can't do it: the scale won't allow it."

"But who cares about the scale in the country?"

"What do you mean? The scale's the same everywhere."

"But, my dear chap, we have no scale in the country. Just draw me six windows and don't worry about the scale."

"Can't be done," Pectoralis persisted. "In fact, it's quite out of the question: the scale won't allow it."

The police captain just looked at him and then whistled.

"I'm sorry for you, old man," he said, "but it seems there's nothing to be done about it: I shall have to ask somebody else to draw me the plan."

And off he went, telling everybody:

"Imagine what a blithering idiot Hugo Karlovich is: I say to him, I want so many windows for my country house, and he says: the scale won't allow it."

"Not really?"

"It's true, I swear to you, that's what the fool told me."

"What a fool!"

"Yes, isn't he, though? I told him: Just think of it, old man, I'm going to build the house in my own village, what kind of scale or map will not allow me to do what I damn well like there? But no, couldn't talk that fool over."

"Well, it's obvious: the man's a born fool."

"Of course he's a fool. Whoever thought of a scale in a country house? He must be a fool."

"Yes, that's true enough, but who's to blame for it, I ask you. Why, we are!"

"Of course we are."

"Why did we have such a high opinion of him?"

"Why indeed?"

In a word, Pectoralis's prestige had suffered an eclipse and if he only knew what such a turn of the tide in the affairs of men meant everywhere and, particularly, in Russia, he wouldn't have embarked on such a perilous enterprise as nailing up Safronov's gates. But Pectoralis did not believe in the turn of tides and he didn't lose courage, which, as we shall presently see, he showed more now than his whole past warranted one to expect. He knew that the chief thing was not to lose courage, for, as Goethe had said, "to lose courage is to lose everything." That was why he appeared in court with Safronov the same strong-minded and determined Pectoralis that I had once met at the cold station of Vassilyov Maydan. It is true, he looked much older now, but there was the same firm expression on his face, the same courage, the same tremendous self-confidence and self-respect.

"Why didn't you get a lawyer?" his acquaintances whispered to him.

"I have brought a lawyer with me," he replied.

"Who is he?"

"My iron will," Pectoralis replied briefly at the very moment when it was no longer possible to talk to him, for the judge had just then entered.

CHAPTER XVI

I DISLIKE the description of court cases so much that I shan't bother you with all the details of what took place during the hearing of Safronov's action, but I shall come to the point at once.

Safronov was stepping from one foot to another as he stood in his long brown frock-coat which had suffered considerably from his journeyings over the fence and related his story very respectfully to the judge, shaking his head good-naturedly and waving his hands about weakly, while Hugo stood facing him, his hands crossed on his chest like a second Napoleon, either keeping silence altogether or giving short replies in a calm and firm voice.

The whole uncomplicated affair became clear beyond any possibility of doubt in a few minutes: Safronov's lease did not mention either the gates or his right of passage through Pectoralis's yard, and from the tone of the judge's voice it became clear that, while he sympathised with Safronov, he could see no possible line of defence for him and was, in fact, quite unable to help him. That part of Safronov's action was lost; but to everybody's surprise the moon turned to us with the side which nobody had seen before. The judge was looking through the documents which dealt with Safronov's losses as a result of Pectoralis's high-handed action. They were not exaggerated in any way: altogether from the day Safronov had been forced to give up his business they were calculated to amount to fifteen roubles a day.

The computation was precise, clear and definite. Safronov could have incurred a loss of that amount, if his business had been conducted properly, but it never had been conducted properly owing to his general carelessness and negligence.

But so far as the court was concerned the matter was quite clear: the daily loss, as claimed by the plaintiff, was entirely feasible and, therefore, proven.

"What have you got to say to that, Mr. Pectoralis?" asked the judge.

Pectoralis shrugged his shoulders, smiled and replied that that wasn't his business.

"But it is because of your action that he is suffering those losses."

"It isn't my business, your Honour," replied Pectoralis.

"And you don't want to settle with plaintiff?"

"No, your Honour, never!"

"Is there any reason why you shouldn't come to some arrangement?"

"Your Honour," replied Pectoralis, "it is quite impossible for me to come to any arrangement with the plaintiff. I am a man of an iron will and everybody knows that once I make up my mind, I stick to my decision and nothing in the world can change it. I shall not unlock those gates."

"Is that your last word?"

"Yes, your Honour, it is my last word."

So Pectoralis just stood there with his chin stuck out and the judge began to write, and he didn't write very much, either, but what he did write seemed very much to the point.

His decision was a complete triumph for Pectoralis's iron will, but at the same time it also meant Hugo's utter ruin and it was, so far as Safronov was concerned, just as Zheega had foretold, a piece of unexpected good fortune.

The verdict of the court did not open the gates which Pectoralis had nailed up, it left the German his full rights to titillate his iron will, but it also bound him to compensate Safronov for his losses to the tune of fifteen roubles a day.

Safronov was naturally very pleased with this decision, but to everybody's surprise Pectoralis, too, expressed himself completely satisfied with it.

"I'm very satisfied," said he. "I said that the gates will remain locked and locked they will remain."

"Yes, but that will cost you fifteen roubles a day!"

"Quite so, but he hasn't gained anything."

"He has gained fifteen roubles a day."

"I was not referring to that."

"But, let me see, what will it come to now? Twenty-eight working days a month. . . ."

"Except the Lady of Kazan day. . . ."

"Yes, except the Lady of Kazan day, of course, that means two hundred and eighty and one hundred and forty, making altogether four hundred and twenty roubles a month. About five thousand a year! My dear Hugo Karlovich, why, that's a hell of a victory for him! He never earned as much in his life: it's just like hanging a millstone round your neck for the rest of your days."

Hugo Karlovich just blinked, for he felt, of course, that the thing was costing him rather a lot of money, but he showed his mettle and on the first day of the month he paid into court the whole sum, to Safronov's great delight and his own undoing.

And so it went on. On every first day of the month Safronov paid into court fifteen roubles of the monthly rent he owed to Pectoralis and took away with him four hundred and twenty roubles which had been paid into court by Pectoralis.

It was altogether a wonderful piece of luck for Safronov who now had the time of his life. Never before had he lived as he did now, nor had he ever dreamt of being able to live on so grand a scale, just like a gentleman of independent means. He closed his sheds and outhouses and went about whistling merrily all day long, treating himself to innumerable cups of tea at the different inns or standing pints of vodka to his friends and helping himself to some himself, and then he'd climb up the ladder and get over the fence and sleep peacefully and assure everybody he met, "I don't feel a scrap of ill will against the German," he'd say. "It was God who sent him to reward me for my uprightness. All I'm afraid of now is that he should die before me. But I have every reason to believe that he won't, for he promised to come and eat pancakes after my funeral and I know him to be a man of his word. In fact, I told my wife to be sure to give him plenty of pancakes and in the meantime may the Lord grant him many years of health and happiness to work for me."

And as Safronov was truly a man who bore no ill will against any man, he did really feel exceedingly well disposed towards Hugo Karlovich and whenever he happened to run across him, he'd take off his hat to him even if Pectoralis was still at some distance from him and he'd bow to him, shouting the while:

"Good morning, Hugo Karlovich. How are you, my dear bread-winner?"

But Hugo could not understand this genuinely heartfelt concern for his welfare on the part of Mr. Safronov. He mistook it for a desire to make fun of him and he used to get very offended.

"Go away, you blockhead," he'd say. "Go and climb over the fence where I have made a way for you."

And Safronov would reply with the utmost good humour:

"Why are you so angry with me, dear Mr. Pectoralis? Why be so cross with me? I don't mind climbing over the fence and I shall go on climbing over the fence as long as you wish me to, but I respect you greatly for all that and I should hate to offend you."

"I shouldn't advise you even to try!"

"But I'd never dream of offending you, dear Mr. Pectoralis, I'd never dream of offending you. Besides why on earth should I offend you? Quite the contrary: I always pray to the Lord for you every morning and I see to it that my whole family does the same."

"I don't want your prayers!"

"But, my dear Mr. Pectoralis, you may not want them, but we do, for we want the Lord to keep and preserve you for many years to come. That's why I keep on telling my dear children, 'Don't you forget,' I say, 'my dear little ones, to pray to the good Lord that our dear benefactor should go on living for a hundred years and crawl on all fours for another twenty."

"What did he mean by crawling on all fours?" Pectoralis reflected. "Live for a hundred years and . . . crawl on all fours for another twenty . . . Is it good or bad to 'crawl on all fours'?"

He decided to find out what it really meant and, having learnt that it was a bad thing rather than a good one, this greeting became a source of constant annoyance to him. But Mr. Safronov stuck to his text and kept on shouting at the top of his voice:

"May you live and prosper and also crawl on all fours."

While the family of the man who had lost his action in the courts had to communicate with the outside world over a fence, it lived, thanks to the tribute collected from Pectoralis, in a state of affluence which it had never known before and, in Zheega's words, led a life of joy and happiness. Pectoralis, on the other hand, having won the action, could ill afford the tribute imposed upon him and, as he paid it month after month, it began to make serious inroads into his capital and not only swallowed up all his income, but threatened him with utter ruin.

Pectoralis, it was true, showed a bold front to the world and never complained about his bad luck to anybody and he even managed to look cheerful, as a man had a right to do who had publicly stood upon his rights and won general acclaim thereby; but in that cheerfulness of his a careful observer could detect a certain suspicion of make-believe. And, indeed, obstinate mule though he was, he could not help foreseeing the end of it all and he could not very well be expected to wait for that comic and desperate ending with a cheerful countenance. The whole position could be put quite simply in a nutshell: whatever Pectoralis did by way of business and however hard he worked, everything had to go to satisfy Safronov's claim. Pectoralis could not possibly earn more than five or six thousand during the first years as an independent business man and there was nothing left of his earnings not only for the expansion of his business, but even for his own domestic needs. For that reason his business began to show quite unmistakable signs of decline from the outset—and his melancholy end could already be foreseen.

Pectoralis's will was strong, but his means were too slender to enable him to afford such expensive whims and the capital he had accumulated in Russia was going down the drain in the country in which he had earned it. Pectoralis was faced with a great temptation and it seemed he had made up his mind to perish rather than haul down his flag and surrender alive, and the story of his life might have ended very tragically, if chance had not given it a most unexpected ending.

CHAPTER XVII

ONE year had passed and then another without any change in the situation as I have described it to you: Pectoralis went on paying and getting poorer and poorer, while Safronov went on drinking and, finally, drank himself into such a state of hopeless intoxication that he could be seen reeling down the streets of our town at any time of the day or night. Thus the court action brought little advantage to either party; but there was somebody who did manage the affair much more wisely. That was Mrs. Safronova, Maria Matveyevna, who was as simple-minded a creature as her husband, but who had the advantage over him in realising that once they had got all the money the German possessed, their life on easy street would come to an end. "What would happen to us then?" she asked herself.

This realisation, of course, was founded on a sensible estimate of the situation and it had important consequences. Maria Matveyevna saw clearly, which, by the way, it didn't take much to see, that as the second year was drawing to a close, Pectoralis's factory stood idle, there being no more orders to keep it going, and that Hugo himself was walking about in the hardest frost without a fur coat, in an old coat that was worn threadbare, and just to show that he was not downhearted, he began to sport a black ribbon on his *pince-nez*. He had hardly any property left and, what was worse, hardly any reputation, either, except perhaps the reputation of a clown, which he had acquired by his iron will. But *that* reputation was quite frankly of no use to him whatsoever.

To add to his troubles, another misfortune had befallen him at that time: his better half had left him, and the way she had left him showed the utter brazenness of the woman and her treachery, for she had taken with her all the valuables she could lay her hands on. To add insult to injury, everyone seemed to take Klara Pavlovna's part, asserting that there was nothing left for her to do but to run away, first, because Pectoralis's house had such extraordinary stoves which were lighted in the corridors, but did not warm the rooms, and, secondly, because he himself had a most extraordinary character and such a devil of a character, too, that it was quite impossible to live with him, for whatever queer idea he got into his head, he had to carry it out. Indeed, surprise was generally expressed that Mrs. Pectoralis had not run off earlier and picked him clean at a time when he still had plenty of money and before he had squandered it all in paying Safronov's damages.

Thus it was that the unfortunate Hugo was plundered right and left and, on top of it, people went on saying that it was his own fault and that it served him right, and it was impossible to deny that there was some foundation for that opinion. To be sure, it was not right that he should have been plundered, but it was quite true that it was impossible to live with him, and that was why he was left all alone in the world and, one was already justified in saying, was as poor as a church mouse; still for all that he did not give in and kept his iron will as unsullied as ever.

But Safronov, as I told you, was not in a much better position, for he spent all his time at inns and pubs of all sorts and every time he met the German he maddened him by wishing him to live and prosper for a hundred years and crawl on all fours for another twenty.

If that at least could have been avoided, if that indignity, if those insults had not been inflicted upon Pectoralis almost daily, he would not have felt so bad about it. So, to cap the climax, Pectoralis brought an action against Safronov for defamation of character, since in the German's opinion there was no reason in the world why he should crawl on all fours.

"Why," Pectoralis used to say, pointing an accusing finger at Safronov, "it is he who can often be seen crawling on all fours after leaving a pub!"

But once again Safronov had it all his own way and Pectoralis suffered an ignominious defeat. For, in the first place, the judge did not share Hugo's views about the offensive nature of the expression "on all fours" and he saw no reason why the German should not crawl on all fours, and, secondly, the judge found that to crawl on all fours after one hundred years of prosperous life was in the mouth of Safronov an expression of the utmost benevolence and showed the defendant exceedingly well disposed towards the plaintiff, whereas the identical words used by Pectoralis in connection with Safronov's pub-crawling were used with an *outspokenly offensive intention*, for which Hugo Karlovich laid himself open to a fine.

Hugo's ears tingled when he heard the court's verdict and he thought it a crying shame and a typical example of Russian injustice. But, none the less, he was sentenced on the demand of the triumphant Safronov to pay ten roubles damages to the pub-crawler and that threw him into utter confusion. Pectoralis had to part with his last farthing to pay Safronov's damages and, having done that, he felt that there was nothing left for him to do but to curse the day wherein he was born and to die taking his iron will to the grave with him. And he would probably have done so, had that not been contrary to his expressed intention to "outlive" his enemy and to eat pancakes at his funeral repast. Pectoralis could not possibly go back on his word!

Pectoralis was to a certain extent in the same position as the unhappy Prince of Denmark inasmuch as two desires and two wills battled in his breast, and, being already a broken man, he could not make up his mind which was more profitable for the soul of man—to lay hands on himself and his iron will or to drag on a miserable existence for the greater glory of his iron will.

The ten roubles he had paid into court as a consequence of his failure to grasp all the manifold shades of meaning of the Russian idiom of crawling "on all fours," were his last and he had no more money left to pay his contribution to Safronov's upkeep next month.

"Oh, well," he said to himself, "let them come to my house and see for themselves that I have nothing left . . . I have nothing left and I haven't eaten anything to-day, either, and to-morrow . . . to-morrow will be the same and the day after to-morrow will be the same and then . . . then I shall die. . . . Yes, I shall die, but my will at any rate will remain an iron will."

While, however, Pectoralis was in such a truly desperate situation and was going through the most agonising moments of his life, an unexpected crisis loomed ahead, which I really don't know whether to describe as fortunate or unfortunate. For, you see, an event of the greatest importance was at the same time taking place in Safronov's life, an event which could not but bring about a most drastic change in the whole situation and bring to an end the fight between those two heroes in a most unexpected and incredible fashion.

CHAPTER XVIII

HERE I must make it clear that while Pectoralis and Safronov bandied conclusions with one another and Hugo, to his undoing, paid into court in monthly lump sums all his worldly goods, the receiver of those goods, confirmed drunkard though he was, was still in a better position. For that he had to thank his wife, who did not leave her husband as Klara Pavlovna had left hers, but, on the contrary, took her husband in hand and saw to it that he didn't waste all Pectoralis's money. It was Maria Matveyevna who took to court the monthly rent and it was she who took away from Safronov the tribute paid to him by Pectoralis. To avoid any trouble with that drunkard of a husband of hers and to make him submit to her arrangements, Maria Matveyevna doled out to him fifty copecks every day, which Safronov could spend as he liked and which he always spent in the same way, namely, on drink, and at night he'd return home up the now all too familiar ladder and over the fence. No matter how intoxicated he was, he always followed that highly original route. The Lord who, according to popular belief, extends his special protection to infants and drunkards, showed mercy to Safronov in pitch darkness and in rain, in times when the streets were covered with snow and in times when they were covered with a treacherous crust of ice. Safronov climbed the ladder without any mishap, reaching the top of the fence and then tumbling over it on to a heap of hay which had been placed there for his safe homecoming. And he intended to carry on like that for as long as one hundred and twenty years which he always wished Pectoralis to live and to crawl. For it never occurred to him that a German would have no money in Russia, being firmly convinced that whoever it was who had no money, it was never a German.

But Mrs. Safronov in her female simplicity of mind and without "preconceptions" thought differently and, having got all the money which her husband had recovered as damages from Pectoralis, she put it away for a rainy day and thus laid up a little capital for herself. As she did not intend to go on climbing over fences all her life, she finally bought herself a little house, a nice, clean, cheerful house, built on a high foundation with an attic and a high gabled roof, in a word, a dream of a house which, moreover, was next door to her old home where the iron Hugo had ruined her husband's business.

The purchase of the new house took place at the time when Mr. Safronov had been summonsed by Mr. Pectoralis to answer for that "all fours" greeting of his and on the very day when the ex-foundryman had won his unexpected victory over the German and received ten roubles' damages, his family was moving into their new home and settling down in comfort such as they had never before experienced.

Safronov himself took no part in the moving, nor did his wife and children, who had long ago given him up as totally undependable, expect his help and they did everything by themselves, just as they wanted and knew best.

Having received so considerable a sum as ten roubles, Safronov concealed it from his wife, reached a pub safely with it and went on a spree, the gayest and wildest spree of his life. His family had spent three days and three nights in their new home, but he was still crawling from one pub to another, standing drinks to all his cronies and wishing the German to live for a hundred years and to crawl on all fours for another hundred. He generously added another eighty years, for he was overflowing with brotherly love at the time, bawling at the top of his voice:

"Lord, what a fool I am, what a fool! The late Zheega was right when he told me I was a fool and now abundant and unexpected grace has been given to me through that German! But why? What have I done to deserve it? 'What is man that thou art mindful of him, or the son of man that thou visitest him?' Where was that said?"

"In the Scriptures."

"Aye, in the Scriptures, to be sure, but how much are we mindful of him? Oh, I'm afraid, we're not mindful of him at all, not at all!"

"We are weak."

"Aye, that's it; we are weak, we are worms, not men, a disgrace to mankind. But when the Lord wills it, He will preserve even a worm, and He will make you so comfortable that you won't ask for anything better, you won't dream of asking. If you are weak, He will send you a German and all you have to do is to live by his exertions."

"Take care, old man," his friends warned him, "that German of yours may get fed up and open the gates."

But Safronov was too maudlin by that time to fear that.

"He won't open them," he replied, "not for anything, he won't. He'd be ashamed before his own nation. The Germans have such a rule: once they say something, they stick to it, come what may."

"Have they, the swine?"

"Yes, sir, they're made that way, especially as he himself made it so clear in court. 'I have an iron will,' he said. Well, how do you expect him to get the better of it? That's why he suffers such a lot."

"He suffers all right."

"The Lord save any man and especially a Russian from such a will: it'll strangle him!"

"Aye, it'll strangle him all right."

"Let's have a drink! Why talk of such things at night? It isn't lucky. Well, may the Lord grant him to live a hundred years and may he outlive me."

"That's right, let him outlive you."

"That's what I said. Let him outlive me and have at least that as a consolation."

"Aye, what a generous fellow you are, Safronov, me lad!"

"Yes, I'm a generous man, the soul of generosity, that's me! Let him outlive me by all means, but . . . my friends . . . just for a tiny little bit."

"That's it, for a couple of hours."

"Just for a tiny little bit . . . like that . . . see? . . . just up to here . . ." and he drew an imaginary line on his glass of vodka.

"That's right."

"Up to here. . . . Just a tiny little bit. . . ."

Having again indicated the line up to which he wished Pectoralis to outlive him, Safronov and his cronies emptied their glasses and continued to drink each other's healths for some considerable time and they finished up by drinking to the health of the former court clerk Zheega, adding a further wish for the salvation of his soul, for it was, after all, Zheega who was responsible for their treat, and they had just intoned, in loud though rather unsteady voices, a requiem for him when there occurred that strange beginning of the end which has up to this day remained a complete mystery to everybody.

As soon as the drunkards had sung the requiem for the departed Zheega, a loud knock was heard at the window of the pub from the dark courtyard outside and a fearsome face appeared at it and the frightened publican immediately put out all the lights and turned the whole company out neck and crop into the pitch dark street. The revellers found themselves up to the knees in filth and in a trice had lost each other in the thick and damp autumnal fog in which poor Safronov sank like a fly in soap suds and lost his senses completely.

Hardly able to stand on his legs, he tried for a long time to put in his pocket an unopened pint bottle of vodka which he had snatched as he was being bundled out of the pub, and then he wanted to call someone, but his tongue, after working so hard without a stop for three whole days, felt so worn out that it stuck to the roof of his mouth and would not move. And that was not all, for Safronov's legs were as little amenable to his will as his tongue and they, too, refused to move; in fact his whole body seemed to have gone on strike: his eyes didn't see, his ears didn't hear, his head alone seemed still to function, for it was overcome by a desire for sleep.

"Ah, my dear fellow, the devil take thee, you won't take me in by such tricks," Safronov addressed himself to his head. "That is how Zheega went to sleep and didn't get up again, and I'm damned if I'll let that German outlive me long. I don't mind if he outlives me, but only for a little bit."

So he bucked up a little, took another ten steps and, feeling that he was now over the knees in filth, stopped again.

"Oh dear," he said to himself, "if I'm not careful I shall be drowned, and it's so foggy, too, quite as bad as in England. Where the hell am I? How did I get myself so deep in mud? Where's my house? Eh? Seriously now, where's my house? And where's my ladder?"

"The devil has eaten it with a dram of *kvas!*"

"Eh? Who said that? Who said the devil has eaten my house with a dram of *kvas?* Come forth! If you're a good man I'll treat you to a drink of vodka, if not, come on, let's have a Russian war!"

"Come on!" a voice said from out of the fog and at the same time somebody gave Mr. Safronov a terrific punch on the nose which flung him into the mud.

"Well, I'm done for now," he thought. "My memory's gone and I don't know what is happening to me, and where the hell have all my friends disappeared to? The drunken sots! Serves you right, my boy, you shouldn't have been drinking with drunkards! No, I shall never again drink with drunkards. . . . Eh? What was that? Who keeps on talking to me? Hi, you there, what are you trying to find on me? You won't find anything! I've hidden the pint of vodka under me! Ha-ha-ha! Stop pulling me by the hair! Stop it, I say! It hurts and it won't do you any good, anyway. And now by the ears? Well, perhaps you'd better go on pulling me by my ears, it brings back my memory to me, but don't pull so hard! It hurts, I'm telling you. Well, I think I'd better get up now."

And, whether by his own will or by compulsion, or partly by his own exertions, he got up and apparently started to walk. Not that he was absolutely certain of that, but it seemed to him that he was either walking, or else the ground was slipping away from under his heels, but something was happening, of that he was quite sure, somebody was leading him, holding him up without saying a word. Only once did he say, "Oh, so that's who it is!" and just led him on.

"What's that? Who's holding on to me? Eh? Lord, I hope it isn't the devil! It couldn't be anybody else, could it? Still, what does it matter who it is so long as he leads me to the ladder? I know my way from there. . . ."

And so his guide brought him to the ladder and said:

"Here you are, start climbing now, but hold tight! Come on now, get hold of the handrail!"

Mr. Safronov had got back his speech during the walk and, finding that he was no longer tongue-tied, he said:

"Wait a minute, wait a minute! I know my house better than you: my ladder has no handrail!"

But his guide did not waste any words on him: he just started pulling at his ears as if he were stripping the bark from a birch-tree.

"Do you remember now?" he asked.

"Well," thought Mr. Safronov, "I suppose I'd better humour him," and he began to climb the ladder.

And, having started to climb, he climbed and climbed and still there was no end to that ladder.

"Well, I'm hanged," Mr. Safronov reflected, "I'm sure it isn't my home!"

For the higher he climbed, the more clearly did he begin to perceive that when he used to climb up his ladder, it used to get lighter and lighter with every rung he climbed, and it wasn't long before he would see the stars and the moon and the clear azure of the sky. . . . It was true that the weather was very dirty just then, but all the same the whole thing was extremely fishy, for the higher he climbed, the darker it got. Why couldn't he see anything and what was that strange, choking smell of soot and ashes? And there seemed to be no end to it, no top to that dearly wished for fence, where Mr. Safronov knew that he would have to start to descend, he should have reached it long ago—then, suddenly, a terrific blow on his temple, from which not sparks, but shafts of light began to dance before poor Mr. Safronov's eyes and those shafts of light lit up—well, who do you think?—they lit up the former clerk of the court, Zheega!

Now, don't run away with the idea that Safronov saw it all in a dream or something of the kind. No! It was just as I'm telling you. Safronov had been climbing up an endless ladder and he came face to face with Zheega whom he recognised at once in the light of that inward illumination, and he said:

"Well, well, well. . . . The Lord's will be done, how are you, old man?"

And Zheega, who was sitting on a stone seat, kept on nodding to him and replied:

"Hello, glad you've come. There's been a special issue of grub for you here for some time now."

"Oh, so that's where I am! Gracious me, it's dark here in your hell, isn't it? Well, I suppose it can't be helped, can it? This seems to be my destination."

And Mr. Safronov sat down, took out the pint of vodka from his pocket, drank as much as he could from it and handed it to Zheega.

CHAPTER XIX

WHILE these strange adventures befell the tipsy Safronov who had lost his way in the fog and was now spending his time with the late Zheega on some mysterious devilish height which he took to be the pitch dark regions of black hell, all the members of his family were spending a very disturbed night in their new home. Although they were all dead tired what with the moving of their belongings to the new house and what with the hard work of settling down, their sleep was continuously interrupted by a most inexplicable din which began before midnight and went on without stopping up to the very dawn. The mistress of the house and her children first of all heard somebody walking in the attic over their heads, very softly like a hedgehog at first, then he seemed to be getting very angry and started moving something about and throwing it about and, generally, creating a terrible racket and just would not let them sleep. Some of them even seemed to hear a strange muttering, a quiet ringing of bells and other quite incomprehensible noises. On awakening they would listen in fear and trepidation to the ghostly noises, cross themselves, and in the end they decided unanimously and without a single voice raised in dissent that the disturbance upstairs could be nothing else but the work of some evil spirits who, as every true believer knows, are in the habit of getting into a new house before the arrival of the householders and making themselves at home in the attics, haylofts and other empty spaces on the top of the house and, generally, in places where icons are not hung.

The same thing had quite obviously also happened with the worthy Safronov family, that is to say, the devil had made a bee-line for their new house before they had moved in. That was what must have happened, for Mrs. Safronova as soon as she had entered her new home, at once chalked crosses with her own hand on every door and, in taking that wise precaution, she did not overlook either the bath-house or the door leading to the attic. It was therefore quite clear that after that no evil spirit could possibly have entered the house and if, as it seemed now certain, it had, must have done so before.

Yet there seemed to have been a way in which it could have happened even after Mrs. Safronova had chalked her crosses on the door; for when, after the troubled night, day had come at last and with its approach the noise made by the devil had died down and the inmates of the haunted house had shed some of their fears, Maria Matveyevna, who was the first to leave the bedroom, saw that the door leading to the attic was wide open and that the chalked cross made by her own hand was consequently hidden behind it, thus leaving a free passage for the devil. On discovering this grave blunder, Mrs. Safronova at once instituted an investigation to find out who was the last to climb into the attic. After a thorough interrogation of every member of the family and frantic denials of guilt by the younger members of it, suspicion fell on one of the younger girls and it was indeed confirmed by strong circumstantial evidence later. The girl in question was the barefooted Fenka who was born with a harelip and for that reason was little esteemed by the rest of the family. If anybody did show some pity for her, it was her drunken father who refused to regard the fact of the birth of the child with a harelip as due to any intrinsic fault in the girl and who never beat her or even spoke angrily to her. The poor girl lived a life of utter seclusion, was ostracised by the rest of the family and was given little food, being a scullery-maid, sleeping on the floor, and walking about barefoot, without a warm coat and in threadbare rags instead of clothes. The evidence produced by Mrs. Safronova's cross-examination clearly established that Fenka was the last to go upstairs late the night before to "stop up the chimney" and one could not help drawing the inevitable conclusion that because of her childish fears she must have rushed down head over heels and forgotten to close the door behind her and just left it open like that with the side on which the cross had been chalked against the wall, thus bringing to naught that infallible safety device against Satan. Later on, it was quite plain, the devil had made good use of that unforgivable oversight, streaked through the open door into the attic and was, of course, overjoyed at being able to disturb the sleep of a family well known for its piety. To be sure, the devil couldn't help doing that, since he had his own duties to perform, but Mrs. Safronova was in that respect quite an unabashed egoist and made no allowances whatever for anybody's needs, urgent as they might be, and she began to put things right first of all by calling the guilty party to strict and quite unjust account. Getting hold of harelipped Fenka, who was cowering behind the stove, Maria Matveyevna dragged her to the door by the hair and there she began to shake her, saying:

"To make sure the devil doesn't go through this door again after you, I'm going to shut it now with your own forehead, you naughty girl!"

And so she shut the door by giving it a mighty push with the little girl's forehead and then fastened it with the latch. But no sooner was it done than the evil spirit upstairs started another riot and kicked up a frightful row with quite unnecessary violence. Before even the pitiful howling of the child had stopped, something began to turn round and round over the very heads of the assembled family, somebody began to run about and, to cap it all, a brick came sailing through the air and crashed against the door.

Well, of course, that was going a bit too far. Mrs. Safronova, who from her childhood knew all the traditional and well-attested stories about devils and the numerous tricks they played in Christian homes, was naturally aware that they sometimes threw things about, but, to tell the truth, she never really believed it and she had always thought that that was just added on to make the stories more exciting; but that the devil should dare to raise an infernal din and throw bricks at people in broad daylight—that she never expected and for that reason it was not surprising that her hands relaxed their hold on the child, who immediately slipped away and darted out into the yard where she sought safety in running from one shed to another. But as soon as a hue and cry was raised for the apprehension of the girl about whose guilt no doubt could be entertained any more, the devil began to rage even more fiercely and began to throw more bricks about. His hands must have been perfectly "materialised," for whole bricks and bits of bricks began to fall among those who were chasing the girl and they were thrown with such force and violence that they all began to fear for their lives and with a shout, "The Lord have mercy upon us," all of them, as though of one accord, rushed into the open hen-run, where they squatted in a frenzied heap in the safest place, namely, under the roost.

There could be no doubt that they were perfectly safe there, for the devil could do nothing to them in such a place because the midnight cock usually crows on the roost, and the midnight cock, as is well known, possesses certain mysterious powers about which the devil knows something which gives him good reason to fear them. Still, they couldn't very well stop there for ever, for the hens were due to return towards the evening and the position occupied by them *under* the roost would then become uncomfortable in quite a different sense.

CHAPTER XX

So as soon as the people who had hidden themselves in the hen-run recovered little by little from the panic with which they had been seized, something which usually happens to superstitious folk and cowards the world over also happened to them: their terror began to give way to a certain scepticism. The first to make a move was Mrs. Safronova's maid Marfutka, a very brisk young woman, who did not relish the idea of remaining cooped up in a hen-run for long without being able to move about. She was followed by Yegorka, Mrs. Safronova's only man-servant, a lame, but very quick-witted lad with ginger hair, who was in the habit of whispering to Marfutka on any and every occasion. Both of them now turned to their favourite pastime and, having whispered to each other for some considerable time, they arrived at a most startling conclusion: their combined brains, which had apparently worked in complete harmony for some time, penetrated into the very heart of the mystery and the opinion they formed pointed to a suspicion that if things were not as they should be, they were not so for quite a different reason.

In fact, it occurred to them that last night's racket and this morning's cannonade was not caused by the devil at all, but by some wicked man, who, according to their deductions, was none other than, and, indeed, could be none other than, the German Pectoralis.

"The villain must have climbed into the attic out of sheer malice and envy and now he's throwing bricks about!"

Mrs. Safronova threw up her hands in astonishment on hearing that, so likely did that supposition appear to her. And thereupon scouts were sent out of the hen-run to spy out the land and to reconnoitre the territory occupied by the enemy and to take all the necessary measures to cut off the way of retreat to the villain.

Yegorka and Marfutka immediately sallied out of the hen-run, ran hand-in-hand to the shed, took off the padlock from the door and locked the attic door with it; then, after having whispered their fill in the passage, they went to carry out the tasks they had allotted to themselves: Yegorka ran to spread the news among the neighbours and to call them together to help in apprehending the German who was lurking somewhere in the attic, and Marfutka mounted guard at the attic door with a pair of tongs in her hand, ready to attack the German should he try to get through the locked door by one of the knavish tricks known only to Germans. The German, however, held his peace and did not show himself to Marfutka; but as soon as Yegorka rushed out of the gate and started running to the market-place as fast as his legs would carry him, he collided face to face with Hugo Karlovich. That so astonished the poor lad that at first he did not know what to do, but he immediately recollected himself and, seizing the German by the scruff of the neck, began to shout, "Help!!!" Pectoralis, who certainly did not expect to be collared by a raving youth, immediately retaliated by hitting Yegorka over the head with his rolled-up umbrella and pushing him into a puddle. The terrible emotional storm that arose in Yegorka's head from that soft, but smart rap with the umbrella and his headlong plunge into the puddle, so unnerved the poor lad that he remained sitting in it and just went on screaming:

"Beshrew thee! Begone! Avaunt!"

All the suspicions with which Marfutka had filled Yegorka's susceptible mind were now dispelled. However simple-minded he was, he could not help perceiving that if the German had not crawled through the locked door, it had to be concluded that it was not he but somebody else who had been making all that row in the attic. And here Yegorka's rather feeble mind, unsupported by Marfutka's livelier imagination, again began to incline to the theory that it was the devil after all who had been causing all that disturbance in the house. And it was this theory that he expatiated on at great length to his rapt audience in the market-place, which hailed the news with great delight and straightway rushed in a big crowd to Mrs. Safronova's house where, according to Yegorka's circumstantial account, such amazing, although, as every spiritualist will tell you, quite common occurrences were taking place, occurrences, I might add, which certain learned men to-day regard as proving the close proximity to us of beings from the invisible world.

CHAPTER XXI

IN the course of the day the whole town called on Maria Matveyevna and all of them listened several times to the story of the supernatural events which had taken place in her new home the night before and again in the morning. Certain members of the local police force also put in an appearance, but everything was hidden from them lest (which God forbid) something worse might befall. Among the visitors was also the maths master of the local grammar school who was a correspondent of some learned society. He demanded to be given the bricks which the devil had been throwing about, for, it seemed, he wished to send them to St. Petersburg. But Mrs. Safronova quite firmly refused to comply with his request on the ground that it might involve her in all sorts of troubles. Marfutka, however, more wide-awake than her mistress, immediately rushed to the bath-house and brought back a brick from behind the furnace.

The maths master took this piece of material evidence to the local chemist's shop where it was subjected to a minute examination by the mathematician and the chemist. Both of them smelt it, licked it and then poured some acid over it, exclaiming afterwards in one voice:

"It's a brick!"

"Yes," said the teacher of mathematics, "it's a brick all right. No doubt about it."

"Quite right," said the chemist.

"I don't think we'll trouble to send it after all."

"No, I don't think so, either."

But the believers who cared nothing about chemical tests spent their time much more profitably and got a greater thrill out of it, and some of them, who were more zealous and more patient than the rest, remained in Mrs. Safronova's house until it was granted to them to hear through the door how somebody seemed to sigh and moan in the attic, just like a soul tormented in hell-fire. There were among them also a few intrepid spirits, one of whom went even so far as to suggest that the attic should be examined through the dormer window, but the suggestion appeared so utterly improper, if not indeed rash, that it was immediately and unanimously turned down. Moreover, in turning down that suggestion the fact was taken into account that such an examination was not entirely free from danger, since it was out of that dormer window that the bricks had been hurled and the bombardment, for all they knew, might be resumed at any time. Anybody, therefore, attempting such an examination might be expected to run a great risk with serious consequences to himself.

Mrs. Safronova, being a woman, resorted to the well-tried female expedient of bewailing her bad luck.

"Of course," she said, "if I had a husband like any other woman, a husband who was useful about the house, I mean one who was master in his home, it would have been his bounden duty to climb on the roof and have a good look through the attic window, but my poor husband suffers from such a terrible weakness and he hasn't been home for the past five days."

"You're quite right, Mrs. Safronova," her neighbours replied. "Even the devil wouldn't dare hurt the master of the house."

"I shouldn't be so sure about it," said one lady, "he might get hurt all right."

Nothing had so far been heard of Mr. Safronov and nobody knew even where, that is to say, in what pub, to look for him. It was quite possible that he had been paying visits to the pubs in the neighbourhood and was lying dead drunk in some remote village.

"Don't worry about him, dear," her visitors were saying to Maria Matveyevna. "What you have to do now is to think of something to get rid of Satan in your house."

"But what am I to do? Won't you, good people, advise me what to do?"

"Well, what advice do you expect, dear Maria Matveyevna," said one of her lady visitors. "There's only one of two things you can do: either call in Foma the cobbler to entice the devil out of your house or send for the priest to sprinkle holy water all over the place."

"Don't mention that Foma to me, my dear! He's a real devil, he is. It's bad as it is here and if Foma came, heaven knows what would happen!"

"Quite right, dear, you can't expect one devil to drive out another."

"Well, if that's so, then there's only one thing left for you to do—sprinkle holy water round the house."

"As a matter of fact," said Mrs. Safronova, "I thought of it myself last night, only it slipped my mind as I turned over in bed, but I'm going to do it right away, bake some pasties and raise the icon and then let them consecrate the house with holy water. . . . Oh dear, and at such a time poor Mr. Safronov would be away!"

"You can't possibly wait for him now, can you?"

"Of course I can't wait for him, but I wish he was here all the same, for the dear man loves this service so much, you know, and he always insists on carrying the vessel with holy water in front of the priest and joining in the singing of the prayers. I don't know what to do without him and I'm blessed if I know who to ask."

"Call in the archpriest, he's the senior one in rank and it stands to reason that the devil will be more afraid of him."

"No, dear, I don't think I fancy asking him, seeing how addicted he is to smoking. Always puffing cigarettes, he is, may the Lord forgive him. I think I'd rather have Father Flavian."

"Yes, I suppose Father Flavian will do."

"Too fat, if you ask me."

"Yes, I suppose so, but he's such a dear little pumpkin of a man and ever so kind-hearted. It was he, you know, who consecrated the Ilyin's house the other day. Such crowds I never saw, my dear! Oh, but he did it so beautifully! I only hope he can manage to sprinkle the holy water everywhere in this house, for, you see, the poor dear is so fat that he just can't crawl into every nook and cranny and he sprinkles it just anywhere from a distance, just as it suits his fancy."

"We'll see to that."

"Well, of course, if there's someone who knows all about it, everything will be all right."

"You see, my dear Maria Matveyevna, you'll have to watch him carefully so that he sprinkles it crossways and says all the necessary words while doing it. But do you think Father Flavian will be able to go through the attic door with that big belly of his?"

"Couldn't you make the door wider for him or will it cost too much money?"

"I'm afraid I couldn't afford it, dear."

"Tell you what, dear Maria Matveyevna. Let Father Flavian consecrate the house, but have Deacon Savva climb into the attic to sprinkle the holy water. You simply must ask him, dear Maria Matveyevna, he's as thin as a lath and he's quite sure to get through anywhere. That's your best plan, for poor Father Flavian might slip on the ladder with that paunch of his and break his neck."

"God preserve us from such a calamity, dear. He's such a nice, kind-hearted old man and I hope he keeps alive for many a day yet. I remember I had very difficult labour once and I sent to ask the archpriest to open the altar gates for me, but he wouldn't do it for anything."

"I suspect you didn't give him enough, dear."

"Oh, I don't know, I sent him a rouble, but Father Flavian just flung them wide open for me for half the price!"

"I should hate to say a word against him, dear Maria Matveyevna, but let him stay downstairs and let Deacon Savva climb upstairs with the water and the sprinkler. Do that, my dear, for really he doesn't care what happens to him, poor man. His wife, you know, goes off her head once every month, so I suppose he must have got sick and tired of life long ago."

"That's right, dear Mrs. Safronova, he's such an obliging man, the deacon is, he'll go anywhere you like and sprinkle everything beautifully, but you must see that he isn't in too big a hurry or just does the sprinkling anyhow. Remember, he has to do it crossways."

"Don't you worry, I'll look after him all right," said Mrs. Safronova. "I might even go with him to the attic myself. I wouldn't mind doing it a bit so long as something came of it."

"Now really, Mrs. Safronova, how can you say such a thing! If everything's done nice and proper like, something's bound to come of it. But you ought to do it as soon as possible and, mind, see it's done in a godly way."

"But, my dears, what could be more godly?" replied Mrs. Safronova. "I'll tell Marfutka to start baking the pasties straight away and I'll send Yegorka to Father Flavian to ask him to come here directly after to-morrow's early mass."

"That's just lovely, my dear Maria Matveyevna."

"But, of course! Why should I put it off? Do you think I like living in a house with the devil and just waiting for the villain to start throwing things about? Oh dear, if only I had my pasties ready, I'd not have waited even until to-morrow with the service!"

"My dear Maria Matveyevna, you simply mustn't think of having the service without the pasties. The clergy can't carry on without them, you know, especially Father Flavian who likes everything as doughy as himself," and the other lady visitors having concurred in that opinion, it was unanimously decided that the hapless family should somehow or other put up with the devil's knavery for another day and night and that in the meantime the pasties should be baked and Yegorka sent to Father Flavian to ask him to be so good as to come with Deacon Savva after early mass the next day to consecrate Mrs. Safronova's house with holy water and drive out the devil and then partake of Mrs. Safronova's delicious, puffy pasties.

Father Flavian, a corpulent old man, all puffed up and soft like a feather bed, with a long grey beard and wearing a cassock over his spacious paunch and a greasy clerical hat, listened attentively to Yegorka's account of the trouble the devil had been giving to Mrs. Safronova's household and, hearing the urgent appeal to him to come and drive the devil out, said in a thin, squeaky, childish voice:

"All right, my boy, tell them to get everything ready. We shall come and we shall prevail, only tell your mistress to bake one or two pasties for me and fill 'em with carrots, for my stomach has been getting rather weak lately. But what about Vassily Safronov? Hasn't he come back home yet?"

"No, Father, he hasn't."

"Well, I suppose we shall have to carry on without him then, only don't forget about those pasties, let them get those ready . . . the rest we shall do ourselves. . . . And, oh, I almost forgot, I shall want a towel, for, of course, in this case I shall be dipping the big cross myself."

Yegorka ran back home at a hop and, passing under the dormer window, even challenged the devil by cocking a snook at him.

Everybody in the house felt much better, having reconciled themselves to the idea of spending one more night in the haunted house, and to make quite sure that nobody got frightened, they all went to sleep in one room, Yegorka alone staying in the kitchen to keep Marfutka company, so that she shouldn't be afraid to get up at night and knead over the dough, which was rising beautifully, being kept in a warm place at the edge of the stove and covered with a fur coat.

The devil, meanwhile, kept quiet, as though realising what big preparations for his utter discomfiture were on foot. During the whole of the day he played not a single knavish trick against any member of the household, but there could be no doubt that he was still in the attic, for several people had heard him snoring. Towards evening, when a hard frost had set in, he was even heard to groan and chatter with his teeth and during the night Mrs. Safronova and, indeed, anybody else who woke up could hear his groans very clearly, but no one took any particular notice of it and everyone just muttered, "Serve him right, the enemy of Christianity," and, making the sign of the cross, turned over on the other side and fell asleep.

But, alas and alack, such scorn was rather premature, for it made the evil spirit lose his patience completely and when the bell tolled for a third time in Father Flavian's church, a most pitiful groan was heard in Mrs. Safronova's attic and at that very moment something came down with a crash in the kitchen.

Maria Matveyevna jumped out of bed and, forgetting her fears, rushed to the kitchen in her nightdress to find out the meaning of that crash and, as she opened the kitchen door, all she could do was just to gasp at the new abominable trick played by the devil! For there in front of her by the oven on which the dough for the pasty was rising in a large earthenware basin, stood Yegorka, covered from head to foot in dough, and round him lay the bits and pieces of the broken basin.

Both Mrs. Safronova, Yegorka and Marfutka, who was sitting on the top of the stove with her bare feet hanging down, were so utterly dumbfounded that they just shouted in one voice:

"Oh, may he roast in hell!"

Such was the ill-omened beginning of the day which was to be memorable for the dauntless fight of Father Flavian and Deacon Savva against the mysterious creature who had been creating such a turmoil in the attic and whose impudence had gone so far as to throw out of the basin on to the floor the whole of the dough which was to be used for the making of pasties for the clergy.

And when did he do it? What was the time he chose for that foul deed of his? Why, just when it was too late to start making any new dough and when the tall, gaunt beadle was rattling the ring on the gate, bringing the tin sprinkling cup!

What was Maria Matveyevna to do now? How was she to mend the business which had such a bad beginning and which threatened to have even a worse ending?

To tell the truth, all that was much more important than anything that had happened to Pectoralis, on whose fate, however, this seemingly irrelevant matter had a very decisive and portentous influence.

CHAPTER XXII

MRS. SAFRONOVA was terribly upset about the mishap with the dough; she simply did not know how she was to tell Father Flavian that there were no carrot pasties for him, and she decided not to say a word about it to him, not at any rate until he had finished the service and consecrated the house. As a wise and experienced woman, Maria Matveyevna preferred to wait and see, being convinced that time was a great conjurer who could bring help when there seemed no hope of any help. And so it happened. The consecration of the house began directly the clergy arrived and before the service had come to an end the whole affair took such an unexpected turn that there was no time even to think about pasties filled with carrots.

This was what happened: no sooner did Deacon Savva intone at the end of the service the prayer calling upon the Almighty to grant long life and happiness to the master and the mistress of the house than an impatient knocking began at the attic door, which still remained padlocked, and a voice which seemed to be very familiar, although it sounded rather weak, said:

"Open the door! Open the door for me!"

At first, needless to say, this caused a tremendous sensation and everybody rushed to Father Flavian in mortal fear. . . .

The spectacle which was revealed when the door was opened was indeed most unexpected: on the bottom rung of the ladder, by the door, stood Mr. Safronov himself or the devil who had taken his shape. The second alternative was indeed more likely, since the apparition, or the devil who had cleverly made himself up to look like Safronov, did not entirely succeed in looking like the original; he was, for one thing, much thinner than Safronov, with a bluish, deathly pallor on his face and with eyes that looked almost dead. But the insolence of the creature! Not in the least daunted by the sprinkler, he at once went up to Father Flavian and, cupping his hands, waited for the priest to sprinkle some holy water into them, which Father Flavian did. Then Safronov kissed the cross and, as if nothing unusual had happened, went to greet the members of his family. Mrs. Safronova had willy-nilly to acknowledge in that half-dead man her lawful wedded husband.

"Where have you been, my dear?" she asked him, her heart melting with pity and compassion for him.

"I sat where the Lord had brought me as a punishment," replied Mr. Safronov.

"So it was you who were knocking?"

"Yes, I suppose it must have been I who was knocking."

"But why did you throw bricks about?"

"Well, why did you knock the girl about?"

"Why didn't you come down yourself?"

"How could I have come down without having received a proper dispensation? When I heard the priest raising his voice in prayer to the Lord to grant me a long life, I came down immediately. . . . Let me have some tea, dear, some hot tea, I'll climb on to the stove and you'd better cover me up with a sheepskin," he said hurriedly in his weak, hoarse voice and, supported under the arms by Yegorka and his wife, he climbed on to the hot stove, where he was covered up with sheepskins, while Deacon Savva walked all over the attic with the sprinkler, without, however, discovering anything out of the ordinary there.

After such a discovery there could, of course, be no question of any large spread for the clergy; Safronov's appearance in such a wretched state made everything assume a rather haphazard character and Father Flavian was quite satisfied with a cup of hot tea, which he drank sitting in an armchair by the stove where Safronov was trying to warm his frozen body and replied in a rather desultory way to the trivial questions put to him.

All Safronov knew of the events of the last few days was that he had been somewhere, climbed up to some place and found himself in hell, where he had a long chat with Zheega who told him that Satan himself had got fed up with his quarrel with Pectoralis and that all that business was now drawing to an end. Accepting that decision, Safronov resolved to stay where he had been brought for his sins and he bore all the torments they inflicted on him, of cold and hunger, with exemplary stoicism and he even suffered without protest when he heard his own daughter's cries and moans, but when he heard the beautiful church singing and, particularly, the prayer for the long life of the master of the house which he loved so much and when Deacon Savva mentioned his own name, he was suddenly overwhelmed by quite different thoughts and he decided to come down on earth even for a short time to hear Savva and take leave of his family.

The poor man could not tell a more coherent tale of his adventures and Father Flavian forbore to question him any more. Mr. Safronov was indeed in a most pitiful state and did his best to get warm, but he kept on shivering and was quite unable to warm himself. Towards the evening he recovered consciousness for a short time and expressed a wish to obtain absolution for his sins and after another day he really did die.

All that happened so unexpectedly and so quickly that Maria Matveyevna had barely time to recover from the shock of her husband's return when she had to start making arrangements for his funeral. Preoccupied with these sad duties, she did not pay any attention to a remark made by Yegorka who had gone to order a coffin an hour after Safronov's death and who brought back the strange news that "the German has unlocked the gates," the gates in their old yard he meant which had been the cause of all that long-drawn-out dispute that had brought disaster both upon Safronov and Pectoralis.

Now that Pectoralis's enemy was dead, Hugo could, without compromising his iron will, open the gates and stop paying the ruinous fine, which he did.

CHAPTER XXIII

THE clergy, the guests and the widow herself, having filled Safronov's grave with frozen earth, had only just returned to Maria Matveyevna's new home and had barely sat down at the table to enjoy the repast in memory of the departed master of the house, when the door was unexpectedly opened and in walked Pectoralis, looking haggard and pale.

His appearance naturally took everybody by surprise and none more so than the grief-stricken widow who did not know what to make of it—did Pectoralis come to offer his condolences to her or to mock at her? But before she could make up her mind which of the two alternatives was the more likely one, Hugo Karlovich said to her quietly and soberly and with his customary dignity that he had come to keep his word which he had given to her late husband a long time ago: to eat pancakes at his wake!

"Well" said Maria Matveyevna, "we're all true Christians here and we all of us have received Holy Baptism and we extend our hospitality to every man or woman who cares to come and sit down at our table. So, please, sit down, sir. We have made a large number of pancakes, enough for all the beggars in town to sit down with us and partake of our meal."

Hugo bowed and sat down, a place of honour even being given him at the table between fat Father Flavian and lean Deacon Savva.

Notwithstanding his rather starved appearance, Pectoralis seemed to be in the best of health: he sat there with the mien of a conqueror and he behaved himself rather indecently at the wake of his enemy. But just because of that overbearing behaviour of his an extraordinary thing happened to him there which made a worthy ending to the story of his iron will.

I don't know how the argument about his iron will started between him and Deacon Savva, but during that argument the deacon said to him:

"Why are you always picking quarrels with us, Hugo Karlovich, and showing off your iron will? It is not seemly."

And Father Flavian supported Savva and said:

"It isn't nice, my dear sir, it isn't nice. God will punish you for that. God always punishes people for injuries done to Russians."

"But I have outlived Safronov all the same, haven't I? I said I was going to outlive him and I have outlived him."

"But what's the use of having outlived him, my dear sir? How do you know for how long you have outlived him? The Lord in his inscrutable wisdom always metes out just punishment for any offence done to us. Look at me. I am old and my poor legs are so swollen that I can't even trample on mice any more, but even I may outlive you yet."

But Pectoralis only smiled.

"What are you showing your teeth for?" the deacon broke in. "Aren't you afraid of God even? Can't you see how overweening in your pride you have become? No, sir, mark my words, you won't outlive Father Flavian: all will be up with you soon."

"Well, we shall see."

"What shall we see? Why, there isn't much left of you to see, is there? Skin and bone, that's what you are. Look at Safronov! He lived a simple life and he departed this world at his own pleasure."

"Some pleasure!"

"Why? Wasn't his end good? He ended his life just as he wanted, tippling to the last, always drinking your health."

"The swine!"

"There he goes! The swine, indeed! Why insult him? He may be a swine, but before his death he had fasted in the attic and, having confessed his sins to Father Flavian and obtained absolution for them, he died the death of a true Christian and carried out every rule laid down by the Church, and now he's probably already with his forefathers, resting in the bosom of Abraham and talking his head off, telling them all about you and I can imagine how heartily they must be laughing. But you, of course, are not a swine, sitting at his table and abusing him. Now, tell me, who is the bigger swine, you or he?"

"You're the bigger swine, my dear sir," Father Flavian chimed in gravely.

"Didn't care a rap about his family," Pectoralis said dryly.

"What? What did you say?" the deacon went on. "He didn't care about his family? Have a good look round, my dear sir. He left his family a dry corner and some provenance and you yourself are sitting in his house and eating pancakes at his table, but you haven't got a family of your own and when you die there won't be anyone to mourn for you and there'll be nothing to remember you by. Well, who has done better by his family you or he? Just think it over . . . and remember you can't play fast and loose with us, for God is on our side."

"I refuse to believe that."

"Whether you believe it or not, it is as plain as a pikestaff that it is much better to die as Safronov did than die of hunger as you're doing."

Pectoralis looked a bit embarrassed at that: he must have felt that those words contained more than a grain of truth so far as he was concerned, and cold terror entered his heart and with it Satan himself entered it; he entered it together with a pancake Savva had offered him, saying:

"Here's a pancake for you, eat it and keep quiet, for I can see that you can't even eat pancakes as well as we do."

"Why can't I?" asked Pectoralis.

"Well, don't you see what a mess you're making of the pancakes? Crumpling them, cutting them up, munching them."

"What do you mean by munching them?"

"I mean you just munch them, transferring them from one side of your mouth to the other."

"Do you mean I shouldn't even chew them?"

"What do you want to chew them for? A pancake is just like a piece of pastry: it goes down your throat by itself. Just have a look at Father Flavian. See how he eats them? Well? It is a real pleasure just to watch! He takes it by the end, covers it well with thick cream, rolls it up nicely, puts it in his mouth and then gives it a flick with his tongue and lets it slide down where it belongs."

"It isn't healthy to eat like that!"

"It isn't healthy, isn't it? What else are you going to say? Do you really think you know better than anybody else? Why, my dear sir, you'll never be able to eat as many pancakes as Father Flavian!"

"I will," said Pectoralis sharply.

"Don't boast like that, my dear sir!"

"I will," Pectoralis repeated doggedly.

"Don't boast, I said. You've just done with one trouble, do not call another one on your head."

"I will, I will, I will!" Hugo went on repeating.

And so an argument started between them and, as this argument could be decided there and then, a pancake-eating contest began between Pectoralis and Father Flavian to everybody's delight.

Father Flavian himself did not take any part in the argument: he just listened and went on helping himself to the pancakes, but Pectoralis found the match rather more than he had bargained for. Father Flavian rolled up his pancakes one after another and swallowed them without showing any ill effects, but Hugo got white and red in the face and just could not keep up with Father Flavian. And the witnesses of this contest just sat there and heaped fuel on the fire by constantly egging him on and brought things to such a pass that he should have snatched up his hat and shown a clean pair of heels long ago, but he evidently did not know the saying that discretion is the better part of valour. He went on eating and eating until he suddenly dived under the table and began to wheeze.

Deacon Savva bent down and tried to pull him back.

"No shamming, my dear sir," he said, "no shamming! Get up and eat as long as Father Flavian is eating."

But Hugo did not get up. They crawled under the table to lift him up, but by that time he had breathed his last. The deacon who was the first to realise that the German was not shamming just slapped his thighs and exclaimed:

"Well, what do you say to that? Boasted he knew how to eat and now he goes and kicks the bucket!"

"Is he dead?" all exclaimed in one voice.

But Father Flavian just crossed himself, sighed, whispered, "God's will be done," and reached out for another pile of pancakes.

So Pectoralis outlived Safronov only for a very short time, and did so under circumstances which were certainly unworthy of his character and his ability.

He was buried hastily at the expense of the Church and, of course, without any funeral repast in his honour. None of us, his former colleagues, knew about it. And I myself, your faithful servant, got to know about it only by mere chance. I arrived in town on the day of his funeral during the first and most terrible snowstorm of the year, and I suddenly saw as we turned into a lane a funeral procession coming towards me and Father Flavian stumping along in his fur hat with its three flaps turned down and singing "Holy Father," and just at that moment my horse fell through a snowdrift and the breeching strap snapped. I crawled out of the sledge and began to assist my driver, but we botched the whole business and in the meantime an old lady in a sleeveless padded coat emerged from behind some tumble-down gates and another from the same kind of gates on the opposite side of the lane and they started shouting to each other.

"Who're they burying, dear?" asked one.

And the other replied:

"Oh dear, it wasn't even worth coming out for: they were taking the German away to the cemetery."

"Which German?"

"Why, the one who choked himself with a pancake yesterday!"

"And is Father Flavian burying him?"

"Yes, dear, it was him, bless his dear heart, it was Father Flavian."

And the two old ladies went back and slammed their gates. That was how Hugo Karlovich came to his end and that was what the people in our town had to say about him, which I, who remembered him from the time when he had so many great expectations, found not a little sad.

DEATHLESS GOLOVAN

(FROM *TALES OF THREE UPRIGHT MEN*.)

Perfect love casteth out fear. ST. JOHN.

CHAPTER I

HE himself is almost a myth and the story of his life is a legend. It needs a Frenchman to tell such a story, for it is only a Frenchman who knows how to explain to others what he does not understand himself. I am saying all this in order to ask the reader to forgive the all too obvious shortcomings in my story of a man whose biography a much greater master than I would have found difficult to write. But Golovan might soon be altogether forgotten and that would be a great pity. Golovan is worthy of attention and although I never knew him well enough to paint a complete portrait of him, I shall try to pick out and present certain features of that mortal man of lowly origin who had every right to be known as "deathless."

The nickname of "deathless" which was given to Golovan did not express derision, nor was it a meaningless, empty-sounding word. He was nicknamed "deathless" because of the existence of a strong conviction among the people that in dealing with Golovan they were dealing with a man who was different from other men, a man who was not afraid of death. How could such an opinion arise among a people who always walked in the fear of the Lord and who never for a single moment forgot that they themselves were mortal? Was there a good reason for it, a reason which gradually emerged as a result of circumstances, or was the nickname given to him by simplicity which is so closely related to folly?

So far as I was concerned, I was inclined to accept the second view as the much more probable of the two, but what other people thought of it I can't say; for as a child I never stopped to think about it at all and when I grew up and was capable of forming my own opinion, the "deathless" Golovan was no longer among the living. He was dead, and he did not die in a very nice way, either: he perished during what is known in Orel as "the great fire," having been drowned in a pit of boiling water into which he had fallen while saving someone's life or rescuing someone's property. However, "a big part of him survived extinction and remained alive in grateful memory," and I want to try to put down on paper all I ever knew or heard about him, so that his memory, so worthy of respect, should go on living.

CHAPTER II

DEATHLESS GOLOVAN was quite an ordinary man. His face with its rather heavy features had become engraved in my memory ever since the early days of my childhood and remained there for ever. I met him at a time of my life when, they say, children are unable to receive lasting impressions which they can remember for the rest of their days, but it was different with me. The circumstances of my first meeting with Golovan were preserved by my grandmother in the following note:

"Yesterday, 25th May, 1835, I arrived from Gorokhova at Mary's (Mary was my mother). Semyon Dmitrich (my father) was not at home as he had been summoned to Yeletz where a terrible murder had been committed. There were only women in the house, ourselves and the maids. The coachman had gone with him (my father), only the house caretaker Kondrat remaining at home, and during the night a night-watchman used to come from the office (the chief district Criminal Investigation Bureau where my father served as Government Councillor) and spend the night in the hall. At noon to-day Mary went out into the garden to have a look at the flowers and to water the pinks and she took little Nicholas (myself) with her, the child being carried by Anna (my nurse who is still alive). On their way back for lunch—Anna had only just opened the gate—the house dog Ryabka in a sudden fit of madness slipped his chain and hurled himself upon Anna, but no sooner had the dog put his paws against Anna's chest than Golovan gripped him by the collar, squeezed his neck tightly and flung him into the cellar through the open trap-door. There Ryabka was later shot with a rifle, and the child was saved."

I was that child and however strong the evidence may be that a sixteen-months-old child cannot possibly remember what happens to him at that tender age, I do remember the episode very well.

I don't, of course, remember where the mad Ryabka came from or what Golovan did to the dog after the breath began to rattle in its throat as it struggled with its four legs and wriggled with its body in Golovan's iron grip; what I do remember is just one moment . . . *only a moment*. It was like a flash of lightning on a dark night when for some reason you see a large number of objects at once: the bed curtain, the screen, the canary which gives a violent start on its perch and the glass with the silver spoon, on the handle of which the magnesia had left little dark stains. Such, I suppose, is also the characteristic of fear which has large eyes. It was such an isolated instant that I can still see it as if it only happened a minute ago: the dog's huge, spotted head, its dry coat, very red eyes and wide-open mouth full of darkish froth and its bluish, almost as vivid as if they were painted, jaws . . . its sharp teeth ready to snap at me, but suddenly its upper lip draws back, its open mouth is pulled back towards its ears, and deep inside, like a naked human elbow, its protruding gullet begins to move spasmodically. . . . And over all that stands a towering human figure with a big head and that figure seizes the mad dog and carries it away, and all during that time the face of that man is *smiling*.

The man I have just described was Golovan. I am afraid I shall not be able to draw his portrait just *because* I can see him so clearly. Like Peter the Great he was over six foot tall; he was broad-shouldered, wiry and muscular, dark-skinned, round-faced, blue-eyed, with a very big nose and thick lips. The hair on his head and his trimmed beard were very thick, of the colour of pepper and salt. His head was always closely cropped and so were his beard and moustache. A calm and happy smile never left his face: it seemed to play on every feature of his face, but particularly on his lips and there was also a constant twinkle in his eyes, his wise and good and also seemingly a little ironic eyes. Apparently Golovan had no other expression, at least I can't remember any other. To conclude this rough sketch of Golovan, I must mention one idiosyncrasy or peculiarity of his gait. Golovan was always hurrying along, as though he was afraid to be late somewhere, but he always walked with a kind of skip. He did not limp, but, as they used to say locally, he "cut capers," that is to say, he trod firmly on one of his feet, namely, the right one, and hopped on his left one. His left leg, it seemed, refused to bend, but had a kind of spring in some muscle or joint. People with an artificial leg usually walk like that, but Golovan's left leg was not an artificial one; that peculiarity, however, was not natural to him, as he himself had caused it, and therein lay a mystery which I am afraid cannot be explained straight away.

Golovan dressed like a peasant, both in summer and in winter, on a hot, sultry day and on a day when the temperature dropped to forty degrees below zero. He wore a long uncovered sheepskin coat, which was glossy and dark with age. I never saw him wearing any other garment and my father, I remember, used often to joke about that sheepskin coat of his, calling it "eternal."

Golovan used to tie his sheepskin round with a large, peasant belt, ornamented with silver harness-plate which had grown yellow with age in some places and dropped out altogether in many others, either with the wax-end or holes showing. But his sheepskin was kept meticulously clean and was free from vermin. I knew that better than anybody, for I was often carried about by Golovan inside his capacious coat and always felt very comfortable there.

The wide collar of his sheepskin was never buttoned, and, as a rule, he wore the coat open to the belt. That was the "bosom" which served as a very large receptacle for the bottles of cream which Golovan used to deliver to the kitchen of the Orel Gentlemen's Club. That had been his occupation ever since he had obtained his "freedom" and received a "Yermolov" cow for his upkeep.

The powerful chest of "the deathless one" was covered only by a linen shirt of Ukrainian cut, that is to say, with a straight collar, always spotlessly clean and invariably fastened round his waist with a long coloured band. That band was either a ribbon or just a piece of woollen or even cotton material, but, whatever it was, it lent to Golovan's exterior a touch of something fresh, something gentlemanly, which suited him very much, for he was, in fact, a *gentleman.*

CHAPTER III

WE were Golovan's neighbours. Our house in Orel was in the Third Gentlemen's Street and was third from the steep bank of the river Orlik. It was rather a beautiful spot. At that time, before the fires, the steep bank of the river formed the edge of the town proper. To the right, on the other side of the Orlik, there stretched the low hovels of the suburb, which adjoined the town and came to an end with the church of Vassily the Great. At the side was the very steep and difficult descent to the bank of the river and behind, beyond the gardens, was a deep ravine and beyond that was a common where many years ago a powder magazine had been built and where soldiers used to drill and engage in mock battles with sticks —the earliest scenes of my childhood which I remember and which I loved to watch more than anything else.

On that common, or rather on a narrow strip of land which divided our gardens from the ravine, the six or seven cows which belonged to Golovan used to graze together with the reddish bull of the same "Yermolov" breed which also belonged to him. The bull was kept by Golovan for his small, but fine herd of cows and he was also "lent" to different houses where Golovan used to lead him by a rope whenever his services were needed. That brought Golovan in an additional income.

The milch cows and their strong mate formed Golovan's chief means of subsistence. As I have already mentioned, Golovan delivered milk and cream to the Gentlemen's Club, and his dairy produce enjoyed a high reputation, mainly owing to the excellent breed of his cows, but also because he looked so well after them. The butter sold by Golovan was fresh and yellow like the yolk of an egg and it smelt good; his cream did not "run," that is to say, when the bottle was turned upside down the cream did not pour out, but came out very slowly in a thick, heavy mass. Golovan never sold anything of low quality and for that reason he had no business rivals and in those days the Russian nobleman not only ate well, but had the wherewithal with which to pay for his food. In addition, Golovan used to supply the Club with eggs of an unusually large size laid by a special breed of large Dutch hens, of which he had a great number and, last but not least, he "prepared calves" which he alone seemed to know how to fatten in quite a masterly way and always at the right time, for instance, for a large conference of noblemen from all over our district or on some other special occasion when our nobility flocked together for a celebration of one kind or another.

As a result of all these circumstances, upon which, as I said, his livelihood depended, it was in Golovan's interest to live near the streets inhabited by the gentry, for he used to supply many well-known personalities in whom our townspeople at one time had no difficulty in recognising Panshin, Lavretzky and the other heroes and heroines of Turgenev's "Noblemen's Retreat."

Golovan, however, did not live in our street, but in a near-by gully. The building which was known as "Golovan's House" did not stand in a row of houses, but on a small terrace half-way down the ravine on the left side of the street. The terrace covered an area of about forty-two square feet. It was a big plot of land which at one time or another had slipped down the ravine and stopped half-way where it seemed to have settled firmly. It was not considered sufficiently safe by anyone and, as a matter of fact, it was never claimed by anyone as his property. Such a thing was still possible in those days.

Strictly speaking, Golovan's house could hardly be called a house or a farmstead. It was a large, low-roofed shed which occupied the whole space of the subsided piece of land. It was quite possible that that shapeless building had been erected long before that plot of land had thought of slipping down the ravine and that at that time it had formed part of a farmyard whose owner had not bothered to run after it and had ceded it to Golovan for as small a price as that strapping fellow could afford to pay. I seem also to remember to have heard people say that the shed had been given to Golovan in return for some service, for he enjoyed doing people all sorts of services.

The shed was divided into two parts: one half, bedaubed with clay and whitewashed, with three windows looking out on the Orlik, served as the living quarters for Golovan and the five women who shared the house with him, and the other half had stalls in it for the cows and the bull. The low attic was inhabited by the Dutch hens and the black "Spanish" cock, famous for his longevity and reputed to be "a magic bird." It was in that cock that Golovan was said to grow "the cock's stone," which comes in useful for all sorts of things, being absolutely an infallible means for bringing good luck, recovering territory lost to an enemy in war and transforming old men into young. Such a stone took seven years to grow and was deemed to have reached maturity only when the cock stopped drinking.

The shed was so large that the two parts—the living quarters and the cattle-pen—were very spacious, but in spite of the very great care with which they were kept, it was impossible to keep them warm. It was the women, however, who wanted the warmth, for Golovan himself was completely insensible to any climatic changes and slept both in summer and winter on a bed made of interlaced willow wands in the cattle shed next to his favourite red Tyrolean bull, "Vasska." He was absolutely indifferent to cold and that peculiarity of his formed one of the "mythical" sides of his personality which, combined, helped to make him into a legendary figure.

Three of the five women who lived with Golovan were his sisters, the fourth was his mother and the fifth was called Pavla or, occasionally, Pavlageyushka, although more often than not she was referred to by the people of our town as "Golovan's sin." I was so used to hearing her called that ever since the early days of my childhood that it never occurred to me that there was anything improper in that name. To me Pavla was simply a very kindly woman and I can still remember her tall figure, her pale face with the bright red spots on the cheekbones and the remarkable symmetry of her wonderful black eyebrows. Such black eyebrows, so symmetrically arched, can be seen only on the paintings showing a Persian woman reposing on the knees of some elderly Turk. Our girls, however, knew the real secret of those eyebrows, a secret which had been imparted to me very early in my life: what happened was that Golovan, being a sorcerer and having fallen in love with Pavla, smeared her eyebrows with bear fat while she was asleep and he did it because he did not want anybody to recognise her again. After that, needless to say, there was nothing remarkable about Pavla's eyebrows; but another consequence of that piece of witchcraft was that Pavla got attached to Golovan against her own will and by a power that was quite obviously supernatural.

Our girls knew all about it.

Pavla herself was an extremely placid woman and she was always silent. So taciturn was she that I don't remember ever hearing more than one word at a time from her and one, too, that was absolutely necessary, such as, "Hullo," "Sit down," and "Good-bye." But in every one of those short words there was a world of kindliness, good will and tenderness. The same feelings were expressed by her quiet voice, the look of her grey eyes and, indeed, by every movement of her body. I also remember that she had unusually fine hands which is rather rare among people belonging to the working classes and she was so keen on her work that she easily excelled even among the members of Golovan's hard-working family.

Every member of that family had plenty of work to do: the "deathless one" himself worked ceaselessly from early morning till late at night. He was both herdsman, milkman and maker of cheese. At dawn he would drive his cows out to graze on the common behind our gardens when the grass was still heavy with dew and he kept on driving his magnificent cows from one gully to another, choosing the best grazing place for them where the grass was more lush. At the time when people at home were only beginning to get up, Golovan would already arrive with the empty bottles he had collected at the Club in return for those he had left there that morning; he would himself place in our ice-box the jugs with new milk and discuss some business with my father and by the time I had done with my lessons and gone out for a stroll in our garden, he was sitting at the back of our fence again, looking after his cows. We had a little gate in the fence through which I used to go out to talk with Golovan. He told the one hundred and four sacred stories so well that I learnt them from him without ever having to look into a book. It was there that the poor people used to come to him for advice and as soon as one of them came, he would say, without beating about the bush:

"I've been looking for you, Golovan. Want to ask your advice."

"What's the matter?"

And the man would tell Golovan immediately what was wrong, whether he had any business or family troubles, or whatever it was that was worrying him at the time. More often it was family troubles. Golovan would listen patiently while plaiting an osier basket or from time to time giving a shout at his cows, and all the time he would smile and then he would raise his blue eyes to the man and say:

"I'm not at all good at giving advice, you know. Why not ask God for advice?"

"How am I to ask Him?"

"Oh, that's simple enough. Say your prayers and then do everything as though you were about to die. Now tell me, what would you do if you were about to die?"

The man would think it over and tell him.

Golovan would either agree or he would say:

"But if I were about to die, I think I'd have done this."

And he would explain what he would have done in such a case with his usual cheerful mien and his customary smile.

His advice must always have been good, for people used to act upon it and thank him for it.

Could such a man have had a "sin" in the person of that mildest of women, Pavlageyushka, who at the time was, I should think, in her thirties and who did not live to be forty? I could not understand the meaning of that "sin" and remained guiltless of ever offending her or Golovan by harbouring any suspicions of however vague a character. But there were some grounds for such suspicions, very good and, to judge by appearances, irrefutable grounds. What was she to Golovan? A stranger. Nor was that all: he had known her long ago, he was owned by the same master as she and he had wanted to marry her, but their marriage never took place: Golovan was given as a personal servant to General Alexey Petrovich Yermolov, the hero of the Caucasus, while Pavla was at the same time married off to a groom by the name of Ferapont, or Khrapon, as his name was pronounced locally. Golovan proved a very good and efficient servant, for he could do everything: he was not only an excellent cook and pastrycook, but also a clever and smart orderly. Alexey Petrovich paid for Golovan's services to his master, and also, it is said, lent Golovan enough money to buy his freedom. I don't know how much truth there is in that story, but the fact remains that Golovan did buy his freedom from his master after his return from the Caucasus and he always spoke of General Yermolov as his "benefactor." Alexey Petrovich, on the other hand, made a present to Golovan on his obtaining his freedom of a good cow with a calf which were the beginning of his "Yermolov" herd.

CHAPTER IV

I DON'T know when Golovan settled in his shed in the gully except that it coincided with the beginning of his "free life." At that time he still had to think of his mother and sisters who remained serfs, for Golovan was the only one to obtain his liberty and, in addition to his own family, he had also an aunt who later became my nurse who had to be bought her freedom. His dearly beloved Pavla or Pavlageyushka was in the same position. Golovan considered it his first duty to buy them all out and to do that he wanted money. According to his trade, he could have become a cook or pastrycook, but he preferred to take up dairy farming instead and he started on his career as a dairy farmer with the help of the "Yermolov" cow. It was said, however, that he chose dairy farming because he was a "milker." That might simply have meant that he was always busying himself with his milk, or it might have been a direct hint at his religion in which he appeared rather strange as in many of his other actions. It was, of course, quite possible that while he served in the Caucasus he had got acquainted with the members of the Russian dissident sect of "milkers," a sect which based its beliefs on the direct interpretation of the Bible and which is supposed to have got its name from St. Paul's declaration, "I have fed you with milk, and not with meat." And if Golovan was not a "milker" it was suggested that he might have borrowed some of that sect's ideas. But that relates to the various oddities of his character, of which later.

Golovan's dairy farming throve greatly: after three years he was the owner of two cows and one bull, then of four, and he made so much money that he was able to buy out his mother and every year after that he bought out a sister, and he brought them all to his roomy, but rather chilly den. So it came about that in six or seven years he had bought out his whole family, but the beautiful Pavla had slipped through his fingers. At the time when he could have bought her freedom she had disappeared. Her husband, the groom Khrapon, was a bad man—he did something to displease his master and, as an example to the rest, he was enlisted into the army without any payment.

In the army Khrapon was sent to Moscow where he "ran in the races," that is to say, he became an outrider in an army fire brigade in the ancient Russian capital and he sent for his wife to join him there. But very soon he committed some offence and ran away, and his deserted wife, being of a quiet and meek disposition, got afraid of the vicissitudes of life in the capital and returned to Orel. There she found nothing with which she could support herself and, driven by want, she went to Golovan who, of course, took her in immediately and placed her in the same large room with his mother and sisters. What his mother and sisters had to say to the installation of Pavla, I really don't know, but her living in the same room with them occasioned no quarrels. All the women lived very amicably with one another and Golovan's mother and sisters got to love poor Pavla, while Golovan showed the same kind of attention to all of them and only singled out his mother for his particular respect. His mother was so old and infirm that he used to carry her out in his arms and place her in the sun in summer, just like an ailing child. I can still remember how the old lady would "go off" into a hacking cough and would always pray to be "gathered in."

All Golovan's sisters were old maids and they all assisted Golovan in his business: they looked after and milked his cows, fed the hens and spun a curious-looking yarn which they would weave later into even more curious-looking cloths, the like of which I never saw in my life afterwards. The yarn was called by the rather ugly name of "spittle." The raw material for the yarn was brought from somewhere by Golovan in small bales and I saw it myself and I can still remember it consisting of small, tangled ends of multi-coloured cotton yarns from three inches to half a yard in length and each one of them always had a knot in it, a more or less thick one, or just a twist of some sort. Where Golovan got hold of those broken ends I do not know, but it was evidently some useless factory waste. That was, in fact, what his sisters told me.

"This, my dear," they said, "is what's thrown out in the cotton mills where they spin and weave cotton material. Whenever they get to such a knot, they tear it off, throw it down on the floor and *spit* on it, for it gives them such a lot of trouble as it does not go through the reeds. Our brother collects them and we make warm blankets from them."

I used to watch them patiently unpicking those broken threads, winding the resulting multi-coloured yarn on long bobbins, then spinning it into thicker threads, stretching them on pegs on the walls, sorting out those which were more or less of the same colour for the border and, finally, weaving out of that "spittle" through special reeds their "spittle" blankets. These looked rather like the fleecy blankets we have to-day: each had the same kind of double border, but the material itself was always mottled. The knots seemed to disappear in the stretching and although they were still visible, they did not affect the lightness or the warmth of the blankets which sometimes were quite beautiful. They were, moreover, sold very cheaply, less than a rouble apiece.

This home industry went on without interruption in Golovan's household and I dare say they didn't find it difficult to dispose of those "spittle" blankets of theirs.

Pavla also took a hand in the tying up and drying of the "spittle" yarn, but, in addition, out of gratitude to the family who had given her shelter, she did the heaviest chores in the house: went down the steep slope to the river to fetch water, brought in the fuel and so on and so forth.

Logs were very dear in Orel even in those days and the poor used to heat their homes with the husks of buckwheat or with dung, and the latter in particular demanded a great deal of attention.

Pavla did all that with those slender hands of hers, always in silence, looking out upon the world from under her Persian eyebrows. Whether she knew that people had nicknamed her "Golovan's sin" I can't say, but that was certainly how she was known in our town and the people never change a name they bestow upon a man or woman. And, indeed, what else could one expect? Wherever a woman who is fond of a man lives in the house of the man who loves her and who wanted to marry her, there, of course, must be sin. And so at the time, when, as a child, I knew Pavla, she was unanimously considered as "Golovan's sin," but that did not detract a jot from the general esteem which Golovan himself enjoyed among the people and he kept his nickname of "deathless."

CHAPTER V

GOLOVAN began to be called "deathless" in the first year of his settling alone above the river Orlik with his "Yermolov" cow and her calf. He had earned that name as a result of the following quite authentic circumstance which nobody remembered during the recent "Prokopyev" plague. In that year Orel went through its usual plague period which first broke out among the cattle in the villages in February on the day of St. Agatha the Milkmaid. It happened as was the custom and as, indeed, it is written in the *Universal Book*, which in the chapter entitled *A Chilly Vineyard* proclaimeth: "As soon as summer draweth to a close and autumn approacheth, the plague breaks out among the people. And at such times every man hath to submit himself to God and to His Holy Mother and to amend his living through the strength granted unto him by the true cross, and most of all let him fortify his spirit against that ghastly horror and let him not give way to grief; for thereby his heart may be overcome by a fatal weakness, and he may soon find himself afflicted by ulcerous sores and his brain and heart may become infected and the disease gain mastery over him and he may die apace." All that took place at a season which is all too familiar in our district: "when thick and dark mists arise from the ground and the wind from the land of the midday sun beginneth to blow and thereafter rains come down and the earth smoketh from the sun; then go not abroad in the open air, but stay in thy cottage where thou must beware of opening any window, and beware of resorting to the town, for it is best to flee far from infected places unto places which are free from infection."

When, that is to say, in what year, the plague broke out which made Golovan famous as "deathless" I do not know. People did not worry over such trifles in those days and did not raise an outcry over them as it happened over Naum Prokopvyev. The local trouble was strictly limited to its own locality, where it began and where it came to an end, and the people put their trust in God and the Holy Virgin; and it was only if at the time there happened to live in such an afflicted locality a leisured "gentleman of education" who exercised a great influence over the people, that some highly original measures were taken for the combating of the plague: "in the courtyards great fires of oaken logs were lit so that the smoke spread and in the cottages of the villagers the air was purified by the burning of wormwood, juniper logs and rue leaves." But all that could be done only by "a man of education" who, besides, also happened to be a man of means, but death carried off "apace" not the educated man, but the man who had no time to sit in a warm cottage and who could not afford to light a fire of oaken logs in his yard. Death walked cheek by jowl with hunger and the one supported the other. Those who were hungry went about begging food from those who were as poor as they, and the sick died "apace," that is to say, quickly, to the husbandman's great relief. There was no long-drawn-out agony, nor were any recoveries heard of. Everybody who fell ill died "apace," everybody, that is, *except one*.

What kind of pestilence it was, was never medically established, but it was known popularly as "bosom," or "abcess," or "ulcerous sore," or just "pimple." The plague started in the corn-growing districts where, owing to a bad harvest, the people ate cakes made of hemp-seeds, hence it was also known as "the hemp-seed sore." In the Karachevsky and Bryansk districts where the people mixed a handful of wholemeal flour with pounded bark, there was a different kind of plague, also a fatal one, but not the "ulcerous sore."

The "sore" first appeared on the cattle and then spread among the people. "A purple sore doth appear under the breasts or on the neck of a man who is straightway overcome by an aching in his bones and an unquenchable burning in his bowels or a coldness in his extremities and a shortness of breath—no sooner doth he breathe in the air than out it cometh again, and a drowsiness doth fall upon him and he cannot shake it off; there is a bitter or sour taste in his mouth and he begins to vomit; and a change cometh over the face of the man, which turneth yellow, and thereafter he dieth apace." It might have been anthrax or some other kind of eruptive malady, but whatever it was, it was a fatal and merciless one, and I repeat the most popular name for it was "sore." As soon as a pimple or "sore" appeared on the body, it would get a yellowish head on it with a purple ring round it and after a day gangrene would set in and then death would come on "apace." The quick death was, however, generally described as "a great release" to the sufferers. The end came gently, without agony, a death which the peasants look upon as very merciful, and the only trouble was that the dying suffered terribly from thirst. That was all the brief and simple nursing the patients demanded, or rather implored for themselves. But even that kind of nursing was not only dangerous, but quite impossible to obtain: the man who gave a drink of water to his dear one to-day, fell ill himself to-morrow and it was quite a usual occurrence for two or even three bodies to be laid out on one day in the same house and the one who was the last to catch the infection and fall ill, died without having anyone to look after him, without anyone to give him that last comfort about which our peasants are so anxious: "that there should be someone in the house who could give the dying man some water." At first the only surviving member of a family would place a pail of water at the head of his bed and would get himself a drink with the help of a jug until he would get too weak to lift a hand; then he would twist his sleeve or the hem of his shirt, wet it and put it into his mouth and so he would die and grow stiff in death.

A great personal calamity is a bad teacher of charity. At least it tends to have a bad effect on ordinary people, people whose moral consciousness does not rise above the average of ordinary compassion. It blunts their feelings, which are too overcome by their own sufferings, and it hardens their hearts which are too full of their own troubles. But to compensate for this general decline in the moral standards of society, such times of general affliction produce among the people heroes whose self-denial and whose fearless and self-sacrificial zeal raises them above the crowd. In ordinary times such people attract no attention and very often are indistinguishable from the rest of the population. But let a "sore" begin to play havoc among the people and there will emerge from their midst such a chosen man who performs miracles of self-sacrifice which make him into a mythical being, a legendary, a "deathless" figure. Golovan was one of those chosen ones and during the very first epidemic he excelled and eclipsed in the popular imagination another remarkable local man, the merchant Ivan Ivanovich Androssov.

Androssov was an old man of great honesty who was loved and esteemed for his goodness and justness; for in any affliction that befell the people he was the first to "extend a helping hand" to the sufferers. Nor did he hesitate to do all he possibly could to help those who suffered from the plague, for he possessed a manuscript which abounded in remedies against the plague and he kept on "copying and multiplying it." People used to obtain those copies from him and read them in different places, but no one could understand a word of it and "they knew not how to apply the remedies." The manuscript, for instance, said: "If a sore doth appear on the crown of the head or in any other place above the waist, let a great quantity of blood out of the *median* vein; if it appeareth on the face, let blood immediately from under the tongue; if it appeareth near the ears or under the beard, let blood out of the *cephalic* vein; if, however, it appeareth under the breasts, it signifieth that the heart is touched and then open the *median* vein on that side." For any place "where a pricking is felt" the manuscript gave detailed directions which vein to open, whether the "salfenian," or "the vein against the thumb," or "the spatic, seminatic, or basic vein," with the warning to "let the blood flow freely, until it turneth green and changeth." And it further enjoined to treat the patients with all kinds of curious remedies including "marked earth, Armenian earth, malmsey, mithridates and monus Christi," and a man entering a room where a plague-stricken man was lying was told "to hold in the mouth an angelica root and in his hands wormwood and have his nostrils smeared with scabious vinegar and his lip with vinegar." Nobody could understand what all those strange words meant and, besides, it all read as if it were written in official language, as if it were a decree issued by the Government where the same thing is repeated in many different ways and the meaning is obscured by a superfluity of "whereases." Nobody had ever heard of such veins and nobody knew where to look for them, nor had they ever heard of "malmsey," or "Armenian earth," and they went on reading the writings of the old kindly gentleman more "to soothe their sorrows." Of all his injunctions they could only carry out his last one, namely, "flee from the infected places and go not into the company of them which be infected." That was in fact what many people did and Ivan Ivanovich himself strictly observed the same rule and kept indoors in his well-heated cottage, going out only occasionally to distribute copies of his manuscript which he pushed under the gates, trying to hold his breath and holding in his mouth the angelica root. Only those were supposed to be able "to resort to infectious persons" who possessed "deer's tears" or the bezoar stone, but poor Ivan Ivanovich had neither. It was true that so far as the bezoar stone was concerned, it might have been possible to obtain it at the chemists' shops in Bolkhovskaya Street, but one of the chemists was a Pole and the other a German and neither of them had any particular love for the Russians and, if they had such a stone, they kept it for themselves. That they did so was abundantly proved later when one of the two Orel chemists had lost his stone, for immediately his ears were seen to turn yellow (he was crossing the street at the time), one of his eyes grew smaller than the other and he began to shake in a palsy, and although he immediately took measures to bring on a sweat, ordering a hot brick to be put to his heels, he did not perspire and died in a dry shirt. Many people tried their best to find the stone which the chemist had lost and somebody was said to have found it, but it was not Ivan Ivanovich, for he, too, died of the plague.

And at such a dreadful time when the educated people rubbed themselves all over with vinegar and managed not to breathe their last, the "sore" raged among the poor wretches who lived in the hovels of the Orel suburbs more than ever. People began to die off in thousands and without any help whatsoever, and then suddenly Golovan appeared in this valley of death, displaying an amazing fearlessness. He probably knew, or thought he knew, of some remedy, for he used to place upon the sores of the sick a "Caucasian plaster" prepared by himself, but the "Caucasian" or "Yermolov" plaster was of precious little use. Golovan did not cure those who were stricken down by the "sore" and in that he was not much more successful than Androssov; but his help both for the sick and the hale was important in the sense that he showed no fear in entering the hovels of the people infected with the plague and he gave the sick and dying not only fresh water to drink, but also the skimmed milk which was left over after he had taken the cream off for the Gentlemen's Club. Very early every morning, long before dawn, he would cross the river Orlik on the gates of his shed which he had taken off their hinges (there was no boat to be had) and with the bottles of skimmed milk in his capacious sheepskin he went from one hovel to another to moisten the parched lips of the dying from one of his bottles and to put a cross on a door with a piece of chalk wherever life's drama had drawn to a close and the curtain of death had fallen on the most recent of its actors.

From that time Golovan, who had been little known before, became one of the most popular figures in our town and in the poor suburbs in particular the people looked upon him as their best friend. His name, which before was known only to the servants of the gentry, now began to pass from mouth to mouth among the common people who very soon regarded him as "a man who not only can take the place of the late Ivan Ivanovich, but can be held even in greater esteem than he both by God and men." And it did not take them long to find a supernatural explanation for Golovan's fearlessness: Golovan, it was quite plain, knew something and on the strength of that mysterious knowledge of his he was "deathless."

Afterwards it appeared that that was so: the cowherd Panka was the instrument through which the mystery surrounding Golovan was explained to all, for Panka had seen Golovan perform a most extraordinary act, which, indeed, merely confirmed the opinion already formed about Golovan's supernatural powers, for which there were a number of other proofs.

Golovan seemed immune from contagion and while the plague raged in the suburbs neither he nor his cow and her calf suffered any harm; but that was not all: the most important thing was that he had deceived and brought to naught, or, to use a local idiom, "bested" the plague itself and he performed that miracle without hesitating to shed his own blood for his beloved people.

It was Golovan who had the bezoar stone lost by the chemist. How he had come to possess it was not known, but it was generally assumed that when Golovan was taking his cream to the chemist for a "one-day ointment" he caught sight of the stone and hid it. Whether it was honest or dishonest to "hide" somebody else's property was a question that was regarded as of little moment in this connection and not only did it not arouse any severe criticism, but it could hardly be expected to arouse any criticism. If it was not a sin to take and hide away food because food was given by God to all, how could it be deemed to be a reprehensible act to pick up and retain a medical substance, if it had been given for the general good? This is, I am afraid, the way public opinion judges about such things in our town and I am merely reporting it. Golovan, on the other hand, having concealed the chemist's stone, acted generously and saw to it that it brought help and salvation to all good Christians.

All that, as I have already mentioned, was discovered by Panka and public opinion merely put the mark of its approval upon his discovery.

CHAPTER VI

PANKA, a cross-eyed peasant lad with mousy hair, was a herdsman's help who in addition to his usual duties used to drive out "on the dew" early every morning the cows belonging to some Russian baptist merchants of our town. It was during one of those early excursions of his that he had witnessed the event which was destined to raise Golovan to so high a pinnacle of popular esteem and veneration. That took place in spring, I suppose soon after—

Fair Yegory, gallant and gladsome youth,
On th' emerald Russian fields came riding
In gold up to his elbows apparell'd,
His legs to the knees in silver encas'd,
The sun on's brow and the moon at his back,
With wandering stars on each side adorn'd,
And all the people, loyal and true, their herds
And flocks drove out to greet him.

The grass was still so short that sheep and goats found it barely enough to sustain them and the thick-lipped cows could hardly nibble at it, but under the wattle fences, in the shade and in the ditches, wormwood and nettles were already growing in rich profusion which, for want of anything better, the cows were quite glad to eat.

Panka drove out the cows of the baptist merchants very early, while it was still dark, and he drove them along the bank of the Orlik past the suburbs to a glade directly opposite the Third Gentlemen's Street, where on one side, on the slope of the hill, was the old, so-called "city" park and, on the left, Golovan's house clung precariously half-way up the ravine.

It was still cold in the mornings, especially in the hours before dawn, and Panka, who was only half awake, felt very cold indeed. Panka's clothes, it goes without saying, did not provide any protection against the chill morning breezes, for, truth to tell, they were all in holes. The poor lad shivered and stamped about, trying to warm himself and praying in vain to St. Fedul for a breath of warm air for his fool, but instead the wind seemed to get even more and more icy. As soon as he'd close his eyes, the cold blast would blow through a hole in his clothes and waken him again. However, youth prevailed in the end: Panka pulled his ragged overcoat over his head like a little tent and fell into a doze. He did not hear what hour it was, for the green steeple of the Church of the Redeemer was far away. There was not a soul to be seen only the fat merchants' cows were panting and from time to time a playful perch would give a sudden splash in the Orlik. The cowherd snoozed away in his torn coat. Suddenly he gave a start, as though somebody had nudged him in the side: Aeolus must have found a new hole through which to blow. Panka started up, opened his sleep-laden eyes, was about to give a shout to one of his cows, the one without horns, to stop her from wandering off too far, but instead he just gasped speechlessly. For it seemed to him that someone was coming down the steep slope of the hill. Was it a thief who wanted to bury his swag in the loamy soil? Panka's interest was aroused: why shouldn't he lie in wait for the thief and catch him redhanded or, perhaps, shout, "Let's go halves," or, what was even better, try to remember the exact spot where the stolen goods were buried and then swim across the Orlik in the daytime, dig it all up and take the lot without going shares with anybody?

Panka was all eyes now, his gaze glued to the other side of the river. The day was just beginning to break.

He saw somebody coming down the slope and, on reaching the river, beginning to walk on the water as if it were dry land, without making a splash, but just leaning against some kind of a crutch. Panka was struck dumb.

In the monastery in Orel they were just then expecting the appearance of a new saint, and the monks and, indeed, many members of the congregation who came to pray in the monastery church had heard voices coming from the crypt from beneath the floor. All those expectations of a miracle began soon after "Nicodemus's funeral."

Bishop Nicodemus was a spiteful old man who had gained an evil reputation towards the end of his earthly career by his desire to curry favour with authority and supply the army with another cavalry squadron, for which purpose he had pressed into the army a large number of monks, among whom were many who were only sons and even deacons and sextons with families of their own. They used to leave our town for the army in large parties, shedding bitter tears. Those who saw them off also wept and the people who, as a whole, did not particularly love the priests who lived on the fat of the land, joined in the general weeping and offered them alms. Even the officer who was in charge of the party was so sorry for them that, wishing to put an end to their tears, he ordered the recruits to sing a song, and when they burst out into a song which they had composed on the spot—

Our bishop Nicodemus,
Is an arch-fiend out of hell—

the officer himself was said to have started crying. Those universal tears were merely an expression of the general feeling of disgust against the evil deeds of a bishop which cried to heaven. And, to be sure, when those cries and lamentations reached heaven, "voices" began to be heard in Orel. At first the "voices" were hardly distinguishable and people were not certain where they came from, but soon after Nicodemus had died and been buried in the crypt under the cathedral church, the "voices" became audible and were said to belong to a bishop who had been buried in the crypt before (I believe it was Apollos). The bishop who had died earlier did not like his new neighbour and demanded, quite unabashed, in plain language, "Take the carcass away, he stifles me!" And he even threatened that, if "the carcass" were not removed, he would "go away and appear in another town." Many people had heard it. After the evening mass at the monastery church and just before they were about to go home, they'd hear the old bishop begin to moan, "Remove the carcass!" Everybody wished that the demand of the good bishop should be carried out, but the authorities who did not always heed the wishes of the people refused to remove the body of Nicodemus, and the new saint who was about to reveal himself was generally expected to "vacate the premises" any moment.

So quite obviously that was what was happening now: the saint was going away and the miracle was only witnessed by a poor cowherd who had been so taken aback that he had not only failed to stop the saint, but didn't even notice where the saint had disappeared to.

The sun was just rising. Man usually gathers up courage with the light of day, and with the return of courage curiosity also awakens. Panka wanted to walk up to the water over which the mysterious being had just walked, but no sooner did he reach the bank of the river than he saw the wet gates held fast to the bank by a pole stuck into the sand. The mystery was therefore cleared up: it was not the saint who had been leaving the monastery at all, it was just deathless Golovan who had simply ferried across the river on his gates. Golovan must have gone to comfort some children, whose parents had died of the plague, and taken them some milk. Panka could not help feeling rather surprised: didn't Golovan ever go to sleep? . . . And how could he, such a huge man, ferry safely across the river on such a primitive contraption—one half of a gate? It was true the Orlik was only a small river and its waters, dammed up down-stream by lock gates, were as stagnant as a pond, but all the same how did he manage to ferry across on gates?

Panka wanted to see how it was done himself. He stood on the gates, took hold of the pole and, just for a lark, ferried across the stream and, having reached the other bank, got off to have a look at Golovan's house, for by that time it had got quite light. But just at that moment Golovan shouted from the other side, "Hi, there! Who's taken my gates? Bring them back!"

Panka was not exactly a brave lad and his experience of life had not taught him to count on anyone's generosity. He therefore got the wind up and did a silly thing. Instead of taking the ferry back to Golovan, he hid it in one of the clay pits, of which there were a great number thereabouts. Panka lay hidden in that pit and, although Golovan went on shouting to him for some time from the other side, did not show himself. Seeing that he couldn't get his ferry back, Golovan threw off his sheepskin, stripped naked and, strapping his whole wardrobe with his leather belt and putting it on his head, he swam across the Orlik. The water was still very cold at the time.

All Panka was concerned about was that Golovan should not discover him and give him a hiding, but his attention soon became attracted to something else. Golovan had swum across the river and had started to dress, but suddenly he sat down, examined his left knee carefully, seemed to discover something just under it and stopped dressing. All that had happened so near the pit where Panka was hiding that he could see everything very clearly by just peeping over the top. It was quite light already, the sky was crimson with the dawn, and although most of the citizens were still in their beds, a youth appeared from behind the city park carrying a scythe over his shoulder and with his scythe he began to cut some nettles and put them in a wicker basket.

Golovan noticed the mower and, standing up in his shirt, shouted to him in a loud voice:

"I say, boy, give me your scythe quickly!"

The youth brought the scythe and Golovan said to him:

"Get me a large burdock, please!" and as the boy turned away from him, he took the scythe off its snath, squatted down again on his haunches, pulled out one of the calves of his legs with his hand and cut it off with one stroke. He then threw away the cut-off piece of flesh, as large as a village flat cake, into the river Orlik, while he himself squeezed the wound with both his hands and collapsed on the ground.

Seeing that, Panka forgot about everything, jumped out of his pit and started shouting for the boy.

The two youths took hold of Golovan and dragged him to his cottage where he recovered consciousness and told them to fetch two towels out of the chest of drawers and twist them round his wound as tightly as possible. They twisted them round with all their might until the flow of blood stopped. Then Golovan told them to put beside him a pail of water and a jug and to go about their business. Before they left him, however, he asked them to tell no one about what had happened.

They went away, stunned with terror, and told everybody everything and those who heard the story immediately realised that Golovan had not done it just for fun, but that he, full of pity for the people who had been struck down with the plague, had thrown a piece of his own flesh to the "sore" with the intention that it should go down all the Russian rivers as a sacrifice, from the little Orlik into the Oka and from the Oka into the Volga, all across great Russia until it reached the wide Caspian Sea, and that by this act of his Golovan had taken upon himself the sufferings of all the afflicted, being himself safe from death, for he possessed the life-giving stone of the chemist and he was a "deathless" man.

This legend seemed to be what everybody wanted to believe and, as a matter of fact, the prophecy was fulfilled. Golovan did not die of his terrible wound, while the great pestilence really came to an end after that sacrifice and happy times came back again: the fields and meadows were overspread with thick, lush grass and young Yegory, fair and gallant, could roam over them at will on his brave steed, apparelled up to his elbows in gold, his legs encased in silver up to the knees, the sun on his brow and the moon at his back and on each side adorned with wandering stars. Then the linen was bleached in the fresh April dew and in place of the brave knight Yegory, Jeremiah the prophet rode out into the fields, carrying the heavy yoke and dragging ploughs and harrows behind him, and on St. Boris's day, comforting the martyr, and thanks to the efforts of St. Mavra, the corn began to grow sturdily and covered the fields in a bluish mist, St. Zossima passed across the land with his crutch, on the knobbled head of which he brought the queen bee, the day of St. John the Blessed, father of Nicholas, had gone, and on the ninth of May St. Nicholas's day, too, had been celebrated and Simon Zilot arrived when the earth herself celebrates her birthday. It was then that Golovan crawled out of his shed and lay down in the sun, propped up against the mound of earth by his house and since that time he began little by little to walk about and to look after his farm again. His health apparently did not suffer in the least, except that he began to "hop about," skipping on his left foot as he walked.

People no doubt had a very high opinion of the touching bravery of the terrible operation he had performed upon himself, but, as I said, that opinion was not based on any rational explanation of his action. People preferred to give free play to their imagination, they created a fantastic legend out of a natural event and transformed the simple, kind-hearted Golovan into a mythical figure, something of a magus, a sorcerer, who possessed a magic talisman, and could do anything he wanted without running the risk of death.

Whether or not Golovan knew with what magical powers popular fancy had invested him, I do not know. I can't help thinking, however, that he did know it, for people very often came to ask him to do things which only a magician could do. As for Golovan, he seemed to have given "encouraging replies" to such demands and did not, as a rule, get angry whatever people asked him to do. In the suburbs his help was constantly sought after as a cow doctor, a medical man, an engineer, an astronomer and a chemist. He could rid animals of the mange and the scab by some kind of "Yermolov" ointment, it seemed, and the same ointment apparently also cured people of all sorts of skin diseases and it cost only a farthing for three people. He also relieved the headaches of patients who had high temperatures with the help of a salted cucumber, knew what herbs had to be collected between the twenty-fourth of May, St. John's day, and the twenty-ninth of June, St. Peter's day, and he was an excellent water-diviner, showing people where to dig wells. That, however, he could only do at a certain time, namely, between the beginning of June and the day of St. Fyodor the Well-digger, that is to say, only so long as "the waters under the ground could be heard flowing." Golovan, in fact, could have done anything else that a man might desire, had he not vowed to God not to do everything people asked him to do provided the "sore" came to an end. And, as everybody knew, he had sealed his vow with his own blood and he kept it faithfully. That was why God loved him and spared him and the people who had a fine sense of knowing how far one could go in asking a man for a favour, never asked Golovan to do something he could not perform. Such is the etiquette which the people never dream of violating.

Golovan felt so little encumbered by the mystical cloud with which popular fancy surrounded him that he did not seem to make the slightest effort to destroy the legend which had grown round him. He must have known that it would have been quite impossible to do so.

When I eagerly scanned the pages of Victor Hugo's novel, "The Toilers of the Sea" and came across Gilliatt with that marvellously conceived stern sense of duty of his, coupled with his no less remarkable forbearance for the weaknesses of other people which reaches the height of perfect self-abnegation, I was struck not only by the fine conception of that character and the power of genius which created it, but also by the perfect kinship between the Guernsey hero and the living man whom I had known by the name of Golovan. One and the same spirit lived in both of them and their hearts, so like one another, beat with the same self-sacrificial zeal. Nor was their fate very much different: a kind of mystery surrounded them all through their lives just because they were so pure and transcendent in spirit, and neither the one nor the other enjoyed a particle of happiness of his own.

CHAPTER VII

GOLOVAN, like Gilliatt, was "doubtful of his faith." It was generally assumed, however, that he was a dissenter, but that did not matter very much, for in those days Orel was full of dissenters of every kind, as, no doubt, it still is, including "old believers," believers that were not so "old," baptists, and even flagellants and just "God's people" who were sent by man's judgment into far-away exile. But all those dissenters adhered strictly to their own faith and firmly denied any other faith, holding apart from each other, keeping themselves to themselves both as regards prayer and food in the strong belief that they alone knew "the way to salvation." Golovan, however, behaved as if he himself knew nothing about the best way for achieving salvation and he gladly shared his bread with any man who cared to ask for it and, if asked, did not hesitate to sit down at anybody's table. He even took milk for the children of the Jew Yushka, but that un-Christian-like act on the part of Golovan found some excuse in the eyes of those who loved him: for the people realised that in favouring Yushka, Golovan tried to get from him the secret of "Judah's lips," which the Jews were believed to keep from the whole world and which made it possible for any man to tell a lie in court without being found out, or to obtain "the hairy vegetable" which enabled Jews to quench their thirst without drinking any liquor. But what they could not understand was that Golovan should be great friends with the coppersmith Anton who enjoyed a very low reputation indeed in regard to those moral attributes which they themselves esteemed highly. For Anton did not agree with any man's opinion about sacred things and he was known to draw very mysterious lines of the "zodiac" and even to write something or other.

Anton lived in the suburb in an empty attic room, for which he paid half a rouble a month. Although his room was bare of furniture, it was said to be full of all sorts of terrible things, so that no one except Golovan ever visited him. It was known, however, that Anton kept in his room a "plan" called "the zodiac," and a glass which could "bring down fire from the sun"; in addition, he had a skylight in his room through which he was known to clamber on to the roof at night where he used to squat down like a cat behind a chimney, "put out a spy glass" and, at a time when all good Christians were asleep, he looked at the sky. Anton's attachment to that instrument knew no limit, especially on a starry night, when he could see all the "zodiacs." As soon as he came home from the workshop where he was employed as a coppersmith, he would go straight to his attic and immediately climb out on the roof and, should there be any stars about in the sky, he would sit there the whole night through, just star-gazing all the time. He could have been forgiven that occupation of his, if he had been an educated man or, at least, a German, but as he was just a common or garden Russian, people did all they possibly could to make him give up that hobby of his, trying to force him off the roof with long poles or throwing dung at him (once they even threw a dead cat at him), but he ignored it all and did not even notice that he was being poked with a pole. Everybody laughingly called him "the astronomer," and he really was an astronomer.[1]

He was a very inoffensive and honest man, but a freethinker; he would stick to his point that the earth turned round and that we sometimes walked about upside-down. For talking rot like that Anton was beaten up and earned the reputation of being a born fool and, having got that reputation, he began to enjoy the privilege of a born fool, that is to say, he was allowed to think as he liked, a privilege freely bestowed on all born fools in Russia, and indeed his theories were quite often extremely wild. He thus refused to

[1] My former school friend and the now well-known Russian mathematician, K. D. Krayevich, and myself knew that enthusiast towards the end of the 'forties when we were in the third form of the Orel grammar school and shared the same digs in the house of Mr. Lossev. "Anton the astronomer" (rather an old man at that time) had really quite an adequate knowledge of the stars and the law of their revolutions, but the most remarkable thing about him was that he himself manufactured the lenses for his telescopes out of the bottoms of thick glasses and through them studied the skies. He had always been poor, but he did not mind his poverty, for he was in a state of constant excitement over his "zodiacs." (N.L.)

acknowledge that the "sevens" in Daniel's vision was a prophecy about the Russian Empire and he used to say that the beast with the ten horns was just an allegory and the beast that was like a bear was an astronomical figure, which he had on his maps. Similar heretical views were held by him about "the eagle's wings," the phials and the mark of anti-Christ. But as he was considered to be mentally defective people forgave him all that. He was unmarried, because he was too busy with the stars to get married and also because he could not afford to keep a wife and, besides, what fool of a woman would ever dream of marrying an astronomer?

Golovan, on the other hand, who was considered to be completely rational, not only spent a great deal of time with the astronomer, but didn't even make jokes at his expense. They were even seen together at night on the astronomer's roof, taking turns in looking through the spy-glass at the "zodiacs." It is not difficult to guess what thoughts those two figures, standing side by side on the roof at night, aroused in the minds of the people, figures round which romantic superstition, medicine magic, religious credulity and gross ignorance had woven the most fantastic stories. . . . Finally, circumstances themselves put Golovan in a somewhat curious position: thus it was impossible to say to which parish Golovan's house belonged. His cold shed seemed to hang in mid-air, as it were, and no clerical strategists could determine whether or not it belonged to their parishes. Golovan himself did not seem to care about it and if questioned somewhat persistently, he would reply:

"I belong to the parish of the Almighty Creator," but there was no such church in the whole of Orel.

Gilliatt, in reply to the question to what parish he belonged, just raised a finger and, pointing it at the sky, said:

"To that one"—and in essence both replies were identical.

Golovan liked to listen to the exposition of any faith, but he did not seem to have any opinion of his own about it and when asked point-blank, "In whom dost thou believe?" he would reply:

"I believe in the one God the Father, the Almighty Creator of everything visible and invisible."

That, of course, was just begging the question.

However, anyone thinking that Golovan was a sectarian or that he avoided anything that had to do with the Church would be mistaken. No, he even used to go to see Father Peter in the Borissoglyebsky Cathedral and ask him "to examine his conscience." He would come and say:

"Admonish me, father, I'm somehow greatly dissatisfied with myself."

I remember Father Peter very well, for he used to visit us; and once when my father said to him *apropos* of something that Golovan seemed to be a man of a sterling conscience, Father Peter replied:

"No doubt about it: his conscience is whiter than snow!"

Golovan liked exalted thoughts and he knew Pope, but not as people usually know a writer whose works they have read. No. Having approved the sentiments expressed in the "Essay on Man," which was presented to him by his patron Alexey Petrovich Yermolov, Golovan learnt the whole poem *by heart*. I can still remember how he used to stand leaning against the lintel of the door and listen, for instance, to a story about a recent rather melancholy event and, sighing suddenly, he would say:

> Awake, my St. John! leave all meaner things
> To low ambition, and the pride of Kings.

The reader need not be surprised that a man like Golovan should quote Pope's verses. The time he lived in was a cruel one, but poetry was in fashion then and its inspired words were dear even to men of noble blood, and from the gentlemen this love of po try descended to the plebeians.

But now I am coming to one of the most important events in Golovan's life, an event which did seem to put him in rather an ambiguous position even in the eyes of people who do not as a rule believe all sorts of nonsense. Golovan was apparently guilty of some rather unsavoury misdemeanour at some remote period of his life. It came out quite unexpectedly and in a way that could not possibly be overlooked. There appeared in the streets of Orel an individual who was not of the slightest account to anybody, but who seemed to possess an extraordinary power over Golovan and, indeed, behaved to him with the utmost insolence.

That individual and the story of his appearance in our town forms an exceedingly characteristic episode in the history of manners of that time and is not altogether uninteresting in itself as an illustration of low life in those days. I must therefore ask the reader's indulgence if I digress a little and take him to a place far from Orel, to much warmer climes, to a river flowing gently between banks carpeted with grass, to "a feast of popular faith," where everyday, practical affairs have no business at all, where everything, *absolutely everything*, happens as an act of faith, which lends every event its own vivid distinctness. We must be present at the display of the relics of a new saint, which was an event of supreme importance to the representatives of all classes of society in those days, but which to the common people was an epic in itself, when, as a bard of that time used to say, "a sacred feast of faith was celebrated."

CHAPTER VIII

THE road traffic which began at the time of the start of the festivities no contemporary account adequately conveys. The human, though sordid, side of the whole business escaped the chronicler of those stirring events altogether. Travel in those days bore no resemblance to our modern orderly travel in post-chaises and on railways, with stops at well-run inns and taverns where everything can be got at a fair price. To go on a journey then was an heroic enterprise and in this particular case an act of pious heroism which, however, was entirely worth while in view of the forthcoming solemnities in the cathedral.

There was so much poetry in those church solemnities and also something special, something rich in colour and full of various shades of religious ecstasy, which was characteristic of the life of the Church at the time and which was as boundless as popular simplicity and the infinite aspirations of the living spirit.

Great multitudes left Orel for those solemnities. Most of the devout pilgrims came, of course, from the merchant classes, but there were also a large number of middling landowners and crowds of common people. The last went on foot. Only those who were bringing sick and ailing with them "for a cure" managed to obtain a cart and some ancient horse to take them to the place of pilgrimage. Occasionally, however, people carried the sick on their backs and did not mind doing it, for at the inns specially reduced rates were charged to the sick and their relatives and sometimes they were not charged anything at all. There were also quite a few who simulated ailments on purpose: turned their eyes up, or two men would take turns to push a third one on a handcart "to obtain thereby some money wherewith to buy wax candles, oil, and for other rites."

That was what I read in one of the contemporary accounts of such a pilgrimage, an account written by hand and never printed, neither was it written to an official pattern, but evidently transcribed "from life" and by a man who preferred to stick to the truth instead of indulging in the tendentious lies of that time.

The traffic on the roads was so dense that in the towns of Livny and Yeletz, through which the pilgrims had to pass, all the taverns and inns were full. It even frequently happened that important and well-known people had to spend the night in their carriages. The price of oats, hay and groats rose all along the highway, so much so that, according to my grandmother whose reminiscences I am drawing upon here, ever since that time a meal of calf's-feet jelly, cabbage soup, mutton and thick porridge for one man cost fifty-two copecks at a tavern, whereas before that pilgrimage the usual price for such a meal was twenty-five copecks. According to present-day prices even fifty copecks seems quite incredibly cheap, but that was the price of such a meal then, and the discovery of the relics of the new saint bore the same relationship to the rise in food prices in the localities affected by the flood of pilgrims as the burning down of the Mstinsky Bridge did in St. Petersburg. "The prices rocketed and stayed like that."

Among the pilgrims who had left Orel to pay homage to the new saint was the family of S., well-known merchants in their time, grain "collectors," or in plain language rich corn chandlers who "collected" the grain from the peasants' carts and stored it in granaries from where they sold their "collections" to wholesalers in Moscow and Riga. It is a very profitable business which even noblemen, after the liberation of the peasants, did not scorn to engage in; these, however, were used to a life of ease and they soon learnt that they weren't any good at the simple business of grabbing easy profits.

The merchants S. occupied a foremost place among the grain "collectors" and their position in our town was such that even their house was not known by its number, but by some highfalutin name. Their mode of life, needless to say, was extremely strict: they spent the whole morning in prayers, the whole day in squeezing and robbing the poor peasants and the whole evening again in prayers. At night savage dogs were clanking their chains in the ditches which surrounded their house, but through all the windows could be seen the soft light of icon lamps and in the house the loud snoring was occasionally broken by somebody's heart-broken sobs.

The lord and master of the household was, to use a modern expression, the founder of the firm, who in those days was just referred to as "himself." He was a fat little man whom everybody, however, feared like the plague. It was said of him that he could make a soft bed, but would lie hard on it. He called everybody "my dear," but he hit you right between the eyes: a well-known and common enough character, the character of a merchant-patriarch.

It was this patriarch who went on the pilgrimage "in great style": himself, his wife and his daughter who suffered from "melancholy fits" and was being taken to be cured. Every possible remedy known to the romantic popular medicine of the time had been applied to her: she was made to drink the invigorating juice of the elecampane root, she was covered from head to foot with peony petals, which is supposed to remove the influence of an evil shadow, she was given marjoram to smell, which is supposed to be a good cure for diseased brains, but nothing was of the slightest use; and now she was being taken to the saint, her father being in a hurry to be present at the "first event" when the curative powers of the relics are said to be strongest. The faith in the effectiveness of the *first powers* is very great and it is based on the story of the pool of Siloam where only *the first* who entered the water before it became muddied were healed.

The Orel merchant and his family travelled through Livny and Yeletz, experiencing great difficulties on the way, and they were dead tired by the time they arrived in the town where the saint's relics were to be exposed in the cathedral church. But to be present at the "first event" and so benefit from the saint's unimpaired healing powers seemed to be quite out of the question. Such immense crowds were expected to fill the streets on the first evening of the exposure of the relics that the idea of being able to push one's way through to the church had to be given up.

The merchant and his wife were in despair. Their daughter alone seemed to be the only indifferent one of the three, but then she did not know what she was missing. There was no hope whatever of mending matters: there were so many noble families in town who bore such famous names and they were just ordinary merchants and, while in their own town they were people of consequence, here among all that vast conglomeration of Christian grandeur they were just lost. So one afternoon the merchant-patriarch was sitting in his covered wagon, nursing his grievance and drinking tea and telling his wife bitterly that he had given up all hope of reaching the sacred coffin either at the first or the second "event" and that all he could hope for now was to get into the church among the common crowd of farm hands and fishermen. What joy could he expect from that? For towards the end of the solemnities the police were, as a rule, in a fearful temper and the clergy were too fagged-out and they didn't even let the people pray as long as they should and just pushed them out of the church unceremoniously. And, generally, one could hardly expect the same signs of grace at so late an hour after so many thousands of lips had already pressed against the coffin. If he had known what to expect, he would have arrived later, but of course it wasn't *that* that they wanted: they had had such a terrible journey, paid through the nose for their food and lodgings, left the business at the mercy of a hired man and there they were now, stuck at the very gates of the church!

The merchant had tried once or twice to see the deacons, being only too ready to pay for a favour, but it was quite hopeless even to think of it—on the one hand, what he got was some sauce from a policeman in white sleeves and from some cossack with a whip (there were plenty of police and cossacks about, for it seemed they, too, had arrived for the exposure of the saint's relics), and, on the other, he was nearly trampled to death by the faithful who thronged the streets in great crowds. There had been many such "accidents" that day and the day before. Should a large crowd of good Christians, five or six hundred of them, start back at the crack of a whip from a cossack and press together against each other in a solid mass, screams and groans immediately arose from the middle of the crowd and later, when the crush abated, many a female ear was without its ear-ring, which had been torn out with the flesh, and many a finger was not only without its rings, but had nearly been wrenched off its owner's hand, and two or three souls had completely shuffled off their mortal coils and were even at that moment presenting themselves before their heavenly Father.

While the patriarch was recounting all those difficulties to his wife and to his daughter for whom it was so important to obtain the "first powers," some vagabond, whether of urban or rural origin it was impossible to say, was walking among the covered wagons behind the fence of the inn and he seemed to be paying particular attention to the Orel merchant and his family.

There were also a great number of rogues and vagabonds in the town. Not only did they fit in at that festival of faith, but they even found all sorts of profitable employment for themselves; that, in fact, was mainly the reason why they had flocked to the town in their thousands from all over the country, but especially from large and small towns which were famous for their thieves and tramps, that is to say, from Orel, Kromy, Yeletz and Livny where they had earned the reputation of being masters of their art. All the vagabonds who had gathered there were eager to carry on with their trades. The adventurous souls among them acted in gangs, placing themselves in groups among the dense crowds where it was possible to create a crush with the help of a cossack and go through the pockets of the faithful during the panic, or tear off somebody's watch and belt-buckle, or pull ear-rings out of women's ears; but the less enterprising ones among them went about singly, paying visits to the yards of inns and taverns where they complained of their hard luck, "proclaimed dreams and miracles," offered philtres and charms for sale as well as mysterious aids made of "whale's semen, raven's fat and elephant's sperm" and other nostrums "the force whereof moveth continually." These nostrums did not lose their attraction even here, for, to the honour of mankind be it said, human conscience did not allow people to turn to the saint for every kind of cure. No less eagerly did the quiet-spoken vagabonds turn to ordinary robbery and, whenever a favourable occasion presented itself, did not scruple to rob the pilgrims of everything they possessed; for, unable to get rooms at an inn, many pilgrims were forced to live in their wagons and even under them.

There was not much free space in the town and not all carts could find a place behind the sheds of an inn; the rest camped in the open fields on the outskirts of the town where life was even more interesting and varied and richer in all the manifold shades of church and leechcraft poetry, which gave much greater scope to rogues of all kinds to exercise their talents. Indeed, the merchants of iniquity were all over the place. It was there that a brisk trade was done in illegally distilled vodka and two or three carts were filled with red-cheeked young ladies who had gone there to share both their expenses and profits in common. It was also there that the manufacture of sacred relics reached the height of artistry, including chips of the sacred coffin, "marked earth," bits of rotted chasubles and even splinters of "bones." There were among the artists who specialised in the manufacture of these "objects of virtu" men of great wit and invention who performed all kinds of fascinating tricks remarkable both for their simplicity and utter brazenness. Such was the one who had attracted the attention of the devout Orel merchant.

The vagabond listened to the merchant's complaints about the difficulties of getting near the saint's relics before the first medicinal grace had flowed from them, then he went straight up to the patriarch and laid all his cards on the table:

"I've heard your trouble, sir," he said, "and I can help you. You needn't be afraid, for without us you will never be able to fulfil your desire at this crowded and distinguished gathering. You see, sir, we have been at many such gatherings before and we know the ropes. If you want to benefit from 'the first powers' of the saint I shall be able to arrange it for you, provided you won't mind parting with one hundred roubles for your greater joy and happiness."

The merchant gave the vagabond one look and said:

"I don't want to listen to any of your lies."

But the vagabond was in no way abashed and he went on:

"I'm not at all surprised to hear you say that, sir, for you no doubt judge me by my unworthiness, but what may seem unworthy in men's eyes, may seem quite different in the eyes of God. I assure you, sir, that whatever I undertake to do, I always carry out. You seem to be concerned about the large number of the great ones of this earth who have come here, but I, sir, don't give a fig for them and even if a whole multitude of kings and princes had forgathered here, they would still not stand in our way, but would themselves make way for us. Therefore, sir, if you still wish to go through all those throngs without let or hindrance and behold the first of the land and be among the first to offer a humble kiss to the friend of God, then do not begrudge me the money I have asked. However, if you do not want to part with one hundred roubles and don't mind sharing somebody else's company, I shall quickly find one or two more men whom I have in mind and then it will be cheaper for you."

What was there left for the pious pilgrims to do? It was, no doubt, a bit of a risk to trust a man who was quite obviously a rogue and a vagabond, but, on the other hand, one did not want to miss one's chance, especially as he did not ask for a lot of money when, that is, the hundred roubles were shared by two or three people. . . .

The patriarch decided to take the risk.

"All right," he said. "Get your company together, my dear man."

The vagabond took a deposit and ran off, having told the merchant's family to have an early dinner and to take each a clean towel and go outside the town to the appointed place in the "poor camp" and wait for him there one hour before the first bell rang out for the evening service. From there the procession, which, the *entrepreneur* assured the merchant, no prince or king on earth would stop, was due to start.

Such "poor camps" on a smaller or larger scale are pitched in a wide enclosure at all such gatherings and I myself saw and well remember them at Korennaya outside Kursk, and as regards the one I am going presently to describe, I have heard eye-witness stories of everything that took place there.

CHAPTER IX

THE site occupied by the poor encampment was situated on a big space on a common between the river and the highway and one end of it adjoined a large and winding ditch at the bottom of which ran a stream and which was densely overgrown with bushes; behind the ditch was a great pine forest where eagles could be heard screeching.

The common was covered with hundreds of carts and wagons of primitive construction which, poor as they were, presented a kaleidoscopic picture of national genius and inventiveness. There were on them ordinary tents made out of straw matting, linen tents which covered the whole of the cart, "summer houses" made out of tufted feather-grass and very hideous-looking awnings made out of bark. The entire bark of a century-old lime-tree was bent and nailed to the cart-body and under it people were lying, feet inside the wagon and heads fore and aft, in the open. Over the heads of the recumbent bodies the winds blew, thus assuring proper ventilation and preventing them from suffocating from lack of fresh air. The horses stood by the carts near the baskets of hay and canvas bags fastened to the side-shafts. The horses were mostly lean and all of them had their collars on, and some of them, those which belonged to thrifty people, stood under "roofs" made of straw mats. Some of the poor pilgrims had their dogs which they should not rightly have brought with them, but those were "faithful" dogs which had run after their masters and overtaken them at the second or third stopping-place and refused to leave them, however much they were beaten and driven back. There was no room for them here, according to the strict rules of pilgrimage, but they were tolerated and, feeling their illegal position, they behaved with admirable decorum, clinging to a cart wheel under the tar bucket and preserving a grave silence. Their good behaviour alone saved them from humiliating expulsion or from the dangerous baptised gypsy who "took off their coats" in no time.

Here in the camp of the poor pilgrims, in the open air, life was merry and bright as at a fair. There was more variety to be found here than at the inns, whose rooms were occupied by a few select people, or under the awnings of taverns where people of middling station spent their days in perpetual semi-darkness. It is true that the fat monks and deacons disdained to visit the camp, neither did one meet real, experienced pilgrims there, but there were plenty of Jacks of all trades here and the business of manufacturing and selling "sacred articles" was conducted on a really big scale. When I read about the well-known case in Kiev of the manufacture of "relics" out of the bones of a sheep, I was surprised at the childish methods of those manufacturers as compared with the daring shown by the masters of whom I had heard earlier. Here the whole thing was done with a brazen nonchalance that took one's breath away. The whole road to the common along the Slobodskaya Street was notorious for the unhampered freedom with which these business enterprises were conducted. For the people who engaged in this trade knew, of course, that such a chance would rarely come their way again and they did not waste their time: at many gates tables were set up on which were displayed a great variety of "sacred" merchandise, such as icons, crosses and small paper bags with rotted wood dust, which the pious purchaser was assured came from an old coffin, and next to it lay the shavings from a new one. All those articles were, according to the assurances given by the salesmen, of much better quality than the articles they could purchase in the real places, because they had been brought by the carpenters and grave-diggers who had been engaged on the most important tasks.

At the entrance to the camp costermongers were busy, hawkers and stall-holders, who sold icons of the new saint which were covered with white paper on which a crude cross was drawn. These icons sold very cheaply and anybody was free to buy them at any time, but it was strictly forbidden to remove the paper until after the conclusion of the first service. Many purchasers, quite obviously unworthy of grace, removed the paper before it was due to be removed and all *they* could see were just bare boards.

In the ditch behind the camp under a sledge which had been turned upside-down with the runners upwards, there lived, by the stream, a gypsy with his gypsy wife and his little gypsy children. The gypsy and his wife had a large medical practice there. On one of the runners of the sledge a large "voiceless" cock was tied by a leg, and out of this cock "stones" came every morning which possessed the magic power of restoring the virility of husbands who were going weak before their time, and the gypsy himself had "cat grass" which was quite indispensable for anybody who suffered from a certain kind of sores. The gypsy was in his own line a celebrity. His fame was such that it was said that when the seven sleeping virgins were opened in the heathen country, he came in very useful there. The gypsy transformed old men into young men, provided a good cure for the weals of gentlemen's servants who were unlucky enough to get a flogging, and he knew how to make a bullet that had stuck in the back of an officer who had been paying attention to a married lady dissolve in his bladder and come out in the natural way. His gypsy wife knew even greater mysteries of nature. She sold two kinds of water to husbands: one to expose wives who committed carnal sins which, if drunk by an erring wife, would not stay in her body, but would come out immediately, and another, a magnetic one, which, if drunk by an unwilling wife, was guaranteed to make her embrace her husband passionately in her sleep and which possessed another even more remarkable power of making a wife who contrived to fall in love with another man fall out of bed.

In a word, people were doing a roaring trade there and the divers ills of mankind found proficient healers in the "poor camp."

As soon as the vagabond saw the merchant with his family, he wasted no words on them, but just beckoned to them to follow him to the bottom of the ditch and disappeared there himself first.

That looked rather suspicious: there was the danger of an ambush where desperate men might be lurking, men capable of stripping the pilgrims of all their valuables and their clothes, but piety got the better of fear and, after a brief reflection, the merchant murmured a silent prayer in which he made particular mention of the saint and ventured down three steps. He was going down with great care, holding on to the bushes, and he ordered his wife and daughter to start shouting for help if anything went wrong.

There was an ambush there, but not a dangerous one: at the bottom of the ditch the merchant found two other men of as great a piety as himself, wearing the traditional garb of merchants, with whom he had "to arrange terms." Here the three of them had to pay the vagabond the agreed sum for taking them to the saint. He promised to tell them of his plan as soon as they had paid him and take them to the church immediately. It was no use thinking it over any longer, nor did any last-minute attempt at bargaining avail: the merchants took out the money, each his agreed share, and gave it to the vagabond, who then revealed his plan to them. The plan was very simple and indeed its very simplicity bore the marks of genius: it was just that he, the vagabond, knew of a man in the camp who was so weak that he could not move and all they had to do was to raise him and carry him to the saint, for no one would ever interfere with people who carried a wasted man to be restored by the saint.

The plan was perfect as far as it went, for it was quite true that people carrying a disabled man would be allowed to go through to the church, but the question was what would happen afterwards? How could they be sure that they were not letting themselves in for some serious unpleasantness should the sick man fail to obtain a cure? However, that difficulty, too, was successfully overcome, the guide merely saying that they need not worry about it.

"We have had a lot of experience in such matters, gentlemen," he said. "You just carry on as if you had gained admittance to the church in the usual way and I have no doubt that you will be thought worthy of seeing everything and kissing the relics of the saint during the singing of the mass.

As for the sick man, it all depends on what the saint himself wishes to do, if he wants to cure him, he will cure him, and if he doesn't, well, who can go against his will? All you have to do now, gentlemen, is to arrange between yourselves how much each of you is going to contribute to the purchase of a bed in which to carry the sick man and of a blanket with which to cover him. I have everything ready in a house near here. All that you have to do is to pay for it. Just wait for me here a few minutes and we shall be off."

So after a little haggling he took two more roubles from each of the three merchants for the bed and the blanket and ran off. In about ten minutes he came back and said:

"Let's go, brethren, but remember don't walk too fast and do not stare at the people in the street, but drop your eyes a little to show your reverence for God and his saint."

The merchants lowered their eyes and walked with due reverence, and before leaving the camp they presently came to a cart with a horse, standing by its canvas bag and looking more dead than alive, and on the box of the cart sat a scrofulous little boy who was amusing himself by playing with the plucked yellow heads of camomile, which he tossed from one hand to the other. In the cart under the lime-tree bark lay a terribly emaciated man of middle age with a face which was yellower than camomile and hands that were also yellow, his body looking as limp as a leather thong.

The women, seeing such utter debility, began to cross themselves and their guide, addressing the sick man, said:

"Look, uncle Fotey, I've brought some good people who are willing to help me carry you to the saint for your cure. May the Lord grant that your health be restored to you."

The yellow man turned round to the strangers and looked gratefully at them, but he said nothing, just pointing to his tongue with a finger.

The merchants guessed that he must be dumb. "Never mind," they said, "don't thank us, but praise the Lord," and they began to drag him off the cart, the men taking hold of his shoulders and feet and the women supporting his drooping arms, more than ever shocked at the feeble state of the sick man, for his arms seemed almost to drop out of their sockets and were indeed fastened to the shoulders by ropes of hair.

The bed stood on the ground by the cart. It was a small, old bed, richly ornamented in each of its four corners with bugs' eggs; an armful of hay was thrown on the bed together with a piece of rather rare calico material on which a cross was crudely drawn in colours as well as a spear and a staff. The guide spread out the hay with practised hands so that bits of it should hang over the side of the bed and they put the wasted man on it, covered him with the calico and, lifting the bed, moved off.

The guide walked in front of them with a small earthenware brazier, making crosses with the smoke.

They had barely left the camp when the people they met began to cross themselves, and when they reached the streets of the town, more and more attention was paid to them: everybody who saw them understood immediately that a sick man was being carried to the miracle-working saint and many people joined the procession. The merchants quickened their pace, for they could hear the ringing of the church bells for the evening service and they arrived with their burden just when the choir was intoning, "Praise the name of the Lord, ye servants of the Lord."

The cathedral could not contain a hundredth part of the gathered multitudes: crowds of people stood shoulder to shoulder in a dense mass all round the church, but as soon as they saw the sick bed and the people who carried it, a general cry arose, "A paralysed man, a paralysed man's being carried, a miracle's about to happen!" and the crowd made way for them.

The street was black with people up to the very doors of the church, but everything happened just as the guide had promised. Even his great trust in the saint's healing powers were completely justified and no one had to hang his head in shame: the wasted man suffered a miraculous cure. He got up and left the church without any help, "praising the Lord and exalting His name." Somebody wrote it all down on a piece of paper and from this eye-witness's report it transpired that the man who had been miraculously cured was a "relative" of the Orel merchant (so, it seemed, the guide had told the reporter) and many people envied the merchant and, it being so late, the healed man did not go back to the camp, but accepted the invitation of his new relatives to spend the night in their cart behind the shed in the yard of the inn.

All that was highly satisfactory. The healed man aroused great interest and many people came to have a look at him and threw him "gifts." But he could not speak much yet and what he said was rather indistinct, for, being unaccustomed to speech, he just mumbled and mostly kept on pointing at the merchant with his healed hand, as if to say, "Ask them, they're my relatives, they know everything." And then they had willy-nilly to acknowledge him as their relative. But quite unexpectedly and in spite of everything that had happened in the church, a most unpleasant development took the merchant completely by surprise: during the night after the miraculous cure of the paralysed yellow man it was discovered that one of the golden cords with its golden tassel belonging to the velvet canopy over the saint's coffin was missing. A secret investigation was immediately set on foot and the Orel merchant was asked whether he had noticed anything when he approached the coffin of the saint and also who were the people who had helped to carry his sick relative. He replied quite honestly that he did not know who they were, but that they had come from the poor camp and had carried his relative just out of kindness. He was taken to the camp to identify the place, the people, the horse and the cart with the scrofulous boy who had been playing with the camomile, but the only thing that was left was the place where the cart had been standing: the people, the cart and the boy with the camomile had vanished without a trace.

The investigation was dropped "to avoid undesirable rumours among the people," a new golden tassel was hung up and the merchant with his family made haste to return home, all of them feeling very upset by that unpleasant incident. But as soon as they were about to start, their healed relative had another pleasant surprise for them: he demanded that they should take him home with them and he threatened that if they refused, he would lodge a complaint against them and he even mentioned the stolen golden tassel.

So that when the time came for the merchant and his family to return home, Fotey found himself on the box with the coachman and they could not get rid of him until they reached the village of Krutoye which lay on their way to Orel. Here the road went down a very dangerous hill and rose again up another very steep hill and many accidents had happened to travellers on that stretch of road: horses slipped and fell, carriages turned over and people were killed and injured. The village of Krutoye had to be left behind in daylight and any travellers who arrived in the village towards evening usually spent the night there. The Orel merchant and his family also spent the night in the village and next morning while driving up the steep hill they were "surprised" to see that they had left their relative behind them. It was said that the night before they had treated Fotey to a good drink from a bottle and failed to waken him in the morning, driving away without him; but fortunately other kind-hearted people made good that omission and, taking Fotey with them, brought him to Orel.

It did not take Fotey long to find his ungrateful relatives in Orel, but he did not receive the welcome that a relative has a right to expect. He began to beg in the streets and he told everybody that the merchant had not gone on the pilgrimage for the sake of his daughter, but to pray that the price of bread should rise. Nobody knew that better than Fotey himself.

CHAPTER X

SHORTLY after the appearance in Orel of the abandoned Fotey, the merchant Akulov from the parish of Michael the Archangel gave a treat for the poor, known as "poor tables." In the courtyard of his house steam was rising from big wooden bowls with mutton broth and metal dishes with thick porridge which stood on large boards, and at the front door every poor person in town was given an onion pie and a pasty. There were hundreds of guests, each bringing his own spoon in his topboot or inside his coat. Golovan was distributing the pasties. He was often asked to such "tables" to distribute the food, for everybody knew that he was very fair and would not dream of appropriating any food himself and he knew who deserved to be given one kind of pasty and who another, whether stuffed with peas or carrots or liver.

So there he stood, "bestowing" a large pasty upon everyone who came to the door, and he gave two or three pasties as "an extra treat" to any person whom he knew had anyone sick at his home. Fotey was among the numerous beggars who came up for their portion. Seeing Fotey, Golovan seemed to remember something and he asked:

"Who do you belong to and where do you live ?"

Fotey pulled a face and said:

"I belong to no one but God and I live under a matting of straw where I find life pretty raw."

But the other beggars told Golovan, "This is the man the merchant brought with him from the saint. It is Fotey, the man who was healed."

But Golovan smiled and he had only time to say, "What do you mean ? It is . . ." when Fotey snatched the pasty out of his hand and smacked his face, shouting, "That's for talking too much!" and, having said that, he sat down at the table.

Golovan swallowed the insult and said nothing to him. Everybody thought that Golovan had acted properly, for it was assumed that the man who had been miraculously healed was behaving so strangely as a result of some divine compulsion. But the question, of course, that immediately arose was, "What transgression has Golovan been guilty of to deserve such a public chastisement ?" That was a mystery which remained unsolved for many years and led to a general conviction among the people that there was something scandalous in Golovan's past, for why should he otherwise be afraid of Fotey ?

And there could be no doubt that there was some enigma there. Fotey soon fell so low in public esteem that people used to shout after him, "Pinched a golden tassel from the saint and spent it in a pub, didn't you ?" But Fotey went on treating Golovan with the greatest disrespect. Wherever he met Golovan, he would stand in his path and shout, "Pay me what you owe me!" and Golovan said nothing to him, but just put his hand inside his sheepskin and, producing a ten-copeck coin, gave it to Fotey. If, however, Golovan did not happen to have a ten copeck coin on him at the time, Fotey, who because of the variegated colouring of his rags was nicknamed "stoat," threw the smaller coin Golovan had given him in Golovan's face, spat at him, attacked him with his fists, or threw stones, mud or snow at him.

I myself remember how one evening, as my father sat with Father Peter at the window of his study talking to Golovan, who was standing outside, "the stoat" rushed into the courtyard through the open gates and shouting, "Forgotten me, have you? You rogue!" slapped Golovan's face. Golovan just brushed him gently aside, gave him a few coppers which he took out from the inside of his sheepskin and led him out of the gates.

Such behaviour was no rare occurrence on the part of Golovan, and the conclusion that Fotey knew something about him was quite a natural one. Many people, of course, became curious to find out the meaning behind this mystery, and their suspicions, as we shall soon see, were well founded.

CHAPTER XI

I WAS about seven years old when we left Orel for good and went to live in the country. I never met Golovan again. Then the time came for me to go to school and I lost sight of that extraordinary peasant with the large head. I heard of him only once, at the time of the "great fire." A large number of buildings were burnt down and much property was destroyed in that fire and hundreds of people perished in it and among them was Golovan. It was said that he had fallen into some kind of a pit which was covered up with ashes and could not be seen and that he was "boiled alive." I made no inquiries about the relatives he had left behind him. After the fire I left for Kiev and returned to the familiar places of my childhood only after an absence of ten years. A new reign had begun and a new order had started. There was the breath of a fresh breeze in the air, the emancipation of the peasants was expected to be proclaimed shortly and the introduction of public trials was hinted at. Everything was new: the hearts of men were aflame with hope. There weren't any diehards left, but one could already meet people who were impatient and expectant.

I was on my way to my grandmother, but I stopped in Orel for a few days to see my uncle who was a judge and dealt chiefly with arbitration cases. My uncle left behind him the reputation of an honest man. He had many excellent sides to his character which had won him the respect even of those people who did not share his views or sympathies. In his youth he was a great dandy, a hussar officer, then he took up horticulture and he became an amateur painter of some distinction. He was a gentleman with a punctilious sense of honour, a gentleman to his finger-tips, *au bout des ongles*. Interpreting in his own way the duties of his position in society, he, of course, accepted the new reforms, but he desired to examine critically the proposed emancipation of the serfs, and he did not disguise the fact that he was anxious to protect the interests of the landowners. He was in favour of the sort of feudal emancipation that had been carried out in the Baltic provinces. He always behaved with the utmost kindness to young people, but their belief that safety lay in an organised movement forward and not backwards seemed to him to be a mistaken one.

My uncle liked me very much and he knew that I liked and respected him, but we did not share the same views about the emancipation of the serfs or about any other political problem of that time. In Orel he used me as a kind of political scapegoat and although I did my best to avoid any political discussions, he purposely led the conversation to the forbidden topics and he liked very much to "shock" me by his reactionary views.

What pleased my uncle very much was to draw my attention to many cases from his judicial practice which, according to him, revealed the inherent "stupidity" of the common people.

I remember one lovely summer evening I had spent with my uncle in "the governor's gardens" engaged in a heated discussion about the characteristics and qualities of the Russian people, a discussion of which I was beginning to get heartily sick. I kept on maintaining, quite perversely, that the common people were *very* wise and my uncle, perhaps even more perversely, insisted that they were *very* stupid, that they had no conception either of law or property and that, generally, they were just Asiatics who would shock anyone by their wild and savage ways.

"And here is something to prove my point, my dear sir," he said. "If you still remember the general plan of our town we have here all sorts of suburbs, big and small, and I don't think anyone has ever made a survey of the property and nobody knows who is the real owner of any building site there. But the fire levelled everything to the ground in a few hours and on the site of the old hovels new hovels have sprung up, but nobody really knows which property is his and which isn't!"

What my uncle had in mind was that when the work of rebuilding began after the fire, several people bought some building sites in the streets behind the church of Vassily the Great and later it was discovered that not only did the vendors not possess any legal documents, but that their fathers and grandfathers had considered the possession of legal documents quite unnecessary. The little house and the site it stood on passed from one owner to another without notice of the transaction being given to the authorities and without any payment of taxes and dues to the Treasury, and, when asked to produce their purchase deeds, they claimed that all the sales had been written down in some "document," but that that "document" had been burnt in one of the numerous fires and that the man who had drawn it up had died and that with the destruction of the "document" and the death of the man who had drawn it up all trace of their ownership rights had disappeared. It was quite true that there were never any disagreements of any kind as regards the present ownership of the property, but all the same such transactions were legally null and void and the rights of ownership, such as they were, depended entirely on the fact that if Protassov said that the house had been bought by his father from Tarassov's late grandfather, then Tarassov did not dispute Protassov's claims on the property; but what was now demanded was legal proof that Protassov possessed the rights of ownership and, as such proof was non-existent, a conscientious judge had to decide whether it was the law that caused the crime or whether it was the crime that made the passing of such a law necessary.

"But why do they always act like that?" my uncle went on. "Because, my dear sir, we are not dealing with an ordinary people who need government institutions which ensure their property rights and who consequently regard such institutions as good and necessary, but with *nomads* who, it is true, have settled down, but who seem to be quite unaware of that fact."

So that was that and we went to bed and after a good night's sleep I went down to the Orlik in the morning for a swim, had a look at the old familiar places, remembered Golovan's house and, on my return, found my uncle engaged in a conversation with three strangers, whom he went on addressing as "my dear sirs." They belonged to the merchant class, two of them were middle-aged, wearing long coats with hooks instead of buttons, and one was rather ancient, with a white head and beard, wearing a long cotton shirt under his short peasant's coat and a tall, brimless hat in the shape of a buckwheat loaf.

My uncle waved his hand at them and said:

"Here you have an illustration of our talk last night. These gentlemen have come to put their case before me and I'd like you to take a hand in our discussion." Then he turned to the three men and added jocularly, although his joke, of course, was apparent only to me and not to them, "This is a relative of mine, a young public prosecutor from Kiev. He's on his way to St. Petersburg and he could explain your business to them there. You see," my uncle turned to me again, "this gentleman here is Mr. Protassov who wants to buy a house from this gentleman, Mr. Tarassov. But Mr. Tarassov has no papers. You understand? None at all! He just remembers that his father bought the house from a certain Mr. Vlassov and this gentleman is the son of Mr. Vlassov. As you can see for yourself he isn't a young man any more."

"Seventy," the old man said shortly.

"Yes, seventy, and he never had any papers, either!"

"Never had any papers," the old man again put in.

"He came here to testify that the other two gentlemen were telling the truth and that he was not claiming any rights as regards the property under discussion."

"I don't claim no rights," said the old man.

"That's what I said, but the people who had sold the property to his 'forefathers' cannot be traced."

"No, sir. They were exiled to the Caucasus for their faith."

"Couldn't they be found ?" I asked.

"No, sir, the water there didn't agree with them and they all died."

"Why," I asked, "did you act, in such a strange manner ?"

"We acted as well as we could, sir. The officials were very cruel to us, we couldn't afford no taxes on our small houses, and Ivan Ivanovich had a 'document' and he wrote everything down in it, and before him, that was before my time, too, sir, there was a merchant by the name of Gapeyev and he had a 'document' and after them we all gave the 'document' to Golovan, but he was boiled alive in a pit and the 'documents' were all burnt."

"So that Golovan acted as a kind of registrar for you ?" my uncle, who was not a native of Orel, asked.

The old man smiled and said quietly:

"Why should he be a registrar, sir ? He was a just man, that's all."

"But how could you entrust everything to him ?"

"You couldn't help trusting such a man, sir. He cut off his own living flesh from the bone for the people."

"Well, well, what a legend!" my uncle said softly, but the old man caught his words and said:

"No, sir. Golovan was no *Legende*, but the truth. May he rest in peace!"

My uncle had made a joke, but it seemed he had got it all mixed up. Even he did not realise that he had supplied the right answer to the questions which at the time had been worrying me so much, overwhelmed as I was by my memories and anxious as I was to find the key to the mystery of Golovan's personality.

But the key was kept for me by my grandmother.

CHAPTER XII

A WORD or two about my grandmother. She was the daughter of Moscow merchants of the Kolobov family and she was married to a nobleman "not for her riches, but for her beauty." Her chief virtue, however, was the beauty of her soul and her clear mind which always preserved the way of thinking of the common people. Having married into the nobility, she submitted to the demands put on her and even allowed herself to be called Alexandra Vassilyevna, instead of Akilina, which was her real name; but she continued to think as the common people thought and, unintentionally perhaps, preserved in her speech the accents of the speech of the people. She said "them" instead of "those" and she had a deep prejudice against the word "morality," which she considered in some way offensive, and she could never pronounce the Russian word for "book-keeper," which is really a Russianised form of the German word ***Buchhalter***. But she never allowed anyone to shake her faith in the common sense of the people and she herself was a walking example of that common sense. She was a good woman and a real Russian lady. She was an excellent housekeeper and she knew how to receive everybody from the Emperor Alexander I to Ivan Ivanovich Androssov. She never read anything except her children's letters, but she liked to get ideas from conversations with people and it was for that reason that she "commanded" people to come and talk to her. Among those were our mayor Mikhailo Lebedev, the pantry boy Vassily, the head cook Klim and the housekeeper Malanya. The conversation was always about something useful or something that had to do with some business she was interested in, but never about just anything. The subjects she discussed were, for instance, why the maid Feklyusha was getting slack about her morals or why the boy Grishka was dissatisfied with his stepmother. After the conversation the necessary steps were immediately taken to help Feklyusha to cover up her plaits and to make the boy Grishka satisfied with his stepmother.

All these things interested her greatly, but the things she was interested in were perhaps not the things that her grandchildren would consider as important.

When my grandmother came to visit us in Orel, she never failed to see Father Peter, one of the priests of our cathedral church, the merchant Androssov and Golovan, who were all summoned to "converse" with her.

I suppose her talks with those people were not useless, either, and that she did not just "converse" with them to pass away the time of day, but more likely discussed some important business, such as the regrettable decline in morality among maids or the dissatisfaction of some boy with his stepmother.

She could therefore be expected to possess the keys to many mysteries, which might seem rather unimportant to us, but which were far from being so to the people whom they concerned most.

Now, at my last meeting with my grandmother, she was already very old, but she preserved her mental faculties unimpaired, nor did her memory or her eyes suffer on account of her age. She still sewed.

And this time, too, I found her sitting at her work-table with the inlaid top showing a harp supported by two Cupids.

My grandmother asked me whether I had paid a visit to my father's grave, whom of our relations in Orel I had been to see and what my uncle was doing there. I answered all her questions and I talked to her at some length about my uncle and told her what a lot of trouble the old legends, or as I pronounced it in the "uneducated" way, "leegends," were giving him.

My grandmother paused and pushed her glasses up on her forehead She liked the word "leegend": she heard in it a naïve distortion quite in the spirit of the common people.

"That was well said by the old man about the 'leegend,'" she said.

"But," said I, "I'd like to know what really happened, granny, and not what happened according to the 'leegend.'"

"What exactly do you want to know?"

"I want to know everything. In the first place, who was that Golovan? I can only just remember him, but he seems to be all mixed up in my mind with what the old man called 'leegends.' But I expect everything was really quite simple."

"Of course, everything was quite simple. But why are you so surprised that the people of our town preferred to write their sales of property down in an ordinary copy-book instead of taking out purchase deeds? I shouldn't be surprised if that didn't go on happening in future. They did not trust the officials, that's all."

"But how did Golovan gain such confidence?" I asked. "To be quite frank, I sometimes can't help thinking of him just as a . . . charlatan!"

"But why?"

"Well, I remember people saying that he had some magic stone and that he stopped the plague by his blood or flesh which he had thrown into the river. Anyway, why did they call him 'deathless'?"

"Well, so far as the magic stone is concerned, it is, of course, all nonsense. People just invented the story and Golovan had nothing to do with it. But they called him 'deathless' because at a time when such a ghastly horror stalked the earth and when deadly miasmas hung over it and all went in fear of their lives, he alone remained unafraid and death did not touch him."

"But why did he cut the flesh off his leg?"

"He cut the calf of his leg off."

"Why?"

"Because he discovered a plague sore on it. He knew that if he did not do something immediately, he would die, so he took a scythe and cut the whole of the calf of his leg off."

"Goodness," I said, "is that possible?"

"Of course, that was what happened."

"And what is one to make of that woman Pavla?" I asked.

My grandmother looked up at me and said:

"What about her? Pavla was the wife of Fraposhkin. She was in great distress and Golovan did his best for her."

"But she was called 'Golovan's sin,' wasn't she?"

"Every man judges in his own way and every man calls things by his own names, but I can tell you Golovan hadn't any such sin."

"But, granny darling, do you really believe it?"

"Not only do I believe it, I *know* it."

"But how can you know it?"

"Quite simply."

And my grandmother told me that before his death Father Peter had said to her what incredible people there were in Russia and he told her that Golovan was a celibate.

Having embarked on her story, my grandmother entered into all the small details of her conversation with Father Peter.

"Father Peter," she said, "was at first doubtful about it himself and questioned Golovan closely and even hinted at his relationship with Pavla. 'I don't think you're doing right,' he said. 'You don't go to confession, but you seduce people. It isn't right for you to keep that Pavla. Let her go.' But Golovan replied, 'Why should I let her go?' 'Why not?' 'Because she has nowhere to go to. . . .' 'Well, why don't you marry her then?' 'That, I'm afraid, is impossible,' Golovan replied, but he did not say why it was impossible, and Father Peter was doubtful about it for a long time, but Pavla was consumptive and she didn't live long and before her death, when Father Peter came to her, she told him everything."

"What did she tell him?"

"That they lived in *perfect* love."

"You mean?"

"I mean angelic love."

"But really, granny, why should they do that? Didn't her husband disappear without trace and isn't there a law that after a woman has been deserted by her husband for five years she can marry again? Didn't they know that?"

"Yes, I believe they knew it all right, but they knew something else even more."

"What for instance?"

"For instance, that Pavla's husband survived them all and never really did disappear."

"Where was he?"

"In Orel."

"But, granny darling, surely you must be joking!"

"Not a bit."

"And who knew about it?"

"The three of them, Golovan, Pavla and that good-for-nothing husband of hers. Don't you remember Fotey?"

"The man who was cured by a miracle?"

"Well, yes, call him that, if you like, but now they are all dead I can tell you that he wasn't Fotey at all, but the deserter Fraposhka."

"Pavla's husband!"

"Yes, her husband."

"But why . . ." I began, but I was ashamed of my own thoughts and said nothing. My grandmother, however, understood what I was going to say and finished it for me.

"I suppose you want to ask why nobody else recognised him, or why Golovan and Pavla did not denounce him? Well, it's really quite simple: no one recognised him because he never lived in the town and, besides, he got old and all covered with hair, and Pavla did not betray him because she was sorry for him and Golovan—because he loved her."

"But legally, according to our laws, granny, Fraposhka did not exist and they could have got married."

"They could according to our laws, but not according to the laws of their consciences."

"But why did Fraposhka persecute Golovan?"

"Because he was no good: he thought of them as the others did."

"And because of him they sacrificed their own happiness!"

"But what is happiness, my dear? There is sinless happiness and there is sinful happiness. Sinless happiness will never commit any injustice against anyone, while sinful will disregard every law and precept of justice. And they deemed the first more worthy of their devotion than the second."

"Granny," I exclaimed, "but what marvellous people!"

"Upright people, my dear," replied the old lady.

But all the same I cannot help adding—marvellous and incredible people. They remain incredible so long as they are surrounded by a mist of legend and they are even more incredible when the mist is dispersed and we see them in all their simplicity. *Perfect* love alone which inspired them put them above fear and even made nature submit to them without their having to bury themselves in sand or fight against the apparitions which tormented St. Anthony.

THE LEFT-HANDED ARTIFICER

A Tale of the Cross-eyed, Left-handed Artificer of Tula and the Steel Flea

CHAPTER I

WHEN Emperor Alexander Pavlovich wound up the Vienna conference, he decided to take a trip across Europe and see what the different countries could show him by way of wonders. So off he went and paid a visit to every country and, being a very easy-going sort of chap, he had friendly chats with all manner of people, and everyone he spoke to tried his best to astonish him by some new kind of invention, for all of them wanted to get him on their side. The Emperor had with him a Don cossack—Platov his name was—and that cossack just hated to see his Sovereign admiring anything foreign and, being terribly homesick, he kept on badgering his Majesty to return to Russia. Every time Platov saw the Emperor showing too great an interest in some foreign invention he would say, while the rest of his Majesty's suite kept a diplomatic silence, "If it please your Majesty, we have much better things at home," and one way or another he'd manage to distract the Emperor's attention.

Now the English knew that and they had thought up all kinds of cunning tricks for the Emperor's arrival: for they had made up their minds that they would extort the admission from the Emperor that everything foreign was much superior to everything Russian, and they very often succeeded, especially at large assemblies where Platov found it a bit hard to say what he wanted to say in French, because, to tell the truth, Platov wasn't much interested in French and, being a married man, he thought all French talk silly and hardly worth while. But when the English began to invite the Emperor to come and see all their arsenals and sawmills and soap factories and what not, being anxious to show him how much better they did things than the Russians, Platov said to himself:

"This has jolly well got to stop. I've put up with it so far, but I'm not going to let it go any farther. I may or I may not be able to say it, but I'm hanged if I'm going to let our side down."

No sooner had he said that to himself than the Emperor turned to him and said:

"Now then, my dear chap, you and I are going to have a lovely time to-morrow, for we're going to have a look at one of their military exhibitions. They've got wonderful things there," he said, "and I bet that when you see them you'll have to admit that we Russians, however much we may think of ourselves, are no good at all."

Platov did not say a word in reply to the Emperor, but just buried his big, broken nose in that shaggy coat of his. When he came back to his lodgings, however, he told his batman to fetch him a bottle of strong Caucasian vodka from his trunk and, filling a large glass to the brim, he swallowed it at one gulp. Then he said his prayers in front of his folding travelling shrine, covered himself up with his shaggy coat and started to snore so loudly that the English in the house couldn't sleep a wink that night.

"Let's sleep on it," he thought to himself.

CHAPTER II

NEXT day the Emperor and Platov went to visit the museums in London. The reason his Majesty took no other Russian with him was because the carriage they had been given had only room for two.

They arrived at a building which did not look particularly large from the outside, but which had a beautiful entrance and miles and miles of corridors and one room more wonderful than the other and, after they had been taken through them all, they were brought to the main room which had enormous statues in it and right in the middle a statue of Apollo Belvebeery under a big canopy.

The Emperor was all the time watching Platov, for he wanted to see whether anything would surprise him at all and also what he would look at, but the cossack did not look at anything. He walked with his eyes fixed on the ground and all he did was to twist his long moustache round and round his finger.

The English at once began to show them all the marvellous things they had in that room and they explained which of them they found most useful in their wars, such as storm gauges, camel-hair coats for their infantry and waterproof treated with pitch for their cavalry. The Emperor looked highly pleased with everything, but Platov was not a bit impressed and, in fact, took pains to show quite plainly that it didn't mean a thing to him.

The Emperor said:

"Really, my dear chap, I can't understand how you can be so indifferent. Doesn't anything here impress you at all?"

But Platov replied:

"The only thing that impresses me, your Majesty, is that my gallant cossacks won so many battles and routed thousands of your enemies without any of the things here"

The Emperor said:

"You're talking through your hat, my dear chap."

But Platov replied:

"That is as it may be, your Majesty, but I'm afraid I can't argue the point with you, seeing as how it is my duty not to reason why, but to do and die."

But the Englishmen, noticing that the Emperor and his cossack officer were having some argument, at once took them to the statue of Apollo Belvebeery and, taking a musket from one of his hands and a pistol from the other, said:

"See the sort of thing we produce in this country," and they gave him the musket.

The Emperor looked at the musket without batting an eyelid, for he had many similar muskets in his own palace in Tsarskoye Syelo, but when they gave him the pistol and said, "This pistol is of an unknown and quite incomparable make, your Majesty. One of our admirals snatched it from the belt of a pirate chief in Kandelabria," the Emperor took one look at the pistol and couldn't take his eyes off it. He sighed and sighed, poor man, and very pitiful sighs they were, and he said:

"Ah, it is indeed wonderful! What perfect workmanship!" And, turning to Platov, he said in Russian, "If only I'd had such a fine craftsman in Russia, I'd be the happiest man in the world and I'd be so proud of him that I'd make him a nobleman on the spot."

As soon as he heard the Emperor talk that way, Platov put his hand in the pocket of his wide breeches and took out a pistol opener. The Englishmen were quite shocked to see him do that and they said, "You will never be able to open it," but Platov paid no attention to them and began to pick the lock of the pistol. He tried it once and he tried it twice and the third time he opened it and, taking the lock out completely, he asked the Emperor to have a look at the trigger, just inside the bend. The Emperor looked and there he saw an inscription in Russian, "Ivan Moskvin of the town of Tula."

The Englishmen looked very astonished and they kept on nudging each other, as if to say:

"Dear, dear, we've put our foot in it this time and no mistake!"

But the Emperor said to Platov crossly:

"You shouldn't have made them look so foolish. Now, I can't help feeling sorry for them. Come on, let's go."

So they went back to their carriage, and the Emperor was at a ball that night, but Platov knocked back an even larger glass of strong Caucasian vodka and slept soundly like a real cossack.

He was glad to have made the English look foolish and to have done justice to the Tula craftsman, but he could not help feeling vexed with the Emperor for being so sorry for the English in a case of that kind.

"Why was the Emperor so cross?" thought Platov. "Damned if I can make it out at all!" and, worried by such thoughts, he got up twice, crossed himself and drank so much vodka that in the end he dropped off into a heavy sleep.

But the Englishmen could not sleep that night, either, for they were greatly worried, too. While the Emperor was having a good time at the ball, they thought out such a new wonder for him that it took the wind out of Platov's sails completely.

CHAPTER III

NEXT morning when Platov came to bid the Emperor a good morning, his Majesty said to him:

"Tell 'em to get ready the carriage for two immediately and let's go and see their other museums."

Platov plucked up courage to drop a hint to his Majesty that it was about time they packed up and stopped looking at foreign products and began thinking of returning to Russia, but the Emperor said:

"No, no, my dear chap, there's plenty more I'd very much like to see. They told me last night that the sugar they manufacture here is simply first-class."

So off they went.

The English showed everything they had to the Emperor, the sort of first-class products they had, but Platov just looked and looked and then he said suddenly:

"Can you take us to the factory where they make the sugar *Molvo?*"

Well, the Englishmen had never heard of *Molvo* sugar before and they kept on whispering to each other, winking at each other, repeating to each other, "*Molvo, Molvo,*" without, of course, realising that it was the sugar we manufactured in our own country, and, at last, they just had to admit that although they had every kind of sugar under the sun, they hadn't got any "*Molvo.*"

Platov said:

"So you haven't got it, have you? Well, what are you bragging about then? Come to our country and we'll give you tea with real *Molvo* sugar from the Bobrinsk factory."

But the Emperor tugged him by the sleeve and said softly:

"See here, don't you go messing up my politics!"

Then the English asked the Emperor to come and see their very last museum where they promised to show him every kind of mineral stone and infusorias they had collected from all over the world, beginning with the largest pyramid from Egypt and ending with fleas which could not be seen by the naked eye and which lived under the skin of animals.

The Emperor went.

They looked at the pyramids and the mummies and all sorts of scarecrows besides and as they left Platov said to himself:

"Thank goodness, everything has gone off fine: the Emperor did not seem to be impressed by anything."

But when they came to the last room, there were English workmen drawn up all in a row in their clean jackets and aprons and one of them held a tray on which there was nothing to be seen.

So the Emperor looked very surprised, for he did not expect to be given an empty tray.

"What does it mean?" he asked, but the English craftsmen answered, "This is our humble present to your Majesty."

"What is it?"

"Well, Sire," they said, "can you see this speck of dust?"

The Emperor looked and, indeed, there was a tiny speck of dust on the silver tray.

The workmen said:

"May it please your Majesty to wet your finger and put it on your hand."

"But what am I to do with this speck of dust?"

"It isn't a speck of dust," they said. "It is a flea."

"Is it alive?"

"Why, no, your Majesty," they replied, "of course it isn't alive. We made it out of our best English steel and in its middle is a spring and there's a hole through which you wind it up. If it please your Majesty to turn the key, it will at once begin to dance."

The Emperor became very curious and he asked:

"But where's the key?"

And the Englishmen replied:

"The key is just in front of your eyes, your Majesty."

So they brought a microscope and the Emperor saw that indeed there was a key beside the flea on the tray.

"May it please your Majesty to put the flea on your hand," they said. "There's a little hole in the middle of the flea's tummy and as soon as you turn the key seven times the flea will start to dance."

It was with great difficulty that the Emperor managed to get hold of the key and even with greater difficulty that he could keep it between his finger and thumb. However, after taking the flea in his other hand, also between finger and thumb, he put the key in and as soon as he began to wind it he felt how the steel flea's feelers began to move, then its tiny legs began to stir and, at last, it gave a jump, cutting a caper in one movement, and next it skipped to one side and went through two variations and to the other side and went through two more variations, and so it danced through a whole quadrille in three turns.

The Emperor immediately commanded that the English should be given a million for the flea in whatever kind of money they wished, whether in silver sixpences or in small banknotes.

The English asked to be paid in silver because they didn't know much about paper money, and then they immediately played another of their tricks: they presented the flea to the Emperor, but they didn't give him a case in which to put the flea and without a case it was quite impossible to keep either the flea or its key, for they could easily get mislaid and thrown out with the rest of the rubbish. The case for the flea was made out of a whole diamond nut in the middle of which a place had been bored for it. The diamond, however, they would not give to the Emperor because, they said, it really belonged to the Treasury and whatever belongs to the Treasury no Englishman dares touch, not even for the Emperor himself.

Platov nearly lost his temper over that, for, said he:

What's the meaning of all this jiggery-pokery? They give your Majesty a present and take a cool million for it, but it seems that isn't enough for them! The case," said he, "always goes with a thing like that!"

But the Emperor said:

"Let it be, my dear chap. Mind your own business and don't go messing up my politics for me: they have their own way of doing things," and he asked them, "How much do you want for the diamond in which the steel flea has to be kept?"

The Englishmen asked five thousand for it.

The Emperor Alexander Pavlovich said, "Pay them!" and he himself put the flea into its diamond case and the key with it, and to make quite sure that he wouldn't lose it, he put it into his golden snuff-box which he ordered to be put into his travelling casket which was inlaid with mother-of-pearl and whalebone.

The Emperor took leave of the English craftsmen very graciously and said to them, "You're the best craftsmen in the world and I'm quite satisfied that my own people can't stand up to you!"

Well, the Englishmen were naturally very pleased about it and Platov could say nothing to contradict the Emperor's words, so he just bagged the microscope and, without saying anything about it, put it in his pocket, "For," said he to himself, "it belongs with the rest and you've got a lot of money for it as it is."

The Emperor knew nothing about that, not until they arrived in Russia, anyway, and they had left England soon after, for his Majesty was getting very depressed on account of the military situation and he wished to go to confession to the priest Fedot in Taganrog. On their way to Russia there wasn't much of a pleasant nature that the Emperor had to say to Platov, for they had disagreed violently with one another: the Emperor was of the opinion that the English had no equals in craftsmanship, while Platov maintained that our men could make anything they saw, but that all they lacked was good education and proper training, and he put it to his Majesty that the English craftsmen had quite different rules so far as their everyday life was concerned, and that every man Jack of them enjoyed full opportunities to manage his private affairs as he liked and that consequently everything had quite a different meaning for him.

The Emperor refused to listen to such talk and Platov used to leave their carriage at every halt and polish off a large glass of vodka to drown his vexation and just chew a piece of salted biscuit and then he'd light his enormous pipe made out of a large root of a tree in which he'd put a whole pound of Zhukov tobacco, and he'd sit down beside the Emperor in the carriage and they would journey on in silence. The Emperor looked one way and Platov looked another, sticking his pipe out of the window and letting the wind carry the smoke away. In this way they travelled together till they arrived in St. Petersburg and the Emperor did not even ask Platov to accompany him to his priest Fedot.

"You're not fit for any religious conversation," his Majesty said, "and, besides, you go on smoking like a chimney and my head is full of soot from that pipe of yours."

Platov was thus left behind to nurse his grievance and he lay down on his couch and sulked and all the time he lay on his couch he went on smoking Zhukov tobacco without stopping.

CHAPTER IV

THE wonderful flea of the best English steel remained in Alexander Pavlovich's whalebone casket until his death in Taganrog. The Emperor gave it to the priest Fedot whom he asked to hand it to the Empress when she had sufficiently recovered from her grief. The Empress Yelissaveta Alexeyevna had a look at the flea's variations and just smiled, but she was not interested in it and did not look at it again.

"I am a dowager now," she said, "and I don't care for any amusements any more," and on her return to St. Petersburg she gave this curiosity together with all the other jewels to the new Emperor as an heirloom.

The Emperor Nikolai Pavlovich at first paid no attention to the steel flea, either, for when he ascended the throne there were all kinds of disturbances and he was too preoccupied to think of it, but later on he began one day to examine the casket left to him by his brother and he took out the snuff-box and from it he produced the diamond nut and in it he found the steel flea, which had not been wound up for a long time and was lying there quietly, just as if it had gone stiff in all its joints.

The Emperor looked at the steel flea and was surprised.

"What a silly thing it is and why has my brother taken such great care of it?"

The courtiers wanted to throw it out, but the Emperor said:

"No, this must mean something."

So they called in the chemist who owned the chemist's shop opposite Anichkin Bridge, who was used to weighing poisons in very small scales, and they showed it to him. He immediately took the flea and put it on his tongue and said, "I can feel a chill on my tongue as if it were made of some strong metal," and he bit on it a little with his teeth and he said, "If it please your Majesty it isn't a real flea, but a flea made out of some metal and it isn't our work; it hasn't been made in Russia."

The Emperor ordered his courtiers to find out immediately where it came from and what was the meaning of it.

The courtiers started to look through all the State papers and letters, but they could find no mention of the steel flea in them. So they started making inquiries from one person and from another, but nobody knew anything about it. Luckily, however, the Don cossack Platov was still alive and was, as a matter of fact, still sulking on his couch and smoking his pipe. As soon as he heard of the commotion at the palace, he got up from his couch, threw away his pipe, pinned on his medals and went to see the Emperor.

The Emperor said:

"What can I do for you, my gallant old man?"

And Platov replied:

"I don't want anything for myself, your Majesty, for I have plenty of drink and food and I'm quite satisfied, thank you. I have come," he said, "to tell you all about that steel flea which I understand has been found," and he told the Emperor all about it, saying, "it all happened in England, in my presence. There's a key beside it and I've got the microscope through which you can see it and with that key you can wind up the flea through a tiny hole in her tummy and she'll start skipping about all over the place and cut figures as she turns from one side to the other."

So they wound up the steel flea and she began to skip about and Platov said:

"It is true, your Majesty, that it is quite delicate workmanship, quite a beautiful piece of work altogether, but it isn't right just to admire it and let your feelings run away with you. It should be given to our craftsmen in Tula or Sesterbek (in those days Sestroretzk was still called Sesterbek) to be examined in order to see if they could not do something more wonderful so that the English should not think that they are in any way superior to the Russians."

Now the Emperor Nikolai Pavlovich had great confidence in his Russian subjects and he did not like to have to admit the superiority of any foreigner and he answered Platov and said:

"You spoke well, my gallant old fellow. Take it and see what you can do about it. I don't want this box now, anyway, for I have plenty of troubles as it is. Take it and don't go back to sulk on your couch, but go straight to the gentle Don and have a heart-to-heart talk there with my Don cossacks about their life and their loyalty to me and ask them what they would like me to do for them, and when you pass through Tula show this steel flea to my Tula craftsmen and let them see what they can do about it. Tell them from me that my brother was very impressed by this thing and praised the foreign craftsmen who made it above everything in the world, but that I have great confidence in my people and I hope and trust that they are not a whit worse than anybody else. I know they will not disappoint me and will do something."

CHAPTER V

PLATOV took the steel flea and, passing through Tula on his way to the Don, he showed it to the Tula master gunsmiths and told them what the Emperor had said and then asked them:

"What are we going to do about it?"

The master gunsmiths replied:

"We are greatly honoured by his Majesty's gracious words, sir, and we shall always be bounden to his Majesty because he has confidence in his own people, but we cannot possibly tell you outright what we'd better do about this business. We have to consider it very carefully, for the English aren't fools, but a very clever people and their craftsmanship has a good deal of sound common sense in it. One can do nothing against the English," they said, "without careful consideration and with the Lord's blessing we may be able to do something. If your honour, like our lord and master the Emperor, has confidence in us, then we should advise you to carry on with your journey to the gentle Don and to leave this flea with us, just as it is in its case and in the Czar's golden snuff-box. Have a good time on the Don and give the wounds you have received in defending your country a chance of healing up and when on your way back you're passing through Tula again stop here and send for us: with God's help we should have thought of something by that time."

Platov did not conceal his disappointment with the Tula craftsmen, that they should be asking for so much time and that they should not tell him plainly what they intended to do. He questioned them closely about it and he spoke to them with great cunning as the people on the Don know how, but the Tula craftsmen were no less cunning than he, for, as a matter of fact, they had already thought of something, but they were afraid that if they told it to Platov he would not believe them capable of accomplishing such a thing and for that reason they wished to put their plan into execution at once and reveal it later.

They said:

"We hardly know ourselves yet what we shall do, but we shall put ourselves into the hands of the Lord and maybe the Czar's word will not have been spoken in vain and to our shame."

So the more Platov tried to match his wits against theirs, the more did the Tula craftsmen outwit him.

Platov wriggled and wriggled, but he couldn't wriggle into their minds and in the end he realised that he would have to do as they wished. So he gave them the golden snuff-box with the steel flea and said:

"Well, have it your own way, but, mind, I know the sort of people you are and since I can't do anything about it, I shall have to trust you. All the same I think I'd better warn you not to try any monkey business with me, such as pinching the diamond and putting some worthless stone in its place and, above all, the Lord help you if you should do anything to the delicate English workmanship and, last but not least, don't take too much time over it, for I'm a fast traveller, before two weeks have passed I shall be on my way back from the gentle Don to St. Petersburg and I'd better have something to take with me to show to the Emperor."

The gunsmiths did their best to reassure him.

"We shall not spoil the delicate workmanship," they said, "and we shall not change the diamond for some worthless stone, and two weeks is enough and to spare, and be assured that by the time you go back to the Emperor, you will have *something* to show to his Majesty which will be worthy of his greatness."

But what that *something* was they did not say.

CHAPTER VI

PLATOV left Tula, and the gunsmiths—three men who were the greatest craftsmen of them all, including one who was cross-eyed and left-handed, with a birthmark on his cheek and his hair above the temples pulled out during his studies—took leave of their mates and their families, packed their bags, taking some food with them, and disappeared from the town.

All that was known about them was that they did not leave the town through the Moscow toll-gate, but went in the opposite direction, and it was surmised that they had gone to Kiev to offer prayers to the saints there and to take counsel of the living holy men of whom there were always a great abundance in Kiev.

But while that was near enough to the truth, it was not the whole truth by any means. Neither the time, nor the distance permitted the craftsmen to go to Kiev, for it would have taken them three weeks to do it and that would hardly have given them sufficient time to do something besides, which would have put the English nation to shame. They could have gone to Moscow instead, which was only "twice ninety *versts*" away and where there are also saints in plenty. And in the opposite direction there were also "twice ninety *versts*" to Orel and from Orel to Kiev another good five hundred *versts*. You cannot do such a journey in a few days and, when done, it would take you more than a few days to rest your tired limbs, for it would take some time before your feet lost their numbness and your hands ceased from shaking.

There were even people who thought that the Tula craftsmen had just been bragging to Platov and, having thought it over afterwards, had got properly scared and fled, taking with them the Czar's golden snuff-box with the diamond and the steel flea which had given them so much trouble. However, such a supposition was also quite without foundation and also quite unworthy of the great craftsmen upon whom the hope of the nation now reposed.

CHAPTER VII

TULA craftsmen are famous for their skill in metal work, but they are also known far and wide as experts in the matter of religion. Nor is it their native country alone that resounds to their glory. No, the fame of their great piety has reached as far as Mount Athos where it is well known that natives of Tula are not only past-masters at church singing, excelling in tremolo parts, but also expert painters of the picture *Eternal Ringing*. It is a no less-known fact that those of them who dedicate themselves to the service of the Lord by entering a monastery become excellent stewards and excel as collectors of monastery funds. At Mount Athos they know that Tula men are a very resourceful people and that but for them the remote corners of Russia would assuredly never have seen many of the sacred objects from the far away Orient, and Mount Athos would have had to do without many useful gifts which are such a shining example of Russian piety and generosity. To-day the "Mount Athos" Tula monks carry the sacred objects all over our country and are real adepts at collecting funds even where there is nothing to collect. A Tula native is full of devotion for the church and is a great practitioner in pious deeds, and for that reason the three Tula craftsmen who had taken upon themselves the burden of justifying Platov's faith in his country and upon whom now the good name of their country depended, made no mistake in failing to take the road to Moscow, but in going southwards instead. They never thought of going to Kiev, the town of their pilgrimage being Mtsensk, a district town in the province of Orel, where the ancient image, "graven out of stone," of St. Nicholas is kept, an icon which in ancient times had sailed down the river Zusha on a large stone cross. This icon of a "stern and most terrifying" aspect shows the full-sized figure of the saint clad in garments of silver gilt, of a rather dark visage, holding a church in one hand and the sword "Victory in Battle" in the other. It is in this "victory" that the whole meaning of the icon lies, St. Nicholas being the generally acknowledged patron saint of trade and warfare, and the "Mtsensk St. Nicholas" particularly, and it was to him that the Tula craftsmen had gone to pray. They had a special service held in front of this icon and another in front of the stone cross, then they returned home at night and, without saying a word to anybody, started on their work in dead secret. They gathered, all three of them, in the house of the left-handed artificer, locked the doors, closed the shutters, lit the lamp in front of the icon of St. Nicholas and set to work.

They stayed there one day, two days, three days, without going abroad, just hammering away at something, forging something, but what it was they were forging nobody knew.

Everybody in Tula was very curious about it, but nobody could discover anything of what the three craftsmen were doing, for they had said nothing to anybody and they did not show themselves in the streets. . . . Many people went to the little house and knocked at the door under any pretext they could think of, either to ask for a light or for a pinch of salt, but the three artificers would not open the door for any reason whatsoever and it was not even known what they did about food. Some people even tried to frighten them, shouting that the house next door was on fire and hoping that they might run out in a panic and that then it might be revealed what they had been forging, but nothing would deceive those cunning craftsmen: only once did the left-handed one stick his head out of the window and shout:

"Let the whole town burn down for all we care: we're busy!" and his head with the pulled-out hair disappeared, the shutter was closed with a terrific bang and the hammering was resumed, the mystery remaining as dark as ever.

Only through some minute chinks in the shutters could people see a fire burning and hear the hammers striking ceaselessly on the anvils.

In short, the whole thing was kept in such terrible secrecy that nothing of what was going on in that little house could be discovered, and so it went on until the return of the cossack Platov from the gentle Don on his way back to the Emperor, and all during that time the three Tula craftsmen did not see or talk to anybody.

CHAPTER VIII

PLATOV travelled in a great hurry and with some ceremony: he himself sat in the carriage and on either side of the coachman sat a cossack with a cat-o'-nine-tails in his hand and they kept on belabouring the coachman unmercifully to make sure that he kept the horses going at full gallop. And should any of the cossacks doze off, Platov himself would poke him in the side with a foot, and they'd drive away at an even smarter pace. Such ministrations had an excellent effect and it was quite impossible to rein in the horses at any station, for they always overshot their mark by a hundred lengths. Then the cossacks would wield their cats-o'-nine-tails in an opposite direction and the coachman would turn round and drive up to the inn.

In this way they came flying into Tula, at first rushing a hundred lengths beyond the Moscow toll-gate, then the cossacks applied their whips to the coachman in an opposite direction and, turning round, they stopped at the steps of the inn where new horses were ordered to be put to the carriage. Platov himself did not leave the carriage, but merely ordered one of the cossacks to bring the craftsmen with whom he had left the steel flea to him and not to take too much time over it, either.

Off the cossack ran to tell the three craftsmen to make haste and bring their work which was to put the English to shame, but he had only gone a short distance when Platov sent more and more cossacks after him to hurry them up.

Having sent off all his cossacks, he began to pick out some onlookers from the crowd of people that had by that time gathered round the carriage and just nearly put a foot out of the carriage himself, too impatient to wait any longer and wishing to run there himself, grinding his teeth in a most fierce way: for it seemed to him that they were not quick enough.

In those days everything had to be done efficiently and expeditiously like that, so that not a single moment should be lost where the welfare or glory of the Russian people was at stake.

CHAPTER IX

THE Tula artificers who were engaged on that marvellous piece of work were just then putting the finishing touches to it. The cossacks were quite out of breath when they arrived at their house and the onlookers from among the public whom Platov had picked out as messengers had not arrived at all, for, being out of practice, their legs just refused to function on the way and the poor men collapsed in the roadway and, fearing what Platov might do to them, they ran each to his home where they immediately hid themselves where no one could find them.

But directly the cossacks reached the house after their breathless sprint, they gave a mighty shout and, finding that the artificers took no notice and refused to open the door to them, they unceremoniously tried to pull the shutters off the windows, but the bolts were so strong that they did not give; they then tried to open the door, but it was barred from the inside with a huge beam of oak. Thereupon the cossacks picked up a big trunk of a tree, which they found lying in the street, put it, fireman's fashion, against the eaves of the roof and in the twinkling of an eye took the roof off the little house. But having pulled the roof off, they themselves were knocked down by a spiral of foul air, for the atmosphere inside the little room where the craftsmen had been working ceaselessly for so many days had grown so thick that when it rushed out through the roof, every man in the street was nearly suffocated by it.

The messengers raised a clamour:

"Hey, you there, you dirty so-and-sos, how dare you knock us down with your spiral of foul air? Don't you believe in God at all?"

But the craftsmen replied:

"We are just driving in the last nail and, as soon as we're finished, we shall bring the work out."

The messengers, however, shouted back:

"He'll devour us alive if we wait as long as that and he won't leave anything over to remember us by."

But still the craftsmen replied:

"He won't have time to devour you, for even while you were speaking, we have driven the last nail in. Run and tell him that we're bringing it this minute."

The cossacks ran off to tell Platov what the craftsmen had said, but they were not too confident, for they thought that the Tula artificers would deceive them; so they'd run and stop and run and stop, always looking round to see if the three craftsmen were coming after them. However, their suspicions were not justified, for the craftsmen did come after them and so fast, too, that they had had no time to dress properly as they should have done in presenting themselves before so important a personage as the Emperor's representative, but were fastening the hooks on their *kaftans* even while running through the streets. Two of them had nothing in their hands and the third one, the left-handed one, carried the Czar's casket with the English steel flea wrapped in a green cloth cover.

CHAPTER X

THE cossacks ran up to Platov and said:

"Here they come:"

Platov at once said to the craftsmen:

"Is it ready?"

"Everything's ready," they replied.

"Give it to me!"

They gave it to him.

The carriage was waiting with the coachman and the outrider in their places. The cossacks immediately sat down on the box on either side of the coachman and raised their cat-o'-nine-tails over his head and held it like that.

Platov said:

"What's all this? Where's your work with which you were going to gladden the Emperor's heart?"

The gunsmiths replied:

"Our work is in that casket."

Platov asked:

"Will you kindly explain what you're talking about?"

But the gunsmiths said:

"What's there to explain? It's in front of your eyes: just have a good look."

Platov shrugged his shoulders and roared:

"Where's the flea's key?"

"Just in front of you," they replied. "Where the flea is, there also is the key: in the diamond nut."

Platov wanted to take hold of the key, but his fingers were so short and stubby that, try as he might, he could not grasp either the key or the flea and he lost his temper completely and started cursing like a real cossack.

He roared:

"Blasted rogues, that's what you are: You haven't done a damn thing and I shouldn't be surprised if you hadn't damaged the thing into the bargain. I'll knock your heads off!"

But the Tula artificers said to him:

"You have no right to insult us like that, but we have to put up with your insults because you are the Emperor's representative. Since, however, you don't trust us and even think that we're likely to be disloyal to the Emperor's command, we shan't tell you the secret of our work. Take it to the Emperor—he will see the kind of master craftsmen we are and whether or not he has any reason to be ashamed of us!"

But Platov just roared at them again:

"You're damned liars, the lot of you! Catch me trusting you or letting you off as easily as all that! One of you is coming with me to St. Petersburg and I'll make him talk there! He'll tell me your secret all right!"

And, having said that, he stretched out his hand, caught the left-handed artificer by the scruff of the neck with his stubby fingers so that all the hooks of his coat flew off, and flung him at his own feet in the carriage.

"Sit here," said he, "like a blasted poodle until we get to St. Petersburg. I'll hold you responsible for all of them. And you," he said to his cossacks, "off you go, and look sharp, for I must be at the Emperor's palace in St. Petersburg the day after to-morrow!"

All the craftsmen dared to do for their mate was to point out to Platov that it was hardly right for him to carry off one of their fellow craftsmen without giving him a chance of obtaining an official document and they also wanted to know whether he would be allowed to come back. But instead of a reply Platov showed them his fist—a terrible, scarred, red fist—and, waving it at them, he said, "Here's your official document!" And to the cossacks he said, "Off with you, chaps!"

The cossacks, the coachman and the horses all started working at one and the same time and carried off the left-handed artificer without a document, and in a day, as Platov had ordered, they drove up to the Emperor's palace and, having driven up at a gallop, they even drove past the columns.

Platov got out, pinned on his medals and went to see the Emperor, telling the cossacks to mount guard over the cross-eyed, left-handed artificer at the entrance to the palace.

CHAPTER XI

PLATOV was afraid to show his face to the Emperor, for Nikolai Pavlovich had a terribly good memory, quite a remarkable memory, in fact, and he never forgot anything. Platov knew that he would most certainly ask him about the flea and he, who never feared an enemy in his life, got into a blue funk and as soon as he entered the palace with the casket, he quietly hid it in one of the rooms behind the stove. Having hidden it, Platov presented himself to the Emperor in his study and began quickly to give his report about the talks he had had with the cossacks on the banks on the gently flowing Don. He argued that he would do his best to interest the Emperor in his report about the Don cossacks and that if the Emperor himself remembered the flea and began to ask questions about it, he would give him the casket and accept full responsibility for the failure of his commission, but that if the Emperor did not mention it, he (Platov) would not say a word about it, either, and would give the casket to the Emperor's valet with instructions to put it away safely; in the meantime he would put the Tula craftsman into a fortress where he would remain indefinitely until he was wanted.

But the Emperor Nikolai Pavlovich never forgot anything and as soon as Platov had finished his report about his talks with the Don cossacks, he asked him immediately:

"Well, how did my Tula craftsmen acquit themselves in the matter of the English steel flea ?"

Platov explained the position just as it appeared to be to him.

"Your Majesty," he said, "the flea is still in the same place and I have brought it back, but I'm sorry to have to report, sir, that the Tula craftsmen were quite unable to do anything more wonderful."

To which the Emperor replied:

"I know that you are a gallant old soldier, but what you are telling me can't possibly be true."

Platov began to assure him that he was telling the truth and he related everything exactly as it had happened, adding that the Tula craftsmen had asked him to show the flea to the Emperor.

Nikolai Pavlovich patted his shoulder and said:

"Let me see it. I know that my people will never let me down. There must be something about the thing that surpasses understanding."

CHAPTER XII

So they produced the casket from behind the stove, took off the cotton cover, opened the golden snuff-box and the diamond nut—and there the flea was lying as it had been lying there before.

The Emperor looked at it and said:

"What the devil ? . . ." but his faith in the Russian craftsmen was not in the least shaken and he ordered his favourite daughter, Alexandra Nikolayevna, to be summoned to his study and when she came, he said to her:

"You have such slender fingers, my dear, take the little key, put it in the flea's tummy and wind up the spring."

The princess began to turn the key and the flea immediately began to move her feelers, but that was all she did: her feet did not move! Alexandra Nikolayevna wound the spring up as far as it would go, but the flea did not even attempt to cut any capers or dance the quadrille as before.

Platov got green in the face and roared:

"Oh, the dirty dogs, now I can understand why they didn't want to show anything to me. It's a good thing I brought one of those fools with me!"

Having said that, he rushed out of the palace, caught the left-handed artificer by the hair and began to tug at it so that tufts of hair began flying about all over the place. But when Platov ceased beating him, the Tula craftsman smoothed the remaining strands of hair on his head and said:

"As it is, all my hair was pulled out by my schoolmaster and I really don't think there was any need to go through the same process again."

"No need ?" Platov roared. "Why, didn't I rely on you and vouch for you and now you've gone and damaged a work of such rare craftsmanship!"

The left-handed one replied:

"We are very grateful to you for having vouched for us, but we didn't damage anything: just look at the steel flea through the strongest microscope."

Platov ran back to tell the Emperor about the microscope, just saying to the left-handed artificer:

"You wait, I haven't done with you yet!"

And he ordered the cossacks to tie the Tula craftsman's elbows more tightly behind his back, while he himself mounted the steps at a run, panting and uttering a prayer under his breath, "The Lord and the Holy Virgin have mercy upon me," and so on. And the courtiers who were standing on the steps pretended not to see him, thinking, "Poor old Platov, he's got himself into a proper mess now and he's sure to be kicked out of the palace," for they just couldn't abide him because he was so brave.

CHAPTER XIII

As soon as Platov reported to the Emperor what the left-handed artificer had said, his Majesty looked greatly gratified and he exclaimed:

"I knew that my Russians would never let me down," and he commanded that a microscope on a cushion be brought immediately.

When the microscope had been brought, the Emperor took the flea and put it under the glass at first upside down, then side-ways and then with its tummy downwards, in a word, he turned it every way, but he could not see anything. Still, he did not give up his faith in the Russian craftsman, but merely said:

"Bring to me at once the gunsmith who is downstairs."

"Your Majesty, he ought to be tidied up a little. I brought him with me just as he was and I'm afraid he's been knocked about a bit."

But the Emperor replied:

"Never mind, let him be brought as he is."

So Platov went and said to the gunsmith:

"Come along, you so-and-so, answer to his Majesty himself."

And the left-handed artificer replied:

"All right, I'm sure I don't mind."

So he went just as he was dressed at the time: in his torn boots, one of his trouser-legs stuck inside his boot and the other dangling outside, all the hooks torn off his threadbare coat and his collar in shreds; but he did not seem in the least concerned about his tattered appearance.

"Well," he thought, "if the Emperor wants to see me, I must go and if I have no official document on me, nobody can blame me for that. All I have to do is to tell him how it all happened."

As soon as the left-handed artificer came in and bowed, the Emperor said to him:

"What does it all mean, my dear chap? We looked and looked at the flea and put it under a microscope, but we can't find anything remarkable about it."

And the left-handed one replied:

"Are you quite sure, your Majesty, that you looked well?"

The lords in attendance on his Majesty began winking at the Tula craftsman, as if to say, "That's not the way to talk to the Emperor! You ought to take an example from us courtiers: let your speech be full of cunning and flattery! Nobody talks in plain language here!"

But the Emperor said to them:

"Just leave him alone, will you? It's you who are the wiseacres, not he. Let him explain as he knows best."

And he at once explained the position to the Tula craftsman, saying:

"We put the flea under the microscope this way," and he put it under the microscope. "Look for yourself," he said, "you can't see anything there!"

The left-handed artificer replied:

"You can't see anything there your Majesty, because our work is so fine that you will never see what we did if you put it that way under the microscope."

The Emperor asked:

"What way are we to put it?"

"You have to examine each foot separately under the microscope and each heel separately to see how the flea walks," said the left-handed artificer.

"Goodness me," said the Emperor, "is it really as fine as all that?"

"I'm afraid it is, your Majesty," said the Tula craftsman. "That is the only way to see our work, if, that is, you really want to admire it."

So they put the flea under the microscope as the left-handed artificer had directed and as soon as the Emperor had a peep at it through the glass, his face became wreathed in smiles and he took the Tula craftsman just as he he was, unkempt and covered with dust, and embraced and kissed him, and then he turned to all his courtiers and said:

"You see, I knew better than any of you that my Russians would never let me down. Why, the rogues have shod the flea's feet!"

CHAPTER XIV

EVERYBODY now walked up to the microscope and had a look at the flea, and, indeed, each of the flea's feet had been shod with real horseshoes. The left-handed artificer, however, pointed out that even that was not the most remarkable thing about the Tula craftsmen's achievement.

"If you had a better microscope which magnified five million times," he said, "you'd have been able to read on each of the horseshoes the name of the craftsman who made it, for each of them bears a name."

"Is your name there, too?" asked the Emperor.

"No, Sire," replied the left-handed artificer. "I made the nails with which the horseshoes have been fastened and those you wouldn't be able to see under any microscope."

The Emperor asked:

"Where is your microscope with which you were able to do such wonderful work?"

But the left-handed artificer replied:

"We are very poor, your Majesty, and we can't afford a microscope, but our eyes are sharp enough."

Seeing that the left-handed artificer had come out of his ordeal with flying colours, all the courtiers began to congratulate him, each embracing and kissing him in turn, and Platov gave him a hundred roubles and said:

"I hope you won't bear me any grudge, my dear fellow, for having torn your hair out."

But the Tula craftsman replied:

"Good gracious, of course not: we're used to having our heads bitten off."

And he said no more, for he had hardly time to say anything because the Emperor immediately ordered the shod flea to be put in a parcel and to be sent back to England as a present, but really to show the English that we did not think it so wonderful after all. And the Emperor commanded that a special courier should take the flea, one who could speak foreign languages, and that the left-handed artificer should accompany him, so that he himself could show to the English what the Russian craftsmen had done and, generally, what fine craftsmen they were in Tula.

Platov made the sign of the cross over him:

"May the Lord's blessing accompany you on your journey," he said, "and I'll send you my own Caucasian vodka to comfort you on the way. Don't drink too much and don't drink too little, but just go steady with it."

And so he did: the vodka was sent.

And Count Kisselvrode gave orders that the left-handed artificer should be taken to the Tulyakovsky public baths and given a good wash, that his hair should be cut at a hairdresser's and that he should be clothed in the dress clothes of a court choirboy, so that it should appear that he was a man of some rank.

So they clothed him in this fashion, gave him plenty of tea with Caucasian vodka to drink, drew in his belt very tightly so that his bowels should not be shaken up during the journey and sent him off to London. Thus it was that the left-handed artificer started out on his foreign adventures.

CHAPTER XV

THE Emperor's courier and the left-handed artificer travelled very fast and they did not stop anywhere for a rest between St. Petersburg and London. All they did was to tighten their belts a notch at every station so that their bowels shouldn't get mixed up with their lungs; but after his presentation to the Emperor, the left-handed artificer, according to a special order issued by Platov, could have as much vodka as he liked at the Government's expense and so he just kept himself going on vodka alone and tasted no food and while travelling across Europe he sang songs, adding, however, a foreign refrain:

Sing merrily, sing merrily,
C'est très joli!

On their arrival in London, the courier went immediately to deliver the parcel to the right people, leaving the left-handed artificer at an inn in a private room. But the Tula gunsmith soon got fed up with sitting in that room by himself. Besides, he also got rather hungry. So he knocked at the door and asked the waiter for food by pointing to his mouth, and the waiter at once took him downstairs to the dining-room.

The left-handed artificer sat down at a table, but he did not know what to do next, for he could not ask for anything in English, but he soon found a way out of that difficulty. He just knocked on the table with a finger and pointed to his mouth and the English at once guessed that he was asking for some food and they brought him some; only they did not always bring him what he wanted, but he would not eat anything that was unsuitable. So when they brought him a blazing plum-pudding, he just said, "No, thank you, I don't know anything about such things and I'm not sure that I could eat it without burning myself," and they took the plum-pudding away and gave him something else. Neither would he drink their vodka, for it was green, just as if it had been mixed with green vitriol. In short, he chose everything that appeared natural to him, and so he spent his time, waiting for the courier in a cool place and helping himself from a bottle.

In the meantime the people to whom the courier had brought the flea immediately examined it under the most powerful microscope and at once sent a full description of it to the police headquarters so that a public announcement could be published about it next day for everybody's information.

"And," said they, "we'd like to see the master craftsman himself right away."

The courier took them to the left-handed artificer's room and, not finding him there, to the dining-room, where our Tula gunsmith had not been wasting his time and had managed to get quite red-cheeked by then, and he said:

"There he is!"

So the Englishmen at once started patting the Tula craftsman on the back, just as if he were their equal, and they shook his hands and said, "Good boy, good boy, a splendid craftsman! We shall discuss everything with you in good time, but now let's drink to your health!"

They ordered a lot of wine and offered the first glass to the left-handed artificer, but he very civilly refused to drink the first glass, for he said to himself, "Who knows, maybe you want to poison me out of jealousy."

"Thank you," he said, "but it's the host who should drink the first toast, so please drink yourselves first!"

The Englishmen tasted the different kinds of wine before him and then they began to fill his glass, and he got up, crossed himself with his left hand and drank their health.

They noticed that he had crossed himself with the left hand and they asked the courier:

"Is he a Lutheran or a Protestant?"

The courier replied:

"No, he is neither a Lutheran, nor is he a Protestant, but he is of the Russian Orthodox faith."

"Then why does he cross himself with his left hand?"

The courier said:

"Because he's left-handed, he does everything with his left hand."

The English marvelled even more and they began treating both the courier and the left-handed artificer very liberally to drinks, and for three days they entertained them in this manner and then they said, "That'll do." So they each had a whole syphon of soda water and, feeling refreshed, they began to question the left-handed artificer where he had been taught his trade and where he had studied and how much arithmetic he knew.

The left-handed artificer replied:

"Our studies, gentlemen, are really quite a simple affair: we know our psalter and the book of Halfdreams, but we don't know much arithmetic."

The Englishmen exchanged glances and said:

"That's just marvellous!"

But the left-handed artificer replied to them:

"That's how it is in our country."

"And what kind of a book is the Russian book of Halfdreams?" they asked.

"Oh," he said, "you see, it is a book in which, if there is anything in the psalter that King David left unexplained, you can find a number of additional explanations of."

But they said:

"That's a great pity, for it would have been much better if you knew at least the four rules of addition in arithmetic. That would have been much more useful to you than the whole book of Halfdreams, because you would then have understood that each engine is so constructed that it can perform only certain tasks according to its power and, although you're certainly very clever with your hands, you don't seem to have realised that an engine such as the one inside the steel flea was made according to the most exact measurements and cannot possibly carry the weight of horseshoes. That's why the steel flea cannot skip and dance any more."

The left-handed artificer agreed entirely.

"We needn't argue about that," he said. "It is quite true that we haven't advanced far in science, but we've always been loyal sons of our motherland."

And the Englishmen said to him:

"Stay with us, we'll make you into a highly educated man and you will become quite a wonderful craftsman."

But the Tula craftsman would not agree to their proposal.

"I'm very sorry, gentlemen," he said, "but I have parents at home."

The Englishmen offered to send money to his parents, but the left-handed artificer refused to accept their offer.

"We are attached to our country," he said, "and, besides, my dear father is a very old man now and my mother is an old lady and they are used to going to church in their own parish and I'd feel very lonely here by myself, for I am still a bachelor."

"You'll get used to it," they said, "you accept our faith and we'll marry you off."

"That," the left-handed one replied, "is quite out of the question."

"Why?"

"Because," he replied, "our Russian faith is the true faith and as our forefathers worshipped God, so must their offspring do, too."

"But you don't know anything about our faith," said the Englishmen. "We are also Christians and we have the same Bible as you."

"The Bible," the Tula craftsman replied, "is the same for everybody. That's true enough, but our books are much thicker and our faith, too, has more in it."

"Why do you think so?"

"We have ample proof of that," he replied.

"What, for instance?"

"Well," he said, "we have miracle-working icons and relics of saints and you have nothing at all and you haven't even any extra holidays except Sunday and, secondly, even if I am lawfully wedded to an Englishwoman, I should find it embarrassing to live with her."

"Why should you?" they asked. "Don't belittle our womenfolk—our girls, too, dress very neatly and they're good housewives."

But the left-handed artificer said:

"I don't know them."

The Englishmen replied:

"That isn't so important. The important thing is that you could learn to know them. Would you like us to arrange a special grand review of them for you?"

The left-handed artificer blushed.

"Why trouble the girls?" he said and, refused even to hear of it. "A grand review," he said, "is a gentlemen's affair and does not become the likes of us. Besides, if they got to hear of it at home in Tula, they'd just laugh at me."

The Englishmen got rather curious and asked:

"But if you have no grand reviews, what do you do in such cases at home to make quite sure your choice is an agreeable one?"

So the left-handed artificer explained to them how things were done in his country.

"In our country," he said, "if a man has honourable intentions about a young lady, he sends an old woman who is conversant with such affairs and she makes an offer and then he pays a visit to the young lady's house and everything is done very properly and he never sees the girl by herself alone, but in the presence of all her relations."

They understood, but they said that they had no such old women and no such customs, and the Tula craftsman said:

"That seems all for the best then, for if I were to undertake any such business, my intentions would have to be honourable and I'm afraid I do not feel so disposed to a foreign nation, so why trouble the girls?"

The Englishmen liked him for the sincerity of his opinions, so they began slapping his back and patting his knees in a very pleasant and civil fashion and they said:

"We're rather curious to know one thing more, though: have you noticed any disagreeable features about our girls that you are so anxious to avoid them?"

But the left-handed artificer said very candidly to them:

"Mind you, I'm not finding fault with your girls, but I don't mind admitting that I dislike the way their dresses seem to billow round them so that it is difficult to say what they are wearing and what occasion they are wearing it for: there's something here and something else pinned on beneath it and on their hands they wear kind of stockings, just like monkeys—*sapajous*—and on top of it all they wear velvet talmas."

The Englishmen laughed and said:

"Why should that bother you so much?"

"It doesn't bother me," he replied, "and I dare say there's nothing wrong with it, only I fear I should feel ashamed to look on and wait till she got out of it all."

"But are your fashions better?"

"Our women's fashions in Tula are simple enough," he said. "Each girl wears her own lace and even our great ladies wear lace."

They invited him to their homes and introduced him to their ladies and treated him to tea and asked him:

"What are you pulling long faces for?"

And he replied:

"We're not used to drinking such sweet tea."

So they let him have a lump of sugar to suck according to the Russian custom. They seemed to think that by holding a lump of sugar in his mouth, his tea would be even sweeter, but he said:

"No, it isn't, for we like it better that way."

The English could do nothing to change his opinions and make him like the English way of life and they only succeeded in persuading him to stay a short time as their guest, promising to take him round their factories and show him how everything was done in England.

"And then," they said, "we shall take you back in one of our own ships and *bring you alive to St. Petersburg*."

And he gladly agreed to that.

CHAPTER XVI

THE Englishmen took the left-handed artificer under their own protection, but sent the Russian courier back to Russia. Although the courier was a person of rank and knew foreign languages, they did not seem to be interested in him, but they certainly were very interested in the left-handed artificer, and they began to take him round and showed him everything. He saw all their factories, their machine shops and their soap factories and their saw-mills, and he liked the way they did things very much, but more especially did he like the way their workers lived. Every one of their workers had enough to eat, and he wasn't dressed in rags, but he wore a good jacket and thick leather, iron-shod boots, so as not to injure his foot if he stepped on a nail or something; he did not do his work because somebody stood with a whip over him, but because he had been taught his trade and he knew what he was doing. In the factories a multiplication table hung in front of every worker who also had a slate by his side, so that whatever his master did, he immediately looked at the table and checked it with understanding, then he wrote something on his slate, wiped something else off it and thus got everything ship-shape: what was written down in figures was later to be seen in the work. And whenever a holiday came, they'd gather in twos, take a walking-stick in their hands and go out for a walk, doing everything with the utmost decorum and observing the utmost politeness to each other, just as it should be.

The left-handed artificer observed their life and watched them at work, but he paid the greatest attention to a matter that used to astonish the English. He'd go round their arms factories, but he didn't seem to be interested in the manufacture of new guns so much as in the way the old guns were kept. He'd praise everything, but whenever he was shown any new guns, he'd say:

"We can do it as well."

But whenever he saw an old musket, he'd put his finger into the barrel, then take it out and rub it on the wall and sigh:

"That," he'd say, "certainly beats ours hollow."

The Englishmen were quite at a loss to understand what he meant, but he would ask:

"Could you tell me, please, if our generals ever saw your old guns?"

He was told:

"Those who came here probably saw them."

"Do you know if they had their gloves on at the time?"

"Your generals," they said, "always wear full dress when they come here and they always walk about in their gloves, so they must have had their gloves on at the time."

The left-handed artificer said nothing, but he suddenly became very home-sick and he said to the English:

"Thank you very much for your kind hospitality and I'm very satisfied with everything and I saw all I wanted to see, but now I should like to go back home and that as quickly as possible."

They could do nothing to keep him any longer. He could not be sent back by land because he didn't know any foreign languages and to send him back by sea was also inadvisable, because it was autumn and strong gales were blowing, but he kept on worrying them, "Let me go home!"

"We have looked at the weather glass," they said, "and we can see that a big gale is blowing up and you might get drowned, for this isn't your Gulf of Finland, but the rough, stormy sea."

"I don't care," he replied. "It makes no difference where a man dies, since we all walk under God, but I must go home, for otherwise I might go off my head."

As they did not want to keep him against his will by force, they fed him, heaped money upon him, gave him a farewell present of a gold repeater, and to shield him from the cold weather during his sea voyage, they gave him a woollen overcoat and a cap which could be pulled down over his head to protect him against boisterous sea breezes. So they clothed him very warmly and took him aboard a sailing vessel which was bound for Russia. There he was placed, got up like a real gentleman, but he did not like to stay below deck with the other gentlemen, because he did not feel comfortable in their company, and he'd go on deck and shelter under a tarpaulin and ask:

"Which way is Russia?"

The Englishman to whom he would address the question would point with his hand or jerk his head, and he would turn with his face to that direction and look yearningly towards his native land.

As soon as they left the harbour and got into the open sea, his longing for Russia grew and grew, so that it was quite impossible to comfort him. A strong gale was blowing, but the left-handed artificer refused to go down to his cabin, but just sat on deck under the tarpaulin with his cap pulled down over his eyes which gazed constantly towards his native land.

Again and again the Englishmen would go up to him and ask him to go below deck where it was warm, but he kept on refusing and, at last, beginning to get vexed with them, he started telling them lies.

"No, thank you," he'd say, "I feel much better here. I'm afraid I shall be sea-sick below deck."

So he just stayed there all the time, except when he had to go down for some special occasion, and because of that an English mariner who, to the left-handed artificer's misfortune, knew Russian took a fancy to him. The mariner could not help admiring him for putting up with such stormy weather, although he was a Russian landlubber.

"You're a fine fellow," he'd say. "Come on, let's have a drink!"

So the left-handed artificer had a drink.

And the merry English mariner said:

"Have another!"

So the left-handed artificer had another, and both of them got drunk.

The mariner asked him:

"Tell me, what is the secret you're carrying away from our country to Russia ?"

The left-handed artificer replied:

"That's my business."

"Well, if that's how it is," the merry mariner said, "then let's have an English bet."

The left-handed artificer asked:

"What kind of a bet is that ?"

"Let's have a bet that we shall never drink by ourselves, but always together and always the same amount of drink, what I drink, you drink, and what you drink, I drink, and he who can drink more, wins the bet."

The left-handed artificer thought: The sky's cloudy, my belly's rowdy and my poor heart craves for the sight of my home beyond the waves, so why not take on his bet and at least have something to cheer me up ?

"All right," he said, "I agree."

"But, mind, no tricks!"

"Don't you worry about that," the left-handed artificer said.

So they agreed and shook hands on it.

CHAPTER XVII

THEIR bet started while they were still on the open sea and they went on drinking until they reached the estuary of the Dvina at Riga, and all the time both of them drank the same amount of liquor and neither of them was able to drink more than the other, and so perfectly matched were they that when one of them took a look at the sea and saw a devil jumping out of the waves, the other one would immediately see a devil too, except that the merry mariner would see a ginger devil, while the left-handed artificer would maintain that the devil he saw was as black as a blackamoor.

The left-handed artificer said:

"Cross yourself and turn away, for it is the devil out of the deep."

But the Englishman did not agree.

"No, sir," said he, "it isn't a devil at all you're seeing: it's a deep sea diver. If you like I'll throw you into the sea and you needn't be afraid, for that deep sea diver will hand you back to me at once."

And the left-handed one replied:

"All right, if that is so, you can throw me into the sea."

So the mariner picked him up by the seat of his trousers and carried him to the rail intending to dump him into the sea, but the sailors saw them in time and informed the captain who ordered that both of them should be locked up below deck and given wines and rum and cold food, so that they should have plenty to eat and drink and be able to carry on with their bet, but he would not send them down any blazing plum-pudding, for he was afraid that the liquor inside them might catch fire.

So they were safely locked up until the ship berthed in St. Petersburg and neither of them won the bet and they were placed in different carriages, the Englishman being taken to the English Embassy on the English Quay and the left-handed artificer to the nearest police station.

CHAPTER XVIII

As soon as the mariner was brought to the English Embassy, a doctor and a chemist were fetched to see him. The doctor ordered that the mariner should be put in a hot bath in his presence, and the chemist at once rolled a pill of gutta-percha and stuck it into the mariner's mouth, and then both of them took him out of the bath, put him on a feather bed and covered him up with a fur coat and left him there to have a good sweat and, to prevent any interference with his rest, an order was given that no one in the Embassy should sneeze. The doctor and the chemist waited until the mariner was asleep and then they prepared another gutta-percha pill for him, put it on a table near the head of his bed and went away.

But the left-handed artificer was taken to the police station, thrown on the floor and asked:

"Who are you and where do you come from and have you got a passport or any other document?"

Weakened by illness, drink and sea-sickness, the left-handed artificer could not say a word in reply, but just kept on moaning. So they searched him, took off his good clothes, confiscated his gold repeater and his money, and the police captain ordered him to be taken in a sledge to the nearest hospital and he told the policeman not to bother to pay his fares.

The policeman took the left-handed artificer to put him in a sledge, but he could not find one for a long time, because the cabbies usually run as fast as they can as soon as they catch sight of a policeman. All the time the left-handed artificer lay on the cold pavement. Then the policeman caught a cabby at last, but there was no warm fox-rug on the sledge, for whenever a cabby sees a policeman and cannot get away, he hides the warm fox-rug under him on purpose to make quite sure that the policeman's feet get frostbitten. So the left-handed artificer was taken in an open sledge and, whenever they had to change over from one sledge to another, they just dropped him in the road, and when they lifted him up again, they'd pull him by the ears, for by then he was unconscious and they wanted to make sure that he was not dead. At the first hospital they would not admit him without a document, and when they took him to a second hospital he was again refused admission for the same reason, and the same thing happened at a third and at a fourth hospital and by daybreak they had dragged him all over St. Petersburg, through narrow byways and alleys, and every time a hospital refused to admit him, the policeman would have to get another sledge, so that in the end he was all black and blue from all that knocking about. Then some assistant doctor told the policeman to take him to the Obukhvinskaya public infirmary where all poor people of no fixed abode were usually taken to die.

There the policeman demanded a receipt and meanwhile they left the left-handed artificer lying on the floor in a passage until a bed was found for him.

The English mariner got up next morning just when they had brought the Tula gunsmith to the infirmary, swallowed the second gutta-percha pill, had a quick breakfast of roast chicken, washed it down with soda water and said:

"Where's my Russian pal? I'm going to look for him."

So he dressed and ran off.

CHAPTER XIX

BY a kind of a miracle the English mariner found the left-handed artificer in less than no time, even before he had been put to bed and while he was still lying on the floor in the passage.

"I must give the Emperor a message," said the left-handed artificer to the mariner. "Just a few words, but it is very urgent."

The Englishman ran off to see Count Kleinmichel and he raised an awful row, saying to the Count:

"How can you allow a man to be treated like that? He may only wear a sheepskin, but he has a human soul, hasn't he?"

The Englishman was immediately kicked out of there for daring to mention a human soul. Then somebody tipped him off, "You'd better go and see the cossack Platov: he's a man of warm human feelings."

The Englishman found Platov sulking on his couch. Platov listened to his story and he remembered the left-handed artificer.

"Why, of course, I know him well," he said. "I've even pulled him by the hair, but I'm afraid I don't know what I can do to help him in his present trouble, for, you see, I've left the army for good and am just a private individual and nobody pays any attention to me any more. But you'd better run quickly to the commandant Skobelev who has had experience in such matters and can do something and, in fact, I am almost certain that he will do something."

So the mariner went to see Skobelev and he told him everything, how it had all happened and what the left-handed artificer was suffering from, and Skobelev said:

"Yes, yes, I know of such an illness, but I'm afraid the Germans are no good at curing it at all. What you want is a doctor whose father was a Russian priest, for such doctors are acquainted with such cases from the days of their childhood and they know what to do. I'll send the Russian doctor Martyn-Solsky to that hospital and let him have a look at your friend."

But when Martyn-Solsky arrived at the infirmary, the left-handed artificer was already at his last gasp, for the back of his head had been split open when they had thrown him down on the pavement, and all he could say before he died was:

"Tell the Emperor that the English don't clean their muskets with bath-brick and that we shouldn't clean them with bath-brick either, or God help us if there is another war, for they won't shoot properly."

And having given that loyal message for the Emperor, the left-handed artificer crossed himself and died.

Martyn-Solsky did not waste any time, but went straight to Count Chernishov and asked him to give the message to the Emperor, but Count Chernishov just scoffed at him and said:

"You'd better stick to your emetics and your purges and don't interfere in a matter that doesn't concern you: in Russia we have generals for that kind of thing."

So the Emperor was not told and the guns continued to be cleaned with bath-brick until the Crimean war and when, during that war, the Russians loaded their guns, the bullets used to rattle about because the barrels were cleaned with crushed bricks. It was then that Martyn-Solsky reminded Count Chernishov about the left-handed artificer, but Chernishov said:

"Go to blazes out of here, you pill merchant, and mind your own business, or I'll deny you ever told me anything about it and then you'll catch it!"

And Martyn-Solsky thought: he most likely will deny having ever heard it from me—and he kept silence.

But if they had brought the left-handed artificer's message in time to the Emperor, there would have been quite a different story to tell about the Crimean war.

CHAPTER XX

BUT all this is now a tale of "old, unhappy, far-off things and battles long ago," and even if it didn't belong to the days that are very "far off" there is no need to be in a hurry to forget it, in spite of the fairy-tale character of this legend and the epic nature of its hero. The name of the left-handed artificer, like the names of many other great geniuses, has been lost for ever to posterity; but even as a myth personified by popular imagination it is interesting, and his adventures can serve as a chronicle of an epoch, the general spirit of which has been truly and faithfully rendered.

Such craftsmen as the fabulous left-handed artificer are no more to be found in Tula; the machine has made less obvious the inequalities between natural talents and endowments, and genius can hardly be expected to compete with application and mere accuracy. While favouring a rise in wages, the machines do not encourage artistic boldness which sometimes broke through all the barriers of the merely possible and inspired popular imagination to create similar fairy-tale legends of this sort.

The workers, no doubt, know how to value the practical devices put at their disposal by science, but they still remember the old days with pride and affection. That was their epic story and one with a very "human soul," too.

THE MAKE-UP ARTIST

A Graveyard Story

Their souls among the blessed spirits
Will find rest—A Dirge.

CHAPTER I

THE opinion is widely held among us that an artist must be either a painter or a sculptor, and among them only those are thought worthy of that title if it has been conferred on them by the Academy. To many Sazikow and Ovchinnikov are just "silversmiths." But that opinion is not shared by people in other countries: Heine used to remember a tailor who was "an artist" and had "ideas," and women's dresses by Worth are even to-day called "artistic creations." For one of those dresses it was recently claimed that "the line of the bodice expressed in itself a world of fantasy."

In America the artistic field is much wider: the famous American writer Bret Harte tells a story about an "artist" who had gained great fame there as a "mortician." He gave the faces of the dead different "comforting expressions," which bore witness to the more or less happy state of their departed souls.

There were several degrees of his art, of which I remember three: "(1) composure, (2) exalted contemplation and (3) a state of heavenly bliss resulting from direct intercourse with the Creator." The fame of that artist corresponded to the high perfection of his work; it was, in other words, tremendous, but unfortunately the artist fell a victim to the mob which had no respect whatever for the freedom of artistic expression. He was stoned to death because he had given the face of a fraudulent banker who had robbed the whole town "an expression of blissful intercourse with God." The happy heirs of the rogue wanted to express their gratitude to their departed relative by such an order, but the man who carried it out paid with his life for being true to his art.

We in Russia also had an artist who was a master in quite an unusual sphere of artistic endeavour.

CHAPTER II

THE nurse of my younger brother was a tall, dried-up, but very stately, elderly woman and her name was Lyubov Onissimovna. She was a former actress of an Orel theatre which belonged to Count Kamensky and what I am about to tell you took place in Orel in the days of my boyhood.

My brother is seven years younger than I and he was, therefore, only two years old when Lyubov Onissimovna looked after him and I was in my tenth year and could follow perfectly the stories she told me.

Lyubov Onissimovna was not very old then, but her hair was quite white: she had a very delicate face with finely etched features, and her tall figure was remarkably slender, like a young girl's. My mother and aunt used to say, as they looked at her admiringly, that she must have been a great beauty in her youth. Her honesty was proverbial and she was very gentle and sentimental and loved everything in life that had a tragic ending and sometimes she . . . drank.

She used to take my brother and myself for walks in the Troitze cemetery where she always sat down on one and the same grave with an old cross and very often she used to tell me stories.

It was there that I heard the story of "the make-up artist" from her.

CHAPTER III

HE was also employed at the theatre and the difference between him and our nurse was that while she "acted on the stage and danced," he was the "make-up artist," that is to say, he used "to make up the faces and do the hair" of all the serf actors of the Count. But he was not an ordinary, everyday hairdresser with a comb behind his ear and a tin tray with grease-paint, but "a man of ideas," in a word, an *artist*.

According to Lyubov Onissimovna, no one could "give a better expression to the face" than he.

Which of the Counts Kamensky owned the theatre where those two artists flourished, I cannot say with any certainty. There were altogether three Counts Kamensky and all three of them enjoyed the unenviable reputation in Orel of being unconscionable tyrants. Field-Marshal Mikhail Fedorovich Kamensky was killed by his serfs for his cruelty in 1809. He left two sons, Nikolai, who died in 1811, and Sergey, who died in 1835.

As a child I still remember seeing in the 'forties a huge, grey wooden building with blind windows painted with soot and ochre and enclosed by a very long, half-ruined fence. That was Count Kamensky's estate of evil fame and the theatre was on this estate. It was so situated that it could be seen very well from the Troitze cemetery and for that reason whenever Lyubov Onissimovna wanted to tell us some story, she almost always prefaced it with these words:

"Have a look at that house, my dears. . . . Isn't it horrible?"

"Yes, nurse," I'd say, "it is horrible."

"Well, I'll tell you something which is even more horrible."

And one of her stories was about the "make-up artist" Arcady, a brave and tender-hearted young man, who was very dear to her heart.

CHAPTER IV

ARCADY "made up and did the hair" of actresses only. The actors had a make-up man of their own and if Arcady did sometimes visit the men's dressing-rooms, it was only because the Count himself had ordered him to make up some actor "as a gentleman." The main originality of this make-up artist's "touch" lay in his ability to lend to the faces of the actors and actresses the most varied and "delicate" expressions.

"Arcady," Lyubov Onissimovna said, "would sometimes be called and told 'We want such and such an expression on the face,' and he would draw back a few steps, tell the actor or actress to stand up or sit down before him, while he himself crossed his hands on his chest and thought. Oh, he was such a handsome man, such a handsome man! For while he was not very tall, he had a very slender figure, so slender that it is quite impossible to describe it, and a thin, proud nose and such kind eyes, the eyes of a real angel, and a thick mop of hair always fell from his head over his eyes so that he seemed to look at you through a cloud."

In short, the make-up artist was a very handsome young fellow and "everybody liked him." He was also liked by the Count who "favoured him more than anybody else, dressed him in excellent clothes," but "was very strict with him." He thus never permitted Arcady to shave or give a haircut to any other man except himself and for that reason he *always* kept him near his own dressing-room and, with the exception of the theatre, Arcady was not allowed to go anywhere. He was not even allowed to go to church for confession or mass, for the Count himself did not believe in God and could not abide priests and once at Easter he let his pack of hounds tear to pieces the priests of the Borissoglyebsk church.[1]

The Count himself, according to Lyubov Onissimovna, was so ugly, because of that evil nature of his, that he looked more like a wild beast than a human being. But Arcady knew how to change, albeit for a short time, even that beast-like expression on his face so that when in the evening

[1] This incident was widely known in Orel. I myself heard about it from my grandmother Alfieryeva, and from the merchant, Ivan Ivanovich Androssov, who was well known for his strict adherence to truth and who *himself* saw "how the hounds tore the clergy to pieces." Androssov got away with his life from the Count only by "committing a sin." When the Count summoned him and asked him, "Are you sorry for them?" he replied, "No, my lord, they deserve it, for why do they gad about?" For that answer Kamensky spared his life. (N. L.)

he sat in his box, he looked more impressive than many of his invited guests at the theatre.

The thing that the Count, being of so evil a disposition, lacked most was just that look of dignity which was in those days considered to be inseparable from "the military mien," the imprint and very stamp of a "gentleman born and bred."

So to prevent anybody from making use of the services of such an incomparable artist as Arcady, "he was kept indoors all his life and was never given any money." At that time Arcady was a grown-up man of over twenty-five years, while Lyubov Onissimovna was nineteen. They knew each other, of course, and what usually happens to people of their age also happened to them, that is to say, they fell in love. But they never could talk of their love to each other, except by dropping veiled hints in the presence of all the other actresses during their make-up. Meetings between them were quite out of the question and, indeed, the thought of arranging such meetings never even occurred to them.

"They guarded us actresses as strictly as wet-nurses are guarded in great houses," Lyubov Onissimovna used to say. "We had special matrons to look after us and if, God forbid, anything happened to any of us, the children of those matrons were exposed to terrible treatment by that tyrant, the Count."

The life of chastity imposed upon the actresses could be terminated only by "himself," the man who had imposed it upon them.

CHAPTER V

LYUBOV ONISSIMOVNA was not only at the height of her beauty at the time, but also at the most important period of the development of her many-sided talents: she sang "pot pourri" in the chorus, danced "the first steps" in the *Chinese Garden Maid* and, feeling drawn to tragic parts, "knew all the tragic parts of their repertoire *by heart*."

In what year it all happened, I don't know, but it was in the year the Emperor passed through Orel (I can't say whether it was Alexander Pavlovich or Nikolai Pavlovich) and spent a night there, and he was expected to attend a performance at Count Kamensky's theatre in the evening. The Count invited all the people of quality to his theatre (seats were not sold for money) and the best show was put on. Lyubov Onissimovna had to sing in the "potpourri" and dance The Chinese Garden Maid, but during the dress rehearsals one of the sets collapsed and injured the foot of the actress who had to act the Duchesse de Bourblianne in the play.

I have never heard of a part of that name, but Lyubov Onissimovna pronounced it just like that.

The carpenters who were responsible for the collapse of the set were at once sent to the stables to be flogged and the injured actress was taken to her little room, but there was no one who could play the part of the Duchesse de Bourblianne.

"I volunteered to play the part," said Lyubov Onissimovna, "because I liked the way the Duchess fell at the feet of her father and asked him to forgive her and later died with her hair falling over her shoulders. I had lovely hair myself, long and fair, and Arcady dressed it simply wonderfully."

The Count was very pleased with the girl's unexpected readiness to play the part and, receiving the producer's assurance that "Lyuba will not fall down on her part," replied, "She'd better not, or you'll answer to me on your back! And now take her *Kamarinov* ear-rings from me!"

The "Kamarinov ear-rings" were a present of both good and bad omen, for it was the first sign of the special favour bestowed on a serf girl on becoming for a short time her lord's mistress. Arcady usually got the order to dress up the condemned girl soon after she had received the present or even immediately after she had received it "in the innocent garb of St. Cecilia" and, dressed all in white with a wreath round her head and a lily in her hand, she would be taken to the Count's rooms.

"You're too young to understand that," Lyubov Onissimovna told me, "but it was the most terrible thing that could happen to a girl and especially to me who was so desperately in love with Arcady. I burst into tears, threw the ear-rings on the table and just went on crying and couldn't even imagine how I should be able to play my part that evening."

CHAPTER VI

BUT in those fateful hours something which was no less fateful and terrible happened also to Arcady.

For that day the Count's brother arrived from his village to be presented to the Emperor, and the brother of the Count was even more ugly than the Count himself. He had been living in his village for a long time and he never wore his uniform and never even shaved, for his face was all covered with moles. But, of course, he, too, had on that special occasion to be dressed and tidied up and, generally, given the "military mien" that was demanded by custom in those days.

And quite a lot was demanded.

"To-day people don't realise how very strict everything was then," the nurse said. "In those days everything had to be done according to rule, and special rules existed for the way gentlemen had to do up their faces and comb their hair and that way didn't suit many people, for if one of them wore his hair as required by the regulations, with a little mop of hair standing up straight above his forehead and small side-whiskers running down his cheeks, his face would look just like a peasant's balalaika without strings. The great gentlemen were terribly afraid of looking like that, and that was why it was so important to get a first-class barber who knew the secret of leaving little paths between the side-whiskers and the moustache and curling or combing out the hair, for the slightest turn of the comb gave quite a different expression to the face."

According to our nurse, civilian gentlemen did not find the ordeal so bad because very little attention was paid to them, all that was required of their faces being a meek and contrite expression; but much more was demanded of military gentlemen, whose lips had to part in servile smiles in the presence of their superiors, but were expected immediately to assume a curl of the utmost disdain in the presence of everybody else.

It was that expression that Arcady knew so well how to give to the ugly and insignificant face of the Count by his wonderful art.

CHAPTER VII

THE country brother of the Count was even uglier than Arcady's master and, moreover, he neglected his appearance so badly in his village and his face had grown so coarse that he himself couldn't help being aware of it, and he had no one to spruce him up, for, in addition to everything else, he was a terrible miser and he let his own hairdresser go to Moscow on the payment of a regular due. His face, as I said, was covered with all sorts of protuberances, so that it was quite impossible to shave him without cutting a pimple here or a mole there.

On his arrival in Orel he summoned all the barbers in town and said:

"Any one of you who can make me look like my brother shall receive two gold pieces, but anyone who cuts me—well, here are two pistols and I'm going to put them on the table. If you do your work well, you can take the gold, but if you cut even one pimple off my face or shave a hair too many off my side-whiskers—I shall shoot you dead on the spot!"

Now, as a matter of fact, he was merely trying to frighten them, for his pistols were only loaded with blanks.

There were not many barbers in Orel at the time and even those mostly frequented the public baths where they let blood or applied leeches, and none of them had any taste or a spark of imagination. They knew it very well themselves and one and all refused to "transform" Kamensky. "Keep your gold," they said to themselves, "and leave us in peace."

"We can't do what you desire of us, sir," they said, "for we are not worthy of even touching so great a person as your lordship. Besides, we haven't got any proper razors, for our razors are just common or garden Russian razors and nothing but an English razor would do for your lordship's face. There's only one man who can help you, sir, and that man is the Count's Arcady."

The Count's brother ordered the barbers to be kicked out of doors, and they were very glad to get off so easily. He himself, however, went to his brother and said:

"Can't you let me have your Arcady before this evening to make me presentable? I haven't shaved for ages and the barbers here don't know a thing about shaving."

The Count said to his brother:

"Our local barbers are of course no damn good. As a matter of fact, I didn't even know we had any barbers here, for even my dogs have their coats cut by my own servants. But I'm afraid I can't possibly lend you my Arcady, for I have made a vow that while I live he will not attend to anyone but me. You don't think I'm going to break my vow even for my own brother, do you?"

His brother said:

"Why on earth not? You made the vow and you can break it."

But the Count replied that that kind of reasoning seemed very flippant to him.

"If I start breaking my vows," he said, "how can I expect my servants to keep theirs? Arcady has been told that I have given that order and everybody knows about it and that's why he enjoys so many privileges, for if he ever dared to apply his art to any other person, I'd flog him to death and send him into the army."

His brother, however, said:

"You can't have it both ways, old man. You can either flog him to death or send him into the army."

"All right," said the Count, "have it your own way. I'll flog him within an inch of his life and send him into the army afterwards."

"And is that your last word?"

"Yes," said the Count, "it is my last word."

"And that's all there is to be said about it?"

"Yes, sir."

"Well, in that case everything can be arranged beautifully," said the Count's brother. "You know, for a moment I really thought that your own brother was of less account to you than your serf. I don't want you to break your word. Just send Arcady to me *to cut my poodle's coat*. What happens afterwards is my business."

The Count couldn't very well refuse him that.

"All right," he said, "I'll send him to cut your poodle's coat."

So the brothers shook hands and parted.

CHAPTER VIII

TOWARDS the evening, after dusk had fallen and the lamps (it was winter) had been lit, the Count summoned Arcady to him and said:

"I want you to go to my brother's house to cut his poodle's coat."

Arcady asked:

"Is that all I shall be required to do, my lord?"

"Yes, that's all," said his lordship, "but don't be long, for I want you to make up the actresses. Lyuba has to be made up for three different parts and after the performance she'll have to be dressed up as St. Cecilia."

Arcady swayed suddenly.

The Count said:

"What's the matter with you?"

But Arcady replied:

"I'm sorry, my lord, I tripped over the carpet."

The Count remarked:

"I hope it doesn't bring you bad luck."

But Arcady's mind was in such a whirl that he didn't care whether it brought him bad luck or not.

Hearing that I was to be dressed up as St. Cecilia, he just picked up the leather case with his razors and scissors and went away, hardly knowing himself what he was doing.

CHAPTER IX

WHILE waiting for Arcady, the Count's brother had candles lit in front of a mirror and two pistols placed beside it and next to them he put not two, but ten pieces of gold, and the pistols were not this time loaded with blanks, but with Circassian bullets.

As soon as Arcady arrived, the Count's brother said:

"I have no poodle, but what I want you to do is this: give me a haircut and a shave and make me look important and I shall give you ten pieces of gold, but if you refuse, I shall kill you."

Arcady just stared and stared at him and then, suddenly—heaven alone knows what made him do it—he began to cut the Count's brother's hair and shave him. He did everything wonderfully and in hardly any time at all and then he put the gold into his pocket and said:

"Good-bye, sir."

The Count's brother said:

"All right, you can go now, but before you go I'd like you to tell me what made you do such a desperate thing?"

And Arcady said:

"My heart alone knows what made me do it, sir."

"Do you mean to say you've got a charm against a bullet and you're no longer afraid of a pistol?"

"No, sir," said Arcady, "I'm not afraid of a pistol. I didn't even think of it."

"Why didn't you think of it? You don't suppose—do you?—that my word isn't as good as my brother's, or that I shouldn't have shot you even if you had just cut me? If you possessed no charm against a bullet, you would have been a dead man now."

At the mention of the Count, Arcady gave a start and replied as though in a daze:

"I have no charms against bullets, but God has given me some sense. If I'd seen you raise the pistol, I'd have cut your throat before you'd have had time to pull the trigger."

And, having said that, he rushed out and arrived at the theatre just in time and began to make me up, while he himself was trembling in every limb. And every time he waved a curl and bent down to blow on it with his lips, he'd whisper to me:

"Don't be afraid: I'll take you away!"

CHAPTER X

THE performance was going well, for all of us were just as if we were made of stone, trained to fear and suffer: whatever our feelings were, we acted in such a way that nobody could have guessed them.

We saw the Count and his brother from the stage, both looking so alike that it was difficult to distinguish the one from the other and, indeed, when they later came round back-stage, it was impossible to tell which was which. Only our master looked so gentle as if butter wouldn't melt in his mouth and those who did not know him as well as we did would really have thought that he had suffered a sudden change of heart. But we knew that he was always like that before one of his wildest acts of cruelty.

All of us were terrified and we just kept on crossing ourselves.

"The Lord have mercy upon us! Whom has he chosen for his next victim?"

We didn't know anything about Arcady's desperate action at the time. Arcady himself, of course, knew very well that he could expect no mercy and he went very pale when the Count's brother looked at him and muttered something in a whisper to the Count. But I have very sharp ears and I caught his words:

"Listen to me; I'm warning you as a brother: take good care when he's shaving you!"

I suspect Arcady, too, must have overheard that whisper, for when he began to make me up for my last scene in which I had to play the duchess, he did something he had never done before: he put so much powder on my face that our wardrobe-master, a Frenchman, began to brush it off me, saying:

"*Trop beaucoup, trop beaucoup!*"

CHAPTER XI

AFTER the performance they took off the dress of the Duchesse de Bourlianne and put on me the dress of St. Cecilia—a white dress without sleeves and gathered on the shoulders. Oh, how we hated the very sight of that dress! Then Arcady came in to do my hair, for he had to dress it "in a chaste fashion," just like St. Cecilia's hair in the pictures, and fasten a slender wreath with a spangle, and Arcady saw that six men were standing at the door of my little room. That meant that as soon as he had finished with me and gone to the door, he would be seized and dragged away to his torture.

The tortures inflicted on our people were such that it was a hundred times better to be dead than to go through them. We had the rack and the string and the iron loop which would be put round the head and tightened—we had all that. Nor did our master fear any legal prosecutions. And under the house we had deep dungeons where people were kept on chains like bears and if one passed anywhere near them, one heard how the prisoners moaned and how their chains rattled. It was true that some people wanted to inform the authorities about it, but the authorities, even if they had ever been informed about what was taking place in our house, did not care or dare to interfere. People were tortured in those dungeons for long periods and some even died there. One of them was kept there so long that he even composed a verse about it:

> Your eyes big coiling serpents will devour,
> Your face with poison scorpions will fill;

and when passing those dungeons you'd repeat those lines and be overcome with terror.

Some men were even chained with bears so that if they moved half an inch, the bear would tear a piece of their flesh with his claws.

But they did nothing of the kind with Arcady because as soon as he came into my little room, he seized the table and knocked out the window and I can't remember what happened after that. . . .

I came round because my feet were terribly cold. I tried to pull my feet up and then I realised that I was wrapped in a bearskin or a wolfskin coat and everything round me was pitch black and I was lying in a sledge which was being drawn by three horses, but where I was being driven to I didn't know. Two men sat huddled up beside me and the one who was holding me was Arcady and the other was our driver who was whipping up the horses for all he was worth. . . . The snow was just flying from under the hoofs of the horses and the sledge was pitching violently, now to one side, now to another. If we had not sat in the middle of the sledge, on the floor, we shouldn't have been able to remain in it, but would have been pitched out and killed.

I could hear that Arcady and the driver were exchanging a few excited words as always happens in moments of great suspense, but I could only catch one word: "Faster, faster . . ." and nothing else.

When Arcady saw that I had recovered consciousness, he bent over me and said:

"My darling Lyuba, they're after us. . . . Are you ready to die if we don't get away?"

I replied that I would gladly die.

He hoped to get over the Turkish border where many of our people had escaped from Kamensky before.

Then we crossed a small frozen stream and in front of us we could see the outline of a house, and dogs began to bark, and the driver whipped up his horses even more and, as he leant heavily against one side of the sledge, it tipped up and Arcady and I were thrown out into the snow and the driver and the horses disappeared from sight.

Arcady said:

"Don't be frightened, we had arranged it all to happen like that, for I don't know the driver and he doesn't know me. I gave him three gold pieces to help me carry you off and he doesn't want to get into trouble. Now we're in God's hands. This is the village of Orlitza; a fearless priest lives here who marries eloped couples and he has also helped many of ours to escape. We'll give him some money and he'll hide us until the evening and then he'll marry us. After that our driver will return and we'll make our escape then."

CHAPTER XII

WE knocked at the door of a house and went into the hall. The priest himself opened the door for us; an old man he was, thick-set with one of his upper teeth missing, and his wife was a very old woman—she blew up the fire for us. We just fell at their feet, crying:

"Save us! Let us warm ourselves and then hide us till the evening."

The priest asked:

"But who are you, my dears? Have you stolen something or are you just runaway serfs?"

And Arcady replied:

"We haven't stolen anything from anybody, but we have just run away from that inhuman monster, Count Kamensky, and we want to get across the Turkish border where many of our people have escaped before us. They won't find us and we've got money of our own and we'll give you one gold rouble for letting us stay the night here and three gold roubles for marrying us, if you agree to marry us, but if you don't, we shall get married over the border."

The priest said:

"Why shouldn't I marry you? Of course I'll marry you. Why wait till you get across the border? Give me five gold roubles and I'll marry you here."

So Arcady gave him five gold roubles and I took off my *Kamarinov* ear-rings and I gave them to the priest's wife.

The priest took the money and said:

"Oh, my dear children, all that would have been easy enough, for I have had to marry couples who were in greater trouble than you, but it is a pity you belong to the Count. I may be a priest, but I, too, am in constant fear of that cruel man. But I'll take a chance and leave everything in the hands of our merciful Father in heaven. Let's have another gold coin, even if it has been chipped a bit, and then you can hide yourselves."

Arcady gave him a sixth gold rouble, one that wasn't chipped at all, and then the priest said to his wife:

"What are you standing about for, woman? Give the girl one of your skirts, or a warm coat or something: I'm ashamed to look at her—she's almost naked."

He wanted to take us to his church and hide us in a trunk under his chasubles, but no sooner did his wife begin to dress me behind the wooden partition, than we heard somebody rattling the iron ring on the front door.

CHAPTER XIII

OUR hearts sank within us. But the priest whispered to Arcady:

"Well, my boy, it seems you won't have time to hide in the trunk with the chasubles. Come on, get quickly under the feather bed!" And turning to me, he said, "And you, my sweet child, go there!"

And he put me inside the case of a big clock, which he locked; then he put the key in his pocket and went to open the door. I could hear that there were many men at the door and two were already looking through the window.

Seven men came in, all of them huntsmen of the Count, armed with iron clubs and riding-whips and inside their belts they had coils of rope and with them was the Count's butler in a large wolf-fur coat with a high collar.

The case in which I was hidden had the front part of it sawn away and covered with a thin piece of muslin through which I could see everything.

The old priest was shaking with fear as he stood in front of the butler, for he must have realised that things looked very black for him. He kept on crossing himself and saying in a loud voice:

"Oh, my good people, oh, my dear people, I know, I know what you're looking for, only I'm quite innocent before his lordship, absolutely innocent, absolutely innocent!"

And as he crossed himself, he pointed a finger over his shoulder at the case where I was hidden.

"I'm done for," thought I to myself as I saw him performing that miracle.

The butler noticed it, too, and said:

"We know everything. Give me the key from that chest!"

But the priest just waved his hand at him.

"Oh dear, oh dear, you must forgive me, I put the key away and I can't remember where."

And while saying this, he kept on stroking his pocket with his other hand.

The butler noticed that miracle, too, and he took the key out of his pocket and opened the chest.

"Come out, my sweetheart," he said, "and I dare say your lover will give himself up without any trouble."

But Arcady had already come out of his hiding-place: he had thrown off the priest's feather bed and stood there in front of them all.

"Well," he said, "there's nothing more I can do about it—you win! Take me back to be tortured, but remember she's innocent; I carried her off by force!"

Then he turned to the priest and all he did was just to spit in his face.

The priest cried:

"Do you see, my dear people, how this wretch insults my sacred office and scorns my loyalty to the Count? Please, tell his lordship about it!"

The butler replied:

"Don't worry, father, he'll pay for everything," and he ordered the men to take Arcady and myself out.

Three sledges were waiting for us. In the front sledge sat Arcady, who had been tied up, and the huntsmen, in the third sledge I sat under a similar guard, and in the second were the rest of the men who had gone in chase of us, and so we drove away.

The people we met on the way stopped to look after us: they must have thought we were going to a wedding.

CHAPTER XIV

WE travelled very fast and we were soon back at the Count's estate and, as we drove into the courtyard, I never again saw the sledge in which Arcady was. I was brought back to my room and then questioned again and again: how long had I been alone with Arcady? And to all their questions I just replied:

"Oh, not even for a single moment!"

So it seemed it was to be my fate to belong to a man I loathed and not to the one I loved—and so it was, and as soon as I came back to my little room and buried my face in the pillow to weep over my great misfortune, I heard terrible moans coming from the room below.

It was so arranged at our place that we, the girls, lived on the first floor and below was the large hall where we studied singing and dancing and we could hear everything that was taking place there. And it must have been Satan himself who made those heartless villains torment Arcady under my room. . . .

When I realised that they were tormenting him, I got up and rushed to the door, intending to go to him . . . but the door was locked. . . . I did not know myself what I was doing, but I only remember that I collapsed on the floor, but there I could hear his cries of agony even more clearly. . . . There was neither a knife nor a nail in my room with which I could kill myself, so I wound my long plait round my throat and I twisted it more and more tightly, until all I could hear was a ringing in my ears, and everything began to swim before my eyes and then I fainted. . . . When my senses came back to me I found myself in some unfamiliar place, in a large cottage, full of sunshine. . . . And there were calves there, lots of little calves . . . more than ten of them . . . such lovely calves, so tender and sweet, and they would come up to me and rub my head with their cold lips, thinking they were sucking their mother. . . . It was then that I recovered my senses, for they tickled me. . . . I looked round, thinking, "Where am I?" Then I saw an elderly woman entering the room, a tall woman in a blue-striped frock of coarse linen and her head covered with a clean kerchief of the same material, and with a very kind face.

The woman noticed that I had regained consciousness and she was very kind to me and she told me that I was in a farmhouse on the Count's estate, in the shed with the calves. . . .

"It used to be there," Lyubov Onissimovna explained, pointing at one of the farthest ruined grey buildings on the other side of the cemetery wall.

CHAPTER XV

SHE was sent to the farmyard because it was thought that she had gone off her head. People who lost their reason and became like beasts were usually sent to the cattle yard, because the people who looked after the cattle were all sedate and elderly people and it was considered that they were just the right sort to keep mental cases "under observation."

The woman in the rough, blue-striped dress in whose shed Lyubov Onissimovna recovered her senses was a very kind-hearted woman and her name was Drossida.

As soon as she had finished her work—my brother's nurse continued—she made me a bed of oaten straw and she spread it so nicely that it was as soft as a feather bed, and then she said:

"I'll tell you everything, my poor child, come what may if you betray me. I am just like you and it wasn't always that I wore this home-spun dress. I, too, knew a different kind of life, only I hate to remember it now, but I'll tell you one thing: don't worry that they sent you to the cattle farm; it is better to be banished here, but beware of this terrible phial. . . ."

And she took out of her neckerchief a little glass bottle and showed it to me.

I asked:

"What is it?"

And she replied;

"This is the terrible phial I was speaking of and in it is the poison of forgetfulness."

I said:

"Give me this poison of forgetfulness! I want to forget everything!"

She said:

"Don't drink it: it is vodka. I couldn't restrain myself and I drank. . . . Some good people gave it to me, and now I can't keep away from it, for I need it. But don't you drink it as long as you can possibly help it and don't think badly of me, if I have a suck at the bottle: I have such pains. But you at least have some comfort in the world: for the Lord has delivered *him* from the hands of the tyrant!"

I just exclaimed, "Dead!!!" and I clutched my hair and it was only then that I saw that my hair had turned white! . . . "What's that?" I asked, unable to believe that it was my own hair that I was holding in my hands.

But she said to me:

"Don't be afraid, my dear, your hair turned white while you were still in your room when they unwound your plaits from round your neck, but he is alive and delivered from all tyranny: the Count has shown him such a favour as he has not shown to any man before. . . . I'll tell you all about it to-night, but now I must have a suck at my bottle. . . . I have to. . . . My heart is on fire!"

And she kept on "sucking at" her bottle until she fell asleep.

During the night when everybody on the farm was sound asleep Auntie Drossida got up quietly and, without lighting a lamp, went up to the window and I saw that she was again sucking at the bottle and then she hid it again and after that she said to me in a soft voice:

"Is your sorrow asleep or not?"

I replied:

"No, my sorrow is not asleep."

She then came up to my bed and told me that after his punishment the Count had summoned Arcady and said to him:

"You had to take your punishment as I warned you, but as you were my favourite I shall show you a favour now: I'll send you to-morrow to be enlisted into the army and I shan't ask any payment for you. But because you were not afraid of my brother, a count and a gentleman, with his pistols, I shall give you a chance to show what you're made of and put you on the road to honour and glory, for I don't want you to feel that your position in the army is not worthy of the noble spirit you have proved yourself to possess. I have written a letter to ask the military authorities that they should send you to the front and you will not serve as a private, either, but as a regimental sergeant and I hope you will prove yourself to be a gallant soldier. Henceforth you will be under the Czar's orders and not under mine. . . ."

"It's much better for him where he is now," Drossida said, "and he has nothing to fear any more, for the worst that can happen to him is to fall in battle and death in battle is better than to be the slave of a tyrant."

I believed her and during the next three years I used to dream about Arcady and in my dreams I saw him fighting the enemy.

So three years passed and all during that time the Lord was merciful to me and I was not taken back to the theatre, but was allowed to stay in the cattle yard, in the calves' shed, as Auntie Drossida's help. I felt very happy there and I was very sorry for the old woman, and when she wasn't drunk I loved to listen to her stories. She still remembered how our people had killed the old Count; he was murdered by his personal valet, for they could no longer bear his hellish cruelty. But I would not taste any drink and I was very happy to do all I could for Auntie Drossida: those calves were just like my own children to me. I got so used to them that after I had fattened one and it was taken away to be slaughtered for our master's table, I'd make the sign of the cross over it and I cried for three days afterwards.

I was no good for the theatre any more, for my feet would not walk properly, they had become very unsteady. Before, I had such a lovely way of walking, but after Arcady had carried me off unconscious into the cold night, I must have got a chill in my feet and my toes had lost their firm grip for dancing. I became a dairymaid like Drossida and heaven knows how long I would have lived in that state of cheerless despondency, if one day as I was sitting in our cottage in the evening something had not happened to give me new hope of a happier life. The sun was setting and I sat by the window unwinding a tangled skein when a small stone came suddenly flying through the window and fell at my feet. The stone was wrapped in a piece of paper.

CHAPTER XVI

I LOOKED round, this way and that, looked out of the window, but there was not a soul to be seen anywhere.

"Somebody must have thrown it over the fence from the street," I thought, "but he didn't aim properly and it fell in our cottage."

I debated within myself for some time whether or not to take the paper off, but at last I decided that it would be better to have a look to see if anything was written on it, for if it was some message, I could keep it secret and wrap it up again and throw the stone back over the fence, so that the person whc had thrown it could pick it up again.

So I unwrapped the paper and began to read, and I couldn't believe my own eyes. . . .

CHAPTER XVII

THE message on the paper said:

"My faithful Lyuba,

"I have fought in many battles and served the Czar loyally and been "wounded many times and they made me an officer and a gentleman. "Now I have come back on leave, a free man, to recover from my wounds "and I am staying in the Pushkarskaya suburb at an inn owned by a "former house-porter, and to-morrow I shall put on my orders and my "crosses and I shall go to the Count and bring the money given to me "for my medical treatment, five hundred roubles, and ask him to let "me buy your freedom in the hope that we may be married before the "altar of almighty God. . . ."

And he also wrote—Lyubov Onissimovna went on, always making an effort to suppress her feelings at this point—that "whatever troubles you have undergone and whatever you have been forced to do, I regard it as part of your cross and not as a sin or a weakness and leave it to God to judge, for I myself can feel nothing but the greatest respect for you." And the letter was signed: "Arcady Ilyin."

Lyubov Onissimovna immediately burnt the letter in the grate and did not speak a word about it to anybody, not even to the old dairymaid, but just prayed the whole night, without a thought for herself, but all for him, "because," said she, "although he wrote that he was now an officer with orders and crosses, I could not imagine that the Count would treat him any differently from before."

She was, in short, afraid that they might beat him again.

CHAPTER XVIII

EARLY next morning Lyubov Onissimovna drove out the calves into the sunshine and began to feed them, dishing out the milk with a bark ladle from a wash-tub, when suddenly she heard a noise from the other side of the fence in the "free" part of the world. She could hear people running somewhere in a great hurry and shouting something very excitedly to each other.

"I couldn't make out anything of what they were shouting to each other," she told me, "but I felt a sudden pain in my heart as if somebody had pierced it with a knife. And as one of our peasants, Phillip, had just driven into the yard with a load of manure, I said to him:

"'What are those people making such a noise about and why are they shouting to each other so excitedly?'

"And he replied:

"'They're running to the Pushkarskaya suburb where an innkeeper killed some officer last night. Cut his throat from ear to ear,' he said, 'and robbed him of five hundred roubles. They caught him all covered in blood and they say they found the money on him.'"

"And as he said that to me I fell down in a dead faint.

"It was true: that innkeeper had murdered Arcady . . . and they buried him just here, in this grave. . . . He's lying under this earth. . . . And you were wondering why I always took you for a walk here, weren't you? Well, I don't come here to look at those houses (she pointed at the sombre, grey ruins), but to sit beside him and . . . take a drop in memory of his soul. . . ."

CHAPTER XIX

HERE Lyubov Onissimovna stopped and, thinking that she had brought her story to a close, took out a little bottle from her pocket and "took a drop" or "had a suck," but I asked her:

"But who buried the famous make-up artist?"

"The Governor himself, my dear, the Governor himself was present at his funeral. What else could you expect? After all, he was an officer, remember. The priest and the deacon called him a 'hero' at the service and when they lowered his coffin, soldiers fired a salute over his grave. And the innkeeper was a year later flogged by the public hangman in Ilyinka Square. They gave him forty-three strokes for Arcady and he survived it and he was sent branded to Siberia. Some of our men got special permission to go and see him flogged and the old men who remembered how the murderer of the cruel old Count had been punished said that forty-three strokes were not enough, but that was because Arcady did not belong to the gentry, for the Count's murderer received one hundred and one strokes. You see, my dear, it is against the law to give an even number of strokes, but they must always give an odd number. The public hangman who flogged the old Count's murderer was specially brought from Tula and he was given three glasses of rum before the execution. He flogged him so that the first hundred strokes were just strong enough to inflict pain, but not to kill, but when he gave the hundred and first stroke, he lashed out with such force that he broke the man's spine. When they lifted him from the scaffold he was already dying. . . . They covered him with a straw mat and carried him back to jail, but he died on the way. And the hangman, they say, went on shouting, "Give me another one to flog—I'd like to kill every man in Orel!"

"Were you at Arcady's funeral, too, nurse?"

"Of course I was, my dear. I went with the rest: the Count ordered that all the theatrical people should be taken to the funeral to see how far one of our men could get in making a name for himself."

"And did you also take leave of him?"

"Why, of course I did, my dear. Everybody went up and I, too, went up. . . . He was so changed that I hardly recognised him. So thin and pale. . . . They said he had been bled white because his throat had been cut on the stroke of twelve. . . . How much blood he had shed. . . ."

She paused and fell into thought.

"And," I asked, "how did you bear up afterwards, nurse?"

She seemed to wake out of a trance and she passed a hand across her forehead.

"At first I hardly remembered how I got home from the funeral," she said. "Must have returned with the rest, I suppose. . . . Somebody must have brought me. . . . But in the evening Drossida Petrovna said to me:

"'You can't go on like that, dear. You are not asleep and you're lying with open eyes just as if you were made of stone. That's not right. You must weep so that your pain can come out of your heart with your tears.'

"I said:

"'But I can't weep, auntie. My heart's burning like a piece of coal and I can't get the pain out of it.'

"But she said:

"'Well, if that is so, then it seems you must have the phial.'

"So she poured a glass of vodka out for me from her bottle and she said:

"'Before, I wouldn't let you drink and I did my best to persuade you not to, but now it can't be helped. Come on, dear, pour it on the burning piece of coal—suck!'

"I said:

"'I don't want to, auntie.'

"'Don't be a silly girl,' she said, 'whoever heard of anyone wanting it? It's a bitter drink, aye, a very bitter drink, more bitter than any poison, but if you pour this poison on the burning piece of coal in your heart, it will quench it for a bit. Come on, my dear, suck!'

"So I drank the whole phial. I hated it, but I couldn't sleep without it, and the next night again . . . I drank . . . and even now I can't go to sleep without it, and I've got my own phial now, yes, I'm buying vodka myself. . . ."

And, turning to me, Lyubov Onissimovna said:

"And you, dear, be a good boy and never tell your mummy anything about it, don't give poor people away: poor people must be taken care of, for they are all great sufferers. And when we go home soon, I shall knock again at the window of the pub round the corner. . . . We shan't go in ourselves, dear, I'll just give them my empty bottle and they'll give me a new one."

I was deeply touched and I promised faithfully never to tell anybody in the world about her "phial."

"Thank you, my dear. That's right, don't tell anybody, for, you see, dear, I can't do without it."

I can see and hear her just as if she were standing before me now: each night when everybody was sound asleep in our house, she'd get up quietly from her bed, so quietly that not a floorboard in her room creaked. . . . She'd listen for any noise in the house, then she'd get up and steal on her long, chilled legs to the window. . . . She'd stand there for a minute or so, look round apprehensively, listen to hear if my mother was coming from her bedroom, then she'd knock the neck of her "phial" very quietly against her teeth, put it into her mouth and "have a suck." One gulp, two, three. . . . The burning coal was quenched and she'd go back to her bed, dive under the blanket and soon begin to whistle in her sleep—whew, whew, whew. . . . She was asleep!

Never in my life have I witnessed such a terrible and heart-rending commemoration of the dead.

THE END